REMAINS TO BE TOLD

DARK TALES OF AOTEAROA

EDITED BY

LEE MURRAY

Clan Destine
PRESS

First published by Clan Destine Press in 2023

PO Box 121,
Bittern Victoria 3918
Australia

National Library of Australia Cataloguing-In-Publication data:

Editor: Lee Murray

Remains to be Told: Dark Tales of Aotearoa

ISBNs: 978-1-922904-49-2 (hardback)
        978-1-922904-50-8 (paperback)
        978-1-922904-51-5 (eBook)

Cover Illustration by Emma Weakley
Internal Illustrations by Emma Weakley
Cover type by Willsin Rowe
Design & Typesetting by Clan Destine Press

Clan Destine
P R E S S

www.clandestinepress.net

Remains to be Told
Dark Tales of Aotearoa

ADVANCE PRAISE

'What a powerful collection of brutal, haunting, visceral stories and poems. But don't worry, this stellar anthology from down under is not one note – originality, wonder, and curiosity keep you guessing, pleading for these dark fates and unsettling myths to find a different, brighter path.

Richard Thomas, Bram Stoker, Shirley Jackson, and Thriller Award finalist

'An assemblage of nightmarishly beautiful and poignant tales of death, despair, and the dark sights only seen in farthest echoes of New Zealand.'

Eric J. Guignard, multiple award-winning and #1 best-selling author

'This expertly curated anthology brims with monsterous mythology, diverse and original voices, and prose that propels the reader from one story to the next with the ferociousness of a rogue wave, a runaway carnival ride, a chattering chorus of insect wings. *Remains to be Told: Dark Tales of Aotearoa* seems to have been excavated from the very soil and riverbeds of New Zealand's unpredictable landscape by the tremendously talented authors who grace its pages rather than crafted with mere paper and ink. A must-read for anyone interested in the darker side of New Zealand, *Remains to be Told* succeeds in showcasing this mysterious, magical place.'

Christa Carmen, Bram Stoker-nominated author
of *The Daughters of Block Island*

'These are stories of the land, about the history and the geography of our odd nation. These are stories that invoke our remarkable blending of cultures. Colonisation and decolonisation stand side by side. The intertwining of Māori myth and oral history with the day-to-day practicalities of raising families in this twenty-first century capitalist world is one of the key threads that unify these stories as they bob and weave around social commentary, entertainment and pointed, bald and wry – even witty – observations. A supremely readable collection that deserves high recognition and a wide readership.'

Sean Monaghan, award-winning author of *Ventiforms*

*Content warning: stories and poems in this book address death (of people and animals), violence, rape, suicide, cannibalism, abuse, mental illness, and trauma.

ARTS COUNCIL OF NEW ZEALAND TOI AOTEAROA

The publisher and editor acknowledge the kind support of Creative New Zealand Toi Aotearoa literary funding in the development of this work.

CONTENTS

FOREWORD

I have never been to New Zealand.

Like most of the rest of the world, my image of New Zealand has been formed by pop culture; thanks to favorite Kiwi son Peter Jackson, I picture New Zealand as mostly looking like Middle Earth, maybe even with a hobbit hole or two thrown in. Taika Waititi taught me that there are vampires living in the suburbs of Wellington, and I've felt for the Māori people in films like Lee Tamahori's *Once Were Warriors*. Although it's not set in New Zealand, *Flight of the Conchords* is still the funniest television series ever made about a two-man band from New Zealand.

If you're one of the truly lucky non-Kiwis, you've been privileged to know some New Zealanders, as I have. My dear friend Rocky Wood, who was one of the world's leading authorities on Stephen King until he sadly departed this life in 2014, was originally from Wellington although he'd spent his adult life in Australia. I met Rocky through our mutual involvement in the Horror Writers Association, which both Rocky and I eventually served as President. If Rocky embodied the qualities of New Zealand then it's a very fine place indeed.

I've also been blessed with knowing Lee Murray, who edited this volume and who, in a relatively short period of time, has blazed an astonishing trail through the horror genre, proving to be a hyphenate powerhouse who has played a significant role in bashing glass ceilings for Asian women writers as well as New Zealand authors.

Which brings me to why I believe Lee asked me to write this foreword: although my ideas of New Zealand may be (falsely, perhaps) formed by media, my knowledge of horror is not. I've spent more than thirty years writing, editing, and studying within the genre, producing both my own fiction and works about other writers' work. I've written about everything from my affection for *The Castle of Otranto* (considered by many to be the first true horror novel) to the brilliant female horror writers of the 19th century to the history of Halloween to the zombies of George Romero. Let's just say I know horror.

And that is why I know that *Remains to Be Told: Dark Tales of Aotearoa* is very good horror.

One of the many reasons I love this anthology is that it's very good horror all set in New Zealand and told by New Zealanders. It has made me reconfigure some of my (mis)conceptions about this astonishing place. These stories feature water prominently (oh, right – it's an island country!) and lush forests (a little like Middle Earth) and alpine mountains (wait – what?), and suburbs recognizable throughout the western world and cities where people meet for coffee. But New Zealand is also a land of living mythology, an intense thread which runs through these tales; Aotearoa (the Māori name for the place) has a history richer than anything a single author could create. That beautiful folklore provides a dense background for many of these poems and stories, spinning a web that catches even those of us who might not be familiar with it. (Oh, and don't forget to use the glossary, thoughtfully provided at the back of the book to make sure non-Kiwis fully understand what they're reading.)

But because this is a horror anthology, all this is wrapped around terrible and disturbing things. All the usual genre tropes are here – monsters, ghosts, serial killers, body horror, post-apocalyptic scenarios – but in the hands of these gifted writers and poets these old standbys feel fresh and reinvigorated, especially being situated within the magical, mystical reality of Aotearoa/New Zealand. This anthology is so much more than a literary travel guide; it's a compelling, beautifully crafted, and genuinely frightening deep dive into both the darkness and the light at the heart of this island realm.

While it wouldn't be fair to say that I almost feel as if I have visited New Zealand now, I can say that I think I have a better understanding of its history, its nature, and its people. For that, I am grateful to all the authors and to Lee Murray.

I have no doubt that other readers all over the world will feel the same way.

Lisa Morton, July 2023
Six-time winner of the Bram Stoker Award®

INTRODUCTION

I love a good anthology. For a reader, an anthology makes an ideal sampler, a fancy biscuit tin of stories and poems by established and emerging writers, all typically working to a theme. With just a small investment of time and money, a reader like myself can dip into the pages of an anthology to discover a new favourite author, gain a fresh perspective, and be entertained. In the case of a horror anthology, this means raising the hair on the back of our necks, having our marrow liquified without risk to our person – and all from the comfort of our armchairs.

By now, the benefits of reading horror are well known, the genre offering readers a vehicle to process fears, gain understanding, and even develop solutions to real-world problems. Plus, as a genre operating on the margins of literature, horror has always welcomed diverse voices tackling subversive and transgressive themes, offering opportunities for readers to see themselves represented in stories which resonate for them on subjects that matter. Sometimes, of course, the benefits are simpler: a rush of adrenalin, a moment's diversion, or the pathos of a good cry.

Despite the many benefits of horror, anthologies dedicated to Aotearoa horror have been few. In fact, I can think of only one: IFWG Australia's 2018 volume *Cthulhu: Land of the Long White Cloud* edited by Steve Proposch, Christopher Sequeira, and Bryce Stevens, which comprises 11 Lovecraftian-themed tales with a Kiwi focus by Aotearoa authors. Others, such as award-winners *Baby Teeth* (2013) and *At the Edge* (2014) edited by Dan Rabarts and Lee Murray, and *Te Korero Ahi Kā* (2018) edited by Grace Bridges, Lee Murray, and Aaron Compton, published by micro-press Paper Road Press (PRP) and SpecFicNZ respectively, included some excellent horror by Aotearoa writers, but these texts are now out of print. And, while PRP's annual 'Best of' series (various editors) and Te Herenga Waka University Press' *Monsters in The Garden* (2020) edited by Elizabeth Knox and David Larson, both feature some darker stories; horror is not the focus.

Local readers shouldn't have to hunt at the bottom of the literary biscuit tin for a horror story set in downtown Auckland, or which represents their experience. So, with the real-life terror of the pandemic behind us and Cyclone Gabrielle blown offshore, the time seemed appropriate for a fresh look at our homegrown horror.

But what exactly is Aotearoa horror? A good question and one, I believe, contributors of *Remains to be Told: Dark Tales of Aotearoa* have answered through their writing, because the essence of Kiwi horror isn't something that can be captured in a single word. Nevertheless, in her foreword to this book, Lisa Morton speaks of the country's 'history, it's nature, and its people', and those broad categories are a good place to start.

It is true that some dark moments in New Zealand's history are reflected in these pages, with Del Gibson weaving another fire into the history of Northland's famous *Duke of Marlborough Hotel* at Kororāreka in 'Buried Secrets', a classic haunted house story with a modern twist. In Jacqui Greaves' 'Fires of Fate', New Zealand women have just been granted suffrage (the first country in the world to do so) when her character, Moira Jacobs, rides into Āpiti with her scissors to give a couple of local blokes their comeuppance. And Tim Jones draws on the 1862 shipwreck of steamer *Guiding Star* in the South Island near Omaui to tell a startling tale of childhood tragedy in a poem strangely congruent with Neil Gaiman's 'The Sea Change'.

It is also true that by its very nature the land of the long white cloud presents myriad terrors, with its towering peaks, rugged coastline, and impenetrable bush. There is the merciless isolation of small towns and farms, and the cold indifference of our bustling cityscapes. My Path of Ra co-author, Dan Rabarts, whose haunting story 'Spare the Rod' opens this book, explains in a 2017 *Halloween Haunts* article for the Horror Writers Association:

'We live on a string of major fault lines, on the spines of any number of volcanoes, surrounded by violent and unpredictable oceans and everything they bring with them, including regular floods, cyclones, and tornadoes. We live with a constant edge of isolation, both in our rural and suburban communities, and even within our own neighbourhoods.'

It's a place populated by its own monsters too, both real and imagined. Creatures like the supernatural Kumi lizard, which demands retribution for the desecration of its sacred land in Denver Grenell's bloody action-horror, 'Ngahere Gold'; or Debbie Cowens' 'extinct' reaper beetle, with its 'scythe-shaped mandibles' and 'black bulbous orbs', perhaps inspired by New Zealand's own dwindling, possibly extinct, Mokohinau stag beetle in her tale 'The Reaper Beetle'. In this anthology, beasts and bugs are everywhere, from worms, flies, sheep and dogs to avenging gods in the form of native birds.

But Aotearoa horror comprises more than just the terrain with its unique flora and fauna: there is something inherently uncanny about this place, a 'savage spirit' that New Zealand author Katherine Mansfield described in her iconic murder tale 'The Woman at the Store':

'There is no twilight in our New Zealand days, but a curious half-hour when everything appears grotesque – it frightens – as though the savage spirit of the country walked abroad and sneered at what it saw.'

That 'savage spirit' doesn't just sneer, it sucks unsuspecting victims into watery graves, yanks them into cosmic hell, or crunches them between bloody teeth. Even amongst the gaiety of an annual A&P agricultural show there exists a malevolent unease, as Kirsten McKenzie reveals in her story 'The Watchman'.

Several of our contributors reached into the spirit realm, conjuring stories of gods and goddesses, of ancient warriors and wairua-spirits, and of ancestral ghosts who haunt the everyday. It's a belief that is pervasive among New Zealanders. Indeed, in his book, *Mapping the Godzone* (1998), American William Schafer noted the significance of Māori mythology and culture in the development of Aotearoa gothic:

'A common cultural link between Pākehā [European] and Māori is a belief in the hauntedness of the landscape, the sense that Aotearoa New Zealand is a land of sinister and unseen forces of imminent (and immanent threat), of the undead or revenant spirits.'

Stories such as Bryce Stevens' haunting 'The Spaces Between', Tracie McBride's powerful 'Her Ghosts', and Celine Murray's poem 'Whaitiri', which is told from the goddess' point of view, reveal New

Zealanders' close connections to the land and the ancestral spirits that embody it.

Remains to be Told: Dark Tales of Aotearoa also includes stories that reveal the nature of its people. There are personal tales of tragedy and trauma, such as Marty Young's ghostly flashback 'Redwoods on Te Mata Peak', which explores the loss of innocence; Helena Claudia's chilling 'I'm a Gemini', a sharp Gen Z take on grief and acceptance; and Gina Cole's 'Blind Date' in which a woman attempts to escape the prison of her mind, an unexpected story with a vibe reminiscent of Marge Piercy's *A Woman on the Edge of Time*.

Social issues are also front and centre. For most of us, harm caused to a child is the worst horror imaginable, yet sadly New Zealand has a poor track record in this regard, ranked at 35th out of 41 developed countries for child wellbeing outcomes in a UNICEF Innocenti Report. New Zealand Police data reveals abductions and kidnappings, while rare, are on the rise, doubling since 2015. In fact, as I write this piece, a frantic search is underway for a missing real estate agent, her kidnapper apprehended at the airport. Such incidences are a source of fear for New Zealanders, so it comes as no surprise to see crimes like this feature in a third of the tales in *Remains to be Told: Dark Tales of Aotearoa*, my own story, 'Dead End Town' among them. Owen Marshall's iconic short story 'Coming Home in the Dark' is another example, the author exposing the worst of the human condition when a family of four picnicking in a lonely spot near Mount Aoraki are murdered by passing opportunists. And in 'Hook' Kathryn Burnett examines social expectations around beauty and aging through a feminist lens – employing body horror with deadly effectiveness.

However, we have yet to fully capture the spectrum of Aotearoa horror. What about that *Flight of the Conchords* brand of horror comedy that Morton alluded to? Paul Mannering takes good advantage of our famous Kiwi self-deprecation in 'A Throatful of Flies'. Here, when an entitled young farmhand slaughters a prize ram, he's forced to retrieve its grisly tag from an offal pit. The result is horrific, what Stephen King might describe as a severed-head-tumbling-down-the-stairs 'gross-out', yet despite its humour, the tale explores the serious themes of privilege and purgatory.

Also running through this work is a quintessential Kiwi stoicism, that stubborn she'll-be-right certitude that everything will be 'sweet as' even when all the signs tell us it is not. Poet William Cook forces us to confront a chilling future in his evocative poem 'Vision of the Apocalypse in Wellington Harbour', for example, and while the images are brutal and visceral, having witnessed the end from somewhere familiar, somewhere many of us have stood, staving it off seems not only imperative but also possible. Finally, Nikky Lee conjures a bleak dystopic future in 'What Bones These Tides Bring', a tale which sees the country crippled by devastating floods and its survivors subject to desperate cruelty, yet she too offers a bone-sliver of hope, a last effort which might allow souls to endure.

Whatever the horror, there is a strong thread of hope in *Remains to be Told: Dark Tales of Aotearoa*. A feeling that in spite of all the things that frighten us, no matter what the future might bring, the spirit of this land and its people will persist, that they're worth fighting for.

Which brings us back to the very point of horror: as a vehicle to both express and address our basest human fears.

It has been an honour and privilege to bring you this showcase anthology of Aotearoa horror, kindly supported by a grant from Creative New Zealand and published by our friends at Clan Destine Press, Australia. I hope readers will devour it, study it, share it, and demand more. Let it be just one of many dark works from Aotearoa's talented horror writers, creatives who 'love their country, love monsters, and love scaring the shit out of people' to borrow a phrase from Australian horror icon Kaaron Warren in her foreword to *Cthulhu: Land of the Long White Cloud*. Most especially, I'd like to thank my writing colleagues for trusting me with their work, and for their passion for Aotearoa – the land, its people, its heritage, and our rich kaleidoscope of cultures – passion which is palpable in this collection, both in its breadth and its quality. Indeed, Morton states it in her foreword: '*Remains to be Told: Dark Tales of Aotearoa* is very good horror.'

Lee Murray, July 2023

SPARE THE ROD
BY DAN RABARTS

Nathan killed his first animal the day he turned fifteen. It wasn't the birthday present he'd been wanting.

Dad roused him at sparrow's fart, to the steady thrum on the tin roof, the rattling gutters. More rain. 'Weather's set in,' Dad muttered. 'Been coming down all night. Need to get all the sheep up to the top paddock.' He clumped away, leaving Nathan in the spill of light from beyond his bedroom door, blinking awake. Dad had probably forgotten it was his birthday, either because of the rain and the sheep, or just because Dad always forgot things like birthdays. More so lately.

'Come on, Nate!' Dad yelled from down the hall. 'Sheep won't round themselves up.'

Nathan rolled out of bed, found the clothes he'd left on the floor the night before, and some decent socks. He hated having cold feet.

Dad was in the back sunporch, decked out in his oilskin and gumboots, finishing off the dregs of a coffee. Rain streamed down the windows and glass doors. Normally this spot trapped the sun, sweltering even on a cold clear winter's day. Today it just offered a blurry view of the immense grey rainclouds pressing down on the sky.

Nathan dropped onto the bench seat, dragged on his boots, grabbed his own raincoat. 'You remember what day it is today?' he mumbled.

'Athletics? Probably cancel it in this,' Dad said, stepping out into the weather, not waiting for an answer. 'You get the dogs. I'll bring the quad round.'

Nathan tugged up his hood and followed. He wasn't sure which was worse: when Dad was completely disengaged from everything going on in Nathan's life, or when he tried to pretend he wasn't, which made it so obvious how far apart they really were.

Shit, it was just a day, a mark on the calendar. School day, too. No point getting caught up in it, what with Dad being worried about losing sheep if the creek rose to flood the bottom paddock. Bigger things to worry about than birthdays. That's what Dad would tell him if he mentioned it, so Nathan put his head down and sloshed through the wet gravel toward the kennels.

The dogs yapped their early morning greetings. Nathan swung the kennel gate open and the dogs roved out, stretching their legs. Brash Rosco and strong but stable Morry loped about, shaking rain off their shoulders, while calm old Bess circled around to Nathan and gave him a look that said: *What's going on? Must be important to get us out in this weather, this early.*

Nathan scratched her behind the ear as Dad crunched up on the quad bike, its low grumble cutting through the hiss of the rain.

'They're working dogs, boy, not pets. Don't go getting attached to them. Next thing you'll be going all gooey over the lambs, and then before I know it you'll be a bloody vegetarian.'

'Sorry, Dad,' Nathan mumbled, and went to open the gate. Dad drove through, followed by the dogs. Pushing the gate closed, Nathan climbed onto the farmbike's back tray. Dad revved up the throttle and the bike lurched forward, Nathan barely hanging on. The dogs ran, Rosco and Morry spreading out in front while Bess stayed close alongside, as Dad sped down the muddy sloping track. Rainwater gurgled across the gravel in sputtering streams where fallen branches and miniature mudslides had fouled up the run-off ditch.

Nathan tried not to think about what his special birthday breakfast might be when they got back to the house, ignored the growl in his belly. Work first, Dad would say. Life later.

The creek was running high around the fenceline in the bottom paddock, dark and muddy and roiling with branches. In summer, the curve of the creek down here made for a great little swimming hole. Way back, before he'd even started school, this was where Mum had taught him to swim. Right now it was a drowning hazard. A hundred-odd sheep were huddled, bleating and bunting each other, over in a corner as far from the creek as they could get, dirty wool dripping with rain, animals just barely smart enough to know fear in the dull roar of rising water.

Nathan jumped down and unhooked the gate. The dogs raced through first, then Dad on the quad. The sheep scattered and flowed back together, driven by the barking black dogs towards the open gate. Dad did a loop of the paddock, checking none of the sheep were caught up in the fence, stuck in mud, or in the water.

Rosco and Morry drove the sheep onto the track, bunching them together, and the whole mob started up the hill. Bess hung at the rear, nipping at the stragglers, nudging them on with the rest.

'Good girl,' Nathan said, as Dad trundled up the paddock and through the gate.

Nathan hauled the gate shut and trudged behind, mud spattering his gumboots. Up ahead, through the rain, there was the red of the quad bike, Dad with his broad shoulders visible against the gloom, standing up on the foot rests, getting as good a view as he could of the flock in front. Bess was alongside the quad, on the downhill side, ready to dart forward and round up any sheep that might break from the fold.

If Mum'd still been here she'd be up now, probably grilling bacon and scrambling eggs. She wouldn't have forgotten his birthday. But the thought, of Mum pottering around the kitchen in her slippers, warming the house for the men coming in from the rain, left him cold and hollow, with the memory of white lights in his eyes, and disinfectant in his nose. Days like this, times like this, he thought about Mum a lot. Maybe Dad did too. Or maybe he tried not to.

Nathan was far away, buried in memories he'd rather not be remembering, when the side of the track gave way. It collapsed with a soft groan, mud and dirt and water pitching down the hillside in a sodden slurry. The quad went with it, along with Dad.

Mud flew away from the spinning wheels, Dad disappearing beneath the quad as it crunched over him. The quad rolled again and came to a sputtering stop on its side several metres down the bank. Flooded, the motor cut out. A hissing, groaning silence rushed in to fill the void the noise had left. The sound of rain on wet earth, of stifled pain.

'Dad?'

Nathan's legs wouldn't move. More of the bank could give way at any moment, but Dad was down there, on the exposed face of the hillside. Not getting to his feet and swearing, shaking mud off his boots. Not yelling at Nathan to come help him get the quad tipped up the right way, and to watch what those bloody dogs were doing. Not anything.

'Dad?' Nathan forced himself forward. Dad was on his side, half-buried in the soft earth. Bloody rainwater pooled in the mud around his strangely twisted frame, before running off down the hill.

Dad gave him a weak wave. It wasn't much, but at least he wasn't dead.

'Dad?' Nathan moved closer to the slip's edge. More mud and gravel broke free, sliding into Dad. Nathan hopped back, his stomach a knot and his heart pounding in time with the downpour. If more of the bank slid away, it might bury Dad beneath the mud. But Dad wasn't getting himself out of there.

Trusting the dogs to keep the sheep out of his way, Nathan backtracked. The rain was coming down harder now. It was getting in his eyes, that's why his vision was a bit blurry. No other reason. Putting some distance between himself and the slip, he clambered down the bank, circling the slip to approach Dad from downhill. The ground sucked at his boots, mud sloughing away with every step.

'Dad?'

'Go, boy!' Dad grumbled, waving him away without looking at him. 'Go call for help.'

'I'll just... If the bank slips... I should move you–'

'No!' Dad tried to twist, but couldn't. 'Might be my back. Move me and I'll end up in a bloody wheelchair the rest of my life.'

Nathan glanced at the sodden mass of earth poised above them, promising to give way at any moment, burying Dad alive. 'If I don't move you, you might die.'

'Better dead than a bloody cripple. Go up to the house, call an ambulance. Bring a shovel.'

Nathan retreated, compelled to do as he was told, but terrified he was going to come back to find a soggy grave, and he'd be using the shovel not to save his father but to dig up his corpse.

'Nate.'

Nathan paused, nodding.

'Bring the gun.'

A moment's confusion, and then Nathan heard it. A soft, low whimpering. He turned slowly, following the sound where it drifted below the white noise of the rain. A dark shape, laid out and half-buried in mud. Black shoulders panting in ragged, painful breaths. Legs splayed at unnatural angles. 'Bess?'

Again, his legs refused to move. Not Bess, no way. That wasn't fair. The ambulance would come, they'd strap Dad to a stretcher and take him to hospital and fix him, and in the end he'd be good as gold. But Bess?

Bring the gun.

He crouched beside the dog, put a hand on her heaving withers, felt the thready rhythm of her heart. Without moving, Bess' eyes rolled towards Nathan, full of pain and uncertainty.

'Go on!' Dad commanded, and Nathan staggered, slipping, then he was running, up the hill towards home.

He skirted the milling mob of sheep by the gate and crossed the fence at the stile. Last thing he needed was a hundred head of woolly chaos swarming the driveway without Dad there to shepherd them.

The house was ominously dark and silent as he pushed through the sunporch, panting, kicking off his boots and shucking his jacket onto the floor. No boots and jackets in the house, that was the rule. He and Dad both used to get in trouble for that one. Afterwards, Dad still made sure they never broke it. Every time Nathan came in the back door, it was like he could hear her voice. *Leave your boots in the porch, and hang that jacket up.*

He hadn't hung his jacket, but this was an emergency. Mum would've understood.

He stumbled into the empty kitchen. His hands were shaking as he picked up the phone handset, hooked his finger into the dial and whipped it around, three times. 111. Waited for it to ring. Several agonising moments crawled by before he realised it wasn't connecting. He hit the switch a few times to disconnect and try again, but there wasn't even a dial tone. Must be another slip, somewhere between here and wherever, this one dropping a tree over the phone and power lines. That's why the house was dark, even though they'd left the porch and kitchen lights on when they went out to round up the flock.

Nathan couldn't call for help. No-one was going to come and rescue Dad.

Head suddenly light, he dropped the receiver back into the cradle.

Bring the gun.

He stared hard at his reflection in the mirror on the wall behind the phone, hollow and haunted and running out of options.

'Your jacket won't get dry lying on the floor, tama.'

Nathan heard the voice, but it made no sense. The stresses of the moment playing tricks on his ears. A soft echo from lost days. He turned to face the old dining table and chairs. The overhead light wasn't on, but an ethereal glow washed the table. Mum was sitting there, hands wrapped around her tea mug, focused on something he couldn't see. Impossible wisps of steam drifted up in the invisible light.

All thought, all words fled Nathan's head. He was cracking up. Mum wasn't there, he'd sat with her in the hospice while the machine blipped over from clinging to life to whatever darkness followed. He'd watched her die. Helped lower her into the ground. She wasn't sitting at the table, quietly contemplating a cup of tea. Telling him off for dumping his jacket. She really wasn't.

'Rain like this, ua nui, brings out the taniwha. Down in the creek, it comes out to play when it floods. Got to watch it, it likes to mess with people.' Something she used to say every time it rained hard. As a kid, he'd always wanted to go look at the creek in the big rains, see if he could spot the monster. As he got older he'd come to understand the warning for what it was, the dangers of nature and the vulnerability of people. There wasn't really a taniwha living in the creek, lurking in wait for an opportunity to gobble people up. Just legends to make sense of the world.

Mum had grown up on this farm. Family roots went deep into the earth around here. Maybe, even though she was gone, part of her remained, tied to the house, to the land. Maybe the rain brought her back. Maybe she was the taniwha.

'Mum? Dad's hurt, and Bess too. I have to help them.'

This was ridiculous, he was talking to a dark and empty room, to someone who only existed in his mind. He'd read about this sort of thing, the power of the human brain to work its way to solutions by whatever means possible, even if those means looked like ghosts, or madness. Maybe he could save Dad after all, but it was going to take Mum to show him how. He didn't need to believe it was really happening, he could just choose to run with it.

'Make sure you eat up,' Mum said, from behind the kitchen island, the table suddenly vacant and falling into shadow. Nathan turned to where she was standing, pushing a plate of eggs and bacon across the benchtop. It wasn't real, couldn't be there, though if he sniffed hard enough he reckoned he could smell hot crackling. Nathan grabbed an apple from the fruit bowl instead and took a bite. 'You won't grow up big and strong if you don't eat enough,' Mum said, squirting phantasmal tomato sauce onto the side of the plate. It was a Greatest Hits reel, all the things Mum used to say over and over again, down through the years. Her wisdom, condensed into fragments of conversations, advice to live by in a handful of syllables. Memories asserting themselves, guiding Nathan to the path he needed to follow to save Dad, before the taniwha consumed him.

Chewing, he nodded to himself. *Eat up, you're going to need your strength.*

'Where are your thick socks? You need good thick socks on under your boots or you'll end up with blisters, tama!'

She was in the sunporch now, sitting on the benchseat to squash feet into her gumboots, pulling on her raincoat. The drizzly morning light passed through her, making her even less real than she already was. Nathan followed her into the porch, hefting his raincoat from its damp puddle on the floor, just as she faded from sight.

'Not in the house!'

It was a shout this time, startling him. Mum was behind him, back at the dining table, her stance one of fierce defiance towards someone he couldn't see. She was younger, too. Although the cancer had aged her hard in those last couple of years, this memory, this ghost, must have been from when he was still tiny. Before he'd started school, even. A memory he didn't remember but which must've been there, buried deep.

'Why do you even need that one? You've got two rifles already. Lock it up in the shed. I'm not having guns in my house.'

Nathan nodded. The gun cabinet was in the shed, but the keys were kept inside. Dad kept the guns in one cabinet, the ammo in another. He unhooked the keys off the ring beside the fridge as Mum disappeared. Then he shoved his boots back on and stepped out into the rain, head down, and made for the shed.

The shed had been there maybe forever, definitely as long as Nathan could remember, a sturdy high-sided structure with corrugated iron roof and rusted cladding nailed onto a solid timber frame. Dad parked up the tractor, the quad, and his rattly old flatdeck diesel ute in here, surrounded by all the piles of stuff that went into keeping the farm running.

He pushed through the shed's side door. The rain thundered on the iron roof, the echoes muffled by the bales of hay stored on the loft level. The sight of them made Nathan's back ache, remembering how he'd had to help Dad haul those bales up the ramp off the back of the ute. He wrinkled his nose at the smells of hay dust, fertiliser, fuel, pesticide, and insecticide that always built up in here when the big rolling doors were pulled shut against the weather.

The shed only had one window, over the workbench, running along the back wall, a long grimy portal on the world outside. Dirty, rainy light struggled to illuminate the dark within. The workbench and window were bookended by a pair of heavy metal cabinets, so old and battered they looked like they'd been through a war. Keys at the ready, he headed for the rightmost cabinet.

'This shit can't be good for you.'

Nathan paused, turning to see Mum, over by the ute, near the pallets that held sacks of chemicals, the fertilisers and pesticides. She had a big white hanky across her nose and mouth, as she scooped a yellowish powder out of a sack and dumped it into a bucket. 'If it's that poisonous to the bugs, what do you reckon it's doing to us?'

Nathan didn't remember hearing Mum talk about this, but he must've at some point, for the memory to be there for him to find. That was how this worked. So what was she drawing his attention to? Not the pesticides, surely. The ute? Dad had given him a couple of driving lessons. He hadn't been very good, but he knew how to start the ute and put it in gear, make it go. Maybe that was it. He could drive the ute down the track; he just had to get Dad up the hill without letting his back move, right? So maybe he just needed one of the camping stretchers which were up on the shelf over there, and some towels and blankets to pack around him so he didn't move. If he could drag the stretcher with Dad on it up the hillside and then lift him onto the ute's open flatdeck, he could strap him down with ratchets, then drive him to the Jacksons' place up the road and get their help. If he grabbed a couple of blankets for Bess too, he could wrap her up and keep her stable, get her to the vet. Maybe he wouldn't even need the gun.

Mum coughed, leaning over and hacking in long, painful gasps.

Nathan watched her fade out.

When he turned back to the gun cabinet, she was there. Older now, and frailer somehow. Her face was drawn, thin around the edges, worn down with the changes that had settled on her when she got sick. The red and black headscarf around her head, like some sort of battle trophy. This was Mum when she still had that streak of grim determination; the cancer might've sucked away her energy, but it hadn't smothered all the fight in her. This was Mum when they'd been told that none of the treatments were working as hoped, and they'd started talking about things like quality of life, and making the most of the months, maybe weeks, that were left. This was Mum, silently raging against the death of hope.

She lifted the key toward the lock, and faded out.

Nathan couldn't move, couldn't breathe. He'd never seen Mum anywhere near the gun; she hated guns. This was no memory. But it had happened.

Ghostly sunlight from a time gone by pooled around the other cabinet. Mum reached in, withdrew a box of ammunition, plucked a single bullet.

The only reason Mum might've been loading a gun was one Nathan couldn't bear to imagine. She was a fighter, had fought right to the bitter end. She'd never given in to despair, not that he'd seen. She'd never given up on life. Never given up on him.

Now she was at the workbench, under the window. She didn't have a rifle, but a handgun, one that Nathan hadn't even known his father owned. Not a weapon for taking out rabbits or possums, not a tool of the farming trade at all. Looked like the ones the police used, all cold black and shiny. Hard to imagine why Dad even had it. It seemed to whisper secrets that needed to be told.

Mum was loading a round into the magazine, slotting it into place. Holding the loaded weapon before her for a long moment, like some holy relic.

This was a fragment of time he'd never known, never seen.

Mum turned the gun, pressing the barrel against her chin, then her forehead. Touched the trigger.

This hadn't happened. It wasn't a memory, not even a ghost, just his mind playing tricks. He wanted to reach out and grab her, wrench the gun away, but nothing would move. Even the strangled cry in his throat caught there in the darkness and refused to break free. He couldn't so much as look away.

Then there was movement, sudden and jarring. The gun flickered out of sight and Mum turned, fists balled. Lashed out.

Nathan had asked Dad about the bruise on his cheek one day, and Dad had muttered something about getting on the wrong side of an angry cow. Could it have been the same day?

An unseen figure gripped Mum's wrists, pressed her back against the workbench, held her while she struggled. Pulling her back from the brink. 'I bloody can!' she growled through her tears. 'Bloody can if I want to!'

Like listening to one side of a phone conversation, long seconds passed, drawing Nathan through what were not his memories, but Mum's, stirred up by the taniwha, woken by the rain and summoned by the promise of death.

'If it was one of your animals suffering like this, you'd put a bullet in them, just like that. Why won't you show me that mercy?'

The light faded, leaving Nathan alone again in the shed, rain bombarding the roof. He waited for the light to return, for Mum to reappear and carry on her story, but there was nothing. No light, no voice. Just like the day she'd left for real. She'd said all she was going to say, shown him what she needed him to see. The rest was up to him.

The metal of the cabinet door was cold under his fingers and a chill ran through him, growing colder the longer he stood there, jacket dripping on the floor. He put the key in the lock, and turned.

Nathan trudged down the track, sloshing through muddy overflow. His shoulders ached with the load on his back, and the weight of the shovel. The weight of the gun.

The guns.

He'd opened up the top gate, let Morry and Rosco herd the sheep into the main section. It wasn't the top paddock, but he didn't want the sheep or the dogs roaming around, getting in the way while he did what he had to do.

A hundred metres or so uphill of the slip, he clambered down off the track and made for the overturned quad bike. Bringing the ute would've been a dumb idea. He was more likely to run over some poor animal, or kill himself if the track gave way again, than make any good use of it. And even if he could drive it, how was he going to lift Dad and his front-rower physique onto the back? As Dad loved to remind Nathan, there wasn't a hell of a lot of him to go round.

Dad was, unsurprisingly, right where Nathan had left him. Soft wet earth had piled up along his shoulders and hips, and he was visibly shaking with the cold. Bess was also still lying where she'd been crushed by the rolling quad, breaths short and shallow. Nathan stopped halfway between them, drove the shovel into the dirt, unslung the rifle from his shoulder and eased the pack to the ground.

He stood, rain sluicing off his jacket, the rifle clutched loosely in both hands, water gleaming on the wet stock and barrel. Feeling somehow older than the fifteen years he was turning today. The rain was coming down harder now, the creek well over its banks and swamping the bottom of the paddock, rising.

'Good lad,' Dad grunted. 'They say how far away the ambulance is?'

Nathan wasn't looking at Dad. He was looking at Bess. 'No-one's coming, Dad.'

'What?'

'Phone lines are all down.' He pulled back the bolt, reached into his pocket for a bullet. 'Sometimes, all we've got is each other. Sometimes, each other is the best we can do.'

'What are you going on about?'

'I can try to make you comfortable. I've brought a tarp and some stakes and poles from the tent to keep the rain off, and I can dig a trench to divert the water away. Once I've done that, I'll go grab my bike, ride over to the Jacksons' place, see if they've got the phone on or if Mister Jackson can bring his ute over and help move you.' He paused, surprised by how calm he sounded. Inside, he was churning. 'And I brought the gun.'

He inspected the bullet, slid it into the chamber. Locked it home.

Dad didn't reply for a long moment as Nathan stood, the loaded rifle in his hands, staring at the rain on the barrel. 'That's a good lad,' Dad said at last. 'Put the poor old girl out of her misery, eh.'

'Wouldn't be good for her to suffer, would it?' Nathan said, deadpan. 'Better just to get it over quick, one bullet, call it done.'

Dad nodded. 'That's right son. Neat and quick and painless.'

'Who for? You? Or her?'

Bess gazed up at him, her eyes full of pain and trust.

'Don't get all sentimental on me now, lad. Put her down and be done with it, unless you want me to die of hypothermia out here before you've even called a bloody ambulance.'

'Did you remember it's my birthday today?' Somehow, Nathan didn't want that detail missed from the moments that were to follow. 'Had you planned anything? Bought me a present?'

Dad frowned. 'Your…? Yeah, course I remembered. I'm your dad, I'm not gonna forget your birthday.'

'Guess it'll have to wait, eh? Work first, then life, right? Can you feel your legs?'

Dad paled at the question, but didn't respond. So that was a no, but he still held out hope that the doctors would be able to fix him.

Nathan stepped over to Bess, swung the barrel around, placed it gently on the crown of the dog's skull.

Happy birthday, son.

It was Mum's voice in his ear, her arms encircling him. Her hands wrapping around his, her finger guiding his to the trigger.

When the echo died away, Nathan blinked back the tears and threw the bolt to eject the hot shell into the grass, where it hissed and steamed briefly. He stood for a long time looking down the paddock, to the creek, where the taniwha lurked. It was awake now, he was sure. The rifle shot, the smell of death would draw it out.

He laid the rifle on top of the pack, then set to work with the shovel. Once the tarp was strung up over Dad and the rain was running around him rather than under him, he reached into his pocket, withdrew the handgun. Pulled the sleek magazine from his other pocket, snapped it home.

'Why'd you bring that? You don't need it.' Dad's voice was far away, muffled by the cry of the rain, the growl of the rising creek, and the faded echo of the gunshot.

'No, but you might.' Nathan looked at Dad then, this broken figure being swallowed up by a broken land. 'None of us wants to suffer, right?' He turned and placed the loaded weapon on Dad's chest. Stepping away, he bundled Bess into a blanket, slung it over his shoulder, and turned to go.

Dad was talking, but Nathan was no longer listening. He'd made Dad safe, like he promised. He'd go for help, like he promised. What happened now, between Dad, the flood, the taniwha, and the loaded gun, was a story that only the rain would ever know. The rain, and maybe Mum.

Carrying his birthday present – a dead dog and a shovel to bury her with – Nathan dug his heels into the mud, and walked away.

THE WATCHMAN
BY KIRSTEN MCKENZIE

The twists and turns of the winding roads pinched as much as the elasticised sleeves of Cindy's too-short dress. To add to her misery, the hem had inched up, leaving her sweaty thighs stuck to the Triumph Herald's leather upholstery. Her father's brand-new pride and joy, and the envy of all their neighbours.

A second-hand dress for a trip to a second-rate fair, at a beach far from home for their annual Easter holiday. For her first fifteen years the Karekare Easter Fair had been a highlight, but this year she wanted to spend the break with her school friends, not visiting a lame country A&P show with her parents and little sister. She was too old for toffee apples and sheep shearing competitions.

Stuck out here, away from the fun and games of the city, she worried her friends would forget about her, and that they'd replace her with someone more exciting. Someone who had at least kissed a boy before. This was the week Cindy had planned on kissing Stanley. They'd been skirting around it for months, stealing glances, brushing arms in the communion line, exchanging half smiles and blushing cheeks, until her mother had reminded her to pack for their annual holiday. Such a stupid family tradition, and one she wouldn't miss when she finished school at the end of the year to study typing and shorthand at technical college.

The car spluttered to a stop, its ticking engine replaced by the dying summer sounds of cicadas gasping their last breaths, the native orchestra supplemented with bird calls from the bush, the nearby canopy punctuated with a smattering of kauri trees abandoned after the collapse of the Karekau Sawmill seventy years earlier.

'It's just as I remember.' Cindy's mother smiled, her floral skirt tangled up in her spindly legs. Legs Cindy wished she had inherited, instead of the sturdy workhorse limbs of her father, all meat and muscle and thick dark hair. The length of her dress stressing the ridiculousness of her legs compared to those of her mother and sister. Her legs could be their own freak-show at the fair, alongside the sheep dogs and the tallest man who'd ever lived, according to the poster on the camping ground's noticeboard.

There was a second poster, featuring the faded face of a girl near her age, with a white bow tied in her hair. Angela Gow. *Missing*. Cindy hadn't come the year Angela disappeared. She'd been recovering from tonsillitis at her grandparents'. But she'd been told of the blind panic and the search parties, and how everyone presumed a rogue wave had swept Angela from the rocks. Elaine said it had been the taniwha Poutini who'd devoured Angela. Cindy had scoffed, too old to believe in the myths her sister loved. Regardless of how Angela died, the poster was a timely reminder to steer clear of the rocks on an incoming tide, where Angela was last seen.

'Get yourselves sorted, then it's a quick walk to the beach. It would be criminal not to enjoy the fine weather before it turns,' her father prophesied.

Cindy knew the script by heart and waited half a heartbeat to hear her sister's reply. A plea for ice cream. It always was.

'Do you think the kiosk is still serving ice cream?' Elaine asked.

They were puppets, dancing to a tune only God could hear.

'We'll check,' her father replied, never one to deny his youngest child anything she asked for, which was why Cindy relied on Elaine to do the asking. Love wasn't equal in the Williamson family.

Tired from the long drive, a windswept walk, and after devouring almost their weight in ice cream, they slept soundly. And woken by the autumn sun, they enjoyed a congenial breakfast on the stretched wooden veranda with no one bothering them. Their holiday neighbours were not yet friends, although they would be by the end of the week, leaving with false promises to stay in touch. No one ever did, not truly, save for a series of annual Christmas cards. Every year. Like clockwork. Cindy briefly wondered if anyone still sent cards to Angela Gow's family, before buckling on her sandals for the short walk to the fairgrounds.

Giant hay bales marked the fair's edge – jaundiced barriers keeping the evils of the outside world at bay, a barrier you couldn't cross without paying the entrance fee, unless you leapt over them like Mary Donaghy with her silver medal high jump at the British Empire and Commonwealth Games the year before.

Then a deviation from the annual script, with time stopping as her father presented her and Elaine with ribbons for their hair. White for her and blue for Elaine, the same shade as Elaine's often complimented sky-blue-eyes. There was no point expecting a brown ribbon. No one made ribbons the colour of alluvial mud.

'Gifts from the campground, they came with the keys,' her father announced, waving the now empty envelope, faint ink scratchings only just visible in the watery light.

Cindy ran the ribbon through her fingers until the smooth white satin caught on a ragged nail.

'Let me tie it in your hair,' her mother offered.

Her mother draped the white ribbon around Cindy's neck while she gathered her daughter's thick hair. And for a fraction of a moment, the ribbon morphed into a silky noose, before her mother triumphantly tightened it around the freshly formed ponytail.

'Thank you,' Cindy managed.

'And buy yourselves a toffee apple each,' her father added, pressing a fistful of coins into her hand.

This was like Christmas in March.

Cindy shot a look towards Elaine, whose face showed nothing more than pure unabashed joy. Elaine's default setting. The sun to Cindy's storm clouds.

'Your mother and I will meet you by the Ferris wheel for lunch,' her father announced, pointing towards the gaudy red of the already ancient giant wheel turning in the sky. 'Look after your sister.'

Together, Elaine and Cindy sidled past stalls selling anything you could ever need; the stall holders entreating them with sugar-coated promises, words lost amidst the hubbub of excited screams and the clanking of machinery.

They lingered at a trestle table of hand-carved wooden figurines. Delicate wood shavings littered the ground as the whittler sat on a high stool, carving his next creation from an aromatic length of ancient kauri. The unmistakable scent of worked leather wafted from another stall, a whisper of nostalgia curling into the air. A blend of tanned hide and earthy musk that tempted the senses with a promise of timeless craftsmanship and stories waiting to be told.

A coconut shy stood like a sentinel amidst the chaos of the fair, its weathered planks bearing the scars of countless strikes and misses. The laughter and chatter of the thronging crowd filled the autumn air with hints of popcorn and spun sugar vying for attention. A sense of anticipation crackled as the coconuts wobbled on their wooden pedestals. And as the softballs flew, the thuds and splinters of shattered expectations echoed. It was here, in this timeless game of skill and chance, that dreams collided with reality, where the cocoon of childhood innocence tangled with the harsh realities of the world.

The girls ignored the leather bags, the handmade soaps and the groaning tables of used books, the paper pages darkened with antiquity, searching for something else to spend their money on. Something more exciting.

Cindy turned to point out a table of bright shining crystals, but Elaine didn't answer. She was sprinting across the field, her ponytail swinging behind her, before throwing herself into a group of mirror-image teens. All legs and arms and hair and rolled-up skirts and lacy white bobby socks, leaving Cindy standing alone. A gang of one.

'Come try your luck, little lady,' called a carny man, beckoning her with twisted talons, all lumps and bumps and obtuse angles. An ostentatious gold and diamond ring on his finger threw distorted rainbows on the giant teddy bears hanging from the roof of his tent. Grotesquely appealing creatures with beady, black eyes.

'Hey there, poppet, do you like the look of these bears? Come on over. You get three balls to knock these milk bottles off the shelf. I bet you can do it in one. You're a big, strong girl. It's as easy as pie.'

Cindy's hand tightened around the coins, coins that promised the sweetness of a toffee apple for both her and Elaine, but she'd never owned anything as special as these bears. How hard could it be? Throwing a ball was the one thing their father had taught them to do. Surely her sister wouldn't mind if she didn't get a toffee apple today?

Snared by the well-rehearsed banter of the carny man, Cindy pivoted towards the allure of the soft toys. Being sixteen wasn't a deterrent, not today, not with a new ribbon in her hair and money to spend.

'Let's see those muscles, beautiful girl,' the tout teased. Nicotine oozed from his pores, staining his skin and his teeth, teeth which jostled for space in a mouth that looked both too small and too large depending on the light.

Cindy swapped a coin for three softballs, their leather outers scarred from the rituals of the past, the stitching rough and ready. Past their prime, but adequate for this game.

She took a step backwards, bent her leg, bit her lip, and hurled the ball towards the opaque bottles. The first ball veered left, as if pulled by an invisible string.

'Strike one,' the carny man called, honeyed commiserations falling from his fleshy lips.

Cindy hefted the second ball, weighing it with both her left and right hands. Rough. Its filthy stitching frayed. An identical twin to the first that she'd thrown.

The ball drifted left, thumping to the ground and dashing her hopes.

'Strike two,' yelled the carny, a dash too jubilant, overstepping his mark. 'One more chance.' He winked, before calling to the gathering crowd, 'Roll up, roll up, today could be your lucky day. This pretty lady has one last throw. Can she do it?'

Could she?

'Cindy!' Elaine's shriek came from far away and long ago, cutting through the metallic clashing of the dodgem cars and the delighted laughs and worried cries of children clinging to the painted horses on the merry-go-round.

Off balance, Cindy's aim went wide. The ball curved left, taking out all three bottles. A clean sweep.

'You won, Cindy, you won. Is it for me? Did you win one for me?'

The tout lost his smile as he stared at the broken bottles littering the hay-covered ground. Try your luck, he'd said. And Cindy had.

'It's not for you, it's mine. I won it,' Cindy said. Why should she give her prize to Elaine when she'd won it fair and square? Cindy missed the wounded look of betrayal flash across her sister's face.

'It's bad luck, you know,' the carny said, a somewhat strained smile staining his face. 'To keep the prize. You're meant to win it for someone special. You don't wanna be breaking the rules now, do you? Isn't she someone special?'

Cindy ignored his question.

'Can I choose which one I want?' Cindy asked, purposely oblivious to the hurt in Elaine's summery blue eyes. Her sister had everything she wanted – all the attention, all the friends and usually all the luck. But not this time.

'Be my guest.'

'The one with the white ribbon, like mine.' Cindy pointed to the bear in the furthest corner.

The carny man tipped an imaginary hat towards her and rescued the bear, his skin rippling in the transition from the sun to the shade.

'Lucky shot. But take care now. Jealousy never ends well,' he said, handing over the bear, his words more a curse than a blessing.

Cindy ignored him. Spinning, she grinned from ear to ear, clutching the bear to her chest, revelling in the cheers from the gang of teenagers. Her prize, and hers alone.

Cindy followed the group of teens as they moved towards the rickety Octopus ride, happy to be included, even if on the periphery of the gang, but even happier with her prize. The Octopus had never been her favourite ride, given it made her nauseous. She'd always sat next to her mother, with Elaine sharing a carriage with their father. It was how everyone preferred it. But this year the teens were old enough to brave the ride sans parents. Too shy to push herself forward, Cindy was left without a partner after they'd all paired up. The bear didn't count, despite its size.

'I'll go with you,' Elaine yelled, trying to climb out of the carriage, obviously happy to abandon her friend for her big sister.

Guilt about not giving Elaine the bear washed over Cindy. The thing was already becoming a burden. The gloss had tarnished as soon as she'd seen Elaine pair up with someone else.

'No, it's good. You go. I'll drop this back at the cabin, and then we can go again together,' Cindy called back.

Elaine gave her a thumbs up before sinking back into her carriage, chattering with the girl beside her.

Cindy masked her regret with a dry smile and an exaggerated wave. Elaine couldn't wave back, with her carriage swinging wildly onto its edge as the ride accelerated until each arm of the Octopus was a blur of colour and screams. Cindy couldn't shake the feeling that the screams were of terror, and not of joyful bravado, and promised herself that she'd make it up to Elaine later.

The smell of stale popcorn and sickly-sweet candy floss mixed with the oily tang of the ride's mechanism turned Cindy's stomach as she raced through the chaotic crowds, intent on returning the bear to their cabin and getting back before Elaine's ride finished. The nausea played tricks on her mind as strangers kept appearing and disappearing, their faces twisted into grotesque masks. She shook her head, focusing on returning to the cabin.

A plume of fire gushing from the gaping mouth of a gaunt performer threatened to singe her hair, so Cindy picked up her pace, pushing past the emaciated fire-breathing man. He laughed his foul flames from the depths of hell, burning forever shadows onto the ground she'd just crossed.

Stepping inside their holiday cabin, a bitter sea breeze tugged at the thin curtains. Placing her prize on the bed, she turned to leave, but something slowed her hand. The bear's glassy black eyes seem to bore into her soul, judgement settling upon her shoulders. Without the rainbows adorning the bear, the toy looked more menacing than she'd remembered. She shook off the thought.

'I'll see you later. You better behave now,' she said, before running from the cabin, the wind slamming the door shut behind her.

Cindy could have sworn she'd been inside for a fraction of a moment, less than a minute, but the sun had shifted. The shadows lengthened. And now time seemed to dance to a macabre tune, bending and contorting on its own twisted clock, with no regard to Cindy and her fears.

After arguing with the crone in the ticket booth who wanted her to pay a second time, Cindy rushed through families armed with prams adorned with balloons bobbing about in the wind. She pushed her way through groups of teenagers, giddy with freedom, arriving breathless at the Octopus ride which was still filled with screaming girls and overly confident boys. The ride slowed to a stop, metal wheels screeching against the rusting tracks, and Cindy scanned the disembarking riders, but Elaine and her friends were not amongst the disgorged passengers.

Her head swivelling like the gaudy clown heads waiting to swallow the ping-pong balls, Cindy searched the milling crowd. Pushing to the front of the queue, she grabbed at the operator. 'I'm looking for my sister—'

'Get off,' he replied, his filthy hands jutting past her to snatch the tickets from the next load of customers.

'She was just here, wearing a white dress with a blue ribbon in her hair.' A brand-new dress, as opposed to Cindy's second-hand number. They'd argued about it before leaving Auckland, but now it didn't matter. All that mattered was finding Elaine and keeping the promise she'd made to her parents.

The ride operator's face closed down at the mention of Elaine's blue hair ribbon. 'If you don't have a ticket, get out of here,' he growled, his malevolent eyes flickering over Cindy's ribbon-less hair.

Cindy stepped back, unsure of what to do next. A gnawing unease unfurled within her as she tried guessing the time based on the watery sun. The sounds of merry laughter and piped music, once so vibrant and alive, had become muffled. Distant echoes of happier times.

'She went with her friends,' the carny man said, the one from the stall with the teddy bears. As he sidled up to her, his sweat-drenched skin brushed against hers.

Cindy recoiled. This was all his fault.

'Which way did they go?' she asked, her voice quavering.

His smile widened, his own black eyes glinting like the bear's eyes back at the cabin. 'I can't remember,' he purred. 'But I've got something for you.'

Cindy took another step back, but he grabbed her wrist, pulling her close, his skin rough against hers.

'Let go.' She tried twisting out of his grip.

The man's smile widened, and she closed her eyes, bracing for the worst. But instead of feeling his hand on her face, she felt something else caressing her cheek.

She opened her eyes to see the man holding a white ribbon, her ribbon.

Cindy snatched it from him, her fingers fumbling with the delicate fabric. She looked up to thank him, but he was already walking away, blending into the crowd.

Confused and shaken, Cindy retied the ribbon in her hair and walked away from the Octopus, her eyes scanning the fairgrounds for any sign of Elaine. But the crowds had grown thicker, with the fair's narrow pathways constricting in time to the music from the merry-go-round.

The merry-go-round.

Relinquishing all pretence of decorum, Cindy ran towards the merry-go-round, her legs pumping faster as she drew closer.

The ride's painted animals soared and twisted against their mirrored backdrop, their eyes staring at Cindy from every angle, burning with an infernal fire. The strands of coloured light bulbs flickered, turning the merry-go-round into a smear of colour, with every rider and animal a blur of motion.

She scanned the riders. As the discordant calliope music played on, the merry-go-round spun faster and faster, as if the ride operator was trying to launch the horses like a boy with a stone in a slingshot. Cindy's heart thumped in time with the gaudy waltz as she pushed her way to the front of the crowd. Was that Elaine?

There, a girl, riding a black stallion, frozen mid-gallop, the girl's white sundress flowing in the breeze and her long, blue ribbon fluttering behind her.

Another rotation, and then another.

Cindy called out to the girl, but she didn't turn around. Cindy tried following the stallion's position on the merry-go-round, but the animals kept changing, morphing into creatures unlike anything God could have designed. The ride slowed to a stop, and giggling girls abandoned their mounts. And the girl with the ribbon proved to be a mirage, with a smear of grease on the bottom of her skirt and a chipped front tooth, taunting her with false hope.

Cindy's heart plummeted, each beat echoing with the weight of her responsibility for Elaine. She cast a desperate gaze upon the sea of people once more, her eyes frantic, when something caught her eye. A tent slithered into view, evoking a disconcerting sense of déjà vu, for she knew with bone-chilling certainty that it hadn't been there before.

Boasting a patchwork of faded blue and green panels that spoke of a time long gone, and a large hand-painted sign proclaiming it as the home of 'Hinepō – Fortune Teller'. The tent's tattered entrance beckoned her in. The flash of Stanley's smile lingered at the periphery of her memory, dampening her fear about Elaine. Elaine would understand if Cindy took a moment to ask about Stanley. They'd been giggling about him all night. It wouldn't take more than a minute…

A kerosene lantern flickered on a small table in the centre of the tent, throwing the shadows of the seated woman onto the blank wall behind her.

Cindy slipped past the canvas flap and locked eyes with Hinepō, the fortune teller.

'Sit,' the woman said, pointing to a wooden stool on the other side of the table, waves of black hair obscuring her face, save for her eyes. Black eyes.

The fortune teller's gnarled hands shuffled a deck of worn tarot cards. As they whispered against each other, a malignant energy seemed to fill the tent, crawling like spiders across Cindy's exposed skin.

A deep keening filled the air and Cindy twisted her head towards the haunting noise, a sudden fear unravelling itself within her heart. Some primal force urged her to follow the lament.

'I have to go,' she said, desperate to flee the deepening shadows in the canvas cave.

The fortune teller shimmered in the oily light, her visage flickering between young and old and back again, the lantern catching the silent mirth in her mocking eyes.

'Family always comes first, girl,' Hinepō called. 'Remember that.'

Stumbling out of the tent and through the crowds, Cindy followed the faraway keening, fear turning rancid on her tongue as she reached the hay bale barricade. Her eyes tracked a worn path through the edge of the sand dunes leading towards the foreshore. Towards the rocks.

Cindy didn't think twice, breaking into a run through the gap in the hay bales and up into the dunes, her thoughts consumed with concern for Elaine. The keening grew louder, and Cindy knew what it was. A warning.

A solitary pīwakawaka danced in her path. The bird's morbid reputation quickening Cindy's pace as she followed the flattened grass track to the beach, a track littered with abandoned shoes and well-worn sandals, not yet fully grown, their sturdy soles holding back the encroaching sands. Leather straps destined to decay as nature's onslaught erased all memories of them.

She paused at the crest of the dune, her heart hammering against her ribcage as she spied the group of teens hopping from rock to rock in the distance, their voices tangled by the wind into something indecipherable.

Shaking off the imaginary hand restraining her, Cindy stumbled down the path, abandoning her own shoes to slide down the sandy embankment. The lordly pōhutukawa sprouting from the cliffs shaded her flight and disguised the pulsing of the rocks as they awakened from their ancient slumber.

'Elaine,' she called, the waves stealing her cries, rendering her voice impotent.

The rocks undulated like a pool of long-finned eels as Cindy tried reaching the group. She tripped, dashing her knee on a rock bitten in two by a giant serpent, the teeth marks sharper than the carving knife at home. Ignoring the rivulets of red running down her leg, she limped her way towards the others. Too far away to hear her, the group moved further down the beach, oblivious to her shouts. The gulls took up her cries, repeating them over and over, the cacophony enough to deafen God himself.

The rocks slick with her blood, Cindy slid across their polished surfaces, her bare feet hardly a match for the vicious remnants of an ancient volcanic eruption. The minuscule pīwakawaka kept following her lumbering steps. An ill omen. A potent for something worse than a scarred knee and a missing hair ribbon.

The booming cries of a wayward matuku heron joined the gulls' wails, the mournful sound sending shivers down Cindy's spine.

Out of breath, the pain in her knee almost unbearable, Cindy paused, scanning the shoreline for any sign of her sister. Nothing. Turning back towards the dunes, she shuddered at the unmistakable silhouette of the carny man watching her, the glowing ember of his cigarette the only colour amidst the pale scrubby tussock.

Her stomach rumbled. Their parents would be frantic. With no watch, she couldn't judge the time, but the sun had dulled, the shadows lengthening around her. Dusk would be upon them soon. That time between day and night where life isn't sure if it wants to carry on. A precipice of time, the edge of which she didn't want to linger on.

Pushing onwards, she tripped again, the rocks grasping at her heels with rapacious hunger. Her hand slid between two rocks as she tried cushioning the fall. The sharp snap of the tiny bones shocked the gulls into silence, with only the grieving matuku oblivious to her pain.

Trapped for an instant, Cindy panicked, pulling at her arm, biting down the agony, the tide creeping closer and closer. Was this how Angela Gow had died the previous summer? Trapped between two rocks, unable to escape?

'Wait,' said a voice behind her.

A fug of tobacco enveloped her, drowning the salty tang on her tongue as the carny man appeared. Cradling her wrist with one hand, he leveraged the rock with the other. His biceps bulged with the strain, veins popping on a neck strung with gold links. Real or otherwise, they glinted in the fading sun, shimmering in the hazy sea air.

'There, you're free,' he said, still supporting her wrist, its angle all wrong, unrelated to her body. A foreigner attached with skin smeared red and held by a stranger.

'Thank you,' she managed. There was nothing else to say.

'You lost your ribbon again,' he said, holding out a tattered red ribbon, fraying at the edges.

'That's not mine,' Cindy replied. 'Mine's white.'

He dropped it, and Cindy's eyes followed its slow descent to a watery grave. The ribbon settled on the naked carcass of an undersized schnapper, whose remaining glassy eye starred up at her in recrimination. But it wasn't the only ribbon caught on rocks.

Cindy counted three, no, four other ribbons decorating the rocks. Correction, five, or maybe six lost ribbons, undulating under the caress of the offshore wind. A rainbow of satin stripes, not unlike the colourful sheen of the pāua shells she and Elaine collected every year.

'The ribbons…' she said, more to herself than her peculiar companion.

And there, on a rock shaped just like her pillow at home, lay a blue ribbon. The satin still pristine in its newness. As if it had slipped free from its owner mere moments earlier. Elaine's ribbon?

'That's…' Cindy took a step forward, her shadow with her.

The ribbon seemed caught, stuck on the rock.

'Can you?' she asked, nodding towards the slash of blue.

He nodded, and Cindy sank onto the rocks, cradling her broken wrist, her knee throbbing, her eyes welded to the ocean blue ribbon. Sinking down deeper, the rocks seemed to subsume her. She closed her eyes, overwhelmed with tiredness and the realisation that she couldn't bear facing her parents until she'd found Elaine. Or Elaine's body.

The cool damp rocks against her skin acted as a balm to the flaming pain in her knee and wrist. She only needed a minute's rest. A minute to compose herself for the inevitable.

A shadow fell over her.

Cindy opened her eyes. The carny man.

'Pillow rocks, from The Watchman,' he said, pointing with his bejewelled finger towards an ancient lava flow cascading down the cliff face. The carny man fiddled with his gaudy ring. 'That's what you're sitting on.'

Cindy struggled to push herself up. 'My sister…'

'She's over there,' he said, smiling, pointing to the rocks. 'Can't you see her? She's where her ribbon was. She called for you, but you took too long to come. What was his name? Stanley? It's so sad that he was more important than your sister.' He shook his head. 'Jealousy really is an ugly trait. I did warn you.' He shook his head. 'You should rest awhile, here, on the rocks. And wait for her, like she waited for you.'

Cindy couldn't comprehend his words. They were riddles in the wind. *Stanley?* What did he know about Stanley? And accusing her of being jealous of her sister. She wasn't. Not always…

Her lungs wouldn't inflate. Gasping for breath, she tried asking what he meant, but he was walking away, running a strip of blue satin between his filthy fingers. Elaine's ribbon.

'Help me,' she said as she leveraged herself up, but the words never left her throat. Her hair snagged on the rocky pillow behind her. She tugged harder.

Reaching with her good hand, she yanked at her hair, but the pretty white ribbon, the one she'd knotted so tightly around her thick ponytail, had been swallowed by the rock. Her hair with it. How? What was happening?

She thought she was hallucinating, so tried again. But then the pain in her wrist and her knee and her body became all-encompassing. An odd pressure grew against her head, stronger, more pronounced. And then against her entire body. Pulsing against her dress. Her new-to-her dress, which really was quite pretty. Almost as nice as Elaine's. The force crushing the summery yellow cotton into the rocky bed, until the threads became nothing more than sea algae. Her beautiful new dress. The colour of summer hay.

The minutes became elusive, stretching into eternity as the shadows swallowed the fading remnants of daylight and the rocks slowly absorbed Cindy's body. Her limbs twisted into unnatural positions, and her face contorted with pain. Another rocky pillow for the day trippers to admire. Another offering to appease the taniwha Poutini.

WHAITIRI

BY
CELINE MURRAY

From the sky I came
To share a feast
And wed a man-eater

Won't you ease my hunger?

Let me whet my teeth on your bones
Slurp at your arteries

Can I not consume your heart?
Or our son's plump fingers?

Won't you ease my hunger?

E taku ipo, let me eat our child
Our most blessed repast
Quench my tenderness

Wait! I was misled
Your name is a farce
Kai-tangata has no appetite

How can you ask me to love
If I cannot devour?

I fly away from your hollow promise
An empty creature
Whaitiri wails on the wind

Disappointment is not a meal
My stomach rumbles
And my eyes flash

You don't know my hunger

E taku ipo, I bide in the sky
With only my broken heart
To nourish me

HOOK

BY KATHRYN BURNETT

'It isn't a fat farm,' said Phil. 'It's a symbian retreat that specialises in curing allergies. You rebalance your immune system by infecting yourself with hookworms.'

He looked pleased with himself as if he'd discovered something extraordinary. Dawny just wished he'd get his haunches out from behind her marble-top counter so she could start scrambling eggs. It was technically 'their' marble-top bench, but she thought of it as hers.

'Only about three hours' drive.' His eyes scanning his iPad. 'A breathtaking retreat nestled in the spectacular and ancient forest. Sounds pretty amazing, right?'

He spun the screen in her direction like it was no big deal to let wriggling worms burrow into your skin and set up house in your gut. The thought of a worm blindly latching onto her insides to feed made Dawny pukish. But Phil was oblivious, on a roll, merrily listing studies that validated the hookworm theory.

'It completely reconfigures your internal ecosystem – imagine if it cured your asthma! You'd be able to get your fitness back.'

Oh yeah, her fitness. That thing, that glorious optimal state that had receded into the past along with her enthusiastic sex drive. The way he talked about 'her fitness' made it sound like she (lazy cow) had carelessly left it somewhere and just couldn't be blowed going back for it. Phil hadn't lost anything. He was determined to stay lean, to preserve the firm contours of his waist and chest. Sometimes she'd see him out running and admire his strong, triangular frame and well-formed shoulders. His long legs, smooth pistons propelling him along the street.

It wasn't the first time he'd paid for her to attend a retreat. Apparently, it *was* his way of being a supportive husband. And maybe he was being nice. Dawny chided herself for being suspicious but couldn't completely dislodge the splinter of disquiet in her gut. She'd clocked the irritation on his face as she laboured up the hill during their walks. Lately, he didn't even bother to hide his disgust when she clutched damp tissues to her dripping nose or made ragged, wheezing sounds as she bent over, chest heaving.

Once upon a time, the preoccupation with her 'spongy bits' had been subtle. Fitness weekends together, gym memberships, he'd even slipped a healthy eating challenge into their life on the sly. But now it felt pointed. Like he was building a case, compiling a list of justifications for his growing contempt. Yesterday, he pointed out the tiny spider veins blossoming on the curve of her nostril. Just another little paper cut, she thought.

Part of her wanted to bark at him to just bugger off then. Like it or lump it as her mother used to say. She'd been a warm, loving wife. She was loyal and smart and fun. It wasn't fair that he was now castigating her for not being young. Back when they were getting serious, Dawny had secretly wondered how she'd managed to hook such a fine-looking masculine specimen and watched her friends and family for any indication that they wondered the same. If she was honest, her feelings had also dimmed, but from what she'd read in self-help books that was common after 25 years. It didn't mean she wanted to lose him. They generally rubbed along okay – and there was the house, the holiday home, everything. Fuck it – there were memories of their life that had mostly been great. And how on earth would she meet someone else at this age? Where would she even start? She made more than him – so that part would be okay but no… Dawny had always been practical and she needed to be practical now. Plus, there was that pathetic, little tender part that just wanted him to love her again.

'It sounds fantastic, Sweetie,' she said, smiling as brightly as she could.

It was expensive, he told her, but her well-being was important so what the hey? She allowed herself to breathe then, to enjoy the tiny tremor of love. Maybe it would work and she'd be free of her constricting, ugly-making allergies.

The group was small and middle-aged. Apart from the stick-thin teenager with rheumatoid arthritis and a constantly bothering mother. Lawrence, the retreat leader, was a 60-something Northland local by way of Montreal. He had that wiry, loose-limbed way about him. The way yoga people do, Dawny thought unpleasantly as she glanced at his naked, tanned feet and silver toe rings. They sat cross-legged on a chilly meditation platform overlooking dark green forest canopy while Lawrence talked them through what to expect.

'Our little friends make their way up through your body to your lungs, then you'll cough them up and swallow them. Easy. They'll attach themselves onto your small intestine and sit there happily working their magic.'

Dawny found him arrogant. He talked about the folly of opting for a sanitised mail order work patch that you slapped on your arm at home. They were too smart and tuned in for that. They'd opted for a more organic and authentic way to fix what humanity had done by living too clean. Just as he had, they were giving themselves over to Papatūānuku – putting their health issues and pain in her hands. Dawny's heart sank when he told them they'd walk a kilometre out to the Worm Well after nightfall.

The forest was dark and sodden. Cold rainwater leaked from the nikau fronds, splattering heart-shaped kawakawa and dripping down to the rotting undergrowth – pat, pat, pat. The raw air bit at Dawny's throat as they made their way along the slippery wooden pathway. Dawny gripped the tissues in her pocket, hoping the moist stench of decay wouldn't set her off. She was at the back of the line in sneakers better suited to a café stroll and could barely make out the path. The pale, bobbing light from her phone caught the slimy wooden slats that crept with dark mould. She'd forgotten how pitch black the bush could get. How unnerving. She turned to peer into the inky expanse. Anyone or anything could be out there, standing between the trees, obscured and watching them… They'd have no way of knowing.

Why was she being so ridiculous? She was on a luxury retreat – and why would anyone want to watch her in her unflattering khaki yoga pants? But her chest tightened regardless. The chill and her overactive imagination conspiring. She stopped to pat her pockets for an inhaler. Sucking it down, she realised the footfalls of the others were fading into the gloom. Something in the bush, rattled. Spindly branches moving for no reason. She cast around, her heart hopping a little. Nothing.

She hurried along the path. It would be impossible to run in these stupid shoes. Then Phil's voice was in her head – why didn't she wear something more sensible? Something scratched at her face and she shrieked, batting it away. There was a dim light up ahead, moving towards her through the darkness.

'Hello?' Dawny hated how querulous she sounded. But even more than that she hated Phil for putting her here in the first place.

'You doing alright, straggler?' said Lawrence. 'We're just about there.'

In the clearing, there was a wooden enclosure, the entrance lit by tiki torches. Lawrence closed his eyes and uttered a reverential prayer to the sky. Dawny caught the teenager's eyeroll and pressed her lips together to stop her smile. Inside, there was a shallow pit filled with dark, pungent mud. Dawny pulled her hood up over her nose and mouth. The fetid stink was oppressive. But Lawrence just beamed.

'Here it is, Folks. Your passport to wellness. It pongs a bit, I know, but we won't be here long.'

Dawny watched the others remove their shoes and socks. The girl stepped into the pit first, the black ooze seeping up over her feet as her mother hovered at the edge.

'It feels rank,' she said. 'But kinda warm.'

'Our unique mud blend is heated from underneath,' Lawrence assured them. 'All the mod cons. Hopping in, Dawny? Just think of it as mud.'

But it was dirty mud, blended with faeces and shit-eating worms. She debated whether Phil could possibly find out if she lied about going through with it. A bald-faced lie embellished with detailed description. But, no, if he found out she'd have to endure his sneering face and yet another 'failure' being added to the list.

Ankle-deep in the wet muck, she walked around with the others as instructed. Trying not to think about the microscopic creatures finding her feet and penetrating the tender, pink skin. Later that night she dreamt of the worms pushing against the wet tissue of her lungs desperate to race to her throat. And then as a slithering, ball-sized mass roiling deep in her gut. She woke feverish, fresh from a dream about her husband digging a grave by tiki torch on the beach of a Pacific resort.

The following night, they went back to the pit. But this time there was almost a party atmosphere. They'd survived the grotesque ordeal and were old hands now – relaxed enough to banter about the filthy stink. Afterwards, Lawrence led them to a private cove.

Dawny lay back on her thick cashmere rug and stared at the scattering of stars across the dark blue sky. The pale slither of moon.

'Extraordinary here, isn't it?' said Lawrence as he headed for the sea.

She nodded. The water rushed towards her feet across sand and pebbles – shush. Somewhere in the background a bonfire was being lit. The tightness in her chest had gone. She was becalmed. Her body an anchored weight, pressing deliciously into the ground. She closed her eyes. Floating on the edge of sleep, she thought she heard a tiny whisper.

Hello.

Was that something…? Probably not. She turned over and slid into oblivion.

In the morning, she opened her eyes to a sun-filled cabin and perfunctory response from Phil to her evening text. Typical, she snorted, typical that he wasn't even missing her. Maybe she'd stay away another couple of nights. See how he liked that. Let him worry about where she was for a change. There was a faint ticking in her wrist bones. She circled the joint and rubbed the veiny underside with her thumb until it stopped.

After the biome friendly brunch, Dawny packed, marvelling at how much energy she had. How much mental acuity. Something twitched under the skin on her left forearm. She rubbed it red and the sensation shimmied to her elbow. Strange. She smiled and pictured one of the worms wriggling under her skin and tickling the expanse of her funny bone. Which was stupid, obviously.

An hour later she was on the road, carving through dense native bush with its muddy colours. The tyres hissed on wet road and the greyness of it merged with a heavy, grey sky to press down on her. She really would have to work on her attitude when she got home. He hated it when she was mopey. She was about to press a CD into the car's player when a quiet voice writhed in the back of her head.

Fuck him. You should definitely stay away another couple of nights.

Damn, straight. That's exactly what she should do.

Dawny pulled into the car park of the first halfway decent motel. The Punga Grove boasted an Executive Suite with a private spa.

Perfect. Exactly what I deserve.

The bed was huge. She spent the first five minutes star-fished on top of it. It was glorious, the type of place where once upon a time she and Phil had enjoyed each other's bodies. But screw him. A soft robe, TV channels and pizza delivery. That was all she needed right now.

It was dark when she woke. Someone whispering close to her ear.

You need to wake up.

She bolted out of the bed, flailing for the light switch and knocking over the bedside lamp. There was no one. She was standing in the room alone. Pressing her palm against her thudding heart, she tried to still her breath. But it was like breathing sand. She heard the rattling wheeze and padded to the bathroom to dig out her inhaler.

She watched herself use it in the mirror, pushing away how tired and flabby she looked under the sickly lighting. Something caught in her throat. A dry, irritating flake. She gave a short bark to dislodge it. It didn't budge. She pounded on her sternum and coughed harder. Her eyes bulged and ran as she hacked. Christ almighty, there was something in her throat. A plug of phlegm shot into her mouth and she spat. In the basin, a writhing cluster of small, white worms. She shrieked and wrenched the hot tap hard. As the mass was swept down the plughole, there was a faint wail. She splashed water on her face – she was clearly in that half waking state when you've been pulled from a nightmare. Had she imagined the worms? Weren't they supposed to be microscopic? And okay, be logical – the worms wouldn't have reached her lung sacs yet. Lawrence had laid it out very clearly…

Next time, you need to swallow them.

Dawny spun. She definitely heard that. But no one. Christ's sake, she was going mad.

Hello, Dawny.

The soft voice was coming from inside her but was not her.

Dawny whimpered. This couldn't be happening. She could still taste the earthy tang of the worms in her mouth and her stomach flipped. She filled a glass of water. Scratchiness pinched at her throat. A brief contraction quivered in her windpipe. No, please don't...

The coughing started again. There was movement in the back of her throat. She gagged as a wet plug tumbled into her mouth. She gulped down the water and then another. And it was done.

She clambered back to the security of the bed and considered ringing Phil. She'd only had the briefest response to her deliberately vague text about staying away longer. He'd be asleep, of course, irritated by her neediness – and the fact that she was losing her mind. But still... something was horribly wrong.

She dialled his number. It rang until it finally cut off. Dead to the world, she supposed.

Or just dead, said the voice. Trembling, Dawny fumbled to open her sleeping pills and threw a couple down. Things always seem worse at night, they always did, she just needed to go back to sleep and that way if the voice came back, she wouldn't hear it. And if there were worms, she'd swallow them in her sleep. Practical as ever, Dawny. Sensible.

In the morning she stood in her robe, heavy-headed and watching the kettle boil.

Hello, Dawny. You seem tired.

The kettle clicked off and her heart spasmed. Please stop, she pleaded, please shut up.

Lawrence. She should call Lawrence.

He seemed pleased. Telling her that it was amazing.

'You've gotta remember you've been through a profound change. You're no longer the person you were – you're tapping into your repressed subconscious – wow, man, not everyone is lucky enough to have that depth of experience.'

'So, the voice I'm hearing is me?'

'Excellent work, Dawny. You're discovering your innermost intuition.'

Dawny drove fast. Every part of her jittered. Her skin prickling with electricity.

Be careful, Dawny, you're tired and unhappy.

'I'm not,' she told the voice. 'I'm fine. I just want to get home.'

What's waiting for you there? A man who despises and belittles you.

He's so repulsed by your sagging bulk and mottled skin that he can't bear to put it in you. You deserve so much more than that, Dawny.

The voice was stronger now. A multitude of tiny voices speaking as one.

'Who are you?'

You know who we are. And we know who you are.

You're beautiful on the inside, Dawny – and we should know.

Blinking away tears, Dawny gripped the wheel hard and tried to focus on the road.

You should turn around and never go back.

Her underarms were a swamp, and wet beads ran down her back. She skidded into the forecourt of a petrol station and ran for the public bathroom. For the briefest second, she was aware of how easy it was to run. She hadn't even thought about it – she just did it.

Inside, she splashed herself with cold water from the small, grimy basin and stared at her dripping reflection. Please don't go mad, she begged, please hold it together. She noticed a barely perceptible twitch in her neck. Something under her skin rippling down across her throat. No, no, no… It disappeared down under her shirt. She ripped it open. A long, thin shape wriggled across her chest to her shoulder. Supporting herself with the basin, she retched and retched.

Don't be afraid. We're here to help you. Make you better.

It was so clear now – she'd obviously lost her mind.

Dawny ran for the car and fired the ignition, her arms and hands tingling. She pictured the worms sluicing through her blood, circulating through her body. Down into her legs and between her legs. She sobbed and put her foot down.

As she sped down through the hills, the bush was two dark shadows racing past on either side.

Phil is a despicable thing. He doesn't care about you because he doesn't care about anyone. He doesn't love you. He never loved you.

'That's not true,' she wept. 'Please stop.'

Remember when you married? He was seeing someone else up to the time you got married.

No!

'Fraid so, Dawny. He's using you cos you're too stupid to realise what's going on.

'So, what is going on?' she asked in a small, desperate whisper. Yes, it was happening; she was having a conversation with the worms. She slapped her cheek hard – get a grip.

We're here to help you. What's going on? Well, let's see – where do you think he is right now? Hmmm? Not at home.

'You don't know that…'

Why do you think he sent you on that retreat? For your health?

Then they laughed. Hundreds of tiny voices laughing at her.

Hahahahahahahahahahahahahahahahahahahahahahahahahaha

Something rippled across the top of her hand. She'd go to a doctor. She'd take something to flush them out. An anti-something or other…

You don't want to get rid of us. You want to get rid of the big parasite. He's destroying you piece by piece. He has to go – and you know it. Where is he now, Dawny? Where? Where? Where? Where?

'I don't know!' Dawny screamed over and over, and the worms went quiet.

Dawny stumbled through her front door calling his name. It was quiet. Empty. And as orderly as she'd left it. She had a sense that no-one had been here for days.

See? See? Where is he?

She ran upstairs calling…but there was no one there. Dawny's head pounded now. The worms had obviously bypassed her lungs and squirmed their way into her brain. She imagined them nesting, writhing in the grey tissue, hooked in and devouring. That explained all of it. Phil had probably told her where he'd be and she'd forgotten. She could be dumb like that – how many times had he told her how dumb she could be? Plus, there was her brain…

Try to relax, Dawny. You need a bath, to relax and think.

She ran a warm bath and lowered herself into it. And the worms stopped writhing.

This is nice. Relaxing.

Dawny was relieved to just breathe again. It was relaxing. She needed to think. Regroup. Work out what to do.

You know what you need to do. You need to kill the parasite.

'I can't. That's not who I am.'

But it could be… You're a good person, Dawny. You deserve to be with someone who sees you like we do. Who cherishes you, wants you. We see you and we want to help you. Protect you.

That night, she sat in the lounge with the lights off and waited in the dark, wondering where her husband was. At 2am she finally went upstairs to bed.

The worms tried to soothe her as she drifted to sleep. *Shush, Dawny, shush. You're going to be okay.*

She woke at dawn, energised and calm. She heard his key in the front door and went down to the kitchen.

He was the first to speak. 'You came back early.' Then Phil gave a small laugh, but it didn't sound like he was amused. 'I don't know why you didn't stay away longer, like you said.'

'Where were you last night?'

'Working. I stayed over at the office – thought you'd have worked that out. Still, critical thinking not really your thing, is it, Dawny?'

He doesn't know who you are. We hate him. We hate him. We hate him. We hate him. We hate him. We hate him. We hate him. We hate him. We hate him. We hate him. We hate him. We hate him.

A tiny worm slithered under the thin sclera of Dawny's eyeball, making its way across to the black pupil. Its tiny head emerged and partially obscured her vision, but she could see Phil moving about in the early morning gloom, pulling off his coat. Her eyes slid towards the knife block sitting on her marble countertop. She gripped her own wrist. That wasn't who she was.

That afternoon, Dawny started digging the pit.

Phil wandered out with a cup of green tea and watched her work. 'That retreat's obviously given you some pep, look at you go. Vege garden, is it?'

'Something like that,' she said, cutting into the soft, dark dirt with a spade. It wouldn't be long before the worms laid eggs that would hatch and then they in turn would lay even more eggs. They'd all need somewhere to feed – that's what they told her – and Dawny, if nothing else, had always been practical. Sensible.

I'm a Gemini

BY

Helena Claudia

Exiting an Uber alone in front of a crowded pub makes me feel like a celebrity, in the worst way possible. Like my social ineptitude is not being observed but is acting as a source of entertainment for a mob of teenaged design students with better shoes than me. Based on that, and the sheer number of them vaping in small, spiky clusters, I want to leave.

I can see the back of Jason's head through the liver-spotted windowpane. He's gotten through about half a pint and is deep in conversation with a stupidly silky-looking bartender.

1. I call on Britney Spears for spiritual strength.

Jason is tapping his thumb on the crescent-marked wooden countertop; the centre stone is missing from his chunky silver ring. I wonder if it's decorative or sentimental.

'Kia ora,' he says absently, flashing me a toothless smile and placing his hand on my arm before turning back to the bartender, who's working her way through an anecdote involving a field and a dog and a mutual friend's car. I slide into the stool next to him. His touch sticks to my forearm like Gladwrap.

The bartender twists a shiny brown tendril around her finger. Her tone rises and she slaps the countertop. They both laugh. I know that, realistically, I'm not the punchline. I smile and choke out a convincing giggle.

'Sorry about that,' he says, as if he hadn't been in uproarious laughter five seconds earlier. 'How are you? Can I get you a bevvy?'

'Hey! Yeah, I'm good. House red would be nice.'

'Cab Sav, please Eden.' He unearths his Visa from behind his phone case with a snap. Cold air kisses the damp patch his hand left behind. 'Thank you so much.'

I'm starving, but Eden doesn't seem like a 'chips for the table' kinda gal. Eden seems like she would order a side salad and a vodka tonic and then breathlessly add them into MyFitnessPal as soon as she could duck into the toilet. She would still be under her minimum calorie requirement for the day, because, despite serving pints for crowds of men with glistening eyes and puffed-up chests every weekend for the past two and a half years, Eden knows that if she does not watch her weight nobody will ever love her.

'I'm sorry I didn't think to reserve a table. They've really popped off recently.'

'I like the bar view; it's good for people watching.'

A group of disheveled men in suits flank my right side, while an elderly woman and her emo daughter share a jug of slushy margaritas to my left. I wonder if they're embarrassed; beyond or in spite of their affection for one another.

'I thought this place seemed like a bit of you.'

'What part of my profile gave it away? I'm a sucker for a 'hidden door' bit. But apparently so is the rest of our generation.'

'I blame Narnia,' Jason mumbles through a mouthful of foam.

I offer him a breathy grin. Like a receptionist. I wish I could have mustered up the serotonin to laugh. A laugh would have sounded good then. Or a quirky IMDb fact. I eye up Eden, cocktail shaker in her hand, down the opposite end of the way. The pause begins to stretch.

'So, how has video editing been treating you?'

He sighs. 'I mean, I do enjoy it, but my boss is acting like a total dickhead at the moment – I reckon some snake in HR passed on the comment I made about his hair in that quote-unquote "anonymous" review last month.'

'What's wrong with his hair?' I laugh. Very convincingly might I add. I'm glad I wasn't born a man. Women are statistically less likely to experience balding. And regardless, it's socially acceptable for us to wear wigs. Masking our ugly bits is a given.

'Oh my god, where to begin? I think toupees, for one, should be outright banned…' Jason continues on this tangent for a while, and I nod at all the right parts. I wonder if he will ask about my work again. My top definitely screams 'office bitch', but the pants might throw him into thinking I work in the creative sphere.

1. *I would like to be a writer.*

Eden's little plaits and sparkles and silver chains have taken time and patience and a fair amount of anxiety. I admire her for that. She looks like an appropriately cool Welly bartender. I think I should try a fringe again.

Jason circles back to my job. 'Rude of me I know – what was it you did again?'

'I'm a freelance writer. It pays the bills for now.'

'What do you enjoy writing about?'

'People, relationships, travel, anything unrelated to corporate jargon.'

Jason tilts his head. 'I would love to know some of your insights on people and relationships. In all honesty, it's all pretty confusing to me at the moment.'

'I might save my undoubtedly life-changing insights for our second date, if you don't mind?' I grin. I trust in my ability to come up with something that sounds inspirational at a minimum.

1. *Or I could read a Vice article about the Keto diet. Cold water therapy. Five ways to reconnect with nature. Eye Movement Desensitisation and Reprocessing.*

When Alex died, I started to dissolve. A sad, fat tablet of Berocca in a sea of other people's ideas about grief. Jason seems pleasantly devoid of any such qualms. I'm almost reluctant to burst that bubble.

He smiles at me. 'I've waited 24 years; I suppose I can hang on until next weekend.'

'What are we doing next weekend?'

The build-up is a little too smooth, and I can see he's sweating. I like this bit. When you could be anything or everything. You won't be. But you could.

'Um, maybe something involving a picnic if the wind doesn't fuck with us – can I text you?'

'For sure. I'm free except for Sunday arvo.' I am 90 per cent sure he will actually text. Maybe 70 per cent if we had sex tonight. A stupidly addictive gamble. I'll always remember the look in Alex's eyes when we first started dating.

We return to our drinks in a comfortable silence. Jason excuses himself for a piss, and I turn my attention to Rita Ora pouting on the flatscreen.

Eden appears like a meerkat. 'So, how do you know J?'

'Uh, Bumble.'

The pit in my stomach reopens.

1. *I like her eyeliner.*

'Oh my god, I can't believe he's still on there!' She laughs. 'Does he still have that photo with the fucking fish?'

'Unfortunately, yes. It was difficult to overlook, but I got there.' I smile back at her. A laugh would have sounded good then. A beefy looking coworker grabs her waist with one hand as he slides past, two jugs of beer jammed in the other fist. I bet he smells like cottage pie.

'I told him he needed to get a Polaroid camera like the edgy Uni boys – the grainy effect always gets me. It's probably just because you can't see their faces as well. But you're pretty cute, so whatever he did obviously worked.' She laughs.

'Yeah…' I say, summoning every ounce of my ability to make small talk. For some reason, nothing is coming out of my mouth. I miss Alex's ability to fill in these awkward spaces. I'm doing a shit job in his absence.

'Would you like a refill on that wine?' Eden eventually offers.

'For sure. Thank you.' I awkwardly chug back the remaining gulp and slide the glass over to her.

It's an enormous relief to see her walk away, even momentarily. Some chiropractor-looking douchebag has launched into a pointed tirade about his worst experiences with female bartenders. He looks very happy. Fuck working in hospitality.

J is taking a while. He's either taking a shit or checking his phone. I let the nondescript bar hum overtake my thoughts. Pretending to be absorbed by Instagram reels has historically proven to be the safest use of my time. A wine appears in front of me and disappears almost as fast.

1. *Alex used to drink whiskey.*
2. *Alex used to kiss me on the forehead.*
3. *Alex's bones are in a jar on the mantelpiece.*

'Sorry, there was a queue.' Jason slides into the barstool. 'Now that we've emptied the tank so to speak, would you like to get some food? They do a mean chips and aioli here but they're also $14. Entirely your call.'

'Ooh, I do love a good chips and aioli. But not for $14. Maybe we can get something on Courtenay Place?'

'Valid call,' he says, unwrapping his jacket from the barstool. I doubt I'll be coming back.

The night is crispened by the wind, and I lean into Jason. He squeezes my shoulders.

1. *I'm in a Lana Del Rey music video; basking in feminine joy, having achieved the ideal armpit to head ratio. Strangers in a city. Everyone wants me. Sunglasses emoji. Red wine emoji. Fingernails emoji.*

There are several faint silhouettes down at the far end of the sheds, shouting over the wind and the waves. I can see puffs of smoke floating sporadically into the wind. We awkwardly clamber onto the rooftops. This is why I never wear tight pants.

I prop my head up on the concrete ridge and watch the clouds wash over the stars. Jason awkwardly sinks down next to me, and I side-eye him. He looks deep in thought. I wish we had some weed. The fish and chips are fucking delicious, regardless.

'So, tell me, please,' Jason asks, spring roll in hand, 'on this beautiful, only kind of windy Wellington day, what specific part of my charming personality do you like the most, and why?'

'I'm not entirely sure to be honest.' I laugh. 'You seem nice and interesting and fun. I wanted to do something different with my Friday evening.'

'Thank you. I am nice, and interesting, and fun,' Jason says, bumping shoulders with me. 'For my part, beyond the fact you're pretty cute, and smart, and funny, I liked what you said in your bio.'

'Really? I thought it was a little on the nose. But I love that you liked it.' I turn to him and smile. He reaches for my hand. His palms are still sweaty.

'Is this okay?' His eyes reflect the streetlight. They look concerned.

'Yeah.'

He smiles. 'I think it's important to know what you want and take steps to make that happen.'

'Let's manifest a future together,' I say dramatically. 'Astrology bitch alert.'

He laughs and squeezes my hand. I squeeze back.

'What kinds of things do you need to make happen in your life?'

1. The darkness makes it okay to admire him.

Jason pauses. 'I would love to have kids at some point. Maybe that's patriarchal or something to mention on the first date, but I would love to have a wife and like, two kids. And definitely a Labrador. And a house. Which is not especially original, I know, but I think I could be happy with a life like that. I just need to work hard.'

'Good for you. Don't work too hard. It's easy to get lost in the sauce.'

Jason chuckles, but it stays in his throat. The hair on my neck tingles. I think about changing the subject.

He coughs, and sighs. 'My, uh, brother. He got all the way lost in the sauce. Was doing so well at his firm, too. Strange feeling, losing half of yourself.'

I can hear the waves crashing against the side of the yachts. They look black and glassy. I know we aren't alone, but it's still peaceful.

'What about you? What, uh, what things do you need to make happen?' Jason twirls the chunky silver ring around his thumb.

1. I am the picture of a skinny, morbid Santa. I bring children the
   kinds of dreams they try to keep buried under their pillows.

'I need to find someone who can be…soft. Without losing their edges.'

'I think I understand.'

We sit together, picking at our cold chips. Strangers laugh on the pavement, and I wriggle through their brains. They have better jobs and shiny dogs and the same bad habits.

1. I wish I was happy.

Jason stumbles into an exaggerated stretch. 'Time to get somewhere warm, you think?'

'Amazing plan. Should I call an Uber?' I offer a hand for him to pull me to my feet.

'No need, my flat is just around the corner.'

The night is brisk and muffled music appears in bursts as we walk along Oriental Parade. A shriveled bonsai and a pair of dirty combat boots frame his doorway. The house has a sour, damp smell. Like laundry after it's been left in the washing machine for a few days.

'Would you like a tea or a Milo?' he asks, sliding his hands around my waist.

'Just water would be awesome,' I say, leaning into his embrace for the appropriate number of seconds before pretending that his Avengers poster-wall has piqued my interest. My skin tingles where his touch was.

'Which one is your favourite?'

'Of the movies? I'm not sure. I like the blue one, though.'

'Me too.' He puts his arm around my shoulders.

'Welly bookshops have the best posters. There are a few more upstairs, but they're based on the comics. It might be the ADHD, but I've always preferred the movies.'

'That's understandable.' I unravel myself and make a beeline for the kitchen.

He picks up a figurine from the coffee table and follows me. 'God, not to sound like a complete nerd, but would you want to watch one of them? We don't have to watch an action movie. Or a movie at all. What do you want to do?'

'Um, a glass of water would be a good start. But I'm happy to watch whatever you wanna watch.'

'Oh duh, I'll put the kettle on and get you that water. Give me a minute and I'll set the TV up upstairs.' He fumbles with the mugs as the kettle begins to grumble. 'My flatmate's away doing conservation work in The Sounds.'

I raise my eyebrows and nod. There is a speck of dried tomato on the side of my glass. He pauses by the door, fingering the entranceway. 'The TV stuff won't take long. I was just wondering: can I kiss you?'

I don't really want to kiss him. But he looks thoroughly breakable.

'Of course,' I say.

He puts his hand on my lower back. His shirt is a little bit sweaty. He slurps aggressively at my bottom lip, and I can feel the hot stinging pressure of blood being sucked to the surface.

He pulls away, and grins. 'I've wanted to do that for ages. See you soon.'

I stand in the kitchen and listen to the sound of his footsteps soften. The capsule in my pocket has a bit of fluff caught on the edges, but it slips open with ease, and I tip it into Jason's mug. Garfield grins back at me. He hates Mondays.

1. Did Alex's parents ever decide to move the cat's ashes or are they still sitting side by side with his like a depressing menagerie?

I scrunch the sweaty, plastic casing between my thumb and forefinger; it falls into place with my other pocket debris. Like nothing ever happened.

Random thumping continues to resound overhead, and I decide to finish making Jason's Milo and head upstairs. A good little wifey. Genuinely shocking that he takes four sugars.

I can tell that he's vacuumed recently. No corner fluff. Impressive for a man in his 20s. The flat is old with tall mouldy ceilings. All the doors have pretty indented patterns and stubborn keyholes. The door to his bedroom has a peeling Teenage Mutant Ninja Turtles sticker slapped haphazardly on the left-hand side. The handle creaks as I twist it and cologne bursts onto the scene like an overeager toddler.

Jason turns. 'Oh, thank you!' He wraps his fingers around the handle and pulls me in to kiss him with the other hand. Bold. I tense my stomach and pucker my lips.

'What are we watching?' I smile, pulling away but keeping my hand on his arm.

He grabs my hand and leads me to the bed. 'Well, you said you haven't seen *Guardians of the Galaxy*, so obviously we've got to watch *Guardians of the Galaxy*.'

'Well, obviously,' I respond playfully, flopping down next to him on the navy duvet. He has two sad flat pillows jammed against the headboard. A spiderwebbed bauble lampshade illuminates the room in pale marigold. Fine masculine decor.

I hear his mug click down on the nightstand, and he turns over to face me. He looks like he's waiting for instructions – or exam results. He wants to fuck. You can always tell.

I put my hand on his cheek. 'Can we watch the movie?'

'Yeah sure. Of course!' he says, a blush creeping along the back of his neck. He wriggles up and grabs the remote.

Our shoulders and thumbs are pressed together as the movie booms around us. I focus on the hot chocolate, which he has started to drink in painfully slow sips. I genuinely still enjoy *Garfield*, and the sequel, *A Tail of Two Kitties*. The headboard is digging into the back of my neck.

I can't tell how full the mug is, but I'm guessing it will take him another 15 minutes to finish.

1. *Which gives me about 45 minutes to think about Alex. How he would bring me flowers and iced coffees and always text me when he got home.*

The movie dialogue calms, and he pulls me in for a kiss; I sink down onto his chest instead. It's warm and soft and I can hear his heart beating lightly. I resist the urge to check my phone. I hear his heart skip a beat and I wonder if it has already started to work or if he's anxious. I hear the telltale slurp that accompanies the dregs of a drink and I wonder if he notices a grainy, bitter aftertaste. Probably not. He obviously has a powerful suction technique.

'I remember watching this when I was in Year 10. I haven't been to an actual movie theatre in years,' Jason whispers, kissing the top of my head.

'We can go on a movie-theatre date if you like,' I reply softly.

'I would like that.' He chuckles and squeezes my shoulders.

I listen to his heart rate slowly build, and he starts to fidget. A raccoon with a gun yells something on-screen, and his chuckle turns into a violent cough.

It's working.

'Sorry,' he says, sitting up suddenly. 'I think I need another drink.'

I hear his footsteps pad down the stairs, and then a distant fit of coughing. I pick up the remote and mute the movie.

I can hear the tap running.

The sharp cracking of a mug on hard tile.

I twitch.

It shouldn't take too long.

I stand tentatively in the doorway.

'Jason?' I call down the stairs.

Silence.

1. *I want to cry when I see the Milo splayed over the black and white kitchen tiles. Like dirt on a painting.*

I turn off the tap. Jason is bleeding from the temple and curled up on the cold lino. They say that most people die with their eyes open, but his face is all scrunched up. They say that Alex didn't have any eyes left when the volunteers found him – he didn't do that part to himself. Two days in the open elements does a lot more damage to a body than you would think.

Jason's chunky black shoes thump rhythmically against the stairs. Heavy, but far from unbearable. I drag his body into the centre of the hallway. Take a deep breath in, and out. The hard part is over. I rummage through my purse for a lighter. A stick of incense twirls the scent of warm spices into the room, and I close my eyes.

'Alex?' I stroke his hair. 'Alex? It's time to wake up now.'

His eyelashes are thick and long and beautiful. Boys always get the best eyelashes. I climb onto his stomach, using both hands to delicately pry open his eyelids.

Nothing.

Odd.

My sleepy boy.

In the morning, he'll be surprised to find that the shape of his nails and knees and chin are different. But he'll be in my arms.

I wonder if he'll be upset with me. God, it would hurt so much if he were to be upset. Surely not. Alex and Jason have never gotten along.

1. *Jason cheated at cross country and copied Alex's homework.*
2. *Jason kissed Tabitha Florence even though he knew Alex really liked her.*
3. *Jason stole Alex's absolute favorite limited-edition Lord of the Ring chess set and sold it on Trade Me so he could buy tickets to Bay Dreams.*
4. *Just last month, Jason asked Alex if he could borrow $200 to invest in an NFT he saw on Tik Tok.*
5. *Jason thought it was cool to date his dead twin's girlfriend.*

Jason was quite clearly a dickhead. Alex will be glad to have this second chance.

They shared eyes, not intentions.

I loop the rope around Alex's armpits and slowly hoist him onto the bed. The back of his hand thwacks against the side table and I cringe. It's okay. He's safe, he's warm, he likes to sleep on his back. I can take care of him. I snuggle into his chest and listen to my heart pound through Jason's sweater. My cheeks ache. I'm so tired.

1. *We'll need to buy new clothes tomorrow.*
2. *We can do that before we go to the movies.*
1. *Alex will understand everything.*

REDWOODS ON TE MATA PEAK

BY MARTY YOUNG

The curiously named Sleeping Giant lay before them, dominating the skyline – but there was nothing peaceful to his slumber. Te Mata, the Chief of the coastal Wairarapa tribes, had choked to death trying to prove his love to Hinerakau, daughter of a Pakipaki chief from the Heretaunga Plains.

She had tricked him into eating his way through the hills, so their people might move more freely between the plains and the coast. But no feat of love, this had been her way of exacting revenge on his warring tribe's past. And now, Te Mata's prostrate body filled the horizon southeast of Hastings. Near his feet, the massive bite mark he'd made in the hills, forever known as the Gap. Pari Karangaranga.

Wayne's own throat constricted as if the earth was thick in his lungs, clogging his airways. It was a struggle to breathe, and he gripped the handlebars of his BMX, forcing down the emotions. Stopping the tears, before they flowed again. Stopping the anger, before he screamed once more.

It was just a stupid chair, so why did it matter so much?

He led the way, as he always did, down Havelock Road out of Hastings and into Havelock North, the smaller town on the foothills of Te Mata Peak. It was a trip the four of them did every weekend, and it was a hell of a ride up to the summit. Today, he needed it more than ever.

He needed to find a way to breathe again.

He peddled his blue BMX harder, daring someone to call out and tell him to slow down – or for someone to just say *something*. He couldn't even hear his brother Darren or Nick chatting behind him like they always did. No one had spoken since they'd started out.

Any other weekend, his best friend Mark would've been riding next to him, and they would've been cracking up at everything. Telling their younger brothers to hurry up, to stop bitching and *grow hair on their pair*.

But when only silence kept pace with him, he looked back, wondering if he was somehow alone. Darren was two lampposts behind him. No doubt red in the face with that determined look he always wore. The Sidewinder he rode was bigger and heavier than his old BMX, and he struggled with wheelies on it. Most of the tricks he used to be able to do on his BMX he couldn't do anymore, and that at least made Wayne smile.

The red crossbar pads on his own blue BMX were his pride and joy, and he couldn't imagine wanting to get a new bike. He'd saved for weeks, every cent from his paper run going into his top drawer until he had enough for the pads and the Mongoose race plate. He had stuck a big black Fox sticker on the plate, the fox-head logo skewed to the left.

But now, all that did was keep the chair firmly in his mind because it was the same, wasn't it? Just another pointless thing to fight over.

Behind his brother was Mark, who still wasn't speaking to him after their falling out at school on Thursday. That stupid padded chair was the only one in the class and there was always a fight for it, but that day, he and Mark had grabbed it at the same time, and for a reason he still couldn't understand, they'd fought over it.

Best friends weren't supposed to fight.

They hadn't spoken all day on Friday and worse was seeing him with Philip and Scott. Making new friends. Laughing without him – not that

Mark had laughed much lately. And not that Phil or Scott were dickheads; they were okay. But that didn't make it any easier, either.

Mark's brother Nick, who, with his red hair and freckles, looked more like his twin than his younger brother, was currently languishing even further behind. He'd said Mark was still pissed about it.

'He's only here 'cos mom made him come,' he said as they stood out front of their house this morning, waiting for Mark who was taking forever. Usually, he was always there, waiting for them. Today though, he was sullen and slow-moving, and they had waited almost ten minutes before he joined them with his bike.

'And he woke me up again in the middle of the night,' Nick said. 'His nightmares are getting worse, but he doesn't want to talk about them. He's been weird lately.'

Mark hadn't spoken about them to Wayne either, even before their fight. Only once had Mark let it slip that he'd been having nightmares where the night had grown legs and come after him. But when Wayne had prodded, Mark had gone silent. He had refused to say anything since, and now…

Was a chair really going to ruin their friendship? It sure seemed like it, and that was just… It shouldn't have been possible. They'd been best friends forever, living only six houses away from one another for as long as Wayne could remember.

It was a *fucking* chair!

So why was it so hard for either of them to apologise?

Because maybe it wasn't just a chair. Maybe it had never been about the chair. And that's what really gutted him. Mum said sometimes people just outgrew each other but how was that even possible when they had so much growing left to do? Couldn't they do that together?

But that thought ignited another memory – of them playing with Wayne's *Star Wars* figures a few Sundays ago. They'd been setting up their Rebel base when Wayne spotted Mark staring off into the distance, Han Solo laying discarded at his feet.

'Do you think we're getting too old to play with dolls?' he'd asked when Wayne prodded him, and although Wayne brushed it off at the time and ramped up the excitement to distract from the concern, the question had certainly wormed its way deep inside him.

Dolls?

Angry thoughts pushed his legs in angry cycles. They weren't dolls. And *they* weren't too old. The landscape about them changed as they cycled onwards, creeping higher, and that realisation only made Wayne cycle even faster. Why did the world have to change?

When he reached the lookout they always stopped at, about halfway up, he'd opened up a large distance over the others. He wiped away sweat from his forehead and let his bike fall to the ground. His legs burned from the effort of cycling up a mountain without gears, even though he'd walked part of the way where the road had become too steep, but that was good because it had also burned away some of his anger.

They hadn't asked him to slow down, though...

And they were cycling slowly, with Darren and Nick side by side, weaving unsteadily across the road in animated conversation. Mark was further behind them, looking back every so often as if watching out for cars.

He never rode last. No way would he let his brother beat him here.

Wayne turned around and walked towards the edge of the lookout. *So what? If he wants to be last, let him.*

Then laughter reached him on the fading wind, and he ground his teeth. It drifted off, away from him, leaving that silence again. Hanging thick and heavy about him. His stomach was knotted with something he didn't like at all – fear.

'About time you got here,' he said when his brother finally reached the lookout.

Darren knew better than to say anything, though. He dropped his bike and went to the other side of the lookout, with Nick following him.

Morphing and swirling, forming shapes and jagged outlines, tendrils of silence sneaked out from Wayne to lash about Darren and Nick, stealing away their laughter, making them mute.

Wayne said nothing when Mark got there almost ten minutes later.

On a clear day like today, it was possible to see as far as the Mahia Peninsula to the northeast, on the far side of the Bay, the Ruahine, Kaweka and Maungaharuru ranges to the west past the Heretaunga Plains. Once they got to the peak, they might even be able to see Mount Ruapehu rising from the centre of the North Island. That was always something special.

Introduced redwoods stabbed the landscape before them, and from the lookout, Wayne stood over the first of those trees, giving him a strange view into their branches, exposing him to secrets he shouldn't have been privy to – not that he could understand their language. If only he could, perhaps then he'd know how to speak with Mark.

But even that forest was silent, save for the faint whisper of wind. As if the trees had picked up the tension between them, becoming infected with the same silence emanating from them. Perhaps they didn't want to be here, either. They were a long way from home.

'Hey, check it out,' said Nick, who was standing on the other side of the small metal railing of the lookout, his feet inches from the drop-off. His words were like a gunshot into the silence. 'That looks like a car.'

Darren crowded into him, trying to catch a glimpse of what he'd seen between the trees at the bottom of the gully, and reluctantly, Wayne joined them, driven on by curiosity.

'Woah!' Daren said, pointing too, now. 'It is!'

The rusted Ford Cortina lay at the bottom of the gully, twisted and bent out of shape, and only just visible between the massive trees.

'It looks like someone drove it straight off the road,' said Nick.

'Why would they do that?' Darren asked. 'That's nuts.'

But Nick was right; the metal was crumpled and dented, and the front end was smashed in where it would have impacted the ground first. The wheels were bent at odd angles.

'How have we never seen it before?' asked Nick, and it was a good question. They stopped here every weekend – although it was different today and the answer was almost immediately obvious.

Wayne glanced over at Mark, who hadn't moved to see the car, and for a moment, their eyes met. But Mark quickly turned away.

If it had been a usual weekend, they would have resurrected Te Mata with their chatter and laughter. They wouldn't have been standing here in silence, too uncomfortable to interact with one another and instead taking in the scenery alone.

'We should go have a look,' said Wayne, needing to fill that silence with something.

The gully was deep, the car was partially obscured by the overhanging cliffs and the thick underbrush. It would be a steep climb down to it.

'No,' said Mark. It was the first thing he'd said to Wayne the whole day. 'I'm going to go home.'

'What?' Nick said, his excitement swapping out for confusion, but even that was quickly replaced with annoyance. 'Jeez guys, work it out already, would you? You're ruining the weekend. If you go home, I have to go home, and I don't want to!'

Wayne's cheeks grew hot and he stared down at his shoes.

'I… This was in my dream,' Mark said after a few seconds. 'We stopped here and saw a car at the bottom of the gully. But…'

'But what?' Wayne pushed.

'How could you dream about it?' asked Darren.

There was a curious look on Mark's face: panic and terror, loss and loneliness, all blended into something unknown. Then it was gone. 'I don't know. But in my dream, something was waiting inside the car, and as soon as we saw it, it knew we'd seen it, and it started creeping out towards me, until it surrounded me and I was blind, like it was suddenly midnight. I couldn't find my way home. It's spooky being blind,' he said in a rush.

'It's not even lunchtime,' said Darren, squinting up at the sun. 'I don't think we have to worry about getting lost at night. My dad'll go nuts if I'm not home well before then.'

'You don't get it,' said Mark, but he didn't explain. The troubled look in his eyes grew more intense.

'Come on, Mark,' Nick said. 'It's just a stupid dream. Nothing's going to happen.'

'Yeah,' added Darren. 'How can the night be inside the car in the middle of the day?'

'Don't be a wuss,' said Wayne, unable to help himself. The dream just sounded like an excuse for him not wanting to be here. Another way of avoiding having to apologise over the chair. 'We've been riding up here for years and we've never seen anything scary.'

'Too bad,' Mark said, his expression changing into something fierce. 'But you're right. We always do this. Every weekend. And I… I just don't want to anymore. There're other things I'd rather do.'

'Like hang out with Phil and Scott.'

'So what if I do? Maybe they're more fun to hang out with! *At least they don't play with dolls.*'

'They're not dolls!'

'Screw you guys.' Nick threw up his hands in frustration. 'I'm going to go take a look.'

'Well, I'm going to wait up here,' said Mark. 'But then we're going back, Nick. I don't care what the rest of you do. Stay or go, I don't care.'

'Whatever,' said Nick. 'C'mon, Darren.'

'Yeah, okay.' Darren followed Nick over the railing, and they began climbing down the steep slope towards the car.

Wayne and Mark stared at each other, neither moving. But the car called. And Mark had wanted that chair, and now he wanted to sit this one out, and Wayne didn't want to.

'I...' But Wayne didn't know how to finish that sentence. I'm sorry? But why should he have to apologise? Why didn't Mark have to?

Because neither of them was sorry, and the chair was irrelevant. His mother had been right. Something had fundamentally changed, and it had snagged on their friendship, tearing the bond between them.

'You wanted to play with the *Star Wars* figures just as much as I did,' Wayne said, still needing to understand.

'Well, I don't anymore.'

'But *why*?'

Mark's expression changed, and he opened his mouth to speak. There were dark shadows under his eyes, and Wayne didn't know how he hadn't noticed them before. But then Mark closed his mouth in silence, his shoulders sagging.

'Can't you just tell me?'

'Just go,' said Mark, turning from him. 'Fucking enjoy your chair.'

The words blasted him like a death knell of their friendship. So instead of hunting for words that might mend, he turned to the gully and angrily called out, 'Wait up, guys!'

The tear grew worse with that action; he felt it deep, felt the mortal wound he'd just caused. There would be no coming back from this, even if he didn't understand how they'd reached this point. Things would never be the same between them again – and maybe that's how it was supposed to be because *fuck it*. He'd had enough. If Mark didn't want to be friends anymore, then fine. Let him go play with his *new* friends.

But there were tears there, simmering with the anger, threatening to burst out. And that fear too, the fear that had been building within him ever since the fight. Fear that something was wrong, deeply wrong.

Darren and Nick waited for him to join them, but they didn't say anything. He pushed past them and descended into the gully, using shrubs and rocks to slow his descent.

Behind him came the sound of footsteps and for a fleeting moment, he imagined it was Mark with a change of heart. But it wasn't, and there was something so final about that thought that it scared him even more. He glanced back up to the road.

'It'll be okay,' his brother said, but Wayne turned around and resumed his climb down towards the car. No, it wouldn't.

Redwoods rose over them as they moved deeper into the gully, massive tree trunks with their branches held high, shading the light. Their trunks were covered with thick, fibrous bark that had deep grooves forming irregular patterns, like they'd all been broken, too. The whole world had shattered.

'Listen,' Darren said, and they paused. Then he whispered, 'It's so quiet.'

He was right; there were no birds chirruping, no wind through those sky-high branches. Nothing but a stillness that made Wayne want to hold his breath to stop his heartbeat from being heard.

But heard by what? It was a silly, childish thought – one that was fortunately broken by the sound of an approaching car up on the road. A bird called out from somewhere ahead of them, the rush of wings to go with it, and everything was right again.

'Weird,' said Nick, still in a whisper.

The car waiting for them at the bottom of the gully was a rusted, mangled hulk of a thing. The blue paint was mostly gone now, and the windows were shattered. Ferns and weeds grew up around the wheels, and moss covered the hood.

'Far out, look at it,' said Wayne as he approached the old Cortina. 'Can you imagine being in this when it crashed?'

'No way,' said Darren, walking around to the front of the car. He mimicked a car bursting out over a cliff and falling to its death, where he made exploding sounds and threw up his arms. He spun – then froze. 'Hey, guys? Is that a cave?'

The entrance to a cave was a few metres away from the car, almost invisible due to the overgrown vegetation; they'd never have seen it if they hadn't climbed down here. A jagged, uneven mouth had been formed by the relentless flow of water, and that opening was easily big enough for them to enter walking upright.

'Hey, Mark!' Nick called out. 'We've found a cave!'

Mark didn't reply, and Nick paused.

'He's okay,' said Darren.

'Yeah, but I wish you and him would sort things out,' he said, pointing at Wayne. 'He said you almost pulled the chair out from under him.'

'What? That's not true. We both wanted it.'

'It's a chair. Why did it matter?'

'It doesn't, and that's the point.'

'What?'

'Don't worry. You won't understand.'

'C'mon guys,' said Darren, forever the peacemaker. 'Just forget about it for now.' He made his way over to the cave's entrance but didn't go in. The sound of trickling water echoed inside.

'We should come back tomorrow with torches and rope,' he said, the thrill of adventure gleaming in his eyes. 'I wonder how far it goes, and what's in there. Dinosaurs would be so cool…'

Nick was still at the car, and after casting one final look back up the slope to where his silent brother was, he returned his attention to the Cortina, grabbing one of the door handles and depressing the button. Surprisingly, the door popped open a couple of inches, despite the twisted state of the car.

Like a release of pressure from the interior, even though all the windows were broken.

'I didn't expect that,' he said as he pulled the door open further. It creaked open a couple of inches before getting stuck.

'No, don't!' Wayne yelled, not entirely sure why, although Mark's words blasted through his mind and the look he'd glimpsed suddenly became clear.

But it was too late. Something shifted within the car, a rising, sighing bulk of midnight that began to unfurl from the confines of the Cortina. It didn't matter that the windows were smashed; whatever it was, it had waited for someone to open to door, to free it that way.

And now it came for them – for Wayne. A thick, inky cloud darted towards him. He screamed, or tried to, but no sound came out. And even as he drew breath to try again, the darkness enveloped him, sucking him deep into its lonesome void. He could hear Mark calling for him, like he'd been trying to do all along, but he couldn't respond to that, either.

Then someone was shaking him, and the darkness was receding. It was Darren, grabbing him by the shoulders, worry etched into his face.

'That was Mark!' he said, pointing up the slope towards the rest stop high above them. Already, Nick was clambering his way back up to the road, and Darren let go of him and sprinted after his friend.

Wayne shook his head, trying to clear it of the residue of darkness that clung on. His thinking was slow, distorted, as was the world around him. Gone were the vibrant colours of the forest; now all was a dull, faded grey as if tainted by whatever they had let free from the car.

He clambered to his feet (had he fallen over?) and followed his brother, still sorting through words and their meanings. What was wrong with Mark?

Then, behind him, the car shifted with a creak and a groan. Wayne spun in time to see the door Nick had pulled open, open further. The darkness that had spilled from it was withdrawing, seeping back into the deformed interior, but not before he glimpsed something inside it. A face, familiar, but terrified–

Then the door closed, and this time, its creak was more like a chuckle.

Wayne screamed then, his head suddenly clear enough to allow him to run back up the slope as fast as he could. He ran, but–

–they were too late.

Time… Fucking time and its relentless trek ever onwards with scant regard to anything or anyone. It just rolls on over the top of everything, eventually. A steamroller.

Wayne sat in the car, his mind consumed by the past as he stared up at Te Mata Peak. It was hard to believe that so many years had passed since the last time he had been here. And yet the landscape looked little changed.

Time rolled on, but the memory of that day remained as clear as ever. Time hadn't erased it one bit, or even dulled it. The past was forever stained by the abduction of his best friend, a mystery forever unsolved. A wound that forever bled.

The loss of a loved one is hard enough, but never having answers…
that's a different kind of pain.

'I'm sorry, Mark,' he said quietly. 'I wanted to go look at that crashed
car. Just like I wanted that fucking padded chair. If we hadn't fought
over that, I would have listened. I wouldn't have left my best friend alone
on the side of the road when he'd needed me the most.'

But there was no one around to answer, to forgive him his deeds from
long ago, so he lapsed into silence again.

Mark's brother Nick never recovered from what happened, and Wayne
had long since lost contact with him, so there was never an option of
talking with him about that day, or why Mark no longer wanted to be
mates. Wayne's own brother pretended none of it ever happened. He
closed down, walled himself up – but then he had also lost Nick that day,
albeit in a different way. It was too much for a ten-year-old to endure.

So it was just another question that would forever go unanswered. It
could go onto the pile. Hopefully, one day he could burn the fucking lot
of them – but that would never be a solution. Their ghosts would just
continue to haunt him, just as they had done for decades.

Besides, he knew it had never been just about the chair. Perhaps they
had been changing, growing apart, and he hadn't wanted to acknowledge
that. They were best mates who spent every day together, and the idea
that one of them had outgrown the other, that Mark had grown bored
of him – was too much to bear.

But the years, they twist and turn, sprouting truths where perhaps
none had been before, or they slowly revealed truths that wouldn't have
otherwise been visible. Exposed through the erosion of time.

Because there'd been that look on Mark's face. Only there for a
moment, but in the aftermath of what had happened, that look had
grown clear – he had been terrified, wanting help. But no one was
listening.

Wayne, his best friend, wasn't listening, and perhaps that was why
Mark had sought out other friends. Not because they were no longer
mates, but because his new friends listened.

Had there been problems at home, or at school? Wayne just didn't
know; if there had been, they'd been well hidden. But then, wasn't that
always the way – until it was too late?

That suspicion, coupled with those fatal last words (*fucking enjoy your chair*), all served to stake the memory in his mind, pin it firmly in place so time could never take it from him. It was him and Mark both reaching for that stupid padded chair at the same time, then turning to look at one another.

The police launched a nationwide investigation, but Mark was never found and no one was ever arrested. His parents had been interviewed, Wayne remembered that, and they had split up soon after, but neither had been charged with anything. Same with Mark's teachers.

Perhaps now, with all the advanced computing power and linked databases, the police might have more luck, but Mark just vanished into thin air back then, leaving behind a trail of unanswered questions.

It was like he'd been…erased. Like he'd been a mistake the universe wanted to rectify. And all they were left with were these weird memories of someone who might have existed but one day didn't.

He didn't die, he just…*wasn't* anymore. Other than a memory. The darkness had taken him – as stupid as that sounded. But it was true, and that memory was also stark and vivid, despite the weight of years.

When Nick had pulled open the door, something had surged from the car and come straight for him – *hadn't it*? Or was it all part of a jumbled memory spiked by loss? Had they all seen it emerge like a sinister fucking creature, or only him? Mark had dreamt of that happening – and how was *that* possible?

He'd never asked, never told, for fear of what it might mean. He didn't believe in the supernatural, but sometimes he did. Like now, staring up at Te Mata Peak.

And the sound that Cortina had made when it reclaimed whatever it had been, as if it had chuckled.

'Fuck off,' he whispered, fighting back the urge to shiver.

Hadn't he also glimpsed Mark within that shade as it had returned to the car?

He was parked at the same lookout they'd stopped at all those years ago. The car was down in the gully below…

Go check, the day whispered at him. Pull open the door…

'No,' he said, more firmly this time.

Because what would happen if he creaked open that door and the black roiling cloud of night sought him out again – or worse, it took someone else that he loved?

Bullshit, he thought, unable to voice anything. That way lay madness and he wouldn't go there. He couldn't – because sometimes it was better to believe in supernatural monsters than in real ones.

And yet, despite that hope, more vibrant here than anywhere else, the supernatural always sank back below familiar questions that refused to leave him alone: could it have been him taken instead of Mark? Or his brother? Had it been a random abduction, or was there more to it? Had someone been preying on Mark, and this was their opportunity? Was that why Mark hadn't been himself the last few weeks of his life?

They'd been best friends, so why hadn't they talked to each other, properly talked?

If only he'd let him have that stupid fucking chair.

If only he'd apologised. Not for the chair, but for not understanding.

If only he had listened.

If only he had paid attention.

If only, if only, if only…

He gazed up at the peak.

'Wake up, damn you,' he said to the Giant. 'Tell me what happened to Mark.'

But Te Mata kept silent.

Blind Date
by Gina Cole

Dallas sat at a small round table outside the Sunset Café, waiting for her date Chichi to arrive. What kind of a name was that anyway? A name for a lapdog, a small white fluffy pedigree. And this was not a date; it was an appointment. She turned up the collar on her black wool coat, tugged it close to the back of her neck and held the stitched end points over her nose with her gloved hands to block out the freezing wind howling down the footpath. Would Chichi ask to move inside next to the roaring fire? There was one – a roaring fire that is. Dallas peeked in through the café window. The waitress threw a log on top of a smoky grate. Orange sparks flew up into her face and hair. A small flame ignited at the corner of her apron. She whacked at the orange lick with her bare hands over and over until it died and left tendrils of smoke curling up into the air. She made frantic movements with her fingers to brush away floaty embers caught in her fringe, scurried behind the bar, turned on a tap and held her red palms under the streaming water. The smell of burnt hair and singed cotton wafted out from the interior of the café, swirling on the heels of a stout middle-aged man and woman exiting onto the footpath. The man glanced at Dallas and drove his hands into his coat pockets. The woman tugged at his sleeve urging him to move. They walked briskly towards the cliff. Dallas twisted in her seat, not wanting them to notice her.

The life of an assassin is a lonely one. After this kill, she needed to go somewhere for a break. A tropical oasis to soothe her soul, an island in Fiji so she might commune with the ancestors. Followed by a visit to a fairground with thrilling rides. Disneyland in Paris. Not California, Hong Kong or Shanghai but Paris. Maybe a cruise along the Amazon River. But the more she thought about touristy destinations, the more she realised she wanted peace. She longed for a day at a white sand beach in the middle of a scorching summer. The sun sparkling on the ocean, diamonds lifting into the air. To swim in the sea, the water smooth against her skin. It's always summer somewhere in the world.

After her phone chat with Chichi, she was certain the little table on the footpath was the perfect place to meet. She checked herself over. What about the black felt fedora and black leather gloves? Too much? She yanked the hat low over her forehead, pushed her fashionably oversized sunglasses up the bridge of her nose and sank into her trench coat. Yes, all this garb was acceptable attire on a chilly day in late autumn. Puka leaves large as hands danced along the gutter, although Dallas saw no trees anywhere in the street. What effect was she going for here? Spy? Hip hop artist? Fashion maven? Whichever one it was, it would be clear to anybody with half a brain that she was trying to hide her face. No one would remember her. Or they would have differing recollections of her. She had mastered a certain obscuration of form, made herself genderless and forgettable, a blank upon which people might imprint their own impressions. That was the look she was going for, blank.

She hunkered lower as the waitress approached holding a twee serving tray made of woven cane and laden with two steaming cups of coffee. The harried waitress brought with her a wisp of smoke and burnt wood.

'One espresso and one cappuccino. Can I get you anything else?'

'No thanks. My friend will be here any minute.'

'There's a free table inside if you'd like to get out of this cold wind.'

The waitress shivered in a mini skirt, diaphanous top with a burn hole at the shoulder, and black apron with a raggedy burnt corner. A wind gust swirled her brown hair across her eyes. Why she was taking the time to ask, to converse? She was shaking with cold, and it was clear to Dallas that she wanted to get back into the warmth inside.

'The view is better out here.'

The waitress would have no reason to question her on that issue. Sunset Café was positioned high on a hill near a steep cliff with a view looking west over a vast ocean expanse. The waitress hugged the tray to her chest and hurried back inside the café. Dallas turned her attention to the horizon shimmering in a curved line where it met the sky. She imagined tanned summertime tourists wearing shorts and singlets packing out the café, laughing and chatting while lingering over iced tea and gazing at the magnificent sea view. Tonight, the street was cold and empty, except for a few scruffy sea gulls hovering on a thermal updraft rising over the cliff. She reached across to Chichi's still hot cup of coffee, rotated it so that the handle faced the empty seat, and sank back to wait.

Paper flyers skittered along the asphalt. Dallas retrieved one caught up against her chair leg, fluttering and snapping in the wind. She smoothed the crinkled paper to see the image of a woman standing in front of a merry-go-round, her hands planted on her hips, the words 'Come to the Fair' written across her t-shirt. Dallas' eyes glitched for a moment and she read 'Come to the Fire'. She blinked it away. The woman on the flyer reminded Dallas of someone she'd had a conversation with many years ago while sitting in the sun at a hexagonal picnic table. Any threads of the faded conversation eluded her, something to do with a marathon, the marathon of life. A sudden flurry blew the paper from her hands. It floated out beyond the cliff and disappeared. The sun blazed into Dallas' eyes as it began its descent in a glorious red show. She continued to watch in case she missed the huge orange ball dipping into the sea. But the sun did not move.

When she turned back to her coffee, she spotted a woman striding towards her wearing a cream coat. Blue hospital scrubs peeked out from inside the coat as it flapped around her long legs. Blinking rapidly, the woman approached the table. She kept turning as if to ensure no one had followed her, as if she were being pursued. Her hair was tied back off her face. Dallas stood up to receive her but stopped short of offering any physical greeting.

'Hello. You must be Chichi.'

The woman pulled up mid-stride, a frown line deepening between her eyebrows. 'Um yeah. Dallas?'

'Yep. I ordered coffees. Cappuccino for you, right?'

Dallas gestured with an open hand to the seat opposite her, in the manner of a cop directing traffic. In a way, she was directing the situation.

'Thank you,' said Chichi, once again checking behind her before she sat down.

They remained silent, regarding each other, reaching for their cups, sipping coffee. The sun hovered. It had grown bigger, brighter as though moving towards them rather than dropping below the horizon. Chichi gazed out to the view over the sea.

'I've never done anything like this before.'

'Yeah, you don't look like the usual type.'

'What's the usual type?'

'Oh, you know. Kind of desperate.'

Chichi drew herself up, inhaled, changed position and straightened her shoulders. She opened her eyes wide and relaxed her face. The frown disappeared.

'Great. How does this work, Dallas? Is that even your real name?'

Dallas scoffed. 'Nobody uses their real name in this game.'

Chichi drew her coat tight around her body and crossed her arms and legs. 'Well, like I said. This is all new to me.'

Dallas had no desire to drag out their rendezvous any longer than necessary. She would get in and out as quick as possible like an opportunistic carnivore, a large cat.

'Okay. Let's talk business. I understand you have a patient who needs tending to.'

It was Chichi's turn to scoff. She slumped her shoulders and almost laughed. 'You call the people you kill patients?'

Dallas flicked her head towards the other two outside tables. There were no people seated at either of them. But there were still a few patrons left in the café. You can never tell who might be listening.

'Keep your voice down.'

'I'm sorry. It's just ironic because I work at Mercy Hospice, and the woman I want you to…I mean the patient I need you to tend to, also works there. She's a nurse, same as me.'

Dallas straightened her coat sleeves. She baulked at the stench of deep-fried food, cooked in rancid oil, billowing from a vent on the side wall of the café.

'Mercy Hospice? My grandmother was there.'

'Oh? What was her name?'

Dallas looked Chichi dead in the eye. 'Martha Thomas.'

'Martha was your grandmother? Well, yes, I knew her very well. Lovely person. That was so recent. I'm sorry for your loss. Funny, I never saw you with her.'

'I never saw you with her, either. Strange she didn't mention you,' said Dallas.

'She was a bit confused at the end. They get that way. Can't remember people, can't swallow, can't do much at all really. They're completely helpless.'

Dallas would not be drawn. She was a tricky one, this Chichi. Dallas had come across her kind before. A little bit irrational and, if not handled with great care, extremely dangerous. She scanned the beautiful horizon, suppressed an urge to go towards it. The sun had stopped moving altogether, as though listening in to their conversation.

'So, tell me about the patient.'

Chichi hunched over and looked around to make sure no one heard her speak except Dallas.

'Her name is Sister Soala. She's killed ten women at Mercy Hospice. I want you to tend to her. Can you do that?'

Dallas held her tongue. She tried to calculate in her mind how much longer this charade would last. Not much longer. She almost yawned. It was plain to her that the woman was deranged. But who was she to question the woman's motives? This was shaping up to be one of her more unusual jobs. An easy one but strange all the same.

'I don't see why you need my services. Why haven't you reported her to the police?'

'She knows I'm on to her. She threatened me. I'm terrified. She's far too clever for the police. They won't find anything and then I'll be exposed. I'll be her next target.'

Dallas toyed with her cup, swivelled it back and forth on the table. She eyed Chichi over the top of her sunglasses and sighed. 'And how did you find me?'

Chichi sat up straight, jutted her chin out and lifted her chest a little. 'I saw what you did last month.'

'What are you talking about?'

'You turned up your grandmother's morphine drip. You killed her.'

Dallas shifted uneasily, crossed and uncrossed her legs. The story was all topsy-turvy.

'So you did see me with her. Why did you lie before?'

'Never mind. I understand why you did it. She was in a lot of pain. Didn't have much time left. Anyway, I looked into your grandmother's file. Found your details. You're a tech specialist. Is that even true? Is she even your grandmother?'

'That's what I told the hospice. But how did you find out about my... side line?'

'From the dark web.'

'Ha! You don't strike me as someone who would visit the dark web.'

'I didn't. There was a cancer patient at hospice: Martin. He was a computer hacker. I told him about Soala, and I told him what you did. And somehow, he found you. Don't ask me how. I have no idea how the dark web works.'

Dallas leaned over, steepled her fingers, rested her elbows on the edge of the table. There was no point ordering another coffee. The less opportunity for the waitress to identify her, the better. Best to have as few witnesses as possible. She didn't think the waitress would remember her. There were too many barriers in the way of an accurate recollection. Dallas would be just another customer who had ordered an espresso. The coat, hat, sunglasses and gloves covered everything. And Dallas had made sure to check for CCTV. She had taken no chances with this job.

'Look, sorry about this, but I'm too close. I can't do it,' she blurted.

Chichi's face fell and a second later she brightened. 'But you must do it. I have video footage of you killing your grandmother.'

'So, you want to blackmail me? I was only doing what she asked me to do,' said Dallas. Tears formed but did not fall. She ruffled her coat lapels and got up to leave. Chichi caught her gloved hand.

'At least your grandmother could choose how and when to die, and she had time to say goodbye. If you don't do what I ask, I'll send the video to the cops.'

Dallas returned to her seat, eyed Chichi once more over her sunglasses. 'What's this video you claim to have? Let me see it.'

'Alright, I can show you. But don't try anything. I've backed it up in the cloud.'

Chichi dipped her hand into a side pocket in her cream coat and took out a mobile phone. She tapped on the display and brought up the video, turned the screen to Dallas and held it high so Dallas could watch. Dallas leaned into the table, squinted at the phone as the video played. Tears now flowed over her cheeks, leaked through the gap in her collar and rolled in wet trails between her breasts. She lifted her sunglasses a little to wipe the tears from her cheeks, careful not to let Chichi see her eyes. A figure in the video moved in and out of shot.

'Hang on. Is that you in the background, in the reflection?'

Chichi frowned and inspected the phone. 'No, that is not me. That is her. Soala.'

Dallas leaned back, tugged on her coat collar again, pulled it tight over her face, crossed her legs and hugged her sides. Coiled up like a spring. 'You two look remarkably similar. You could be sisters.'

Chichi scoffed. 'She's Samoan. I am Pākehā. We're not even related.'

Dallas snorted behind her black collar. She'd almost had enough of this woman. 'Look, I don't understand. Why don't you tend to the patient yourself? You're a hospice nurse. You have access to drugs.'

'I can't. I'd lose my nerve. I'm too scared.'

'Well…my services aren't cheap. You need to pay up.'

'I am paying you. With your freedom.'

Dallas arched her eyebrows. Non-plussed. This amateur was annoying her. 'Look, if I'm going to do this, and I'm not saying I will, I'll need some detailed information about the patient.'

Chichi shot a side glance at Dallas. She raised her trembling hands from her lap and gesticulated like a mechanical scarecrow. 'All I can tell you is that she's always on the shift before mine. The graveyard shift. I can't tell you anything else about her. We're not chums.'

'Okay,' said Dallas, keeping her voice low to calm the waters. Chichi was obviously nervous.

'Good. Also, I don't want to know when or where it will happen.'

'Trust me. You won't know a thing.'

Dallas picked up her coffee and took a sip. Chichi grabbed her cup, lifted it up to toast Dallas and gulped down the last dregs of her cappuccino. Dallas stared out to sea and waited for the sun to lower beyond the horizon. But the sun loomed stubbornly above the ocean. Chichi coughed and spluttered and choked. Her phone fell from her hand and clattered onto the table.

'You okay?' asked Dallas.

'What have you…'

Chichi continued coughing, grabbed at her throat, and stared at Dallas. She snatched at the air and slumped forward in the seat. Her head dipped, and her hands collapsed onto the little round table her mobile just out of reach. To any observer Chichi would appear to be sitting upright with her head bent over. Not an unusual posture in this time of constant phone checking. Dallas reached over and grabbed Chichi's phone. She tapped into the screen.

'As you requested, you didn't want to know when or where. And the video? I have erased it, Chichi. Or should I say, Soala. Oh, and one last thing. Martin helped clear out your savings account to pay me. So, thank you.'

Dallas replaced the phone in the mark's hand. She took hold of her own phone, tapped the screen, put it to her ear. 'Hi Martin. I have tended to the patient as per your request. Job done. How's grandma?'

Dallas stared at the mark for a second. Rearranged her coat, got to her feet and left. She walked as fast as possible towards the cliff, glancing back to see Chichi slide off her chair onto the ground.

The sun sat in the same position above the ocean, its rays bursting across the sky. She stood at the edge of the cliff. On the rocks below lay the broken bodies of the couple who had left the café earlier. The rocks all around them were splattered with blood. Dallas took one step into the air and jumped. The waitress ran and jumped after her.

No, no, no, no…not this again. She didn't mean to. If only she'd been more careful. She had stupidly gone right to the edge of the cliff to look at the water. The sparkling water. Only to look at the water. That was all. The bright, bright water. Diamonds of light, lifting, lifting into the air. She had been so happy at that moment. That fateful moment just before the ground beneath her front foot gave way. She'd scrambled, cartwheeled her arms backwards, tried to regain her balance. And then she was airborne. Her heart pumping in her ears, the wind whistling into her face, the rocks rushing up to greet her, a panicked scream howling from her mouth.

Falling.

Falling.

Falling.

An ancient pōhutukawa tree broke her fall. If it wasn't for that tree she would have died, smashed on the rocks. But the branches caught her. She bounced from one branch to another, snapped twigs and broken boughs scratching and catching at her, gouging at her skin, slicing raw and bloodied flaps that hung from her face and arms. Her bones were broken and fractured in a million places – vertebrae, back, wrists, arms, legs, skull.

The tree flipped her over. She landed on her head on the rocks. She can never remember the landing except for the pressure in her head. And then nothing. Blackness. The rib and spine damage made it hard to breathe. Her breath rasped and gurgled through her blood-choked airway as she lay like pulp, almost dead on the rocks in excruciating agony. She'd wanted to scream through her shattered teeth, but no sound came out. She tried to blink away the blood seeping into her eyes. She tried to move, but her body grated and creaked like a bag of smashed glass. And the pain, the pain washed into her even as the sea washed in and out.

Blackness.

And here she is again. With no escape, despite her careful plotting. If only they would let her go. Let her go gently towards the permanent sun. Like she had done for her grandmother. Her grandmother had told her what to do near the end. Had given Dallas firm instructions. Why hadn't she left instructions? Why hadn't she?! Why don't they give her a view of the sea, a view of the water? Please, please let me go. She wanted to go, to be with her grandmother.

Next to her, the waitress fell at the same rate. They hit the rocks one after the other. Dallas fell through the rocks. She woke in her room in the hospital. The overhead light blazed at the end of her bed. The waitress came to check her chart. Two doctors in white coats and scrubs marched into the room, a senior and a junior, with a group of medical students straggling dutifully behind them. Dallas' eyes tracked their movements. She read the name tag of the senior, 'Dr Soala Martin', and the junior, 'Dr Chichi Sun'. Dr Sun grinned like a ridiculous clown at a fairground stall.

'Good morning, Dallas,' said Dr Soala, leaning over to make sure that Dallas saw her face. Dallas would know her cloying perfume anywhere. A combination of stale smoke and industrial cleaning liquid.

'How long has she been in this state?' asked an eager student with bright red hair.

How could anyone stand to be around Dr Soala when such a revolting smell emanated from her person?

When Dr Soala spoke, her answer matched the enthusiasm and energy of the young student. 'Dallas has been in a state of persistent locked in syndrome for three years now. She sustained a brain stem injury after falling from a cliff. Unfortunate accident. But we know she's in there. EEG results are off the charts. Elevated levels of brain activity in all quadrants.'

Dallas blinked into her secret sun hovering above the sea.

Vision of the Apocalypse in Wellington Harbour

by William Cook

One foot in the dead low tide, a lump of flesh and bone on the wet stones
I stand, frozen in time as the long white clouds darken this ghost land
Roiling and tumbling across the back of the predatory sea fog
Creeping stealthily across the cove, inch by encroaching inch

The black hills undulate with the death throes of the dying
Darkness flecked with crematory ash falls from the stars
As the bay begins to blacken with the shadows of the end
Fit for Babylon's capitulation and a night without dawn

I am witness to the first angel's descent
And the marked ones' howling, as they tear each other limb from limb
The second harbinger fills the sea with the blood of the dead
That which once lived beneath rises bloated, hollow, lifeless

As the third herald's wrath draws blood from the mountain streams
  and tributaries
The red moon burns like the sun, so brightly through the ashen clouds
Oppressive heat ripples the horizon and scorches the earth where I stand
It is apparent this land, these people, spilt the blood therein

The world shudders as the fallen hit hard, burned and blackened
And then the fifth angel wets the head of the demon who now
  straddles the hills
A deafening thunder roars from the belly of the beast
The tide lifts with the sonic boom, washing the city with death

Glass and steel detonate as the harbour retracts into the merciless night
In the centre of the cove a stone altar stands and on it a twisting
  serpent dances
Tracing flaming sigils in the thick, cloying air with its tongue
As embers erupt and ascend into the blackened air

And then the seventh sign comes with the tempests of a million years
Staccato bursts of radiation cut the sky as the ground heaves
And lightning stabs the hills, tremors dropping me to my knees
As the harbour splits in three, the abyssal fissures scream deafeningly

My ears bleed, my flesh chars, my mind is destitute and collapsed in
  upon itself
As the blood tide laps my heels, through swarms of blowflies I climb
Until I can climb no more, sat down among the dead things I weep
On the broken back of hills where the demon once held court

Wishing like a child for hope, I watch the blood-choked harbour ripple
  with death
Floating corpses strewn like rose petals on the surface
Carrion birds spinning through the boiling blackness above
As the harbour and all its ages, sink beneath the turgid tide

Now the end is here, I gasp one last breath of living horror
The revelation fulfilled, the dying nightmare lingers with a final vision
A celestial beast boiled in blood and stars, lurches through the light
Eclipsing life with the promise of eternal sleep and merciful fate
Then there's nothing, nothing left at all.

BURIED SECRETS

BY

DEL GIBSON

Aroha and Shaun Fletcher move into their Parnell Street house in Rawene, and everything is great. Until they begin to hear noises. Aroha knows when you build a house from scratch, there are the usual settling in sounds – moans, groans, and creaks. It's to be expected. What they didn't expect is the incessant knocking, scratching, and tapping on the walls, the doors, and the windows. The stomping, sometimes pacing, footsteps they often hear on their wraparound deck. But Aroha figures it's the local kids messing about, trying to scare them, now they no longer have an empty lot to play on.

A month after they move in, they're relaxing on their deck. Aroha looks across the Hokianga. Motukaraka historical church's steeple is practically glowing red in the sunset. The mouth of the harbour snakes its way towards Opinoni – the panoramic view is spectacular. Aroha breathes in the salty air, relishing the moment. She's glad they moved to such a beautiful location. One of the main advantages is that it is far enough from the hustle and bustle of Auckland, it makes her feel like she's in another country.

However, not only are they experiencing scary happenings in the house, there is also an old Māori man who watches them from across the street for hours. Aroha hasn't pointed this out to Shaun, as her husband has been distracted lately. She believes the isolation of Rawene is getting to him, provoking his short temper.

They look comfortable in their dream house. I want to stay away, yet I've been returning for months, ever since they began rebuilding on the land.

I can't help myself.

When the locals told me that my house was haunted and the land beneath it cursed, I didn't believe them. I should have, then perhaps my wife would still be alive, and I wouldn't have done what I did. But by the time I'd learned the history of our homestead, it was already too late — we'd moved in, and the situation was out of control.

I was a sceptic, paid no attention to the gossip. Then odd occurrences started happening; items vanishing, shadowy figures appearing in the rooms, cupboards opening and closing, loud thuds rattling the house, and, worst of all, the blood dripping from the ceiling in the bathroom.

It's the place that devours souls, the land contaminated as it is with entities, some good, some evil. Like dust motes dancing in the sun, the dead wish to come to life in the light...to be freed. Their spirits wandered the home, endlessly pacing, knocking, their disembodied voices and blood curdling screams leaving me shivering in pure terror.

I was tormented.

She was too heavy in my arms. It was useless. Abandoning all hope, I burned the homestead, crying as the flames lit up the night. I'd left her inside, laying in our bed, a broken mess — my Mildred. Perhaps I should have gone back inside to retrieve her, but by then I'd already done the most diabolical thing possible.

Regret is guilt, and guilt gnawed away at me, until there was nothing left but an empty abyss of hopelessness.

Aroha is slow to wake. As she waits for the shower to heat, her reflection in the mirror says it all – her face is like ashes, brown eyes sallow with dark rings of fractured sleep. She looks like one of the undead.

After her shower, she finds that Shaun's left a note on the benchtop saying he's gone to get groceries from Kaikohe. As she sprinkles muesli in a bowl, glass smashes somewhere in the house. When she investigates, she finds one of their wedding portraits in pieces. Strange! None of the windows are open, so it can't have been the wind. She hurries to clean it up, because she doesn't want Shaun to see the mess. His nerves are frayed enough. It takes a while to get all of the glass out of the carpet.

Shaun's watching the late-night news, with Aroha snuggled in beside him on the couch, when three loud knocks pound on the front door. Shaun gets up to answer it, but there's nobody there. It's probably kids pranking them. He's sick of it. He'll rip into them if he ever gets the chance! He's only just settled back on the couch when three knocks bash on the back door. It makes them jump in fright.

This time Aroha answers it. 'There's no one there,' she says when she returns.

'Bloody kids,' Shaun mutters.

In bed, Aroha tosses and turns next to Shaun. He must have drifted off at some point.

Suddenly he and Aroha are wrenched awake: the smoke alarms are blaring, ripping through the silence, scaring the wits out of them. Aroha covers her ears, while Shaun rushes around turning them all off.

Aroha falls back to sleep, but Shaun lies awake, unable to sleep after the drama with the smoke alarms.

It's midnight when Shaun decides to go for a run. He leaves quietly through the back door and takes the long way around the harbour. While he runs, he marvels at the sight of the full moon reflecting off the water's surface. It's breath-taking.

Shaun rests on the jetty, where the water smashes against the worn wooden posts, spraying him with a cool, refreshing mist.

'You're up late,' says a voice in the dark, half scaring Shaun to death. He turns. It's an old Māori man dressed all in black. No wonder he didn't see him.

The man comes closer, stepping under the sole light casting a yellow glow onto the jetty.

'Can't you sleep?' the old man asks.

'No. Why are you out this late?'

'I couldn't sleep either. I find it nearly impossible these days.' The man sighs.

'Okay. Well, I love to run, and it's quiet this time of night. Anyway, I'm heading home.' Shaun walks away.

'Hey, you!' the old man shouts.

Shaun stops and turns around.

'You and your wife are the new owners of the Parnell Street property, correct?'

'Yes, what about it?'

'No reason,' the old man says. 'It's a small town. Everyone knows everybody's business around here.' The look that crosses his face appears menacing, making Shaun's skin crawl.

Shaun dashes off home.

Aroha is still asleep when he climbs in beside her. She is warm, while he is corpse cold.

In Auckland, Sarah, convenor of the Ghost Hunters NZ team, receives an urgent email from the proprietor of the Duke of Marlborough Hotel, in Russell in the Bay of Islands.

A case for the team to investigate.

Ms Harriot Simpson explains the hotel's most active areas are downstairs in the main dining room, the lobby and the office. 'It's been scaring guests away,' she says.

In return for the team's help, they'll receive free accommodation, travel, and all expenses paid. Sarah tells the other team members about the invitation to film their investigation at the oldest hotel in the country. Arthur and Wiremu both gladly accept.

I've become obsessed with the couple. This is the fifth family to live here. The original owners, Dr William Sinclair and his wife Julia, built the homestead in 1900, for his doctor's clinic and as living quarters for their family of six. The couple were into witchcraft and mystical beliefs. They held Ouija board sessions, seances, and satanic rituals here – it was some type of cult.

We obtained the homestead in 1984, after the previous owners abandoned it, leaving everything behind. That should've made me wary. I didn't realise that a house can retain fundamental memories breathed

*into its bones by the people who have lived and passed within its walls.
The soul stays attached, clinging to this world, hovering in the darkened
corners where the light cannot reach. Hiding beyond the veil that separates
us from them — forever lurking. They're faceless, distorted, shapeless
beings, morphing and breathing in the darkest spaces.*

The locals called it the Hell House.

Aroha is in the garden when a voice hollers over the fence. 'Howdy
neighbour,' he calls.

'Hi, I'm Aroha,' she says, walking to the wire fence that separates them.
They shake hands.

'I'm Eddie, and that's my wife Sadie.' He points towards a woman
sitting on their deck.

The couple appear to be in their early sixties.

'Would you like to come over for a visit? Just climb over. Here, I'll
help you,' he says, forcing the top of the wire fence down so Aroha can
clamber over.

They walk towards the weatherboard cottage. On the deck, they settle
around a wooden table with matching bench seats. Sadie steps inside for
a moment and reappears with glasses and a jug, cold droplets running
down the side. Windchimes tinkle in the breeze.

'Nice to meet you,' Sadie says, as she sets the tray on the table.

She pours their drinks, and Aroha feels welcome and comfortable,
as if the three of them are old friends reunited. The sun, in the centre
of the sky, is hot, and the drink is deliciously cold. Tui and kererū flitter
and sing in the trees surrounding them. Other than the odd car here and
there, it's quiet.

It's a bit too quiet. It's been difficult for Aroha to get used to not
hearing emergency sirens, trains, planes and other city sounds. The ones
you didn't realise were so loud until you don't hear them anymore.

'How's it been living in the house?' Eddie asks.

'Good thanks,' she says.

Sadie leans in. 'Anything weird going on over there?'

'Not really.' Aroha hesitates. 'Okay, maybe a couple of things, but I'm
certain it's nothing.' She laces her hands together in her lap.

'Do tell,' Sadie prompts, looking sidelong at Eddie.

'Well, when we were moving our furniture in, I was walking by the
front door and I swear I saw my husband Shaun unpacking boxes in the

lounge. But when I went inside to ask him to help me, he wasn't there. He was out the back, stacking firewood we'd had delivered.' She sips her lemonade certain a red blush is heating her cheeks.

'Anything else?' Eddie asks.

Aroha grips her glass. They're asking a lot of questions about the house. Do they know something? No, she's just being paranoid – although they might know of the old Māori man.

'There's an old man stalking us,' Aroha blurts, as shivers rake up and down her spine. She shakes the foreboding away and tells them what has been happening in her home.

'I'm not liking the sound of this. Are you, Eddie?' asks Sadie.

'No love, not at all.' He places his glass on the table, clasps his hands together and cracks his knuckles. 'Aroha, there's a dark energy surrounding you. I felt it when we shook hands. Excuse me for a moment,' he says. Eddie stands abruptly and goes into the house.

'What's he doing?' Aroha asks.

'He's getting his tarot cards. Do you know what they are?'

'Yes. Of course. Mum and I went to see a medium once.'

Eddie returns and sits across from Aroha. Taking her hand gently, he places a rose quartz in her palm. It's warm to the touch as her fingers enfold around it. Eddie consults the cards. The first card is the image of a man facing away while carrying a bundle of sticks.

'The Ten of Wands,' he says.

'What does it mean?' Aroha asks.

Eddie shakes his head sadly. 'A burden is keeping you trapped in an oppressive downward spiral of negativity,' he says. 'You're not facing it, and ignoring it will only make it worse,' he continues. 'It'll be the house.'

'What about the house?' Aroha asks.

As the afternoon wears on, Eddie continues the reading. He and Sadie explain the legacy that she and Shaun have bought.

When Aroha arrives home, Shaun is drinking a beer on the deck. Twilight cloaks the land. She sits and explains what happened over at Eddie and Sadie's house, and the tarot card reading.

He cuts her off midway. 'You did what? You talked about us?'

She says, 'They told me things about the previous homestead, the land and the history.'

'I don't care! You shouldn't go around telling people our business!' He seethes, stomping off into the kitchen for another Waikato beer.

Aroha follows him inside. 'There's an old Māori man who stands out there watching us, across the road under the streetlight. Do you care about that?'

'What old man?' Shaun asks, voice cracking. He wonders if it is the same man from the jetty.

'Horrible things happened here in the original homestead.' Aroha's voice trembles. 'Eddie says it was built by a couple who practised witchcraft. Then later, it was a kind of overflow clinic for victims of the Spanish flu. After the war, they treated soldiers here.' Her eyes are weeping. 'Shaun, there are mass graves beneath this house, from a battle between warring tribes.'

'What the hell are you talking about? Have you gone mad?'

'No. Listen! In the 70s, the Millers moved in. Apparently, at the start they were nice, but over time the dad started lashing out at the neighbours. The couple had vicious fights. One night, another neighbour heard screams and called the police. But when they got here, the family were all dead, killed by the dad. He took himself out before the police arrived.'

'Aroha! What the hell did you tell them?' Shaun yells.

'I had to tell them everything! Look at what's been happening around here. We need to be careful. Eddie and Sadie think we're in danger.'

Fuck this shit! Shaun slams the bottle on the bench top, nearly smashing it.

He storms off into the bathroom. Splashing cold water on his face, in the mirror, he hardly recognises himself. He's a mess, and the alcohol doesn't help. His eyes are bloodshot and raw. Why's he so mad all the time? He'd been trying to get ahead, to offer them a better life by relocating here. Instead, he lost his job. Started gambling. This was supposed to be their fresh start. But it's so suffocating here – this town is too darn small.

The ghost team have set their gear up in the Duke of Marlborough's jaded second-floor conference room, ready to conduct their first interviews. There are three of them: Sarah, whose childhood in a haunted house had infused her with a morbid fascination with the paranormal; clairvoyant to the police, Wiremu; and Arthur, their cameraman, a two-time All-

Black until he had a quadbike accident. During surgery to save his life, he died for three minutes, and woke convinced he'd had a conversation with Jesus under an orange tree.

Their first interviewee is a cleaner named Jules.

'Are you ready?' Sarah asks in a gentle voice, noticing Jules' fidgeting. The girl is clasping her hands together in a knot.

'Yes, I'm ready,' she says.

'Cameras are rolling,' Arthur announces.

'You've worked here for four years. In that time have you seen anything paranormal?' Wiremu asks.

'Yes. Many times. I don't know where to start,' she says, shrugging her shoulders.

'What was your very first experience?' asks Sarah.

'I'd been working here a week. Almost all the guests had checked out, and the hotel was practically empty, except for a few staff downstairs. It was only Mary and I upstairs at the time. Mary's the cleaning manager, she's up north visiting family until Tuesday.' She pauses. 'I was picking up wet towels off the floor in the bathroom, and when I stood upright there was a man looking at me in the mirror. I screamed and ran out. Mary found me in the laundry room hiding behind a trolley.'

'That must have been terrifying! Did Mary see the man?' Sarah asks.

'She didn't need to. Mary's used to creepy things happening around here. She said it would have been the previous owner, Mr Keeler, who used that room for his own accommodation, and passed away in there from a heart attack.'

'You had an interaction with a ghost?' Wiremu asks.

'Yes. Loads of people have seen his spirit here,' she replies. 'They say he was a horrid man, awful to the staff, and the locals hated him.'

'Wow,' Wiremu exclaims. 'So not just any ghost. The previous owner of the hotel, someone people hated. Interesting.'

Sarah is about to jump in with another question, but, gaining confidence, Jules barrels on. 'Once, I was finishing up paperwork in the office, and I saw him walk right through the wall. It was the same apparition I saw upstairs, Mr Keeler. He doesn't really scare me anymore. I think he leaves me alone because I never acknowledge him.'

After admitting to several other paranormal experiences, Jules leaves, warning them to be careful.

Their next interviewee is Thomas, the head-chef.

'I've been here for two years. I like it here, even though some weird shit happens now and again, knocks and bangs and whatnot. The last chef quit unexpectedly one night during his shift,' he says.

'Have you seen anything paranormal?' Wiremu asks.

'I've seen shadows, things out of the corner of my eyes. Several times I've felt something touch me. There have been plenty of noises and voices too. But then I'm often the only one here closing up for the night.' He looks at them sheepishly. 'There are tales about this hotel, and especially the previous owner.'

'Fredrick Keeler?' Sarah asks.

'Yes. Fredrick inherited the hotel from his father Edwin. That family were a creepy bunch. The Keelers were part of a cult over in the Hokianga. Our housekeeper, Mary, she'd tell you some yarns. She's worked here the longest. She says, they would perform rituals and stuff, like those Ouija board things, talking to the dead and whatnot,' he explains, 'and I'm certain I've seen Ed and Fred's spirits a few times. I especially hate going into the dining room to greet the guests. That room freaks me out the most,' he admits.

Wiremu nods. 'Downstairs is definitely giving me bad vibes. I'm looking forward to investigating the dining room,' he says.

When Thomas leaves, Sarah checks in with Harriot, but she's unavailable. She's had to go out of town for the night unexpectedly. Sarah texts her, asking if they can investigate the Keeler suite, where Mr Keeler met his maker.

'No!' Harriot texts back. 'The Keeler suite is off limits. You are here to investigate the dining room first and foremost.'

Shaun's eyes are closed but sleep resists. His thoughts are too invasive. He gets out of bed quietly, enters the dark kitchen and peeks out the window. Aroha was right, the old man is out there, standing under the streetlight, staring straight at Shaun.

Panicked, he wonders what to do. He ducks quickly. Feeling ridiculous at being scared of an old man, he decides to go and face him. He moves towards the front door, but something makes him freeze. Strange sounds are coming from the bathroom. Forgetting about the old man, he treads softly towards the noise.

The door is closed, though a light slithers from under it. Someone inside is crying.

He shivers as he turns the handle. He pushes, but the door is locked.

'Aroha, are you in there?' Shaun rattles the handle.

Behind the door, he can hear the tap in the bathtub is on full blast. The cries increase in volume. He hears mumbled words he cannot understand.

'Babe, I'm coming in.' He pushes against the door with his shoulder. 'Open the door,' he pleads. Still, there is no reply.

Blood leaks under the door, onto the carpet, turning his white socks red. Shaun lunges at the door with all of his might, screaming his wife's name, but it won't give. He backs up about to kick down the door, when it suddenly flies open.

The room is empty, the light out. Everything is normal.

He flees back to their bedroom a petrified mess. Then he crawls beneath the blankets. Aroha has been in bed the whole time! He clings to her. His teeth are chattering. 'Aroha, wake up,' he says, shaking her shoulder.

'What's wrong?' she asks, sitting up.

'I believe you! Everything you said is true. Our house is haunted. I just saw it for myself,' he cries.

'I think we need to get away from the house. Perhaps we can go to that hotel you've been talking about?' she suggests.

Since they can't get back to sleep, Aroha boots up the laptop and books them into a suite at the Duke of Marlborough hotel in Russell, about an hour and forty-five minutes away.

Sarah and the crew are in the Marlborough's dining room with the devices on, cameras rolling, and the lights off in infrared mode. Sarah's under the Estes method, blindfolded, wearing noise cancelling headphones to drown out external sound, and attached to a spirit box with the volume set to high. Static smashes through the frequency changes.

A few minutes in, Wiremu shakes Sarah, who whips off the headphones and blindfold.

The lights are on. She blinks. 'What's going on? Why are we stopping?'

'We have guests,' Wiremu says, looking towards a couple in their mid-thirties, who are accompanied by an older woman.

'I'm sorry,' Sarah says, 'but this room is closed. We have permission from Ms Simpson to film in here.'

'Well, nobody told me. I apologise. I'm Mary Reihana, the cleaning manager, and Harriot leaves me in charge in her absence.'

'We'd heard you weren't back until Tuesday,' Sarah says.

Mary smiles. 'Change of plans. Shaun and Aroha, please have a seat.'

'Wait. Why is the dining room closed?' the man asks, perturbed.

'Please don't worry,' Mary says. 'The kitchen is open. I'll just need a minute to sort this all out. I'll be right back. Please, make yourselves comfortable.' Mary backs out of the room, closing the wooden oak double doors behind her.

The thud makes Sarah jump.

They wait.

When Mary doesn't return, Wiremu tries to open the doors, but they're locked tight.

'She's locked us in!' he shouts.

'What? No way! She wouldn't do that.' Shaun goes over and rattles the terrace doors. Behind the curtains, the doors are boarded up, along with all of the windows.

A violent explosion rattles the building. Sarah is thrown to the floor, hitting her head on a table leg. Her forehead is bleeding.

Alarms blare everywhere; it's brutally loud, yet Aroha's screams carry over the commotion.

The men head to the windows, trying to rip off the boards. They tear at the wood until their fingers bleed, but the boards don't budge. By now, smoke is leaking in under the door, filling the room.

'Hurry, hurry! Please!' Aroha wails.

Arthur coughs and sinks to his knees.

Sarah stumbles to her feet as sirens trill in the distance, giving her hope. She pounds on the doors, screaming for Mary to let them out. Turning around, she sees the smoke manifest into ghostly waifs, darting around the room. One comes at her and screams in her face. She crumples to the floor in a heap, mortified.

Sarah watches, appalled, as Arthur chokes on the floor. Something large and black is smothering him – it smashes his head into the floor, until blood splatters the walls and stains the wooden floorboards.

She can't believe what she's seeing!

The couple, Shaun and Aroha are huddled in the corner, clutching tight to one another.

Wiremu collapses face down to the floor. Horrified, Sarah is frozen, shocked, as a monstrous mass of swirling darkness rips chunks from Wiremu's back. All Wiremu can do is scream in horrendous pain, as his skin is slowly peeled away from his body.

Sarah's vision blurs. The room spins in a smoky haze. Flames warp the doors, making them swing open. Suddenly, Sarah is lifted off the ground onto someone's shoulders and is carried out of the room.

She passes out.

The doors to the room have buckled open. Shaun grabs Aroha and pulls her through the doorway and out into the night. Thomas is holding the limp body of Sarah in his arms. They stand alongside him, watching the hotel burn.

Mary hides behind the hotel and flicks off a text to Harriot. 'Job done.'

'Excellent! I'm on my way,' Harriot texts back.

'Two perished…better than nothing, I suppose. Thomas helped one of the team escape. The couple from Rawene also made it out alive,' Mary writes.

'I'll sort Thomas out when I get back,' Harriot responds. 'Oh, and don't worry, Mary, insurance will cover it,' she adds.

Mary sneaks off into the night, smiling all the way home. The hotel was tired, its bones weary, but now it's refreshed. It's been years since the hotel had new blood, new souls.

Shaun and Aroha arrive home to find their house fully engulfed in flames. Aroha and Shaun stand on the other side of the street, speechless.

The old Māori man steps out from under the streetlight, walks straight past them and crosses the road towards their burning house.

'Hey! Wait!' Shaun shouts. 'Don't go in there!'

The man walks into the inferno and doesn't reappear.

Neighbours are out on the street, watching the chaos. Eddie and Sadie approach them. Aroha is trembling, in cold and in fear.

'What happened?' Eddie asks.

'Fucked if I know. We came home to this,' Shaun replies. 'An old man just walked into it, and he hasn't come back out.'

The emergency services arrive. This prompts Aroha into action. She runs over to the fire crew. 'There's someone inside!' she screams at them.

'Are you sure? Where did they go?' a fireman asks.

'I don't know. He walked in, and we haven't seen him since,' she says, feeling ill.

It seems like a lifetime until the crew come back out. The same fireman from before comes over to Shaun and Aroha, who are still standing with Eddie and Sadie.

'We couldn't find anyone. It's too dangerous to go in any further,' he says.

The crew continue battling the flames. Eddie invites Aroha and Shaun to stay with him and Sadie the night. Shaun agrees as Aroha weeps beside him.

It's noon the following day when they return to assess the damage. It's gone. Everything is destroyed. They both feel defeated. All of that hard work, gone in a smouldering mess. The air around them smells like burnt plastic. Little tendrils of smoke whisk around the ruins.

Only the letter box remains, but it's been knocked over, most probably by the fire appliances. A letter is poking from the slot.

'There's no postage stamp,' Shaun says. 'It must have been hand delivered.' He opens it.

'Who's it from?' Aroha asks.

'Someone called Henare,' he explains.

They read it in the car as a light rain drips from the heavens.

Dear new owners of the house on Parnell Street,

I apologise for what I did to your house, but it's the only way to break the tribal curse. The Sinclair's witchery awoke a dormant evil, through their satanic rituals and summoning. One night, I woke in fear. Something was in the bedroom with us. I switched on the bedside lamp. When I looked over at Mildred, it wasn't her! I swear it was not my Mildred. Instead, a grotesque monster was in our bed. It had huge black gaping holes where its eyes should have been, and it screamed horrid words, I couldn't understand. It ripped at its body, blood and globs of flesh staining the bed. Then it turned on me, scratching and pummelling with its claws, trying to gouge out my eyes. I was terrified. I did the only thing I could do — defend myself. I strangled the monster.

I killed it.

When it stopped struggling, I stood back to look. Upon the bed was my wife. She was dead. Blood covered my hands. I'd been tricked! I couldn't live with what I'd done. So, I set the place on fire, along with the evidence. I thought that would take away the demons, but I was wrong. Then I saw you rebuilding on the land. I wanted to warn you, but I didn't know how to make you believe. I hope when the house is gone, you'll leave this place, and never look back.
Sincerely,
Henare Reihana.

Aroha and Shaun heed the warning. As Aroha drives, Rawene disappears in the rear-view mirror.

Several weeks later, they are settled into their new house in Wellington. Aroha is making dinner when her cellphone rings.

'Hello, Aroha speaking.'

'Hello. It's Tim from State Insurance.'

'How can I help you, Tim?' she asks.

'I'm investigating your claim.'

'Okay,' she replies.

'I've talked to the fire investigators, and we've concluded it was arson. We'll send someone around in the next few days with some paperwork. Lucky you weren't home at the time,' he says.

'Yes, we were very fortunate.' She sighs.

'Of course, the police will want a statement. By the sounds of it there have been a few recent suspicious fires in that region,' he says.

No kidding.

'That's terrible!' she exclaims. 'I'd be happy to provide a statement. Before you go, what of the man who walked into the fire. Does he have any family?'

'Man? I'm sorry, I've no idea what you're talking about. There was no body found inside the house.'

When Aroha ends the call, she's trembling. If they didn't find Henare's body, then where the hell did he go?

She's on the phone with Shaun telling him about the call from Tim, when a shiver attacks her, like someone walked over her grave. Glancing outside the window, she sees a familiar old Māori man, standing across the street, watching their house…

A Throatful of Flies
by Paul Mannering

I was in high school the first time I cut a throat.

Tilt the head back, a long stroking slice with steady pressure. Press harder against the slight resistance. Drag the blade through the delicate rings of cartilage that make the airway. The deep flesh shining with the metallic rainbow colours of spilled diesel fuel. The blood spurts, of course – though I barely noticed, my focus caught instead by the blank stare of the sheep gripped between my thighs. The ram shivered, kicked, and faded. I lay it down and we pressed hooks through the cooling skin at the back of the hock; between the Achilles tendon and the bone on the hind legs. The chain rattled as we winched the beast upside down to drain its blood onto the dark stained concrete.

It's just meat, I told myself.

Three more rams waited in the tight enclosure of the stockyard pen. That afternoon, Wayne, the hired hand, and I cut and hung them all.

We laid their freshly flayed skins out on a table frame ingrained with the grease of years of animal fat. Made of wooden slats older than me, the table came from the woolshed where the rousers used it for sorting wool.

We salted the hides skin side up and left them to dry. The roughly butchered meat went into a big copper pot over a banked fire to be cooked for dog tucker.

The guts and heads went into the offal pit.

The pit was the gateway to Hell. A deep hole covered with roofing iron and old wooden planks. In the centre was a hole about the size of a basketball hoop, enough of a gap to capture fresh offerings.

I stood at the edge of the corrugated iron cover and slopped a bucket load of fresh sheep guts into the centre of the lid. I watched as gravity dragged the mass down into the abyss. It made a wet sucking sound like a toothless giant drinking soup. There was no place on earth I could imagine worse than what lay in the darkness of the offal pit.

And we were done in time for afternoon smoko.

We drank hot tea, black and sickly sweet. Washing down the dense scones tiled with slabs of butter and home-made blackberry jam, the colour reminded me of the sheep's blood congealing on the concrete.

I brushed crumbs off my t-shirt when the boss pulled up and jumped out of his truck. His cold blue eyes permanently clenched against the sun. 'You slaughter the three old rams in the yard for dog tucker?'

'Yeah,' Wayne agreed, barely pausing in his cigarette rolling.

Jobs got done in time for the next. There was always more to do, so you did it when told. They were old rams, past their prime and now only good for dog food. Then, in the slow way most of these workers had, Wayne added, 'Four of 'em.'

'Four?' the boss said.

I swallowed the lump in my throat. Stared at the brown grass patches and wondered how anything grew in the summer heat.

'Yeah…' the hand said, his gaze dropping to the drought-scorched ground.

I'd cut the throat of a prized stud ram. A sheep with balls bigger than my fists. Each squirt of seminal fluid worth more than its weight in gold. Somehow the wrong sheep got in among the tired old bastards and I'd killed the most valuable animal on the farm in one cutting stroke.

The boss raged at the hired hand for another ten minutes. I sat frozen in my seat. Counting blades of withered grass.

'Get me the ear tag. Then pack your shit and fuck off,' the boss said and walked away, got in his truck, and drove off.

I couldn't be fired. I was here on holiday. My parents had been friends with the boss and his wife since before I was born. Wayne was being punished for my crime.

We headed down to the offal pit in awkward silence.

The severed heads were in there. We'd rolled them like bowling balls across the sheet metal cover and watched them drop through the hole.

Now we peeled back the layers of sun-warmed iron. Stacking the metal skin. Ripping off a dressing over the foulest wound I have ever seen.

The stink was a physical thing. It swelled like a balloon and trapped you inside. I clutched my nose and tried to back up. Flies roared in an angry swarm, barely rising in the summer heat over the black-stained edge. Wayne fetched a pole with a gaff hook on it and fished for the fresh heads. I didn't get close enough to see inside the pit. I stared at the stained black of the earthen walls. The flies were a carpet and wallpaper, so fat with decay and foulness, they could hardly fly when the light of day washed over them.

'Fuck an' shit,' Wayne swore, the flies rising around him in a cloud as thick as a swarm of bees. 'It's fuckin' gone.' He brushed the black fog of buzzing insects away from his face and backed away, stirring the hot summer air.

I staggered, gagging and spitting at the stench so thick I could taste the foulness in the back of my throat.

'Put the fucken' cover back on it,' Wayne yelled and tossed the gaff into the dust. As unpaid summer help I ranked somewhere below the dogs in the pecking order. I did what I was told, the collar of my sweat-stained t-shirt pulled up over my nose – like smelling my own sweat made any difference.

Wayne lived in a ramshackle hut of concrete block construction with a wooden beer crate for a coffee table. It was far from the main house, nearer the stockyards and the offal pit. I was only here for two weeks, so I got a decent room in the boss' house on the hill overlooking the valley up here in the high country of the South Island.

The hired hand walked back to his quarters, leaving me to drag hot sheets of corrugated roofing iron over to the wide-open pit.

I watched as the bastard loaded his gear and, with his dogs barking on the back of a dirty ute, he drove off the property. He didn't even glance at me as he shot past. He would have a new job on some other farm by tomorrow morning.

Flies were settling on my sunburnt arms and stumbling in thick clusters over my face as I blinked the sweat out of my eyes and tried to drag the sheet metal without dropping it into the cauldron of foulness.

I don't know how it happened, blinded by the stink, the sweat in my eyes, the heavy black flies kissing my face with tiny bumper-car crashes. Maybe a shoelace untied.

There's a moment when you lose your balance on an edge. The heartbeat before you fall. Adrenaline surges and you freeze with shocked certainty that you are going to die.

I fell. Out of the sunlight, into air that felt thick. A second later I landed on my back in the offal pit.

It was like landing on a waterbed. A wet squishing sound and a slow trapped ripple wafted out from where I hit. I bounced and floated. The square of sky above me, no more than my body length away, filled with the black static and deafening roar of a TV tuned in to the end of the world.

Enraged and aroused, the flies swarmed into the air with bloated bodies as fat as thimbles. I drew in a shocked breath to scream. My mouth filled with hard shells and battering wings. Sinking, I choked, waving my arms, and fighting against the foulness.

Twisting, I struggled to sit up, to get my feet under me so my head would stay above the rotting soup. The flies were blinding. I pressed my face against my sleeve, mouth open as I scraped my tongue against the rough cotton of my shirt, spitting flies and tasting chemical foulness. A cloying stench clogged my nose and brought tears to my eyes.

The flies filled the air. Millions of them. Untold generations breeding in this paradise of rot. I could barely see for the thick carpet of yellow egg clusters. They floated on dark pools of black liquid like spilled rice. The putrefying landscape writhed with maggots. Thick, white slugs, gorging on the endless decay while their parents danced in the shadows.

My feet sank, dragging me down to my chest as I screamed and struggled toward the nearest wall. Flies were in my mouth, gagging me.

My head tilted up. My legs struggled in a goo too thick to swim through but liquid enough to drown in. The flies surged over me, covering my exposed skin. I clenched my teeth and tried to breathe. Flies settled in a mask on my face, crawling on my eyes and pushing up my nose. I felt them force their way under my lips, wings buzzing against my gums.

I coughed and retched, and then took a desperate breath. I choked on a mass of crawling insects that invaded my mouth and with the instinct of the drowning, I swallowed the lump, clearing my throat so I could gasp the foul air.

My filth-encrusted fingers scraped against the rock-hard earth of the wall. It had been dug out years ago, the ground scarred by steel claws, leaving grooves and small handholds. I clung to the wall, shaking my head to get scant enough space to breathe. My stomach was roiling, a strange fluttering sensation deep in my throat.

I gripped the wall with white knuckles, my body pulling against the sucking draw of the visceral slime. I worked my sneakers off with my feet. Feeling with sock covered toes, I found a purchase on a sunken sheep skull somewhere below and rested my weight against it.

Clinging to the wall, I waited for the swarming tempest around me to settle. Behind me, the cold guts and bodies of sheep swollen with putrefying gasses seethed with life. My impact had torn a hole in the foul crust and the flies settled on it like an oasis in an endless desert.

I twisted my head and looked for another way out. There was no ladder, no steps cut into the black clay walls. I blinked and tossed my head, shaking the dripping bile away from my vision.

Square mesh wire, sometimes used to make temporary pens for lambs, hung down the opposite wall. Some discarded piece of trash that no one had thought to remove from the pit. It might take my weight. It might be my way out. Except it was about three metres away across a cesspit.

I started shivering. Above ground it was high summer. The air warm as an oven, dry as biscuits, and the promise of rain a myth. Down here, it was cold as death. Any warmth generated by decay was in the top layer only. My body was buried in deep chill, and it seeped into my bones. The foulness staining my skin as permanent as a tattoo.

Tightening my grip with one hand, I reached up. It wasn't far. If I could get a handhold on the knob-like clods of the wall I could get out. I reached and scratched, pushing my fingertips deep into the small holes. Straining, I pulled myself up and reached with my other hand towards a small knuckle of hardened dirt.

Like quicksand in an old movie, the shit sucked at me as I dragged myself up. My socks slipped off my feet, which were already numb with cold as I scrabbled for purchase on the dirt wall. My skin glistened with rancid fluid that soaked my clothes and made it hard to move. I shivered with shock and chill, reaching up, trying to see another hand hold, so close to the sky.

The dry clay under my toes broke and I screamed as I scraped down the wall. I plunged into the bog of viscera and went under. My eyes closed instinctively against the darkness, and I fought the urge to vomit as sharp bones scratched my skin.

Desperately swimming up, I broke the surface, thrashing and puking. Flies again rushed to embrace me. They filled my throat, crawled in my mouth and came out of my nose on streams of snot. Half crawling, half swimming, and moaning in horror, I splashed my way to the wall, where I hoped the hanging net fence would be my way out.

I felt the wire, rather than saw it; my eyes were covered in stinking bile. I wiped at my face, flies lifting and settling again on every pore. My fingers clawed at the fence, and I hauled my body up. It held.

Sobbing, I wiped my face against my filthy shirt. The flies swarmed and coalesced as I blinked the black ooze from my eyes.

A shape formed in the swirling cloud, shadows cast in dark relief by the light from above. An almost human form appeared against the wall to my left. Sheep bones and rags of wool tufted flesh cloaked in a living suit of flies. The fly-clad bones dripped with ichor and the features of the face in the black cloud sharpened. Glittering eyes formed and focused, regarding me with a ravenous glare.

The shifting mask of flies writhed and formed a pulsing mouth and through the deafening buzz a voice whispered.

He tamariki mātou na Tū-tangata-kino, te ariki o nga namu, a Hine-nui-te-pō. Hoki atu koe ki te ao hei whakatupu mai i ētahi o ā tāua hua; waiho hoki au i raro nei hei kukume i ētahi o ā tāua hua ki raro nei.

'We are the children of Tū-tangata-kino, Lord of the Flies, and Hine-nui-te-pō, Goddess of Death. Return and raise our offspring in the world of the living; leave me here to draw our offspring down below.'

The visage dissolved and the flies engulfed me. Whimpering through clenched teeth, I guessed the foul air caused hallucinations or I'd gone mad with terror.

I climbed. Slowly, hand over hand, my bare feet pressed into the wire as I made my way to the top. The flies raged around me. A hurricane of hard black dots. A roaring swarm that crawled inside my ears, nose, and mouth.

Blind and reaching, my outstretched hand hit the hot metal of the corrugated iron roof. Pushing with my head and shoulders, I crawled out from under the burning iron. Fingers digging into the sun scorched grass and dust, I dragged myself out on to the dead ground.

On my hands and knees, I vomited again and again. I wiped at my eyes until I could see the struggling shapes of living flies crawling in the acid remains of scones and sweet tea. Sobbing, I crawled away from the hole, desperate to distance myself from the pit. Dust and gravel of the track that ran up to the farm sheds pressed against my hands. I dropped, exhausted and retching.

Somewhere, beyond the buzzing of the flies, I heard the roar of a ute, the screech of brakes and the grind of tyres skidding in the grit. A door squealed open, the boss' truck and a voice. 'What in the bloody hell happened to you?!'

I was crying too hard to explain. I don't remember much after that. I heard later that I passed out. The boss dragged me onto the flatbed of his truck and took me to the nearest hose. He washed me down and then, seeing blood from numerous cuts and scratches, and my semi-conscious state, he drove me the two hours into town, still on the back of the truck.

I woke up at the hospital two days later. I was in a plastic-covered bed, draped with heavy plastic sheets like an isolation case. The sun was streaming down on me, and I was sweating in the heat. I thought I was dreaming. I was outside. Attached to tubes, and sensors, with a thick umbilical power-cord going through an open window into the building I was parked next to.

My panicked movements set off alarms and a few minutes later, a nurse appeared. She wore surgical scrubs, a face shield and thick mask. 'How are you feeling?' she asked from the other side of the plastic sheets that hung over the bed, trapping me like a bug in a jar.

'I…feel sick. And thirsty…'

She nodded. 'I'll get you some water.' She walked away.

I had an IV tube going into my arm. The flaccid pouch of liquid draining into me was almost empty. I was wearing a paper surgical gown, stained with a dark taint that looked like sweat.

The nurse returned, and reaching through a gap in the plastic drapes, she handed me a paper cup of water. I drank it and coughed, spitting something solid into the empty cup. Dead flies.

Live ones were buzzing around, crawling on the outside of the plastic sheeting, the nurse waving them away from her face as they hummed around her. I offered her the cup and she hesitated before taking it with a latex-gloved hand. The cup went straight into a yellow plastic bag with a bio-hazard symbol on it.

'The doctor will be along shortly,' she said and left immediately, peeling off her disposable scrubs and pushing them into the bio-hazard bin.

I sat in the heat inside my plastic bubble and wondered what was going on. Did I have a disease? Was I contagious? Flies gathered in curious groups on the outside and I tried not to look at the faces I saw in the shifting swarms or listen to the whispered voices droning in the static roar of their wings.

A doctor dressed in the same paper suit as the nurse appeared outside my plastic cell. 'Yours is a curious case,' he announced to the clipboard he carried.

'What...?' I asked.

'You fell into...' He brushed flies away from a page. 'A pit of rotting animal waste?'

'Uh, yeah?' I felt my urge to puke rising at the memory.

'We've treated you with IV antibiotics and have ah...scrubbed you down a lot.'

'Am I sick? Why am I outside?'

'We can't seem to get rid of the smell.' The doctor sounded almost embarrassed. 'We've cleaned you with everything we can think of and the...smell. It is overpowering. We moved you outside as a necessity for the safety and comfort of other patients and staff.'

'Seriously? I can't smell anything.'

'Olfactory fatigue,' the doctor explained. 'A blessing really. If you could smell what I smell. Well, it's far from pleasant. The good news is your blood work came back clear. We have defeated the infection and you can be discharged shortly.' He started coughing and, sweeping flies off his disposable suit, he backed away before I could ask any of the questions that immediately came to mind.

Mum and Dad picked me up after dinner that night. I hadn't eaten much. The sludge on the plate looked like something I could still taste in the back of my throat. Halfway home, Dad pulled the car over and leapt out. I could hear him puking his guts out on the grass. Mum followed him and they stood outside afterwards, talking in low voices.

They set me up in the backyard. A small tent, camp bed, and an old solar shower. The neighbours complained of course, and Mum expressed concern but asked me not to come into the house. She delivered meals to me, and I sat and stank for a week while my parents spoke to doctors, chemists, and anyone else with a possible solution.

I was doused in perfumes, disinfectants, and air-fresheners. I scrubbed my skin raw. Nothing worked. I was like a superhero who fell into a vat of chemicals and came out with nothing but a foul stink of rot that made the worst body-odour smell like grass after a spring rain.

I was on the news, though I got nothing but the shamed spectacle and horrified pity of the freakshow from my fifteen minutes of fame.

My parents never said anything, but I realised I couldn't stay there. The stench and the flies that clustered on everything I touched were causing visible distress to Mum. After the media interest subsided, I packed up my few clothes and some belongings and walked out in the middle of the night. I've been walking ever since. Staying hidden from people and stealing what I need at night from the small towns I pass through. The smell makes it impossible to be around me. It oozes out of my skin like an oil. I spend my days alone, wandering the wild and empty places. It's not difficult to find food. I can just open my mouth and swallow a throat full of flies. My sense of smell and taste is dead. I now live in the deep bush avoiding the trampers who hike between huts, and the occasional deer hunter.

The children of Tū-tangata-kino, Lord of the Flies and Hine-nui-te-pō, the Goddess of Death are my constant companions. The words whispered from the dark visage in the pit echo in the buzzing of their wings. As commanded, I will raise an uncountable legion of flies in this world, while they prepare the way below.

GUIDING STAR
BY TIM JONES

You are trapped with your bullies at Omaui,
where the land loses its will to resist the sea,
where ragged bush declines to a treachery of coastlines.
A school camp where the days are long, nights endless.
In the photos the children smile. But you do not smile.

The bullies come once the lights are off, armed
with bed legs and laughter. But one more night
is more than you can endure. You would rather face
rain, cold, darkness than the gang of older boys
who gather nightly round your fear-soaked bunk.

You slip away through an unlatched door, a camp parent's
momentary failure of attention. Through its slowly closing eye,
the waning moon fails to spot your shadow. You scurry
across the lawn, the fringe of the forest mere steps away:
manuka scrub bisected by the path you spotted yesterday.

Beneath the forest it is darker. Trapped in the nineteen-sixties,
you have no mobile, no Google Maps. All you have
is dead reckoning and desperation to find the road to Greenhills,
then the main highway that will take you home:
some late-night motorist who will show pity

while you try to imagine what your father will say.
But first, the forest. Night pools around you. Ruru
call in the distance, the low murmuring of wide-eyed,
watchful predators. High above, where the forest thins,
a single star hastens your stumbling steps downhill.

Rain resumes. You have your duffle bag, your duffle coat,
but droplets shiver at your hands and hood as your faint torch
picks out mud and moss. It misses roots. You trip and fall.
Your torch blinks, is gone. You realise you'd rather face
the bullies than the night, but it's too late:

you've stumbled off the path. You flail your way downhill
through wet, resisting scrub, one arm across your eyes,
until the bush ends without warning in beach. Returning starlight
shows the New River Estuary, a sand-lined labyrinth of water,
tide caught between ebb and flow, notorious for shipwrecks.

Later they conclude you must have panicked. Later,
when your parents demand answers, the ashen-faced authorities
say there were no warning signs, that you appeared
to be enjoying your time at camp. They say your footsteps
ended at the high tide line, no body ever found.

But they should search the shipwrecks. That night, desperate,
you saw the *SS Guiding Star* fully fuelled and ready to steam away,
its captain waving you aboard, promising escape, saying
all you have to do to come aboard is reach the gangway
that rises from the water beyond the shifting sands.

Coming Home in the Dark
by Owen Marshall

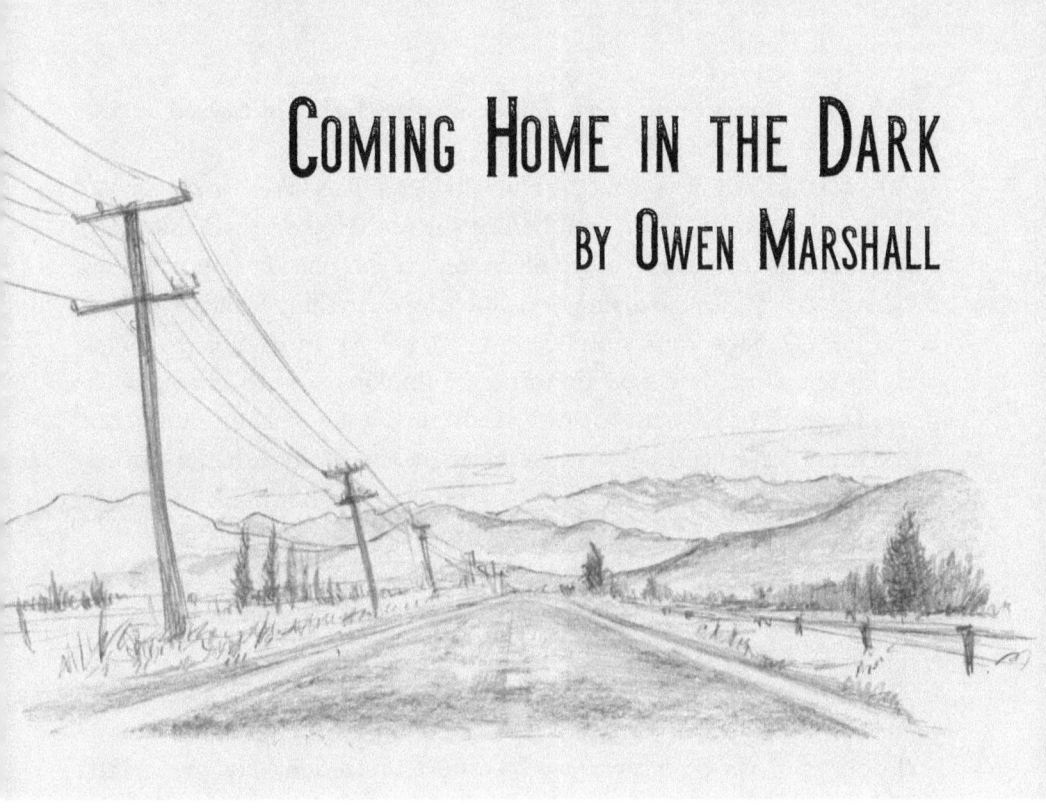

Windswept to a bowl of peerless blue, the sky arched above it all: not oppressive on the landscape, but rather an insistent suction that offered to remove everything into the endless, spun abstraction. The lake had a chop on its milk-green opaqueness. The mountains of black and white rose up ahead. There was a fixed intensity in the delineation of shapes and colours; no compromise, no merging.

'We'll see Cook again soon, I think,' said Hoaggie.

'It's the boys' first time up here,' said Jill.

'So it is, and it should be a view today that they'll remember. I hope that all their lives they can think back to this trip – their first sight of Mount Cook.'

'I wish we were going to ski, though,' said Mark.

At the head of Lake Pukaki was the flat outwash of the glaciers and the cold, braided streams milky with rock flour. Hoaggie noticed how the sun caught and glittered from surfaces and turns of the water as he drove. For a selfish moment he was without family, and felt a pack on his back, boots on his feet, and heard the skirl of the wind on the rock faces.

Jill was telling the boys what the Hermitage was like, based on somewhat hazy recollection of a visit well before she and Hoaggie had shifted to Auckland. Her sons were more interested in the outside opportunities of the place. 'Well, make sure you don't lose anything today. We can't come back. Check your stuff.' She didn't believe in having the twins dressed the same. She said the modern thinking was to encourage a natural growth of separate identity. Both the boys wore linen shorts, but Mark had a jersey and light, suede boots, while Gordon had a ribbed, blue jacket and sneakers. Gordon had more to say, but Mark was more stubborn.

They passed Bush Creek, and Hoaggie recalled for his wife a climb that he and Tony Bede made to the saddle from there. He experienced as he talked a quick reprise of the euphoria of youth, but had no words to articulate it. They passed Fred's Creek and saw a Mercedes abandoned on its side in a ditch of stones.

'Look at that. Yeah, wipeout,' enthused Gordon. He and Mark scrabbled to see more from the back window as they went on.

'Someone overdid it there,' said Hoaggie.

'And can't have had any help for miles,' said Jill.

'You remember when Bruce Trueno broke down on the Desert Road last Christmas and when he came back with the tow truck he found the wheels stolen.'

The outwash was mainly an expanse of shingle, but those parts not recently swept by the channels had rough pasture and matagouri, briar, clumped lichens. Beef cattle were feeding by the road. There was oddity in the sight, because of the close proximity, although distinct by altitude of ice and snow and screes. The inside of the car was more comfortable still: the sun warmed it and the breeze was excluded.

'Moira wants to nominate me as the Regional Arts Council Rep on the grants board,' said Jill.

'Who better if you've got the time. Go for it.' Hoaggie was always gratified when his wife proved her competence in her own right. Successful himself, he felt no threat from the achievements of others. He realised also, that because of his own focus on work, his wife had given much of her time to the family. 'They would be lucky to have someone of your ability,' he said in all sincerity.

'Flatterer.' She rested her hand on his arm. 'You won't say that if you're left to cope when I'm away.'

They came up the final slope to the head of the alpine valley beyond the lake's expanse. Scenery has little intrinsic appeal to the young, but even the twins, accustomed only to the landscape of the North Island, gazed quietly for a few moments at the sheer valley sides and the towering bulk of Cook and Tasman among their barely less impressive fellows.

Then Gordon elbowed his brother. 'Now those suckers are big,' he said.

'I had a talk with Athol Wells at Rotary a while back,' said Hoaggie. 'Did I tell you that?'

'Athol Wells?'

'He's the deputy principal at Westpark. You must remember; I said that maybe he'd have an angle on a school for the boys.'

'I don't want them to go to a boarding school. You know that.'

'Well, neither do I personally. It's what's best for them in the long run though, isn't it?'

'What better environment can you have than your own family?'

'Roddy Sinclair says he's going to Wanganui Collegiate,' put in Gordon.

'Spastic,' said his brother. Hoaggie had almost forgotten they were in the back. He dropped the subject.

Hoaggie turned off the Hermitage road and onto the track that led them to the area where camping was allowed. He was pleased to see almost as few amenities, as few small climbing tents, as he remembered.

When the family stood on a knoll not far from the car, prepared for their walk up the Hooker Valley towards the glacier, they could see over the way they had come and the end of the road. Hoaggie noted that the Hermitage had been developed a good deal, but even so the view was almost entirely unspoiled. He hadn't been to Cook for more than fourteen years and he refreshed himself with all the defiant angles and peaks, the low alpine vegetation, the mutual touch of bright sun and sweet, cold breeze.

'Come on, come on,' shouted Gordon, and as if it were a consequence, almost immediately there was a shivering rumble of an avalanche on Mount Cook, although not on the faces they could see.

'Let's hope no one's under that lot,' said Hoaggie.

'No one would be climbing where that's likely to happen, would they?' asked Jill.

'Sometimes I guess it's just luck.'

The four of them started on the walking track to the Hooker, which wound through the tussock and thorns of the old, heaped moraines. They were out of the breeze from the snowfields for a while and it was pleasantly warm. Jill put her hand on Hoaggie's collar. She ran her nails up and down the back of his neck as they walked behind the twins.

'Maybe you're right,' she said. 'About the secondary school thing.'

'Maybe not,' said Hoaggie. 'What the hell. We can work it out among us all. It's about giving them the right start, isn't it?'

Mark had found a stick, discarded by a previous walker. He flourished it proudly, and Gordon began questing on both sides of the track as they went on, searching for a stick that would restore his equality. They could hear the sound of the swift stream from the little lake at the glacier's snout and the track began to wind over heaped greywacke shingle and boulders.

Below them two other people were climbing up to join the track. The man in the lead was thin and pale; he shrugged his shoulders as he walked. The man behind was immensely solid, the features of his full face seeming indented like those of a snowman. He wore a denim jacket so tight that it pulled his arms back, accentuating the bulge of chest and stomach. Neither of them was old, but men nevertheless, not boys. The big man behind was singing a song from *Phantom of the Opera*, but only the tune was an identification; the words had been replaced by ta and la. The one in front wore a denim top as well, but of a much darker blue against which light stitching stood out. The stoop of his thin shoulders made the sides of the jacket hang below his waist, while the back road up showing the grubby white of his t-shirt.

Having ta-laed himself to the end of the music of the night as he reached the path ahead of Hoaggie and his family, the big man followed his friend with a gait grown suddenly shambling without a melody. Neither man looked back; neither waved.

Gordon sniggered and was joined by Mark.

'Don't be rude,' said Jill.

'What a geek,' said Gordon, doing a quick chesty imitation of the man's walk. It was true they seemed unlikely nature lovers.

'It takes all sorts,' said Jill.

The two men were soon lost in the turns of the track through the moraine and when the family reached the swingbridge there was no sign of them. Hoaggie was happy to share the surroundings with no one but his wife and children: he had deliberately planned on being there before the school holidays began and in that had been very loyally supported by Gordon and Mark. Such feelings of exclusivity were selfish, Hoaggie knew, but part of his response to beauty.

There was the small lake among the shingle and boulders at the glacier's end. Etched icebergs floated there, freed from the rocks that covered the ice flow. Some of them had seams of dirt, or stones, some had flat tints of very old milk. Other ice showed in the banks where the overlay of shingle kept it from the sun. Impressive though it was, Hoaggie knew it to be only the remnant of the ice age days and he pointed out the ledges and striations hundreds of feet up the valley sides where the great rivers of ice had been thousands of years before.

'Hey, yeah,' said Gordon. 'Next time, Mark and I'll climb up there and roll stuff down.'

They walked for an hour up the Hooker and then sat for a while before beginning a return. In the clarity of the mountain air the soaring ridges and coruscating sweeps of snow were deceptively near at hand, and even the stunted olearia, hebe and cottonwood where they rested seemed to have a special sharpness of form. Just occasionally they were caught by the edge of a passing breeze and drew their shoulders in for warmth.

On the way back shortly before the carpark, Hoaggie took a snap of his wife and the twins just below a cairn that commemorated the death of mountaineers many years before. As he lined it up through the viewfinder he had a sudden sense of image within image, of time within time: the shot as it would be with all the others in the album, the wider freeze frame, transient, but stronger just for that instant, showing the four of them together at the foot of the mountains with the grasses and flowers, the spiked matagouri and the sheen of the great snow slopes in the distance. Hoaggie had no god to pray to, but he offered a sort of prayer nevertheless, which was part gratitude for what he had, and part plea for continuance.

'Take another one and let me hold the stick in it,' called Gordon.

The brown grasses were ungrazed and high as Hoaggie's knee. Where the moraine was exposed, the grey stones bore badges of lichens – green, yellow, silver, and silver-blue. Some puffed out a little from the rock like the frilled head of a lizard; others were so fine, so delicate, they seemed more like fossils within the rock than anything that grew on its surface. The small white and pink flowers glistened on the humped bushes amongst the stones, and flies, quick and colourful, were in a euphoria of pollination.

As the family went on to their car and the grassy clearing where camping was allowed, the sounds from the Hermitage carried clearly to them, but subdued in that great natural space. No wind at all in the low clearing, and just a toss of cloud at Cook's summit to show the westerly at work.

The boys wanted to eat at once, but Jill didn't wish to have their picnic near the tents and within sight of the small toilet block. 'There's always red sleeping bags and socks out to air,' she said. 'Always someone with an empty unpleasant laugh.'

So Hoaggie drove back down the valley just a short distance, and took the turn-off to the Blue Lakes and ventured into the tussock grass along its side. There was a bridge not much further on, and on the high side of that a cluster of alpine beech as a feature in the treeless area around them. Hoaggie nosed the Volvo between the matagouri bushes so that the boot was ideally placed to service a grassy area behind it. Jill took out the tartan rugs and told the twins to sort out a good place without stones. The long, dry stalks held up the rugs at first, but Gordon and Mark rolled over and over on them to crush them flat.

'I hope you checked for any stuff under there,' said Hoaggie.

'You mean poop,' said Gordon delightedly.

'Anything,' said Hoaggie.

'But especially crap,' said Gordon.

'That's enough,' said Hoaggie.

Hoaggie and Jill ate on the rugs there, propped on their elbows like Romans, and looking down because of the late-afternoon sun. The boys grappled and snorted through their food, pursued grasshoppers, collected chrysalids, scratched themselves, claimed to see skinks beneath the stones they lifted. Eventually they, too, lay on the rugs, talking in their own close language.

Hoaggie relaxed on his back, his hand across his face as a shield from the sun. He could smell chlorine from the swim a day ago, and the sultanas from the muffin he'd held, and also a scent from the hair on his wrists that had something of tobacco although he didn't smoke.

He was wondering if it was time to consider buying a bach in the

Coromandel, and thinking of the joy the twins would have there, when they stopped arguing with each other and in the pause he heard Jill say, 'Hoaggie.' Her voice wasn't loud, but had an odd formality. He took his hand away and squinted up into the sun. Two men were standing close to them, among the briars. The same men that the boys had laughed at on the track.

The big man put on a silly smile when he realised the family were watching, as if he wanted to appear friendly, but had never checked the expression to ensure that it accorded with his intention. He cracked his knuckles and looked at the food on the rugs. The other man was more interested in the twins. He took several long steps to bring himself up to them, and as they sat up he pushed them down again with his foot. Mark still had something of a smile, as though he thought the man might turn out to be part of a joke his father was playing on them, and he didn't want to be too easily taken in.

'Oh, my God,' said Jill. She put her hands to her face.

Hoaggie stood up, clumsy after lying in the sun all that time.

'Okay, Tub,' said the thin man in the darker denims, and Tub reached Hoaggie at the same time as Jill stood up to help. Neither Hoaggie nor his wife knew much about hurting people, but Tub did. He ignored Jill, who was tugging at him, and concentrated on pushing Hoaggie back onto the boot of the car and then abruptly breaking his right forearm on the curve of the metal. He slammed it a second time, which caused a great deal more pain, and Hoaggie slumped down by the car. The dry grass rustled as he slid into it, and he crushed a spray of tiny white flowers.

Jill was left pulling at Tub and yet trying to back off at the same time. Tub's large hand encompassed her wrist as a precaution against the latter inclination winning out.

'Mandrake?' he said, in a voice both surprisingly high-pitched and equable.

'Enough of this shit,' said Mandrake. He had a sawn-off .22 and he held it to Gordon's head. 'Now that you know we're the bad guys, no one else needs to get hurt, okay. You there, Dad, you give these kids the message just to lie still.'

'It's okay,' said Hoaggie. 'It's all right, boys. Just lie still.'

'There you go then,' said Mandrake. 'Easy as fucking pie.'

Hoaggie was still slumped in the grass with his back to the side of the car. With the pressure of his hand, Tub made Jill sit down again beside the twins. Only Tub and Mandrake were standing. Tub started eating sultana muffins and neenish tarts from one of Jill's oblong green containers.

Mandrake looked off among the grass and stunted bushes towards the road. 'Just a little old family picnic here, folks,' he said loudly, and then grinning, and almost at a shout, 'Nothing to see here.' There was no response. The sun was all brilliance in the high, clear air. Mandrake shifted his grip on the rifle so that it hung more comfortably.

A long way off, the height of a bus showed itself on the way to the Hermitage, and a pair of paradise ducks gave their tuneless call from the flats at the head of the lake. The olearia had fresh and fragrant flowers that glowed like coral amid the leaves and the burnished thorns of matagouri. Cicadas, briefly subdued by the flurry about the car, came back as a chorus. Above everything was the great sharp angle of Cook with a nightcap of cloud streaming from its peak.

Mandrake jiggled his foot playfully on Gordon's back. 'This is some place,' he said. 'What a strange thing bloody privacy is. We could be a world apart here, yet radio waves are going right through us this very instant, aren't they? Full of ski reports and talkbacks and government promises and music from Memphis Tennessee. We hear nothing of it all, though, and they've no idea we're even alive. Things can be so close, yet have no point of contact.'

'My husband's hurt,' said Jill. 'I need to help him.'

'Tub's just broken his arm,' said Mandrake, 'so he doesn't think he's a fucking hero. Take his jacket there and wrap it tightly round his arm. That way it won't jar.'

'He needs a doctor,' she said.

'You play doctor then,' said Mandrake. 'Go on then. Tub will help you.'

Tub took hold of Jill by her hair in a matter-of-fact way and forced her around to Hoaggie at the side of the car. Her face looked very young because of the skin being pulled upwards. With his free hand, Tub kept a grip on the muffin box. Jill wrapped the jacket around Hoaggie's broken arm and, while attention was on that, Mandrake shot Mark and Gordon. Mark died almost immediately, with only a bubbling sound and the shaking of his suede boots, but Gordon struggled to get up from beneath Mandrake's foot and cried out piercingly, 'Look at this.

Look at this,' until he was shot several times. He arched powerfully in his death, and his face had one last primitive instinctual expression before it relaxed.

The shots were not loud, but sufficient to quiet the cicadas briefly again and startle goldfinches, which fled in an alternating series of violent wing-bursts and dipping glides. The sun flashed on the bright feathers of their head-dress. A patch of tussock fluffed up suddenly in a gust of wind, as an animal's fur rises for an instant in alarm.

Jill was held back by her hair as she tried to reach her sons, calling loudly. Hoaggie tried to move towards them too, but Mandrake stepped to the car and put the short barrel of the .22 into Hoaggie's left eye socket to push him back. The crudely sawn muzzle made a cut beneath Hoaggie's eyebrow and blood ran, diluted with tears, as a pink wash on his cheek.

'Enough of this shit,' said Mandrake. 'Get in the car. Open the door, Tub, and get them into the car.'

When both of them were in the back seat, holding to each other for some comfort, Mandrake reloaded the small magazine of the rifle. 'Go out towards the road and look around,' he told Tub. 'See if anybody's about. Make sure everything's okay.'

'I'm still hungry,' said Tub calmly.

'Better still,' said Mandrake, 'wrap the kids in a rug first and find a place for them somewhere. There's tons of stuff you can eat here when you get back. We won't be leaving until it's pretty much dark.'

Tub wrapped the boys in a rug of red tartan and took them away through the high grass and low bushes. He experimented to find the most comfortable carrying position as he went.

'It's actually better for them this way,' said Mandrake at the window. 'Nothing drawn out at all. You know what kids are; as time went on they'd be getting in our way more and more. Jesus yes. Were they twins?' Jill and Hoaggie didn't answer. They hardly heard what he said. 'I reckon they were. I reckon they were twins,' Mandrake said. He checked the fuel gauge on the dash of the Volvo. From the picnic things he took up a wedge of egg and bacon pie and ate it carefully, lifting his lips at each bite so that his teeth were visible.

Mandrake leant on the car in the sunlight while he ate and looked in at Jill and Hoaggie from time to time as if he quite fancied a yarn while they all waited for Tub to come back. 'I don't suppose there's any booze,' he said, partly to himself. He yawned in the sun and ran his free hand over his face as he watched Tub return alone.

The big man settled down very deliberately among the picnic food and began to eat. As he ate one thing, he fossicked for others, saying 'yes' to himself at the most welcome discoveries. He was scrupulous to replace the lids of each container when he'd had enough, in case the bright, darting flies might join the feast.

Jill tried to concentrate on what she had left to love.

'How do you feel, Hoaggie?' she said. He just gazed at her wet face.

'What did she call you?' said Mandrake. 'Speak up.'

'Hoaggie,' he said.

'A special name, is it? Something intimate between husband and wife? Hoaggie, Poaggie, Boaggie.'

'It's short for Hoaganraad. That's my name – Hoaganraad.'

'I like it,' said Mandrake, lifting his head, and his lip to show his upper teeth, in a posture of contemplation and assessment. 'It's friendly and fucking informal. Hoaggie, yes.' His face lifted to the sun again and he shaped the word several times more. 'Wasn't there a Hoagy Carmichael?' he said.

'You may be right,' said Hoaggie. A conversation so unreal was more blessing than the reverse.

'I am right, old son. A musician, wasn't he? What did he play?' He stooped in to look at Jill. 'Come on, I'm sure you're a bright woman.'

'The trumpet?' she said.

'You might be right,' said Mandrake. 'What do you think, Tub? Is Hoaggie a name that takes your fancy?'

'Sounds more like shit to me.' Tub played on his back amid the picnic things with his arms and legs spread like a starfish. He had a stalk of grass in his mouth and he switched it back and forth with his tongue, or puffed his cheeks and made a succession of small poofing sounds that caused the stem to tremble. Maybe the poofing sounds had something in them of the music of the night.

'And what sort of name is Mandrake?' asked Hoaggie. All he wanted was an opportunity to show his contempt. What he saw, though, even as they spoke, was Tub carrying away his sons in the tartan picnic rug.

'I'm a bloody magician, aren't I. It doesn't take all that much with the people I spend my time with.' Mandrake's contempt was equal to

Hoaggie's and the object much the same. 'How's your philosophy, old son?' he asked Hoaggie.

'It's not my line,' said Hoaggie. The tears, pink on one side of his face, shone on his skin. He thought of the twins: their affection and abilities, all the opportunities that had been before them. He wondered who would ever find them. He thought of them lying all alone in the coming night.

'The big fucking mistake, Hoaggie, is to imagine that evil and beauty are antithetical. Don't you think? That's where people go wrong despite one experience after another. There's no natural affinity, but no mutual exclusion either. Don't you think, Hoaggie? Anyway I've pretty much thought that one out to my own satisfaction.'

'What you did to Mark and Gordon. What you did,' cried Jill. She looked away from him, through the window on the other side, where the thorns of the matagouri and the alpine briar made a lattice against the sky. While mentioning her sons she had thought for a moment that the deaths were contestable, that what had happened could be overturned, then her head and shoulders sagged down.

'There's nothing you could have done,' said Mandrake. 'Nothing to be done now. Just one thing impinging on another, as the philosophers tell us. The whole thing is bad luck on your part: just a matter of timing. It's like going out driving and hitting two, or even three, birds when it hasn't happened for bloody ages, and when you get back and have a look, there they are, packed tight into the grille by the impact.'

'I wish we hadn't come. I wish we hadn't come. I wish we hadn't come.' Her voice was muffled by the seat back, but rising almost to hysteria.

'Shut it,' shouted Mandrake, but almost immediately he was reasonable again. His hand steadied her shoulder through the open window. 'It's best for all of us if we do things quietly. A fucking uproar gets nobody anywhere. You've no reason to blame yourself or anything. Take it easy. Bad luck is really just bringing forward what's bound to happen.'

The sun was going down over Cook; different shadows were at play over the rock buttresses, screes and snow fields of the mountains. With the dropping of the sun came an obvious dropping of temperature. The sound of the river became more distinct; the briar and matagouri bushes took on a tinge of purple; the cicadas ceased their song. Tub stood up and tried to pull the sides of his jacket together so that more of his front would be covered. Mandrake still leant on the side of the car. He held the rifle loosely, and partly disguised by the line of his leg. Hoaggie and Jill sat silently in the back seat. Hoaggie cradled his broken arm with the good one and his wife's sobs had subsided to a wide-mouthed, heavy breathing.

'Let's piss off,' said Tub.

'In just a bit,' said Mandrake. 'Better that no one gets a clear look at us on the road.'

'It's got cold.'

'Yeah, but tonight we won't have to be out in it. That's the difference,' said Mandrake. Tub nodded to that. 'I think we should check on our playmates,' said Mandrake, 'to take care of the stuff that might get lost.'

'Bloody right,' said Tub.

Mandrake already had the keys; he took Hoaggie's wallet and Jill's handbag with just a motion of the .22 and gave both to Tub who went through them with the single-minded curiosity occasioned by the unfamiliar. All the money, Tub put it in his trouser pocket; something of a struggle because of the tautness of his belly and his backside against the cloth. He gave the credit cards to Mandrake, who was saying how he was looking forward to getting back into the city – not the fucking sticks he said.

An urgency seized him and he broke off, opened the car door and put the rifle to the back of Jill's head. 'It occurs to me, old son,' he said to Hoaggie, 'That you're just the sort of yuppie bastard to have a cell-phone, and just silly enough to keep it hidden.'

'I haven't. We're on holiday, for God's sake. There's nothing at all.'

Mandrake looked carefully at him, at the same time lifting the short barrel of the .22 through Jill's fair hair, which parted noiselessly, brushing the metal and falling into place again with its own smooth weight. 'No, of course you haven't,' said Mandrake. 'Silly fucking me, eh. You know, I'm prone to an odd paranoid notion that people are out to get me. Funny that.' He closed the door again and stood in the last of the light, laughing. Hoaggie and Jill could only see the contrast stitched denim jacket, but they could hear the laugh, which was subdued, like that of a panting dog. Tub joined in for a time on a higher and less controlled note.

Mandrake decided that he would do the driving. He had Jill come into the front seat beside him, and Tub sit with Hoaggie in the back. 'This is a class car,' he said as he nosed from the grasses onto the road. The flat outwash before the lake was becoming an indiscriminate mix of dark evening shades, and only Mount Cook and its fellows were still sharp against a westward edge of sky, ember lit by the sun. 'Tub and I recently had an unfortunate experience with a Mercedes,' he said. 'It was a great car too, but I don't think we quite had time to get used to it. Eh, Tub?'

'Bummer,' said Tub. He confined Hoaggie to a small portion of the Volvo's generous squab as he settled down to rest. His obvious feeling that neither Hoaggie nor Jill could pose any threat whatsoever increased Hoaggie's sense of helplessness.

For a time, as they drove in the gathering darkness with the steep hills on one side and the leaden expanse of glacier-fed lake on the other, Mandrake quizzed his captives about their lives for information that might be helpful to him. He was disappointed to find they had no home in the South Island. Soon though, he indulged his fondness for speculative, even intellectual talk. 'You wouldn't know it, but I'm a bugger for the reading. I reckon I would have done all right at university had things being different,' he said, 'but sooner or later the point of every lesson that you can be told about occurs in the course of your life anyway. It's the capacity to see to the core of things, to put aside that fucking self-deceit, that's the important thing. Don't you think?'

'You're a murderer, and a senseless bastard,' said Hoaggie. The great, dimly seen platter of Tub's sleeping face was close to his shoulder and the man's breathing had become an adenoidal whine.

'You're a murderer,' said Jill distantly and she wept for the proof of it. Mandrake drove on beside Pukaki, which was assuming a pale luminosity as the mountains around it retreated into darkness.

'As to a bastard,' he said. 'You're right there in any way you like.'

'You're not right in the head,' said Hoaggie. 'Who kills people for the sake of it?'

'I'm on the outside, Hoaggie. Don't you fucking get it? I'm on the outside of this whole thing that the rest of you have got going. Nothing connects me with it except bringing it down. That's all an outsider has, you see. What the books call a negative capacity.'

'You'll get caught.'

'Wonderful, Hoaggie, but what's that to me now? Don't you see? I've always been caught, so there's a difference. I'm teaching a few people, and you're one of them, that I'm determined to have all the things I can't claim within your rules. Get it? You never asked me to any dinner party, old son, yet here I am with my hand warmed by your wife's thighs and my heart by this philosophic discussion. Boredom and truth, they're the two things that have done for me. I tend to break down if my life's too flat. Yes, Hoaggie, boredom's a killer and so is truth.'

Mandrake's long mulish face came alive when he talked, and he was his own best listener. 'I reckon truth is the worst affliction anyone can have. Most people are shielded by stupidity, convention, or privilege, but I wasn't lucky enough. By the time I was fourteen I was on my own and could see what a fucking rat-arsed world we've got here and entirely rigged against pricks like me. Everything comes to nothing, Hoaggie, soon enough. Nothing anyone does ever matters.'

'None of that's an excuse for the things you do. It's pointless, it's horrifying.'

'You know, sometimes I horrify myself. Can you believe that?' Mandrake gave his panting laugh. 'But the more you get into it, the more you need the kicks. You get so far down the line that there's no way back even if you wanted it. You're fucked one way or another.'

Jill was stiff and quiet, her head turned away from Mandrake and against the glass of the window. Hoaggie wept for a while, the sound of that conjoining within the car with the noise made by sleeping Tub. Hoaggie attempted to adjust the coat twisted as a support for his fractured arm. The Volvo swept on past the lake towards the Tekapo road.

'Did I tell you that Tub and I spent last night in the open?' said Mandrake. 'Well, near enough. Jesus, it got cold. You wouldn't think it at this time of the year so much, but I suppose it's the height and being so far inland.'

They met only one or two other cars in the night. The Volvo headed back towards Tekapo through the desolate Mackenzie Country. The lights on full swept the thin avenue of seal before them or, on the bends, caught the barren undulation of the landscape beyond, with not enough vegetation to hide the rabbits that moved there. Just the fierce spaniards made profiles and a few small pines wind-sown across the stony ground. In the dark felt of the sky hung a gibbous moon and the bright barbs of stars.

Mandrake took his free hand from Jill's leg and marvelled at it all.

'Look how there's light on some of the peaks,' he said. 'White on white until they glow. I wonder if any bastard climbs there at night, do you think. Jesus. I remember, oh years ago, when I spent a few weeks in the Hokianga and some nights, after we'd had a fair bit of shit, we'd row this old dinghy out and just sit and talk and watch the lights of Rawene down the harbour. We'd smoke and lie back, rocked by the swell. It always seems to me that the sky is closer when you're out on the water.'

Jill had begun weeping and to Mandrake it made her less attractive: it also distracted him from his conversation. 'Quit all the blubbing,' he said. 'It gets on my nerves.' But she was past the point of caring even for the things that Mandrake could do.

'Leave her alone,' said Hoaggie.

'All this fucking snivelling,' said Mandrake. 'What's the point.'

They came down past the few shops and the hotel at Tekapo. A brief oasis of lights in the night and the lake like a pale carpet spread into the mountains. Tub woke and said that he wanted to get some booze, but Mandrake said maybe at the next pub, Burkes Pass. 'Jesus,' he said to Jill, 'haven't I been telling you to shut up?' On a long climbing straight with not a house for miles, he pulled abruptly to the side of the road, cut the lights and, leaving the driver's seat, went round the front of the Volvo and pulled Jill from her place. He held her among the low lupins as a shearer holds a sheep, steadied in a crouch with one hand and a knee. Her crying altered not at all in intensity; without resistance she held any position into which he forced her. Hoaggie managed to get a door open before Tub reacted.

Mandrake shot Jill twice beneath the ear and then Hoaggie once in the flesh of his upper leg. 'Get that prick back inside,' he told Tub, and he rolled Jill through the soft, rustling lupins into the grassed ditch flanking the road. She lay there very low, very relaxed, almost as if she was pressing herself into the scented earth. The noise of her weeping had been with them for so long that the silence which succeeded it was a noticeable release. Mandrake walked back to the driver's side and had a stretch there, his long arms reaching up as if for a hold among the stars. Tub quietly held Hoaggie in the back seat; nothing seemed to disturb the equanimity of the big man's life.

'That's a whole lot better,' said Mandrake. He made himself comfortable in the car and placed the .22 carefully at his feet again. He shrugged his shoulders in the denim jacket as he had done on the track to the Hooker Glacier when Hoaggie had first seen him, and then began driving again up the lonely road through the tussock to the pass. 'Women have a tendency to whine, don't you think, Hoaggie? And besides, I've been quite considerate. The worst thing for you would be to go first, imagining me at play with your wife. Aren't I right?'

'Bugger you,' cried Hoaggie. What else could Mandrake threaten him with once Jill and the boys were dead. 'You're nothing – nothing at all,' he said in a voice that had become almost a whisper again.

'The odd fucking thing is that I can't get it up these days! Your wife's okay for looks. I took to her voice and the way her hair was done, but I can't get it up anymore. Some sort of punishment, I suppose, Hoaggie, and you'll be pleased to hear that. Yet I can sleep like a baby.' Mandrake bounced his head on his chest and gave his panting laugh.

'You're nothing,' said Hoaggie harshly. He rocked a bit. 'Jesus,' he said. With his good hand he tried to hold his handkerchief to the wound in his thigh.

'Come on, Hoaggie,' said Mandrake. 'Be a man. No one dies from a fucking .22 in the leg. Most likely you'll hardly even bleed.' At the crest of the pass the lights for a moment pointed up to nothingness and then the car dipped over the highest place and the beam caught again the sealed road, the median white dashes, the treeless hills above.

'Does it look any different out there, Hoaggie, than when you came up? I often think that's the thing, how little connection there is. Indifference, Hoaggie, that's all there is in nature. In a community, a family too, I suppose, people can babble on to conceal it, but when you're on your own, when you come down to it, then it stares you in the face if you've got any brains at all. No wonder so many people get pissed, or turn to religion.'

'Your apple barrel meditations are rubbish,' said Hoaggie. 'You've killed people for no reason, no reason at all.'

'Well, you're an educated man, Hoaggie. I'm just a fucking bum trying to get some share of the action and make sense of things. But I reckon that I have reasons: it's just that for you they're not good enough.'

'You could have had the money, the car, without hurting any of us.'

'But that's not it, Hoaggie. I want you to see me, to take me seriously.

Get it? From time to time I need intelligent conversation. I will have attention paid to me, see?' Mandrake struck the wheel in his vehemence.

Before Burkes Pass Hotel and the three or four other buildings, isolated, a little higher on the slope, there is a graveyard with wooden gates and a line of oak trees facing the road. Consecrated ground no bigger than three or four urban house sections. Mandrake pulled into the dirt track and stopped there. He cut the lights and told Hoaggie that they were going to take a breather. 'Tub will give you a hand,' he said solicitously. 'What with your arm and leg the way they are.'

It seemed very dark at first, as if there were nothing present but themselves, and then, as Hoaggie's eyes adjusted to the absence of headlights, his surroundings gradually came up before him. First the sky as a sheen with a hump-backed moon and a scatter of stars, then the dark but individual masses of the oak trees, and the pines on the other boundaries, with a glimmer among them in one quarter from the hotel.

It was a lawn cemetery or, rather, a rough pasture one, with the older monuments at the higher end catching enough light to show the symmetry of their shapes. Mandrake walked in further from the road and Tub took a good deal of Hoaggie's weight as they followed.

'Jesus, what a life you have,' Hoaggie said to him, but Tub just turned his great, flat snowman's face to him and said nothing. Hoaggie felt and heard dry acorns beneath his shoes as he went through the gateway and the night breeze drew through the trees of the cemetery with an easy sigh.

'I could stay here all night talking, just about,' said Mandrake. 'I love the night. It's the other side of the coin, isn't it? People think that it's just some sort of pit that separates one day from another, but there are sights and sounds and smells that exist only then: there's animals and all sorts that have their whole life when most of us are sleeping. It's an alternative, Hoaggie, isn't it, and that's always a good thing. I always feel uneasy when there's only one choice, one way of looking at things.'

Tub had drawn off towards the trees and was having a piss, which cascaded long and loud into the rank grass. It reminded Mandrake that time was passing. 'The thing is,' he told Hoaggie, 'that Tub's keen to get down to the pub and that's fair enough. He doesn't ask much. He's a fucking natural man and doesn't pretend to love his fellows, but he's very loyal.'

Hoaggie sat down on the cold concrete bed of one of the graves. His arm ached, his leg ached, but the real anguish was that of loss. It occurred to him quite without irony, that he would like to read the inscription on the headstone, so he would know his companion for the night. He could see the graves more clearly then, and realised that the night was their natural time – cold and quiet and peaceful. No matter what Mandrake, Tub, and Hoaggie could do there, the place was one of serenity. The trees, the old stones, the wrought iron surrounds of some of the oldest plots caught the more subtle light of the night. Hoaggie was amazed by the coherent detail that formed about him.

Mandrake looked at the shadowed graves with interest. 'Everyone living must be considered an optimist, for they've had the alternative of suicide after all,' he said. 'Hold on to your philosophy, old son. That's the bloody thing to do,' and he lifted the hand which held the sawn-off .22 and began the gasping that was his laugh.

Ngahere Gold
by Denver Grenell

The campfire crackles and spits as the old man places another branch of mānuka on the burning pile. Orange sparks dance skyward in pursuit of the spiralling plume of smoke. The two children lie by the fire, wrapped in sleeping bags and rugs, the glow from the blaze flickering in their sleepy eyes. Remnants of the night's dinner is scattered on the ground before them – greasy plastic plates, charred sticks that had held sausages, then marshmallows, over the flames, and shredded tinfoil that still houses some potatoes, slow-cooked in the embers.

The old man reaches into his poncho, removes a thin bone flute and raises it to his lips. He blows softly on the kōauau, releasing a mournful tune into the air. His long fingers make subtle movements over the holes, causing the notes to waver slightly.

The boy listens, transfixed by the plaintive melody.

The old man lowers the flute and nods to the sky and then to the trees that surround the campsite. The song has ceased, but the magic it conjured remains, filling the air with its invisible aura.

The boy breaks the silence. 'Koro? Can you tell us a story?'

'I just did, young one. Well, it was an oriori. Lullaby.'

'I want a scary story.'

The old man smiles. 'Tama, if I tell you a scary story, you'll be up all night. And we can't be having that. This old timer needs his beauty sleep.'

'Yeah, so does Tama, cos he's U.G.L.Y,' the girl teases.

'Marie, please.' The old man's voice is warm but firm.

She lowers her eyes. 'Sorry, Koro.'

'Yeah shush, dunghead,' the boy teases his sister.

Before she can retaliate, the old man raises a leathery hand in warning. 'Quiet now. Or you might wake up the mighty Kumi lizard.'

The girl's eyes widen.

Seeing he has their attention, the old man continues, 'Kumi lizards are supposed to be extinct, but some say they still live out there in the bush – watching, waiting.'

'Waiting for what, Koro?' the girl asks.

'For someone to violate the sacred laws of the forest or break tapu by taking that which is not theirs. And then–' He pauses for dramatic effect. 'And then the Kumi come. And they get very hungry you see, as there are only small creatures to eat in the bush. Birds and bugs. The odd possum. But chubby tamariki like you would make a tasty feast indeed.' He smacks his lips theatrically.

The children giggle nervously.

'Tama would be eaten first. He's the chubbiest!' The girl laughs at her brother.

'Shut up,' the boy wails. He picks up a cold, uneaten potato and threatens to throw it at his sister.

The old man's hand goes up once more, commanding silence. His left eyebrow rises at the same time, indicating his displeasure. The boy sheepishly puts the potato down.

'The Kumi are placated by the songs of the bush. They don't want to hear the trivial bickerings of tamariki.'

'I think they must be extinct, or someone would have seen one,' the girl says earnestly.

'Some say they retreated when man cut down the trees to make cities, towns and farms. And some say the Kumi were transformed by their anger and sadness. Became hardened. Vengeful.'

The smile drops from the girl's face.

'It's just a lizard, you wuss!' the boy chortles.

'Hush!' the old man warns. 'They could be watching us right now. So beware.' A sly smile creeps across his face. 'And on that note, te moe pai and sweet dreams.'

The old man lies down on his makeshift bed and pulls his red sleeping bag over his shoulders. There's a quiet chuckle and then silence.

The children look at each other fearfully. The fire sputters as the gum in the mānuka branches bubbles and pops. The siblings snuggle down on their foam bedrolls and stare at the stars glimmering through the treetops. Morepork call out. Possums cackle in the darkness, taunting them.

The boy folds his pillow over his ears to drown out the eerie choir of the night. He closes his eyes tightly. Eventually, his fears give way to peaceful slumber.

The children sleep, oblivious to the sharp cooing of the morepork. Or the old man's snoring. Or the padding of large feet, creeping just beyond the periphery of the campsite, an unseen form retreating into the dark of the forest.

'Tama! Stop! Don't take another step.'

Tama focused on the small object dangling at eye level from a translucent length of fishing line – a barbed fishhook. 'Jesus!'

Dean grabbed the hook between his thumb and forefinger and cut the line with a short-bladed knife. 'One more step and pfffft. No more eye, cuz.' Dean held the hook up in front of Tama. Sunlight gleamed off the thin piece of steel. 'We tread carefully from now on, aye? We're close.'

Tama nodded and waited for Dean to take the lead, which he naturally did, given that he was the instigator of the day's mission. He was like a dog, always rushing ahead excitedly, eager to be the first one to arrive at their destination. But there was a considered, careful air to his movements today, even prior to their encounter with the fishhook.

Tama's lanky friend crept forward through the trees. Dean had dressed in head-to-toe camouflage for their outing, which Tama had thought odd at first. They hadn't planned on going hunting – just a casual hike in the bush. But the hook that nearly took out Tama's eye told him what they were really here for – Dean was looking for something.

Something that someone didn't want to be found.

On a normal day, a sojourn into the dense North Island bush gave Tama a strong, revitalising sense of peace, a necessary escape from five days of labour at the timber mill, trying to scrape enough money together to pay child support to his ex and make the monthly payments on his ute. Once or twice a month he would hike one of the tracks that wound through the bush-covered Tararua mountain ranges, the great green wilderness acting as a reset button on the trials of the working week. Tama wasn't revelling in the natural beauty today, though. Something troubled him about today's excursion. And it was all to do with Dean.

Tama and Dean had grown up in the small rural town of Featherston, just north of New Zealand's capital city, Wellington. Ever since they were teenagers, Dean always had some sort of scheme going on. At school, it was selling cigarettes he'd pinched from the local dairy or getting his older brother to buy booze for underage teens for a hefty commission. Later, it was selling fifty bags of marijuana cut with grass clippings to make it go further (which also gave him more to smoke for himself). Tama wasn't sure if or what Dean was selling these days and didn't care to ask, but he assumed it to be any number of drugs: weed, speed and whatever else could be smoked, snorted, swallowed, injected or shelved. Dean tended to disappear for weeks at a time, either to avoid someone who was after him or, if he were flush with cash, to head into the city to 'invest' the profits in order to make more.

The main thing they had in common was their love of the bush. Whenever Dean was around for an extended period, he would show up at Tama's place at first light with his tramping boots and a backpack filled with beef jerky, apples, water and weed. A day in the bush with

Dean nearly always ended with a request to borrow some money. 'Just until I'm flush again.' And though countless dollars had yet to be repaid from years gone by, Dean was a loyal mate with a good heart buried somewhere in his skinny, tattooed chest.

There was a snip as Dean's knife removed another rusty fishhook from its wire. Tama shook his head in disbelief. What the hell had Dean gotten him into?

Dean had called him up the previous night, buzzing with excitement, asking if he wanted to go hiking the next day.

'Where are you thinking of?' Tama had asked.

'It's a surprise, mate. Somewhere I bet you haven't hiked before. In fact, I know you haven't.' Even on the phone, the cunning in Dean's voice was evident. Tama could picture him pacing around his dirty, clothes-strewn one-roomer, pumped with adrenalin, and chuffing ciggies as if the smoke was keeping him alive.

'Pick me up at eight,' Dean said before hanging up, no doubt to smoke some more ciggies or, more likely, to indulge in something harder. Judging by Dean's frazzled appearance when Tama turned up at the converted shed that Dean called home, it was the latter. Although he was dressed and equipped for a day in the bush, Dean's bloodshot eyes told a story of chemical excess and sleeplessness. He kept spitting on the ground as if trying to rid himself of some nasty taste.

As Tama had driven up the gravel road to the start of the tracks, Dean had sat with his head resting against his arm, window down, pale and sweaty.

Tama glanced over at his friend. 'You sure you're up for this, Deano?'

Dean didn't even look back at him. 'I'm a box of fuckin' fluffies, mate. Just need some of that bush air in me lungs and I'll be right as bloody rain.' And sure enough, when Tama turned the ute's engine off forty minutes later, Dean had leapt from the vehicle with the boundless vigour of a dog that had been let off its leash. Tama had to jog to keep up with him as he stomped up the hiking track.

After following the track for a couple of hours, Dean stopped, looked around, and then veered right, charging down an embankment into a valley of thick, untouched bush. Tama knew better than to question his mate when he was on a mission. The real question was, what sort of mission were they on?

'Deano. Hold up, mate. Let's have a drink.' Tama reached out and grabbed a three-metre-tall ponga fern to stop himself from stumbling down the steep incline.

Dean was already at the bottom. He turned back impatiently. 'Just a quick one, Tee, then we gotta make tracks.'

Tama half walked, half slid to the bottom of the embankment. Sweat poured down his brow, and his t-shirt stuck to his back like loose, wet skin. The air was still and humid and carried the sweet honey scent of the tarata tree which held a recent bloom of yellow flowers. 'What's with the hustle? Where are we going?'

Dean just grinned, revealing the gaps in his teeth as he backed away. 'I could tell you, but that would ruin the surprise.' Clearly eager to get moving, he turned and resumed his marathon pace. 'I can't fucking wait to see your face when we get there.'

Tama didn't push the issue. Maybe there was a new secret swimming hole or waterfall he'd found out about. Dean was a competent bushman. His wiry frame was well suited to roaming through the thick bush. He bristled with the nervous energy of a junkie hanging for a fix. Worrying. Dean wasn't usually this bouncy on their excursions, and the question of their destination hung over Tama like a nagging itch.

An hour later, he'd had his answer in the form of the steel fishhook. Dean was looking for a marijuana plot. And he needed a reliable pair of hands to help him plunder said crops. Tama's goodwill for his friend evaporated into the humid spring air. But they were too far into the journey now to turn back, and the determination on Dean's face said he'd be pulling those crops with or without Tama's help. If there's one thing Tama knew about Dean, it was that he wasn't completely reckless. He wouldn't go tramping halfway into the bush to steal some crops if there was the slightest chance the owners of the crops would be in the vicinity. For a man who dabbled in the unsavoury areas of life, Dean didn't take overly stupid risks.

More like calculated ones.

Still, whenever Dean was involved in some sort of drama, it was often because of some other untrustworthy party, not because Dean had blundered into the escapade unprepared.

They continued through the dense bush, Tama sticking close to Dean. All at once, Dean stopped. He pointed at the ground. A barely visible razor-thin tripwire stretched from beneath a cluster of ferns on the left to a ponga tree a few metres to the right. Dean followed the wire back to the bush, gently pulling the fern fronds aside to reveal a sawn-off shotgun secured by bent nails to an angled plank of wood. The wire was wound back around the trigger. Dean stood in front of the gun barrel, moving his hand along the trajectory of the gunshot from the barrel to his groin.

'Ouch! You want kids someday, Tee?'

'I've got a kid, dumbass. And I can't believe I actually considered bringing her along today.' In truth, it wasn't his weekend with Ella, but Tama wasn't above using his daughter to make Dean feel bad for leading him on this wild goose chase.

'Right, yeah.' Dean stepped over the tripwire. 'Well, if we find what I'm hoping we'll find, you'll be able to send her to Auckland-bloody-Grammar.'

'How do you know we aren't going to come across a bunch of Red Devils tending to their crops? I mean, it is the Devils, isn't it?'

Dean stopped and turned back to Tama. 'We won't find them. You know why? 'Cause they upped and left town last week. No one's seen them. My mate Dan is tight with that crew. He figures they're doing a roadie up north and will be back to get their crops in the next week. So, we get in now, harvest that sweet green, and flick it on before they get back.'

'They're gonna come looking for us.'

'I've thought of that too, bro.' He reached into his backpack and removed a black and silver bandana – the colours of the local youth gang, the Snakes, a scraggly group of wannabe gangsters who made up for their lack of organisation and smarts with pure brutality. Where some of the older gangs would be happy to administer a swift beatdown to anyone stepping on their toes, the Snakes weren't above bringing knives, steel pipes and shotguns to a fistfight.

'Holy shit. You're gonna set up those young bloods? That's ruthless, even for you.'

'It's a ruthless old world.' He flashed Tama his gap-toothed grin, his go-to signifier that he a) had it all figured out and b) truly didn't give a fuck what anyone else thought anyway.

Before long, the bush thinned out, opening on a sunlit patch of shrubs a half-acre wide, ringed by a border of tall kowhai and birch trees that formed a natural wall around the area.

Dean stopped and sniffed loudly. 'Smell that, Tee?'

The fragrant odour of fresh marijuana stuck to the air like invisible glue – that instantly identifiable natural pungency with a hint of old socks. They pushed forward through the shrubs and laid their eyes on the end goal of their quest – a compact field of chin-high marijuana plants enveloped in the golden rays of the midday sun. The leaves around the base of the plants were yellowed and dry, indicating that it was indeed harvest time. So why hadn't the crop's owners been to harvest it yet?

Dean jumped up and down on the spot with excitement. 'Sweet Mary Jane and her mother! We found it! We fucking found it, Tee! Pure ngahere gold!'

Tama was still breathless from the hike and the thick plant odour didn't help.

'Did you know that in Kyrgyzstan or one of the 'Stans, the harvesters ride naked on horses through the crops to get the resin stuck to their bodies?' Dean murmured, suddenly calm. He stared into the distance as if he were imagining doing just that.

Tama chuckled. 'I am not running through here bare-arsed with you if that's what you're getting at.'

Dean snapped out of his reverie. 'Yeah, nah. No time for that today, pal. We need to harvest these fuckers and get the hell out of here. Time is very much of the essence.'

Dean removed his backpack, took out a handful of black plastic rubbish bags, and handed one to Tama along with a small pair of pruning secateurs. Then Dean approached the plant closest to him, clipped the thick buds off, and placed them in the bag. The buds were tightly bound green nuggets that resembled large green caterpillars. Dean slipped between the rows of plants, snipping off buds with the precision of someone who has harvested crops in a hurry before. Tama joined in. Within minutes, the two rubbish bags were bulging with their plunder.

Dean forced the taut rubbish bag into his 100L hiking pack. 'Alright, Tee, let's hustle.'

Tama nodded and did the same with his haul. He zipped the bag closed and paused.

Something seemed off about the forest.

There was no birdsong. No tui warbling. No kereru swooping through the air. Just an eerie stillness. Static hummed, faint in the distance. Had it been there all the time? Tama hadn't noticed it when they arrived. Probably due to the excitement of finding the crop. Tama stopped and concentrated. The buzzing was coming from the far end of the patch.

'Deano, you hear that?'

Dean was bent over, still trying to force the overfilled sack into his backpack. 'What's that, mate?'

But Tama was striding between the rows. The closer he got to the sound, the more insistent it became, as if whatever was making it heard him coming and intensified in response. As he neared the end of the crops, it crystallised into an unmistakable buzz.

Flies.

Hundreds and hundreds of flies. Which meant there was most likely something dead nearby. The thick smell of the plants had successfully masked the rot, but now the stench grew stronger in tandem with the sound.

Tama pushed aside a large bushel and stepped into an abattoir of death.

The decomposing remains of half a dozen men lay strewn across the forest floor like discarded chicken bones. The bodies had been eviscerated. Tama fell to his knees, overcome by the sight and smell of the slaughter. He looked down and gasped. A large bald head stared at him from eyeless sockets. The birds must have eaten his eyes. The lower half of the man's body heaved with wriggling maggots a few metres away, the legs mostly stripped of flesh. The white of the bones peeked through loose scraps of ragged meat and brown, dried blood.

'Tama, where are you, mate?' Dean emerged from the crops and stood beside Tama, batting at the large flies swarming around his face. 'Jesus – fuck!'

Tama gagged once, then vomited into the ferns.

'Holy shit, man, who did this?' Dean walked slowly among the sun-dried remains. He bent and lifted a shred of leather jacket from the back of a corpse that had no limbs, just a torso and a head. He held the bloody material aloft. A crude print of a grinning devil's face was sewn onto the piece of leather – a back patch. 'Tama, it's them. The Red Devils. Someone got to them.'

Tama spat out the last of his breakfast. 'We shouldn't fucking be here.'

Dean bent again to examine the dead gang member. 'Hello, hello. What's this?' When he stood up, he was holding a large greenstone necklace streaked with the blood of its former owner. Dean scraped off the globs of blood against the trunk of a ponga and then pocketed the jewellery. 'Want not, waste not, I say.'

Tama wiped puke and saliva from his chin and got to his feet. 'Are you for real? You know it's tapu to steal pounamu. It's even worse if it's from a dead person!'

'Doesn't apply to me, mate. I'm just a Pākehā.'

'Dean! For fuck's sake. So what if you're not Māori? Put it back.' Tama glared at Dean until he reluctantly placed the greenstone on the ground. 'Who would do this? And why did they leave the crops?'

Dean spat coarsely onto the corpse before him. 'It's a goddamn mystery, Tee. And one I don't want the answer to, you feel me?'

Tama nodded grimly and turned his back on the open gravesite. The infernal buzzing receded as they re-entered the tightly packed marijuana plants.

A roar cut through the air like the foghorn of a ship. The trees shook with the force of the sound. Tama and Dean froze.

'The fuck is that?' Tama looked at Dean, who remained silent. Branches snapped in the forest behind them, as if a large body was pushing through the foliage. A low guttural growl followed, only metres from Tama and Dean. It was so deep and voluminous, Tama's already tender stomach quivered. Whatever it was, it sounded pissed.

'Go! Now!' Dean yelled, shoving Tama forward.

They broke into a run.

The thing behind them roared again. Closer now.

Branches whipped at Tama's body. Then, a searing pain stabbed Tama in the face. One of the dangling fishhooks had snared his cheek, lodging its barb into the flesh. Tama reached up, grasped the fishing line, and yanked, snapping it and freeing himself. He lurched on, only to have two more fishhooks pierce his skin – one in his left shoulder and another in his right hand.

'Dean!' His voice was like radio static, distorted by frequencies of fear and pain.

Dean stopped running and turned back. The creature – or whatever it was – roared again. Hot wind blasted Tama's skin. The thing's hellish breath reeked of rotten meat. Human meat.

Tama stopped jerking and stood still. Dean ran towards him, wide-eyed and urgent. There was the ping of a wire, and for a split-second, Tama saw the realisation cross Dean's face. Just before the shotgun blast hit him in the thigh. Dean was thrown violently sideways into the ferns. A shower of red sprayed across the foliage.

'Dean!'

Heavy footfalls approached, then a low, purring growl. A long dark shadow fell over Tama. Unseen nostrils sniffed the air around him.

Tama closed his eyes and held his breath. Somehow the name of the beast came to him. It was the great Kumi lizard his koro told him of as a child. Tama couldn't see the creature, but there was a strong compost odour as if the beast had crawled from the stagnant bowels of the earth.

Dean's bloody face emerged from the ferns. 'Tama!'

Wounded, Tama's friend struggled to get to his feet.

'Dean,' Tama hissed. 'Don't move.'

But Dean drew his knife. 'Over here, you ugly fuck!'

The huge form of the Kumi heaved past Tama, knocking him off his feet. The fishing lines snapped as he fell, releasing another jagged bolt of pain. Blood oozed from the fresh wounds, mingling with the sweat. Tama gazed at the creature that lurched forth, out of myth and into reality, a demonic force of nature. It was a cross between a dragon and a bull. Four thick legs held up a solid mass of rippling green muscle. Leaf and swirl patterns were etched into the skin of the beast as if the forest had tattooed its hide. Its head was cat-like but covered in scales instead of fur. A wide Cheshire cat mouth opened to reveal rows of curved yellowed teeth.

Dean howled as the beast approached him, but not with fear. There was a sense of triumph in his voice as if his life's path had led him to this.

Tama crawled to his knees. 'Dean. No.' He tried to shout, but his voice barely rose above a whisper.

Dean swung his blade at the beast, slicing along its snout, opening a long sliver of red above its nostrils. Dean gave a crazed laugh and then vanished into the green, the forest swallowing him whole. There was a muffled shout followed by the sickening crunching of bones.

The beast swivelled to face Tama, and for the first time, he looked into its eyes. They were azure, like sapphires, set into its large green skull. They blazed with a life that was ancient and primordial.

The beast approached, its eyes locked on Tama's. Its lower jaw moved in a circular motion, grinding Dean's body to a bloody paste. It stopped alongside Tama and opened its mouth. A flood of chunky red viscera poured onto the ground, soaking Tama's knees and spattering his face. The beast nudged the grisly pile with its nose then looked directly at Tama again. The brilliant blue eyes told Tama what to do. He reached into the regurgitated mess and dug around with his fingers until they closed around something hard and smooth.

The greenstone necklace.

He removed it from the muck and wiped it on the ground. Red gave way to green, the pounamu shimmering like the blazing eyes of the beast. Tama held the stone up in the palms of his hand. The beast opened its mouth again. Fear held him like a fist, squeezing all sense and reason out of him. He was at the mercy of the beast now. Moments away from being reduced to a pile of red gruel, like Dean. They had trespassed into a forbidden realm and angered its guardian. Death was the toll. Unless…

Tama placed the stone on the creature's wide tongue. The gemstone eyes blazed again, pulling Tama into their hypnotic depths, transporting him to a dark space – a cave. The beast's lair. He saw men with gang patches removing the necklace and other artefacts from the cave. He saw them eviscerated by the beast in the clearing at the edge of the crops. The Kumi – a whirling dervish of green and red – obliterated the men in a tornado of death, leaving their remains as a warning, like mangled human scarecrows. Next, Dean appeared and removed the sacred stone, which had only happened moments ago, but felt like years in the past.

You dumb bastard, Dean. Couldn't leave it alone, could you?

Tama winced as he relived Dean's death. As soon as it had come, the vision receded, leaving a realisation in its wake. It wasn't the land they had violated, but the tapu, the sacred restriction of the stone. The land was for all to use within reason, which is why the Kumi had allowed the crops to grow and flourish.

The beast rose and moved past Tama into the thicket, pushing the plants aside with its mammoth bulk. The foliage closed behind it like green curtains. The footfalls of the Kumi faded into the distance.

Once the beast had disappeared, the birdsong and insect buzz crept in again, having gone silent in fearful reverence to their guardian. Tama rolled over onto his back. The bed of ferns tickled him gently, in contrast to the sharp pain of his wounds. He reached up to his cheek and gingerly touched the hook embedded there. His t-shirt was slick with blood and sweat. The only way the hooks were coming out was if he pushed them through. Tama staggered to his knees, hovering above Dean's shredded remains.

'Dean,' he whispered. 'E noho rā.' The tears came then, mingling with the blood that painted his cheeks. Dean's blood. His lifelong friend. The friend that always had his back.

Not anymore. Not ever. Tama removed his Leatherman from his belt. Opening the tool, he raised it to his cheek, and, clasping the fishhook between the two prongs, Tama squeezed until the metal snapped. Biting back a cry at the jab of pain, he opened the prongs and let the lower half of the hook fall away. Then he clasped the barb and hauled it through the flesh of his cheek. Fresh blood streamed down his face. His face would heal, but he would carry the scars as a testament to the power of the forest and a tribute to his fallen friend.

He picked up his backpack and slung it awkwardly over his good shoulder, ready to walk out of the forest. He scanned the foliage for more fishhooks or tripwires but saw none. As he started to ascend the slope, the ungodly roar of the Kumi shook the forest once more. Despite his injuries, Tama ran, fearing the monster would change its mind and return, that those booming footfalls might bear down on him at any moment. But none were forthcoming.

It was a warning. Begone.

Tama nodded grimly. He set off in the direction of home.

THE SPACES BETWEEN
BY BRYCE STEVENS

Then
Ben knelt against the painted cinderblock wall. He looked down. The carpet under his knees shifted like windblown desert sand. He smelled cooking meat. Through a yellowish haze there was movement, as if bulky animals were approaching. Something splashed against his throat, scalding his skin. He put a hand to the spot and felt only dryness.

He looked up at the row of books and recognised the familiar shelves of the Māngere Public Library. The shelf nearest him rippled, and a greasy mass slid down the spines, obscuring the titles.

A voice close by startled him. 'You alright there, fella?' It was a boy in Otahuhu College uniform.

Ben blinked and stared at him. 'Wha, what?'

The boy was eating a sandwich. 'You had a bit of a turn, bro. My aunty has those.' He piled the bread into his mouth then wiped his face on the lapel of his uniform jacket. Jerked his head towards the window. 'Those kids always pick on us Year 9s. They're not gonna find you here. I told them you were up hiding behind the train station.'

Ben stretched his neck left and right, hearing a familiar click.

The boy reached out and slapped Ben's shoulder. For a moment he looked out the window, watching the rain. 'My aunty also sees stuff.'

Ben narrowed his eyes. 'Who are you?'

'I'm Tupawhai. Call me Tup. You okay there?'

Dry-mouthed, Ben nodded.

The new kid grinned. 'Good stuff. C'mon. Let's get out of here.'

On the main street, Tupawhai dived into a dairy and bought Ben a bottle of water. 'If you've got a bit of time, there's someone you should meet.'

Tupawhai led him into a narrow-fronted house on a side street. The hallway was bathed in dim yellow light. Another yellow glow shone from a room at the end of the hallway. Ben followed Tupawhai's silhouette along the passageway past small tables covered in brightly coloured cloth, one with an old-fashioned brush and mirror covered in pāua shell. The sickly- sweet odour of incense filled the space.

They entered a large room, where tables and couches were covered in the same cloth. Across the room, an owl perched on a wooden stand. Ben squinted in the yellow light. It was a stuffed bird, pinpricks of light shining from its dark button eyes.

Tupawhai's voice, loud in the room, startled Ben. 'Aunty Marama! Auntie, I've bought a visitor.' He nudged Ben. 'Hang about for a sec. She might be out the back. Don't touch anything. Auntie's fussy.'

Jangling music came from a record player. A male voice was singing, something about a nowhere man.

A screen door smacked shut, and he jumped. He glanced down the hallway. Nothing. The song played on. He heard voices coming from where Tupawhai had gone. Nervous, Ben swallowed and waited. At last, Tupawhai returned with a tall woman.

She paused and stared at Ben, then smiled. 'Hello there, Ben. I'm Marama.'

All at once, Ben was tongue-tied.

'It's okay, you're welcome here. You want a cordial?'

'Yes, please.'

Marama smiled again. 'Nephew, can you fetch Ben a drink? And be a dear and put the kettle on.' She showed Ben to a couch. 'Have a seat.'

Ben fidgeted.

Tupawhai called from the kitchen. 'Auntie, can I have a coffee?'

'At this time of the evening? Certainly not.'

'Aww, Auntie.'

'Don't you, Auntie, me, Tupawhai Eyles.' She winked at Ben.

When Tupawhai came back, he coaxed Ben to talk of his visions.

Ben swallowed. 'Sometimes I wake up at night and there is a girl standing at the end of my bed. She's in fog and she's pointing at me. There's something wrong with her face.'

Marama gently touched his arm and held out her hands. Ben put his hands in hers.

'There's nothing to be afraid of, Ben. We share our world with atua, spirit people, kind people. We share space with others, people who have passed, ancestors. Love and memories of good times keep us together. Do you know what I mean? Memories of good times with someone you loved who has gone can make you happy. Sometimes things happen and we can get angry and let hate into our hearts. We need to keep love in our hearts to make those bad things not important. You see where we are, Ben? We're between two harbours: Manukau and Waitemata. Different places so close together with only a thin strip separating them. You know, certain people can see between two worlds. When they're stressed or afraid, they're open to influence. It's nothing to be afraid of. You have such sight, a gift of love, of things you remember.'

Ben finished his drink.

Marama glanced at a wall clock. 'You have people looking for you.'

Ben nodded. 'Yeah, my dad.' He hunched, thinking of his father's belt.

Marama shook her head. 'No, others you have yet to meet are looking for you.' She stood and ushered Ben down the hallway. The three of them lingered on the steps.

Marama put a hand on Ben's shoulder. 'Any time you feel you want to visit and talk, I'll aways be here, okay?'

Ben walked home through the wet, neon-lit streets of Māngere. Rain sleeted in with a cold wind from Waitemata Harbour, spraying his face and school uniform. Ben stopped for a while, taking refuge under the concrete awning of the library building. He crouched by the glass front doors and thought about when he would see his mother again after her latest session of rehab. Something scrabbled above. In the gloom of the solitary streetlight, something pressed out of sight, tight against the façade.

He got up and ran through the nighted streets. *Not real. Not real!* Something heavy hit the pavement behind him. There was a skittering. *Not real…*

Back home, it was late, so Ben used his key, turning it softly to enter silently. His father waited in the hallway. Ben stood still.

'Where the fuck have you been, you little shit? I told you to clean the goddamned garage twice now and what did you do? You fucking ignored me.' He raised his belt and slashed it across Ben's cheek.

Ben felt the first blow. The others were dull thuds across his neck. He kept his eyes screwed shut and teeth pressed together. Smelled the alcohol from his father's breath.

'God knows why I agreed to let your mother take you in from that couple.'

Ben had had enough. He fled through the open front door out into the winter night.

Ben ran through drenched streets to a derelict house behind the old service station near the main street. He crawled under the house and huddled in the darkness, his back next to the brick of the chimney. He smelled something sickly sweet. He put his hand on the packed earth. Wetness. Slime. He pulled a lighter from his uniform trousers and flicked it alight. It was a dead kitten, its tiny body liquifying into the earth. Frantic, Ben shook the ooze from his hand.

There was something just ahead in the darkness. Holding up the lighter, Ben saw something huddled, quivering. He leaned forward. A brown thing, like bread with wrinkles, turned on the packed earth and a face of sorts, droopy, soft and doughy. He swallowed phlegm. He didn't want to, but he couldn't help watching in horror, as the creature shuffled backward in a jerky manner like a puppet being pulled by strings. With a sob he crawled from under the house. *Not real, not real, not real.* He turned back, reaching again under the house with his lighter. It was only a dirty painter's drop sheet and, by the chimney, a corroded water pipe dripped, muddying the dirt. *Not real.* Ben scrambled away from the house, and a warm sigh of air played across his neck.

Now

Ben stayed in his room until the visitors left. Just outside the Auckland CBD, above a second-hand bookshop on upper Symonds Street, the flat was small: a bedroom, bathroom, lounge and a kitchenette. And the walls were thin. Ben had heard enough to know what was going on. Tupawhai was still shuffling some stuff on the lounge table when he came out.

'Y'know, Tup, those dudes are gang members. Their dads used to be Mongrel Mob. I don't need no dealings here with them. If you're gonna insist on doing it, go home to your place.'

Tupawhai held up his hand. 'Relax, they're not bad fellas – it's only a little dope.'

Ben felt his anger rise. 'Yeah, but you're not buying; you're selling for them. There might come a time when you can't get away from them.'

Tupawhai snapped. 'I said okay, bro.'

Ben headed into the kitchenette to grab a beer from the fridge. He should probably shut up now, but he couldn't stop himself. 'What happened to you, Tup? You used to tell all these great stories about Indonesia in the ice age and ancient archaeology and weird-arse animals in the New Guinea jungle.' Ben leaned against the door frame.

His back to Ben, Tupawhai was shoving dope paraphernalia into his shoulder bag. 'Things change, we grow up, Ben. Or some of us do. Others are still stuck in a dead-end kitchen-hand job.' His tone had soured.

Ben was ready to explode. 'I like it there – the people are good; at least I know where I stand with them.'

Tupawhai kicked the lounge table.

Ben stormed out of the kitchen and pointed the bottle at him. 'You can deal all the dope you want, but do it in your own place. You've got ice on you, eh? You're selling ice for them. Get that shit out of my house.'

Tupawhai jerked forward as if to hit him.

Ben flinched and balled his fist. 'I don't want those people here, matey. They scare the shit out of me.' He couldn't stop himself venting. 'Aunty Marama is worried. She's been asking me questions.'

Headed for the door, Tupawhai rounded on Ben. 'Aunty, bro? She's not your fucking aunty. You're not family. What have you been telling her?'

'Nothing. I had to lie. She saved my life, Tup, and I lied to her for you!'

Without a word, Tupawhai stomped out of the flat.

Ben sat heavily on the couch. *Damn you, Tup. Why can't you see? When did you become the stupid one out of us?*

Ben opened his eyes. He wasn't alone in the darkness. The air in his room smelled of sodden leaves after a week of rain. He lifted his head from the pillow, while pulling his feet from the end of the bed. She was back again: the girl in the fog with the strange face. Her shoulder drooped as if dislocated. Black holes winked where her eyes should be. His mattress dipped as if weight had been applied, and a dark shape moved towards him, like a malformed head, and a sigh of warm fetid air played across his face. He scrambled back across the mattress as the thing slowly opened its mouth. Ben leaped off the bed and rushed to turn on the light as the creature curled into the shadows under his bed. A sighing, followed by a low growl, came from beneath the bed. Then... scraping. The skin on Ben's scalp shrunk. Close to panic, he ran through the lounge and grabbed his breadknife from the kitchenette.

Not real...

For the remainder of the night, he sat on the rug facing the bedroom doorway, clutching the knife. Only when it was fully light outside did Ben dare to go to sleep on the couch.

He woke to his phone ringing. He checked the time. He'd slept longer than intended. He didn't recognise the number. Maybe it was Tup, ringing from a friend's phone?

'Hello, yep,' he said gruffly

'Is this Benjamin Brennan?' A woman's voice. He sat up and raised a hand to smooth his hair. Ben hadn't heard his full name since he was a kid. He narrowed his eyes. 'Ahh, he might be here. And you are?'

'Oh,' she said. 'I can call back later.'

Now he felt stupid. 'I'm Ben. How can I help you?'

'I'm Lynley Brooks.' Was that a smile in her voice? 'I represent the Adult Adoption Information Agency.'

Ben stopped breathing for a few seconds, then inhaled and gave a nervous laugh. 'I wondered if this might happen one day.'

Lynley paused. 'You were expecting a call?'

Ben hurried on. 'No. No, I just remember those shows like *Find My Family* and it crossed my mind occasionally. Never thought–' He took a breath and waited.

Lynley said, 'You have birth siblings who contacted our agency in the hope of finding you. I realise this is out of the blue, Benjamin and might not be easy news. If you wish to make no contact, your privacy will be honoured and we will not pursue the matter.' When Ben didn't reply, she continued, 'May I ask how you would like to proceed?'

Ben's hands were shaking as he sat on his couch drinking a beer.

Of all the craziest things.

His heart beating quickly, he replayed the conversation he'd had with a brother he'd never known. The man, Kauri, had sounded hesitant and nervous during their short conversation. Had Ben made a big mistake? Too late now. There was nothing for it but to clean the place and prepare for the arrival of Kauri and his sister Ralene in the coming weekend.

Ben was still nervous when opened his door on Saturday to see two tall Māori.

I fucking knew it. How cool is this?

He stepped back inside and smiled. 'Please, come in.'

They sat on the kitchen chairs drinking wine at Ben's rickety dining table. Ben fiddled with the stem of his glass. They were older than him, perhaps eight years.

He cleared his throat and found it loud in the confines of the kitchen. 'So where are you staying?' he asked.

'Down at the Mercure on Queen Street,' Kauri said. 'We'll be heading back South on Monday.'

They sat in silence for several moments.

Ralene said, 'You probably don't remember, but we used to take care of you as a toddler whenever Mum wasn't around. You have her eyes.' She glanced at Kauri.

'Mum was…' Kauri began. 'We have different fathers.'

Ben looked from one to the other. 'I had a Pākehā dad?'

Ralene laughed. 'Yeah, but you're still Ngāi Tahu Māori from Otago. That's your iwi, your tribe. Actually, Ben, it's not just us; there are four others,' Ralene said.

Kauri reached into an overnight bag and took out a pewter tankard. 'Here's a gift for you, Ben. We had all our names carved into this including yours.'

Ben took the mug and read the names. There were eight, with Kauri, Ralene and five sisters. A Christian cross was etched next to one of the girl's names.

'Katherine drowned when she was eleven,' Ralene said, her hand trembling on the stem of her glass.

'I'm sorry,' he said.

Ralene went on, 'We lost you when you were adopted out at four. Do you remember anything? I'm sorry if this is painful, Ben. I think we're going to be working through this.'

Ben shook his head. 'No, it's fine, really. I don't remember much, but I have recurring dreams of being someplace. Maybe they're memories.' The wine was talking now. 'I've dreamed of a girl in a dark blue dress, walking in fog. She always seems to be floating. I could never get a good look at her face, but I have always imagined her to be sad.'

Kauri took a small sharp breath and exchanged a glance with Ralene.

'Another early memory is me and some friends running down a hillside covered in ferns like we're in danger. Painted warrior people with bared teeth were coming up the hill to meet us. I never knew what to make of this.'

Ralene patted Ben's arm. 'You might have been in a battle with another iwi. Or, it could mean your ancestors are saying hello.'

In the early hours of the morning, Ben phoned an Uber for them. He stood out on the street and felt at ease giving them both a hug. Ralene kissed him on his cheek. He shook hands with Kauri and watched them leave.

Ben arrived home from his shift the next day and saw the two men in the car parked outside. He stopped when they exited the vehicle. Law enforcement. Stern-looking fellows on official business. Tupawhai must be in trouble. He turned to face the men as they stepped up on the footpath.

'Ben Brennan?' said one.

Ben nodded. 'Tupawhai, right?'

'May we come in?'

Ben shrugged. He wasn't about to antagonise them. 'Sure.'

'Mr Brennan, your friend has passed away. We'd like you to come down to Middlemore Hospital to identify him.'

A chill crept into the room.

'Gang related, isn't it?'

'Drug deal gone wrong.'

Ben trembled. 'Come down? Yeah. Sure.' His thoughts raced. 'Did you contact his Aunt Marama?'

The detective nodded. 'She specifically asked for you to be there.'

At the station, Ben crossed the foyer adjoining the reception and hugged Marama. 'I'm so sorry, Auntie.' Marama hugged him tightly. She seemed smaller.

'I can't do this, Benny,' she said softly. 'I can't see my boy like this. I need you to.'

Ben led her to a sofa in the waiting room and held her hands. *My God, look at her. So frail. She's broken.*

'I'll go and see for you, Auntie.'

Tupawhai had been mutilated, his face skinned. Ben balled his hands into fists and could not stop his knees from knocking together. He blinked away tears and wiped his eyes. Tupawhai's index fingers had be crudely sewn to his earlobes, the nails torn from the fingertips. A South Auckland gang sign had been carved into Tupawhai's skinned forehead and above that, patches of flesh showed where tufts of hair had been ripped free. Ben swallowed phlegm and held back a sob of despair.

He turned to the officer. 'You wanted me to see this? This? Okay, it's him. You fucking satisfied?' He shoved aside the detective and he left to find Marama to take her home.

His flat was in darkness. Ben sat on the kitchen floor, ugly thoughts of violence and revenge creeping into his heart. He rocked slowly on the cold linoleum, opened and closed his hands and let the thoughts come. Fury rose. In the darkness, a cupboard clicked open and softly closed. The sound came again, louder and more insistent, now more like a large claw. He opened his eyes, grimacing as they adjusted to the darkness. The dream girl appeared in front of him. Mist swirled about her ethereal form. She moved towards him and bent low, her face close to his. No eyes, just empty black caverns. Ben's chest tightened as fear overwhelmed him. Her face jerked forward, her cold breath fanning his face. A sickly-sweet smell enveloped him.

A voice called from far away. 'Baby brother, help me. I don't know where I am.'

Stifling his terror, Ben raised a hand and reached toward her. An electrical charge threw him backward. The apparition vanished.

Again, the clacking on the lino. In the bathroom, a darker patch in the gloom. The skin about his face tightened, squeezing him. He choked out a sob of terror.

A massive head with twin rows of teeth clung to the bathroom ceiling. With palpable malevolence, it stared at him from the top of the doorway. Whatever body it possessed was hidden. It jerked forward and clacked its teeth, then dropped to the floor. Ben smelled wet animal fur. He scuttled backwards as the creature slapped the bathroom floor. The skin of its face peeled back. Ropey feelers flailed outwards and cracked like whips.

Then, it invaded his consciousness: 'Anger and fear bring me here, child. Tell me, where would you wish me to take you? Between the spaces? All you have to do is wish.'

Ben fled.

He wandered Karangahape Road, huddling under awnings to escape the heavy rain. He stopped outside a bottle store, his back to a wall covered in band posters. Car tyres swished across the drenched street. Nearby pedestrians sounded strange, their words nonsensical. Before the bottle store closed, he bought a large bottle of vodka.

Pulling his jacket closer about his throat, Ben walked along upper Queen Street and crossed a car park to cut through the cemetery. In under the trees at his favourite quiet place, he stepped around lichen-covered concrete slabs and low, rusted wrought-iron fences. He unscrewed the cap from his vodka and poured some into his mouth, feeling the cold sting upon his tongue. He thought of Tup, and of Ralene and Kauri. It was all too much. What was happening? Holding the bottle, he walked through the cemetery back to his flat.

Back home, his mobile vibrated loudly in his pocket. Ben jumped, startled, and answered.

'Ben. It's Ralene.' Ben took a swallow of his drink.

'It's about Katherine.' She paused. 'When we were with you in your flat, and you mentioned dreaming your whole life of a girl in a blue dress, we knew you were talking about Katherine. You were too young to properly remember her when you were adopted out at age four. When you were kids, Mum and our aunties lived in and around Kaitangata just a few kilometres from Balclutha. Like the other girls, Katherine walked the five hundred metres to and from Kaitangata Primary School. One day, she never made it home. She was eleven years old. Mum phoned the police. Me and Kauri searched along the road to the school. The entire town came in on the search. Everyone knew she'd been abducted, but nobody wanted to say it. The police from Balclutha had searched hundreds of square kilometres. People dragged irrigation canals and rivers and scoured woodlands. Katherine was never seen again.'

Ben stood shaking at the kitchen counter.

On the other end of the phone, Ralene was obviously close to tears. Then she dropped the bombshell: 'The blue dress you keep seeing, Ben, was her school uniform. I don't know how you know—'

Ben's mouth went dry.

'Last August we found Katherine. I mean…I mean, two rangers from Pāmu, Land Corp found her remains, her skeleton. The drought last year had taken the dam up in the Glendhu Forest down to its lowest ever. The police from Dunedin had been called weeks before we were notified. DNA had been sampled and, because there were no records back then, dental records were consulted. It took some time before authorities realised who they were looking at.' Ralene began to cry.

Ben sat silent, waiting, tears welling.

Ralene whispered, 'She'd been pushed down among some tangled roots right next to the bank. I've seen photos, awful photos. One of her arms was raised up, stretching between the roots, almost as if she was trying to reach out for help. It was her skeleton, all that was left of her. Twenty-one years, Ben. I watched her walk to school in her blue dress. All they could bring home to me was my baby sister's skeleton.' Ralene broke completely.

Ben felt nauseous. All he could say was, 'I'm sorry, Ralene. I'm so sorry.'

'We brought her home, Ben. Katherine is where she belongs. She's at peace – we're at peace.' Finally, Ralene said softly. 'Would you consider coming home?'

Dusk had bought shadows into the room, slowly creeping across the carpet towards Ben. He thought of the recurring dreams. Ben realised there had been no fog; there had only been swirling water. He gasped. In her final seconds of life, Katherine had sobbing into the dark waters of the lake, her blue dress undulating. Desperate and panicked, tangled in roots, she lifted her arm, reaching for the surface, hoping to find the thing she loved the most – her baby brother.

Now Ben saw the thing behind her that had taken his sister. A roiling blackness, its face slowly peeling back to reveal suppurating flesh. Tendrils emerged black and glistening under the fiery sky, snapping like whips. Transfixed, Ben looked into the eyes of the monster. It was an amalgam of all the ugliness, the dead-hearted brutality of the world. It was hatred personified. It looked like his father.

He woke at dawn, cold and shivering. In his bathroom, he splashed water on his face and changed his clothes. Taking the stairs down to Symonds Street, Ben stepped out onto the footpath. He walked back to his favourite spot beside the gravestones. He looked about, feeling elated. *It's all good. It's all going to be okay. You're going back home, Benny boy – home.*

Closing his eyes for a moment, he pictured himself as a Māori warrior on a fern-covered hillside, poised for battle. He looked up into the blue sky and smiled – he was ready.

The Reaper Beetle

by Debbie Cowens

Neither podcasts nor music could block out the rush of memories as I drove down State Highway 1, the concrete thread slithering through the relentless green of the lower North Island. I was en route to Tracey's funeral though her death still didn't seem real. It wouldn't have been a surprise to me if Tracey had appeared with a sardonic grin when I arrived at my friend Heather's and declared her death a prank and that I was thick as sheep shit for falling for it.

Of course, it wasn't fake. I'd seen news reports of the fatal fall as well as the social media obituaries and memorial pages. She'd been the strongest of us four survivors, fierce and lively. Outliving Tracey in any sense of the word seemed impossible. It was only when I allowed myself to imagine that she might still be alive that the sadness and weight of the loss hit me.

We'd been inseparable at high school. I took Art and Outdoor Ed just to ensure I'd be in her classes, despite having no natural ability in either subject. I needed not just Tracey, but the whole gang, to feel like I was truly myself at that age. Alone, I felt lost in the dark. With them, I was brave.

Tracey guided us – Heather, Rata, Erika, and me – into her way of living, where we balanced our adolescent contradictions through extremes rather than moderation. She didn't just take risks, she ran at them headlong, and we followed her, giggling or exhilarated through every craze and phase: astrology, shoplifting, veganism, binge-drinking, piercing and seances. Yet at school we were model students, diligent in our classes and enthusiastic competitors in sports and clubs. Heather was the first Year 10 student to make the top debate team. Rata was a star netball player. Tracey did everything with passion and skill. She would have been Head Girl in Year 13 had Erika not died. If the OE camp had been cancelled, if we had never set foot in Ruahine Forest.

Twelve years since the fall and now we were going to bury another one of us. It didn't seem possible. I hadn't seen Tracey in person since my own hen party four years ago. For me, she lived on-screen, a life of adventure, travel and cocktails filtered through gurning selfies and Instagrammed vistas.

Since the pandemic, she had faded from my timeline. I hadn't even realised until Heather called me, and I saw all Tracey's social media was now a frozen tableau where other people posted their grief and shock and memories. I'd had to scroll back through time to discover that she had stopped posting. It hadn't been some algorithm restricting my online feed to Parents' group updates in case photos of childless friends sipping martinis led to lethal amounts of envy. I hadn't missed seeing her glamorous online existence, but now I would give anything to vicariously experience a wild night in Ibiza or climb Kilimanjaro with her, even if it didn't inspire gratitude about living in stained yoga pants running around after a toddler.

Underneath maternal anxiety about leaving my 20-month-old, Shelley, for two days, I felt a guilty throb of relief. The backseat, reflected in the rear vision mirror, looked empty with the baby seat transferred to Rob's SUV. Only the small snuggle-bug plush toy lay there, silent and dormant without a toddler squeezing its squeaky voice to life. I was responsible for feeding and transporting no-one but myself for the first time since Shelley was born. It was liberating.

Heather had offered that I could crash at her place. I'd accepted immediately, relieved not to have to stay alone in some random motel.

'Natalie, good to see you. How are you?' Heather's girlfriend Georgia hugged me when I arrived on their doorstep tired and desperate for the bathroom that evening. She was the extroverted, affectionate half of the relationship. We'd only met a few times, but she adopted Heather's friends as her own. She was the one who had posted birthday messages and sent a present when Shelley turned one.

Heather appeared in the hallway as I walked in. Her eyes looked raw, but otherwise she was as attractive and stylish as always: slickly straightened black hair, flawless makeup and creaseless grey suit. I had never seen her professionally attired in person before. All our adult interactions had been social and casual. She looked even more herself as a polished corporate lawyer, and yet it was weirdly disorienting.

'Nat, glad you're here.' She embraced me rather stiffly. 'We've made up a sofa bed in the lounge. There is the other room but…'

'We haven't moved Tracey's things out yet,' Georgia finished for her.

'Tracey was here?'

Georgia looked at Heather who said nothing. 'She's been flatting with us since she got back from Bali. COVID cut short her travel plans, and she didn't have a job or place to stay, so we suggested our spare room while she got sorted…'

'…and then it turned into a more long-term arrangement.' Heather not only ended the sentence but the conversation. She picked up my bag and headed down the hall. 'Let's get you unpacked and sorted.'

Later that evening we dined on lasagna, red wine, and our memories of high school days. It was strange how easily the laughs came when I could feel a torrent of tears threatening to rise up underneath. Half-drunk and nostalgic, we agreed to take our fashionably oversized glasses of merlot up to Tracey's room to toast her memory.

The sight of her bedroom sobered me immediately.

Every inch of the walls was covered in sketches and maps. It was like one of those crazy evidence walls in the films, where conspiracy theorists or detectives pin up every possible suspect, but there weren't any fake moon landings or murder suspects. Just bugs. The artistry was undeniable. Dozens, maybe hundreds of charcoal and pencil sketches of beetles, cockroaches and other insects stuck up everywhere. Tracey had always been talented, but these were impressive. Anatomically detailed like biological diagrams, but strangely lifelike and sentient. I could feel them looking back at me. Many were oddly beautiful, others grotesque: a wasp depicted with its head skewered by spiky fungal growths; a wētā devouring its own shed skin. There were maps of various countries with red crosses drawn on them. Places she had been or was hoping to go?

'Tracey was so gifted,' Georgia said, sitting down on the bed. 'I was encouraging her to try to exhibit her work. It seems a pity that all this should just stay shut up in here.'

Heather sat down next to her and smiled sadly.

'I had no idea she was so interested in…bugs?' I walked over to the large wooden desk, the only other furniture apart from the bed in the room. Several reference books sat next to her sketchpad and pencils. I glanced over the titles: *Scarabs of Egypt, Prehistoric Coleoptera, Endangered Insects of our World.*

Heather nodded. 'It started when she was in Cambodia. She met this guy. I think he discovered some ancient beetle out there that was thought to be extinct.'

'It was the blood stag beetle,' Georgia explained. 'It was apparently a big deal with the beetle crowd. Tracey broke up with him not long after, but by then she had caught the bug.' She smirked at Heather who rolled her eyes. 'Shameless pun I know.'

Georgia shared a few stories about Tracey's travels, relationships, and borderline obsession with catching, cataloguing and preserving any insect foolhardy enough to come into the house. Heather complained about Tracey's late night podcast recording sessions. I listened and laughed along politely, but I couldn't ease into enjoying it the way I had at dinner. I couldn't relax at all in her room. The hairs on the back of my neck stood on end as those beetles on the walls stared down at me.

Their sofa unfolded into a futon-style bed that was more comfortable than I'd anticipated, but sleep did not come easily. I'd showered and skyped with Rob, both at Shelley's bedtime and again after she was asleep, but I still felt as though I had left some task unfinished. Heather and Georgia had retired to their bed at a sensible ten-thirty, but as the minutes approached midnight, I was exhausted and restless.

I hadn't considered myself afraid of insects before, but Tracey's beetles had unnerved me. I'd actually squealed when I thought I saw a bug out of the corner of my eye in the shower. Lying in the lounge with only the flickering blue light of my phone for illumination, dark shapes scuttled between the shadows on the walls and ceiling.

I googled relaxation tips for sleep, but after faint attempts at breathing exercises and a guided meditation video failed to help, I gave up and searched for Tracey's podcast. She had only a handful of subscribers, but there were dozens of episodes, each at least an hour long. I scrolled to the first one and blinked back tears as her voice chuckled through my phone's speaker. She sounded just like she had as a teenager, full of life and passion, only now it was all directed at bugs. She joked in the introduction about how small her audience was and promised to keep it light before immediately diving into the most obsessive detail imaginable.

At some point during the third episode, I drifted into a memory-laced sleep.

'Nat, are you awake?' Tracey whispers.

'Yeah,' I yawn without opening my eyes, the carapace of my sleeping bag crinkling and tightening under my legs as I start to roll over. The cabin smells of stale damp. A low reverberating hum drones in the darkness like a distant jackhammer, although we're still in the bush.

'It's nearly morning,' Tracey says, her voice hushed. Rata and Heather are still asleep in the bunks above us, their breathing deep and regular.

I open my eyes and look over at the window. The faint red haze of sunrise is seeping underneath the blind. 'Do you think they'll send us home today?'

'I don't know. Mrs Green said we would have to talk to the police first. Tell them what happened. She said she'd stay with us, though. We don't have to do it alone.'

I feel like crying again, even though I had cried so hard in the night I thought I'd drained every tear I had. 'The police? But it was an accident.' I bite my lip. 'Do you think they blame us? We didn't tell anyone. They'll say it's our fault. We went after her ourselves. Maybe if everyone had been searching, they would have found her sooner...'

'Stop it!' Tracey slides out of her sleeping bag and kneels by my bed, her face close and her eyes boring into mine. 'We didn't do anything wrong. We went after Erika as soon as we saw she was gone.'

I nod. 'Do you really think she was sleepwalking?'

'Why else would she have left the cabin and wandered off in the middle of the night?' Tracey leans back, the dark hollows under her eyes revealed as her face shifts out of the upper bunk's shadow. Has she slept at all? A flicker of moonlight casts a pale shaft across the dusty portrait of the

camp's founder Dr Henry Moore. A beetle scuttles over the picture. It seems large in proportion to the man, covering half his face. It launches off the image and takes flight. The chattering whirr of beetle wings is loud, painfully loud, as it flies across the cabin towards Tracey.

Tracey lurches backwards. The floor beneath my bunk collapses into a deep gorge. Her body keeps falling, breaking against tree branches and rocks as she plummets. Without breathing or moving, I watch her fall until she hits the earth, broken and lifeless beside Erika.

Now I have the courage to do what Tracey had done hours earlier. This time, I won't just wait, paralysed in shock at the top. I scramble down the slope, my feet finding grooves in the earth as I make a winding path down between the trees and shrubs.

I hurry to Tracey, kneel and grab her by the shoulders. Her body is limp and unresponsive, her legs twisted at unnatural angles, but I lift her head up. Blood trickles from her mouth.

I let go and her head rolls to one side then snaps back to face me, dead unfocused eyes locking on mine.

'I saw the beetle,' she rasps. 'It reaps from within.'

Her head goes slack again, and her mouth lolls open as an ink-black beetle scuttles out of her bloodied lips and across her face towards me.

I leap up, scrambling away, but I trip and fall backwards. Beyond the trees, darkness and stars float above me, and the dark distant shape of the cabin, floorboards shattered, the interior dim.

I woke with a jerk as though I had dropped onto the bed, Tracey's scent, the faint trace of patchouli perfume and peppermint gum, lingering on the air. The fogginess of the dream hung over my eyes for a moment as I struggled to adjust to the darkness and unfamiliar surroundings.

I was not in my own bed. I was in Tracey's room, surrounded by her beetle drawings. And there right in the centre of the wall above the bed, illuminated by a shaft of moonlight from a gap in the curtain, was the very same reaper beetle from the dream.

My breath caught in my mouth, an unvoiced scream closer to the rasping ignition turn of a dead car battery than any human cry. I could hear the chattering of wings still, although the sound was fainter now and I couldn't place where it was emanating from, or if it was simply an echo of a nightmare.

The beetle was almost luminous. Its body glistened and arched off the wall, though it was no more than a charcoal drawing on paper. Its scythe-shaped mandibles were poised in menacing readiness out of a wide head with black bulbous orbs for eyes. I stared at it a long while, half-afraid to blink or move in case it twitched to life once unseen.

I slid myself off the bed and shook off my childish superstitions. I'd had a bad dream, that was all. Sleepwalking and nightmares were hardly surprising after a long, emotional day and too many road trip energy drinks and glasses of red wine.

Nonetheless, I could not deny that Tracey's beetle drawings were both creepy and curious artistic subjects.

I grabbed her journal off her desk, was flipping through her sketches and notes, when I heard a scratching noise from the large top drawer. I slid it open and dropped the journal in surprise.

The drawer didn't hold papers or books or art supplies, but a large plastic-cased vivarium with a reaper beetle perched unmoving on a gnarled stump of wood, its scythe-claws piercing the dried bark. I stared at it, daring it to move, but it was completely motionless. I placed my palm on the vivarium lid, the shadow of my fingers falling across the beetle. It was alive. I was sure of it.

It did not move, yet the chattering continued as I slid the drawer shut, turned off the light and retreated from the room with Tracey's journal.

The sound followed me back to the lounge where I settled onto the bed, and only faded as I began to read.

'What the hell?' Heather's voice startled me from a dreamless sleep.

My mouth was bone dry, and my neck and shoulders ached. I forced my eyes open to find myself half-coiled over Tracey's journal on the sofa bed.

'What are you doing with that?' Heather approached the bed, her arm reaching for the book, but I snapped it shut and drew it towards me.

'I had trouble sleeping.'

'So you just helped yourself to her diary for a bit of a bedtime reading?' She shook her head, disgusted.

'Don't you want to know what inspired her, what drove her research? Do you really think she was just drawing beetles for a hobby? That none of it meant anything?'

Heather stared at me like I was deranged, but then her mask of calm returned. 'Look, Tracey was… She had some issues. Her mental state wasn't the best when she first came back, but these last few months?' She broke off. 'Well, maybe you'd understand better if you'd actually been around and seen her in the last couple of years.'

There it was. The snarky judgement she couldn't repress for long.

'So it's my fault for having a baby, is it?' I asked.

Heather exhaled loudly. 'No, I'm simply saying there's no point trying to find answers in there. She wasn't herself.'

'Is it that easy for you to dismiss it? Have you read this? The connections she found? Maybe some of the theories about ancient death cults and telepathic beetles are a bit out there, but I think she had really discovered something.' I flipped to the pages of Tracey's notes made from Dr Henry Moore's research. 'Look, this naturalist back in the eighteen-hundreds came out to New Zealand. Mostly, he studies wētā and other native insects, but he's an expert on beetles. He becomes an eccentric recluse. The Royal Society of London expelled him from their membership list for some of his more unscientific theories. He was the last known person to have found a reaper beetle, the one worshipped for its gifts of immortality and flight. The ancients used to bury their priests with them, so the beetles would devour their flesh and bestow their powers on them for the afterlife.'

Heather sighed. 'I'm not in the mood for a history lesson. The funeral's in a couple of hours.'

'But it explains what happened to Erika.'

Her condescending expression vanished. 'What happened? That she lost her grip on what was real and refused to get help, or let us help her? I can't hear this right now.'

I wasn't going to be silenced by her, not after all I'd learned. 'Henry Moore spent the last eight years of his life in Ruahine. Now, his theory is that the reaper beetle's eternal life was based on a circular life cycle with years of dormancy and regeneration. If Tracey's right, he brought one with him. Maybe the reaper was lying dormant in the Ruahine Forest, waiting for us, and it found Erika.'

'So Erika was killed by a magic immortal beetle? Tracey, too? What, the beetle had to silence her to cover its tracks?' Heather shook her head. 'Do you hear how ridiculous you sound? Tracey was obsessed. She drifted away from us and ended up throwing herself off a cliff. We didn't even know…' She broke off, her voice trembling. 'I can't do this.'

'You always have to trash anything you don't understand.'

'You always have to copy everything she did. Don't you think it's time you grew out of your obsessive friend phase?'

'Coffee?' Georgia walked in, silencing us before we reopened any further wounds. Peacemaker's intuition or had she been listening?

I nodded, and Heather took the opportunity to follow her out to the kitchen.

I sat alone on the sofa bed. The journal had fallen open on a double page anatomical sketch of the reaper beetle, its black mandibles curved like beckoning fingers.

I could almost hear it clicking its wings underneath the hiss of the espresso machine in the kitchen.

We met Rata and her partner Andrew outside Van Keulen's funeral home and sat with them for the service. Heather had said little during the car ride. I might have assumed it was the gravity of our sad destination were it not for the hostility in her eyes when they flicked up at the rear vision mirror and caught sight of me in the backseat. Was it reading Tracey's journal or what I had said that had annoyed her?

Georgia placed her hand on Heather's as we waited. It was a simple gesture of support and kindness, but it made me conscious of how alone I was, perched between two couples without Rob or my little Shelley.

I recognised Tracey's father and brother, at the front, though they both seemed older than I expected. Otherwise the chapel was filled with strangers. I glanced around the faces of the congregation as the service began in the doomed hope of a spark of connection, a sign that someone else knew about Tracey's research. Someone who might confirm if the legends of the reaper beetle were real? As though summoned, the beetle from the book scuttled through my mind. I shivered as my skin prickled. I put my hand to the back of my neck to reassure myself there was nothing crawling down my back.

We rose to sing a hymn, although I had never known Tracey to be religious, at least not in any conventional sense. In the silence that followed, I became aware of the clock on the wall, its ticking hand scratching around the seconds, and below that a low, resonant hum that filled the space without emanating from any clear direction.

The eulogies began. I concentrated on listening closely to them, hoping for some words to which I could connect my own grief and unanswered questions. There was nothing for me but the sadness of other people's sorrow and memories of a Tracey I didn't recognise. They grieved the vivacious young woman they knew from backpacking or uni or yoga group or art class or volunteering work in Tibet. Even when Heather stood up in front and spoke, it felt disconnected from the truth, the real Tracey, despite her sincere eloquence.

I wondered if anyone else had read her journal, if they knew what she was uncovering. Did anyone know her like I did?

We were a crowd of strangers mourning a dozen different Traceys who all now lay dead in a polished oak coffin.

It was a short drive from the service to the grave, yet the minutes dragged with the foreboding interminability of the dentist's waiting room.

'Do you hear that?' I leaned forward from the back seat to ask Heather and Georgia, as much to break the tension between us as anything. 'That clicking noise?'

Heather shook her head. 'Better not be the car. We only had the fan belt replaced a couple of months ago.'

'Shall I put some music on?' Georgia suggested and turned on the car stereo before waiting for an answer.

'I was old when pharaohs first mounted
The jewel-decked throne by the Nile;
Down the infinite aeons come the beating wings...' [1]

The wailing voice of Sadie Dunwich filled the car and I started to laugh, only a giggle at first, but then I saw Georgia and Heather exchanging a glance and I cracked up in a fit of uncontrolled, crying laughter. They didn't get the joke. But Tracey would be laughing with me if she was with us. Miskatonic's Muse was one of our favourite bands.

It was surprisingly cold at the cemetery despite the blue sunny sky. A chill wind seeped through the crowd flanking the graveside as the coffin was carried from the hearse. The crowd was silent as they lowered the casket onto the green straps and hovered over the open grave. Heather whispered to Rata. Some snide judgement, obviously, from the side eye they directed at me. Contempt masked as concern. I doubted either of them had ever liked me. They resented how close I was to Tracey. Especially now.

A few confident voices struck up a hymn. We'd been directed to sing

'Abide with Me'. I opened the service sheet and was trying to follow the words when a loud scratching arose from inside the coffin.

I lifted my eyes. The wooden lid shuddered. The scratching grew faster and louder, desperate to break through. I threw my hands up to my ears and screamed as the coffin's lid flew open and revealed a mass of black beetles writhing and gorging on Tracey's body.

A hand on my shoulder. I looked back. Rata had taken hold of me, pulling me away from the grave. Everyone had stopped singing and was now staring at me.

'Come,' Rata said gently, leading me away from the crowd.

I glanced back at the grave. The coffin lay motionless and undisturbed. The only sound was my own crying and shaky breath.

'Feeling better?' Rata asked, once I'd had the drink of water she'd insisted upon when we reached her car. 'We can go back if you want or just wait here and meet the others back at the reception. Whatever you want.'

I shook my head. Distant murmurs carried from the graveside. I was uneasy about returning to the crowd. 'You can go back if you like, but I just need a moment.' I leaned against the side of the car, reassured by the weight of solid metal behind me.

She rubbed my arm and leaned on the car beside me. 'I'm not going anywhere unless you want me to. Heather said you'd been…taking it hard?'

'I didn't sleep much. I dreamt I was back there, you know…camp? The night Erika fell.'

Rata nodded. 'Makes sense, I guess. What happened to Tracey stirring up old memories?'

'It was so vivid. I could hear Tracey's voice and everything. And then after she fell…' My throat tightened. I took a big drink to ease the dryness. 'I saw that beetle crawling out of her mouth, like it was coming for me, the reaper beetle.'

Rata turned to face me, her brow knotted in confusion. 'You weren't down there, remember? Tracey and I got there first. You waited at the top while Heather ran back for help.'

'I know what I saw,' I snapped.

'No, you know what you dreamed. That's not the same thing.' The gentleness had gone from her voice. The tone was all rigid authority. 'As for this whole reaper beetle thing? That was just Tracey's weird fantasy.

Do you really think some extinct ancient Egyptian beetle is going to be lurking in the bush on the other side of the world in the exact spot where our friend just happened to fall? Come on, that's a bit too far-fetched.'

'But the last known sighting of the reaper beetle was Dr Henry Moore in 1870, one year before he emigrated to New Zealand and went from renowned naturalist to weird old hermit of Ruahine Forest. And the fact that he died in the exact same place as Erika is what? A coincidence?'

'You're starting to sound like Tracey did. No good comes out of obsessing over the past.' She shook her head. 'She went back there, you know? To Ruahine? Some creepy pilgrimage to retrace Erika's death and then, when she comes back, she's obsessed. Spending her days online going down rabbit hole conspiracies about scarab death cults, drawing beetles and bugs, and calling it research. Heather never should have let her go there.'

'She was onto the truth. I started reading her journals last night. It all makes sense. It's all connected to the reaper beetle. Erika, Tracey, the dream…'

'Erika was a horrible traumatic event for all of us. Maybe they should have given us better counselling back then, maybe we're all a bit messed up with weird survivor guilt, but you are a mother now. You can't follow Tracey's footsteps down some self-destructive delusion.'

'So that's what you think? I'm just copying Tracey, like I always did?' My voice was shrill. Rata's twisted jealousy had pushed me too far. 'You've always resented my connection with Tracey, our bond. You just don't understand because your best friend died alone when you were seventeen and you never even bothered to find out why.'

Rata stared at me in outrage, but she said nothing and walked back to the flock of mourners at the graveside.

The truth always silences the weak.

Georgia came over to me after, as the people dispersed from the graveside. They had sunk the coffin in the ground, but it didn't matter. It wasn't Tracey in there. She was with me, listening to the gentle clicking of wings.

'How about I take you back to our place now?' Georgia suggested. 'Heather's going to go with Rata. Listen, Rata's pretty upset, so it might be good to give her some space?'

Rata had been spreading her poison then. It didn't matter to me if I missed the wake. I'd rather be back with Tracey's work, anyway. No doubt Rata and Heather would love the opportunity to exchange venomous lies about me.

I got in the backseat despite the vacant shotgun position, but Georgia insisted on talking throughout the drive. It was easy enough to drown her out. I concentrated on the chattering vibrations of the beetle wings, and the shimmering black undulations of glistening hindwings when I closed my eyes.

I run through the trees. My feet are light, skipping over the ground and flitting over any bumps or branches. The chattering whirr of the reaper's wings pounds in my ears like my own heartbeat. My shoulder blades twitch. The skin itches to split and release my wings. A long dormant power yearns to be freed.

If I run faster, push harder, I can do it. I will reach the edge and fly straight to her. I will find Tracey in the air and save us both.

My eyes opened. The car had stopped, and I was dizzy at the sudden lack of movement.

'I guess you probably needed some sleep, huh?' Georgia was standing by the car watching me as I pulled myself out and onto my feet.

'I need to go back. I can't stay here.' I walked past her towards the front door.

Georgia followed me and unlocked the door. 'Look, why don't you go have a lie down? We can all have a talk later and…'

I stepped around her and marched straight to the lounge, the clicking of wings growing louder, drowning out her sugary nursery-soft voice as I threw belongings into my bag.

Once packed, I stood and stared at Georgia, daring her to object as I grabbed Tracey's journal and pulled it tight to my chest.

'I guess I'll make you some coffee, if you have to go?' She headed back towards the kitchen, pulling out her cell and texting as she went.

I went to Tracey's room. I ripped the portrait of the reaper beetle off the wall then opened the top drawer of her desk, lifting out the vivarium.

They were mine now. Tracey wanted me to have them.

I hurried out to my car, threw my bag in the back, and set the plastic case on the passenger seat. Georgia rushed down the driveway as I started the engine and drove away.

'I won't let her take you from me,' I vowed, accelerating down the street.

The wings purred and clicked, rejoicing in our speed.

The minutes and miles melted away with the happy whirring beetle beside me and Tracey's podcast playing through the car stereo. My eyelids drooped with the warmth and brightness of the sun streaming through the window.

I pulled in at a petrol station. I needed to fill up to make it to Ruahine anyway. I grabbed a pair of sunglasses and three large cans of Red Bull.

'Big night last night?' The young man at the counter smirked.

'Yeah, uh-huh.' I nodded, swiping my card across the EFTPOS. 'Tracey's funeral was this morning.'

'Oh, sorry. Should have realised with the black and stuff.' He gestured awkwardly at my outfit.

I put the sunglasses on. The price tag stuck awkwardly across part of the right lens, but it didn't matter. It blocked out the glare of the fluorescent lights overhead.

I drank one energy drink as I walked back to my car. It was cold and sweet but did little to slake my thirst. I started on the second as I sat down behind the wheel.

The beetle wings shuddered in the case beside me. She'd woken up with the scent of caffeine, taurine, and whatever else it is they put in those drinks. I opened the case and gently placed her on my left hand. I offered a drop of sweet drink to the beetle with my right index finger, and she suckled.

Then we set off down the road, back to Ruahine Forest, Tracey's voice guiding us like a personal sat-nav.

I could feel the skin between my shoulder blades twitching, eager to taste freedom just as the beetle was.

I hoped we'd get there soon. I knew I'd be safe if I could just stay awake. I could trust her to show me the secret of flight. She was awakened and ready this time. It wouldn't be like the others.

I knew I wouldn't fall.

1. Excerpt from 'Nemesis' by HP Lovecraft in *The Vagrant*, June 1918

DEAD END TOWN
BY LEE MURRAY

Uncle Bradley grunts. His eyes open wide, his mouth going slack, his fat tongue lolling between purple lips. He lets out a gasp.

I breathe through my mouth to block out the smell, not daring to gag. Moments pass, his weight pinning me to the sofa, then he pushes away from me, his lips twisted in contempt. I glance down, past the Salvation Army skirt bunched around my waist, as he staggers backwards, a silvery cobweb still tethering me to him. It dribbles from between my legs, a hideous white tendril snaking across the dark orange sofa cushion where it seeps into the stitching. I close my eyes, so I don't have to see while he pulls up his trousers. His zip buzzes. Still, I don't move. Instead, I trace my fingertip over the scar on my lip, a pink welt extending from the corner of my mouth to my cheek. Uncle Bradley's backhand. Each time it reopens, it takes longer to heal.

'You really need to be more careful on that bike of yours, Kayla,' my form tutor Mrs Arnott had said.

Like she even gives a shit. I haven't used my bike since the summer.

In the kitchen, the fridge door opens and there's the sigh of a beer tab.

Now. Pulling my knickers up and my skirt down, I tiptoe to the front door, push my feet into my gumboots, grab my sweatshirt, and slip out.

I take the back way, cutting through Henderson's paddocks to the forest. Henderson's dog barks when I pass, but I tell him to shut the fuck up and he stops. From there, I climb over the fence and head west towards the creek. Apart from the dog, no one sees me. I'm the only one who comes here. There's no track so it's tricky to get to, the beech trees leaning on themselves the deeper I go, their trunks squeaking where they meet above my head, the scratchy mānuka making a grab for my clothes. I breathe deep. The air is tangy, a mix of lemon and moss. I push on through the scrub, the bushes criss-crossing the backs of my arms with tiny cuts and grazes, little white lines that disappear if you lick them, only I don't, because when I get to the creek, I take off everything but my t-shirt and submerge myself in the water. The creek is shallow, barely coming to my knees, but sitting down with my back to the bank, the water swirls around my legs, rinsing Uncle Bradley's white rot off me. In seconds, my limbs are numb and dimpled, the flesh tinged blue-green, like a decomposing orange.

I sit there for as long as I can bear.

As always, I slip down, letting the water submerge me, allowing it to close over my face, inquisitive tendrils seeking out my nose and mouth. It would be a relief to let it stifle me. I will myself to do it, but something always stops me. I got as far as my eyes once, but, in the end, I was too chicken.

My teeth are rattling, so I crawl out and get dressed. Then I hunker on the bank, my back to a pūriri tree and my arms wrapped around my knees. It's getting dark, but I don't want to leave yet. I stuff my hands into my pockets, pull out my hand-powered torch and squeeze it rhythmically. The torch is small, but it keeps the shadows from crowding in on me, its friendly whirring playing bass to the trickling high notes of the water. In the treetops, the forest murmurs. Mum's people say it's the patupaiarehe talking, the mischievous fairy creatures who live in the mists. The stories say they like to snatch little girls. They're like the Pied

Piper, playing their flutes to lure people away. If it is the patupaiarehe, their words are soft and mournful, like poetry.

I used to write poetry. *Before.* I've stopped now.

'Why is your writing always so dark, Kayla?' Mrs Arnott had said. For a woman of letters, she's pretty dense.

'Didn't you say that poetry's about self-expression?' I replied.

'That doesn't mean you have to be so morbid,' she said.

What was I supposed to say to that? But she was right in a way, because, Uncle Bradley kept recurring in my poems and it was as if I was giving him that power. Although, maybe stopping was playing into his hands too: because I made myself even smaller. Some days, I think I'm crumbling into dust, like a statue left to weather and getting rounder and blunter at the edges. Soon enough, I'll be smoothed away to nothing.

I'm a minor, so I have to go home. I scramble to my feet and start back. The forest doesn't want me to leave either, grey-green mānuka fronds grabbing at my sweatshirt as I scramble through the brush.

I open the front door to yellow electric light and the stench of cigarette smoke. Back from her shift, Mum is lounging on the couch watching *Game of Thrones* with Uncle Bradley.

'Where've you been?' Mum asks, leaning to her left to stub out her cigarette in the ashtray.

'Out,' I reply.

Over Mum's head, Uncle Bradley smirks.

'Out where?' she asks.

'Just walking.'

'She's been fucking that neighbour boy again, I reckon,' Uncle Bradley says. I glare at him. If stares were kitchen knives, his face would be pulp.

Mum turns to him. 'You mean Aaron from up the road? Kirsty and Wallace's boy?' She gives him a playful shove. 'He's harmless. Wouldn't even know where to put it.' She giggles like the girls from school.

Inside the pockets of my sweatshirt, I clench my fists. 'I'm off to bed,' I say.

'I brought you some chips back from the shop.'

'I'm not hungry,' I snap, moving towards the hall.

'Hey!' Bradley says. 'You get back here and say thank you to your mother.' He stands up. 'Kayla!'

I stop.

'Well?'

I stare at a thin bit in the carpet, where the trample of too many feet have worn it to muddy threads. 'Thanks,' I mumble.

He points the remote at the TV, pausing it. 'And you can say it like you fucking mean it,' he snarls.

Mum leans forward and puts a hand on Bradley's leg. 'It's fine, babe. She said she wasn't hungry. The chips'll be cold now, anyway.'

'That girl is spoiled rotten, Leanne. After everything you do for her, the least the disrespectful little madam can do is say thank you.'

'C'mon, Bradley. She's a just a teenager.'

'She's a disgrace.'

'Well, let's not let her attitude ruin our evening, shall we?' Mum says, taking the remote from him and flicking her eyes towards the hall. My cue to bug off.

I don't have to be asked twice.

In my bedroom, I pull the lock across. I bought it from Hammer Hardware and put it in myself. Borrowed a hand-drill and a screwdriver from the Wood Tech room at school. When he saw it, Uncle Bradley just laughed.

Mum's whole life is a fantasy. Like thinking Uncle Bradley is the real deal. As if their relationship is something special.

I squeeze my eyes closed and pull the duvet over my head, trying to get warm.

The thing is, Mum really believes it. Maybe she thinks she's in love with him. Uncle Bradley's not like my other 'uncles'. For starters, he's got a job at the sawmill. Shift work. Pretty decent money, too. Every now and again he gives Mum some of his pay packet, which makes her go all gushy with gratitude.

'Why do you have to make such a big deal about it?' I said once. I mimicked her voice: 'You're so kind to think of us. So generous.'

Her eyes narrowed and she grabbed me by my upper arm, pulling me into the bathroom where he couldn't hear. 'Well, he is generous. You try making ends meet on a benefit, missy. Rent, food, electricity. Your school fees. It all adds up. And he doesn't have to help. It's not like he's your dad or anything.'

That made me think about phoning WINZ because he's not supposed to stay here all the time or she could lose her sole parent benefit. In the end, I didn't. It's not like it would've made a difference. Without Mum's benefit, there'd be no groceries, and anyway, everyone knows WINZ are as useless as tits on a bull.

The TV is still blaring next door when I fall asleep.

In the morning, I take the school bus and sit near the back with Aaron.

'Bags the window,' he says, pushing ahead of me.

Ours is a friendship of convenience. Every day, we get on and off the bus at the same stop; have done since I started school. When you wait in the rain and fog with someone day in and day out, you get to know things. For example, I know that Aaron is gay, and he knows about Uncle Bradley. Not the gory details, but the general gist. It's not as though Aaron can do anything about anything, but it'd been a relief to tell him, and have him believe me.

'Anyone ever tell you, you look like shit?' he says when I slip in beside him, twisting my backpack around until it's resting on my knees.

'Yeah, someone was sick, so Mum picked up an extra shift at the Fish & Chip shop.'

The bus roars, slowly picking up speed. Aaron nods. 'You okay?' he asks.

I stare down the aisle. 'I'm here, aren't I?'

He clutches at the straps of my backpack, leans closer, and whispers in my ear, 'We should go, Kayla. Leave here. We could take the bus to Auckland.' His eyes are big and round and hopeful.

'And then what?' I say. 'Get lost in the big smoke? It's all right for you. You're already sixteen. You forget I'm only thirteen. When you're thirteen, they glue your face on every milk bottle in every supermarket in the country.'

He rolls his eyes. 'And take out full-page ads calling for information about your whereabouts.'

'Someone will start a Kickstarter.'

'They'll call in a psychic.'

'My mum will cry on TV.'

Aaron grins. 'Your mum would love that.'

I smile in spite of myself. 'I know.'

'Think about it though, Kayla. You only have to survive two years. Auckland's big. I can help hide you. When you're sixteen, they can't make you come back. He won't be able to do anything.'

'Two years and two months,' I say, savouring the feel of the words in my mouth.

'So? It's not impossible.'

I think about leaving Mum and how much it would hurt her. Uncle Bradley was right when he said that everything she does, she does for me.

Everything except see what I need her to see.

I pleat the fabric of my skirt in my fingers and shake my head. 'If they find me and haul me back, Uncle Bradley will kill me.'

Now it's Aaron's turn to look out the window. His breath fogs the glass an instant then disappears into nothing. When the bus has bunny-hopped over the potholes outside the Skelton's place, he turns to face me again. 'What about your father?' he demands.

'What about him?'

'Why can't you go and stay with him?' He looks at me hard. Honestly, if he doesn't stop picking that pimple at the corner of his mouth, it'll never heal up.

'I don't know.'

'What do you mean, you don't know? Just ask him.'

'I can't.'

Aaron stares at me like I'm the Prime Minister trying to evade a tricky question.

'Look, I have a father – obviously – I just don't know who he is.'

'Seriously? You don't know anything about him?'

'I know he was a poet and a dreamer. Mum says he wasn't like other boys. He wasn't normal. His family wasn't from around here.'

I pause.

'What?'

'Don't laugh, but she used to tell me the reason he couldn't stay with us because he was a patupaiarehe.'

Aaron scoffs anyway. 'A fairy? A legendary creature from the forest? That's crazy.'

'I know, right?' It is kind of sad. It's not like I'm a little kid who believes in fairy stories, but I like to think my dad was legit, that he had a real reason for not being with Mum and me. Before I started school, I had this picture book of Cinderella and in it there's a drawing of her meeting the prince in the forest. It's silly, I know, but back then I convinced myself that the prince was like my dad, and he was hiding in the forest, just waiting for us to come and find him.

The bus pulls into the bay outside the intermediate school. The doors sigh open, and we all pile out.

Aaron stands up, shouldering his backpack. 'More likely, if your dad split, it's because he didn't want to pay child support.'

'Yeah,' I say, but my heart says something else.

When we get off the bus in the afternoon, Uncle Bradley is waiting at the side of the road. He's never done that before. The back of my throat tightens.

I jump down after Aaron and the doors hiss. The bus pulls out, spitting gravel.

'Hello, Mr Sterns. Kayla's coming to my place today,' Aaron says. 'We've got an assignment.'

Uncle Bradley lifts his chin. 'Like hell she is. And who the fuck are you trying to kid? You're not even in the same class.'

The bus labours down the road. Watching it go, I realise we should've got back on.

Too late now.

Hitching my backpack up on my shoulder, I straighten my back. 'I'm going to Aaron's,' I say. 'It's all arranged. Mrs Waugh invited me over for afternoon tea.'

Uncle Bradley cocks an eyebrow. 'So, it's tea and cookies now, is it? I don't think so.' Quick as ever, he steps forward and shoves Aaron full in the chest, sending him backwards into the road. Aaron stumbles, then recovers, moving off the road and onto the verge again. But now Uncle Bradley's bulky body is wedged between us. Aaron drops his backpack on the gravel.

In my head, I will him to go home.

He stands his ground. This time, when Uncle Bradley shoves him, he springs back like a piece of fencing wire.

'I'll teach you for messing with my stepdaughter,' Uncle Bradley roars.

'She's not your stepdaughter and I'm not the one messing around with her,' Aaron spits.

No! Don't let on you know. He can't know you know ... I stare around Uncle Bradley at Aaron, praying for him to understand.

Uncle Bradley draws a line in the gravel with his toe. 'You're right. She's a slut: there're probably half a dozen like you taking a turn with her behind the bike sheds.'

'Bullshit!' Aaron shrieks, and my stomach sinks.

'No!' I shout, but already he's running at Uncle Bradley, his head down like a wild boar on attack. Uncle Bradley dodges the charge with a neat sidestep. Twisting, he punches Aaron full in the stomach as he comes around again. Aaron doubles over and Uncle Bradley lifts his knee, slamming it into his nose. Blood spurts all over Aaron's t-shirt.

'Stop it!' I croak, my voice echoing over the paddocks. The sheep nearest the fence skitter away. Uncle Bradley rounds on Aaron, punching him in the guts a second time.

Aaron goes down hard. 'Run, Kayla,' he chokes, his arms wrapped around his middle. 'Get away from here.'

'You run, and I'll kill him,' Uncle Bradley says quietly.

I freeze.

'He's bluffing,' Aaron says, getting to one knee, blood in his teeth. 'If he kills me, the police will come after him.'

'Is that so?' Uncle Bradley scoffs as he kicks out Aaron's knee. The action is swift and cruel, pushing Aaron back into the gravel. Uncle Bradley stoops, jamming his face close to Aaron's. 'I could kill you and walk away and no one would even bat an eyelid. Not when I tell them how you've been fucking my stepdaughter, and when I called you out for it, you came at me.'

'Except it's all lies!'

Uncle Bradley shrugs. 'Question of perspective, isn't it?'

'Nobody'll believe you,' Aaron says, but his face has turned as pale as butter.

'Of course, they'll believe me.' Uncle Bradley kicks him in the ribs with the toe of his boot. 'My cousin's the superintendent of the local police.' Grinning, he stamps on Aaron's leg. Aaron whimpers. Like a hedgehog, he curls into a ball, his skinny arms crossed over his head. Uncle Bradley kicks him again and again. In his back. His stomach. His head.

After a while, Aaron goes quiet.

'Please,' I beg.

Uncle Bradley gives him one more kick for good measure. Then, panting, he wipes his hands on his jeans. He turns on his heel, grabs me by the arm and drags me back towards the house. I glance over my shoulder to where Aaron is a motionless lump on the side of the road and pray Uncle Bradley hasn't fractured his skull.

Afterwards, when he's finished his business, I run back to the bus stop to look for Aaron, but he's gone, His backpack, too. I'm about to head up to his house when Mum turns into the driveway. If only she'd come home twenty minutes ago.

Slowing the car, she slides down the window and calls to me. 'Kayla? Where do you think you're going?'

I fold my arms across my chest. 'Nowhere.'

'Well, what are you doing out here on the road?'

'Just checking the mailbox,' I improvise. 'It was empty.'

Mum gives me a suspicious look. 'Come inside, then. I bought some lamb chops for dinner.'

I look towards the Waugh's house, and then trudge after the car, my gumboots scuffing in the gravel.

Aaron doesn't come to school on Wednesday. Or on Thursday. When he doesn't come on Friday, I ride past our stop, get off at Cooper's corner, and walk back to Aaron's place.

His mother opens the door. 'Kayla.'

'Hello, Mrs Waugh. Is Aaron okay? He hasn't been at school.'

'You'd better come in,' she says, opening the door wide.

I take off my gumboots and follow her into the kitchen. It's only four o'clock, but the amber pendant above the dining table is already on. I take a seat. The Waugh's sheepdog pads over, and I give him a scratch under his chin.

Aaron's mother goes to the kitchen bench, where she's been cutting up a pumpkin. She picks up a knife and uses it to slice off the grey skin. 'What do you know about what happened on Wednesday?'

I shrug and ruffle the dog's ears.

'Someone beat Aaron up after school. He wouldn't say who. I had to take him to A&E.'

I pretend to be surprised. 'Is he okay?'

She slices the pumpkin and places the pieces in a pot. 'Yes. But he took the bus to Auckland first thing on Thursday. He's done with this place. His father and I weren't happy, but he's sixteen, seventeen in a week, so there wasn't much we could do about it.' She stares at me hard.

I want to tell her what really happened, but if I do, something bad will accidentally happen to Mum. Something bad could happen to Aaron's mum, too. Uncle Bradley knows where she lives, and Mr Waugh spends a heap of time down the back of the farm.

So I say, 'There are some kids at school–'

'Yes, I know,' she interrupts. 'Bullies. A dead-end town like this – forcing people to pack up and leave just because they step to a different drum.' She puts down the knife and sighs deeply. 'It doesn't do to be different, does it?'

I shake my head. 'No.' The dog nuzzles closer. I give him another pat. 'So where is Aaron staying? Does he have an address?'

Mrs Waugh scrubs away a tear with the back of her hand. 'He knows our number here at home. He'll call us if he needs anything.'

She gives me a piece of ginger crunch and a glass of Fanta.

Before I leave, she says, 'You take care now, Kayla. Any trouble with those kids at school, you know you can always come to Mr Waugh and me.'

I know she doesn't really mean it. It's what people say to be polite, like asking 'how are things going' and not really caring about the answer. I smile and nod. 'If Aaron calls, please tell him I said hi.'

She rests a hand on my shoulder a moment. 'Of course.'

Aaron's dog follows me into the yard and down the driveway to the cattle grate.

'Go home!' I tell him.

His tail down, he heads back towards the house.

Mum will be another hour, so I cut across the Waugh's paddocks, then cross Henderson's to get to the edge of the forest. Henderson's dog is barking its head off at something in the bushes. His ears are cocked and the fur on the back of his neck is standing up. He doesn't even see me when I climb the fence. I step into the gloom. Today, I don't need the creek, so I wade to the other side and head further into the trees.

It's windy. High up where the branches touch, the bark squeaks. Through the rustle of the leaves and the gurgle of the creek, I hear a flute or a clarinet playing somewhere up ahead. It's faint, but there, the melody wistful and eerie, like an Adele song, the kind that makes your heart ache. For a second, I think it might be Aaron. Maybe he hasn't gone to Auckland yet. Maybe he stuck around to say goodbye.

Or to take me with him.

My heart racing, I speed up, plunging deeper into the beech trees, pushing aside the branches, grazing my hands on the bark. It's hard work, the wet ground sucking all the time at my gumboots. The mist rolls around me, cold on my muddy legs.

'Hello? Aaron?'

Three people step out of the trees. My heart stops in its tracks. I can hardly believe it. Patupaiarehe. Tall and willowy, they have fair hair and brilliant diamond eyes. There are three of them, all dressed in skins.

'Kayla,' they say, and I jump to hear their voices in my head.

I hug my arms to my body, my boots sinking in the soft mud. 'You know my name?'

Their answer drifts towards me on gusts of wind. 'We've been waiting for you.'

The drawing of the prince from that old picture book flashes into my head and I can hardly breathe. They've been waiting for me? I'm almost too scared to ask. 'Is my dad here?'

'Yes, yes, we know where,' they whisper in my head. 'We can take you.'

'Take me where?'

'This way. Come.'

I follow them further into the forest, clambering over rotting logs and ducking under fronds. Up ahead, the *patupaiarehe* let the branches swing back and hit me.

'Hey!'

They giggle and smile. Well, they're known for being pranksters. I want to reach out and touch them, only they dart forward on their long legs, keeping just out of reach.

I hurry to catch them up. In the dim light, everything is shadowy and grey and my gumboots slip in the mud. Arms out, I tumble into a ditch. My hands break my fall, pain flaring in the webbing. I bite back a cry. A sharp twig speared me when I tripped. I lift my palm to my mouth and suck away the blood.

It's while I'm standing there, dealing with the cut, that I notice the barking. Somewhere in the distance, Henderson's dog is going ape shit. All at once, I realise how late it is. Behind me, the forest is so dark, the tree trunks are a blur. How did I even get this far?

'It's getting too dark: I'm going to need my torch,' I tell the patupaiarehe. But when I take it out of my pocket, they melt into the trees.

'Hey, come back,' I call.

The forest groans about me, the shadows thick and dank.

'I don't know where to go,' I say.

The patupaiarehe don't answer.

The days go by. A week. I hear nothing from Aaron. No letter. No phone call. Not a whisper.

'You only have to survive two years,' he'd said that last Wednesday morning on the bus. He'd made it sound so easy. Now, with no one to talk to, those two years stretch out in front of me like a dead-end road.

I'm in the kitchen doing the dinner dishes when Mrs Arnott calls my mother and tells her I'm getting behind on my schoolwork.

'What's this all about?' Mum asks when she gets off the phone.

'It'll be because that boyfriend of hers shot through,' Uncle Bradley calls from the living room where he's watching the telly. I imagine his smug look and wish I could stuff the kitchen brush down his throat.

'Is that it?' Mum asks. 'Is this about Aaron?'

'I guess so,' I say and it's not entirely a lie. Since Aaron left, I've lost a lot of weight – I've had to put a safety pin in the waistband of my skirt – and lately I've been forgetting things. It's as if my brain's been getting blunter, worn down like a pencil.

The school makes me see a counsellor. With scraggly hair and big rimmed glasses, she looks like Professor Trelawney and asks me the usual things about what I want to do when I leave school, and if my falling grades have anything to do with the kids at school. I tell her no.

'And what about things at home?' she asks.

'They're okay.'

'Just okay?' Through the glasses, her cheeks are an odd shape.

I shrug. 'It's alright.'

'It's just you and your mum at home, right?'

'Hmm.' I don't mention Uncle Bradley. I can't, I can't mention him or something bad will happen to Mum.

Only, the counsellor must catch me pause because she says, 'You know, anything you tell me is confidential, don't you? That means it's just between you and me.'

'You can't tell anyone?'

'That's right.'

'Like a priest?'

'Exactly.'

I suck in a breath. Maybe I could tell her. Not because she can do anything, but just to be able to tell someone the way I told Aaron. Someone who's not going to pick a fight with Uncle Bradley and get herself beaten up and left on the side of the road. The knowledge makes me feel strangely light, like an old candy wrapper carried along by the wind. I'm opening my mouth to tell her, when she goes on, 'That's how this works: unless you're at immediate risk, nothing you say here will get past me.'

My shoulders slump. Unless you're at immediate risk. *Which means her lips will be flappier than a sheet on a washing line.*

The school makes me go see her a few more times, but each time I clamp my mouth shut, and after a while they give up.

Another day, I'm heading for the creek, when I find Henderson's dog lying up beside the fence. Rolled over on its back like its expecting someone to rub its stomach, the dog's ribs stick out under its ragged fur. Its head is lolled to one side, its tongue sagging from its mouth, covered in mucus. Looks like it ate some possum bait. Mr Henderson must've left it here to bury, away from the livestock. The flies haven't wasted any time getting into the carcass; thick white filaments lick out from behind the dog's eyes. I've seen maggots that got into a lamb once. Aaron and I found the wretched little thing in a ditch. It'd been dead a while because the maggots had eaten the entire body from the inside out. Its skin undulated in waves it was so full of the fat white worms. It was disgusting. Hopefully, Mr Henderson will come back and bury the dog soon. Poor thing. He barked a lot, but he was a good dog.

Backing away from the carcass, I swing my leg over the fence.

Mum's in the bath for one of her long soaks when Uncle Bradley gets me up against the kitchen sink, his hand pressed against my mouth. I'd let my guard down. Mum was home, so I thought I was safe. He hisses in my ear to keep quiet while he fumbles behind me.

The water goes off, but Uncle Bradley doesn't stop. Mum's soaks can take a while.

I see the butter knife lying on the bench. Slowly, I move my hand, closing my fingers around it.

Suddenly, Mum comes out of the bathroom, her bathrobe wrapped around her, heading for the linen cupboard. 'Silly, I forgot to get a towel.' She stops, spying us through the kitchen. 'What the hell?'

Hidden from her by the bench, Uncle Bradley flips up his track pants, flicks down my skirt and steps to one side. 'I had to pin the little bitch down. She tried to attack me with a knife.'

I shudder. The butter knife is still clutched in my fist.

'Kayla? What's going on?'

I stand up, my eyes pricking.

'I told you,' Uncle Bradley roars. 'You wouldn't listen. The kid has abandonment issues. Her daddy's not here and she's got it in her head that it's my fault.'

'Shut up,' Mum says, pushing past him to get to me.

'Mum,' I say, warm tears welling. Gently, she takes the knife from me and drops it in the sink. A hand on each of my upper arms, she fixes me in the eye.

'Look Kayla, honey, I know things are bad for you right now. I get that. Aaron leaving has brought up some things about your dad, but you have to understand, it has nothing, nothing to do with Bradley.'

'I just want him to go,' I whisper.

Uncle Bradley snorts. 'What did I tell you? That kid is all kinds of crazy. Ever since I got here, she's had it in for me.'

'Bradley, would you mind giving me a minute with my daughter?'

'Sure. No problem. See if you can talk some sense into her.' He grabs his cigarettes and goes outside, but not without giving me a look.

'Sweetheart,' Mum says, wrapping her arms around me. 'This has to stop. You can't go around lashing out at the world or people really are going to think you're mad.'

I try to tell her that wasn't like that, but she has to learn it for herself. It's like in *Beauty and the Beast*, where Belle has to choose to love the beast if she's going to rescue everyone from the witch's curse. If I tell her the truth about Uncle Bradley, it won't count.

'Mum please, just make him go,' I gibber.

But she doesn't hear me, and after while I can't hear her either.

The next day, I don't go home. Instead, I get off the bus and go straight to the forest. Mr Henderson must have come and buried the dog because there's no sign of it by the fence. I tuck my school backpack into a hollow where no one will see it, stamp my feet into the gaps in the wire and climb the fence. I suck in a breath, inhaling the ripe smell of soil and leaves. The lush of the trees beckons me in.

I have to go a long way into the brush to find the patupaiarehe. I hear their music at the creek, but it's an hour before I see them.

They hang back, lurking in the trees, laughing.

'I've come to see my father,' I tell them.

'Yes, yes, we can take you to the place.' They urge me forward, flitting in and out between the tree trunks. I follow them further into the forest.

After another hour, I glance backwards. The forest is dense black. It closes about me. This time, I've got no light to hold back the shadows. I'm wearing my school polo and the torch is in my sweatshirt. Maybe I should turn back. Go home. But which way do I go? If I'm going to get back to the creek, the patupaiarehe will have to guide me.

They are the faintest silhouettes now. I feel my way forward, sensing them in the soft squelch of mud and the brush of the branches.

'Hey, slow down.'

Out of reach, the mischievous fairies giggle like I've made a joke.

We keep going.

Finally, the trees part. Before us, moonlight glints off a limestone cliff. A dead end. Looks like we'll have to go back. But the patupaiarehe point upwards and smile. I look up. Above us is an earthy overhang, the roots of a massive tree tangled and coiled in its underbelly. Something's moving up there.

I squint as spindly white vines spool from a slit between the roots, creeping outwards and waving to me the breeze.

My father came here?

The vines sway and undulate like the maggots in the lamb: disgusting but fascinating at the same time. Mesmerised, I watch the glutinous tendrils slide from the recess and curl towards me. Halfway, they strike out, a million barbed threads, grabbing me and pulling me upwards.

No! This isn't right. Why did they bring me here? This isn't where we're supposed to be.

The patupaiarehe reply, 'Yes, yes, we're here, we're here!'

But all I see is the fleshy curtain opening. A beak! And slithering from its yawning depths, a slick white tongue. I thrash and kick: the cords only tighten around me, the barbs digging deeper, lifting me up to meet that beak.

'Help me!' I wail.

The patupaiarehe shrink back into the trees.

Grey slime drops from the beak. It seeps into my clothes, burning them away, searing my skin. I scream. A stinging acid gob falls into my right eye. With one sightless eye, I'm paralysed, helpless. I can only stare in horror as the beak drops further and further, its tongue roiling outwards to meet me, and all the while I'm rising, the vines holding me so tight I can barely tremble.

More foul mucus gushes from the beak, the oily slime smothering my face, and ruining my eye. It's a relief not to see it close over my face. My nose is left free. I breathe in bubbles of vile mucus and scream and scream into its insides, the sound going nowhere.

'We're here,' the patupaiarehe croon.

Yes, we're here, and it's feeding on me, its white coils reaching into my body, their barbed tips sinking through my skin to slurp up my insides.

The pain is searing white and endlessly slow. I can do nothing but endure it. I lay suspended and delirious while its ropey branches snake through my limbs, lifting my fingernails and burrowing into my bones.

For the first time in forever, I wish I'd gone home.

Fires of Fate

By
Jacqui Greaves

Moira Jacob drew up her horse and dismounted at the edge of the Oroua River. Unremarkable and of indeterminate age, Moira travelled alone. Six months ago, the women of this young nation had been given the vote, and although democracy had never treated her well, Moira was encouraged by the possibilities of this new-found equality.

Despite its nervous disposition, the horse followed her lead as she waded into the burbling water. Half-way across the ford the tone of the water changed. Even before the horse flared its nostrils, tossed its head, and shied sideways, Moira felt the malevolence awaken.

The water rushed, twisting around her calves. It dragged at her black skirt and petticoats. The stones beneath her feet, caught by the current, rolled and tumbled away. Moira staggered, but she'd met far worse threats in her lifetime. A small angry taniwha was of little danger. She turned her dark gaze upstream and withdrew her shears from a deep pocket in the folds of her skirt.

'Stop it,' was all she said. The waters calmed. A cream-bellied eel slid by and, with a lazy flick of its tail, disappeared into a deep-dark pool.

From the river, it was a steep climb up a twisting, rutted track. Dense bush crowded in on either side. Chirping pīwakawaka flitted and swooped, snapping at flies and moths disturbed by their passing. All around Moira came the tiny twangs of lifelines cut short by her mere presence. She smiled. On a branch above her head a tūī warbled, its white throat feathers bobbing along with the melody. It stopped singing to plunge its beak deep into a cluster of crimson rata flowers. When it looked at her again, its face was daubed with golden pollen.

The verdant cool of the track gave way to a grim view. Beyond the crest of the hill, the track cut a straight line through charred, flat land studded with blackened stumps. Moira's eyes stung from the smoke hanging thick in the listless air. It reminded her of Hades: all it lacked was the burning stench of sulphur in her nostrils and a three-headed dog. She rode on, the horse skittering beneath her.

Where the track dipped away to the right, she came face to face with the cause of the burn off – a small flock of sheep, which flowed around her like the waters of the Oroua around an immovable rock. Behind them, rode a man on a dull brown pony. He was accompanied by a black and white dog whose blue eyes never left the sheep. The man's eyes were not as focused on his charges as the dog's, resting on Moira several moments too long for politeness.

'Sir, you had best watch your flock,' said Moira.

'Shit,' muttered the drover. He forced his pony after the bolting sheep. The air rang blue with his curses and whistles long after he'd disappeared.

The angry little taniwha would soon enjoy a tasty treat – it wouldn't be the dog though; the dog was a good girl. Moira laughed and rode on.

The closer she got to Āpiti, the more organised the carnage. Rough post-and-batten wire fences formed paddocks where cattle grazed on pasture thriving in the ashen forest remains. In the eight years since the first settlers had arrived in Āpiti, they'd made irrevocable changes to the very nature of the place. The settlers, aided by fair winds gifted to them by the god of weather, Tāwhirimātea, as part of his vengeance against his brother, had burnt Āpiti into existence. The town had started like most others: with a school, post-office and, of course, a hotel. Soon after, came the dairy factory, producing the finest cheese and butter, and a boarding-house to accommodate the growing and oftentimes transient population. And of course, there were churches – competing for souls to revere an introduced god in different ways.

Yet, even amongst all this modernity, industry, and apparent piousness, blackened stumps of forest giants remained. Ghosts of Tāne-nui-a-Rangi's ancient totara, matai and kahikatea. Moira's heart ached for him.

Moira tied up her horse outside the hotel. Thirsty from the smoke and dust, she wondered if they would serve her a beer. It was time to test whether democracy had made it this far yet.

Brownie had just slammed his empty bottle onto the bar when the strange woman walked through the doors. He wasn't the only one who'd noticed the bloody cheek of her, the whole damn room had gone silent. Well, almost silent. From a little further down the bar, Wayne muttered something about 'fucking suffragettes'.

His back to the door, it took Jim, the barman, a moment to figure out what the hell they were all staring at.

'There's a woman,' said Brownie, always helpful.

Jim swung around, a sausage-like finger pointing at the door. 'No women in my bar,' he bellowed.

To Brownie's surprise, the woman stayed right where she was. Her eyes met his and he gasped. As a rule, he was all in favour of the female-kind, and the soft bits they hid beneath those skirts of theirs, but something about this one made his skin crawl. Her eyes were as dark as Wayne's glass of stout, and her smile? – well, he could only describe it as dangerous. If he wasn't surrounded by his mates, he might have whimpered. Instead, he figured he'd curry favour with Jim and croaked, 'You heard the man, get out.'

The bitch just stood there.

'I've ridden this day from Feilding. Where may I purchase a beer to parch my dry throat and find relief from the incessant smoke?' Even though she didn't raise her voice, her words filled the room.

The way the bitch stood and talked just wasn't right. She bloody terrified Brownie. His innards turned to water, and he had an urgent need to shit. From the looks on his mates' faces; he wasn't the only one.

It was Tāne, the old Māori with the tattooed face, who got rid of her. A strange bugger, he appeared out of the bush from time to time, sat in the far corner of the bar speaking to no one, drank a single bottle of beer, then left again. Tāne reached behind the bar, grabbed an unopened bottle, and handed it to the woman. She dropped a couple of coins into his hand and left. Tāne slapped the coins on the bar in front of Jim and returned to his seat in the corner. For the first time ever, Brownie saw him smile.

With the woman gone, Brownie rushed out back to the long-drop. Maybe the runs were caused by something he'd eaten? Must be it. A woman couldn't make a man shit himself just with a look.

He returned to the bar. Bought himself another beer. It seemed everyone had already forgotten the incident. Meanwhile, Tāne sat in the corner with a sparkle in his eyes and a smile on his lips.

Brownie wandered over. 'Why'd yer give her a beer?' He didn't even know if Tāne spoke English.

'Have to respect our kaumātua.' Tāne's voice was deep and resonant.

'Our cow what?' Brownie knew a few of the local words, but this was a new one.

'Kaumātua…our elders.'

Brownie snorted. 'Yer getting blind, old man. She was younger than you.'

Tāne stood up and leaned in so close Brownie could see the tattoos on his face move and swirl like living things. Whatever had mucked up Brownie's guts was messing with his eyes as well.

'I'd apologise, but you deserve everything coming to you, Pākehā.' Tāne placed his half-empty bottle on the bar and strode out.

As arranged, Moira found her well-travelled trunk waiting for her in her private room at the boarding house. With great care she removed her cloak and laid it on the narrow cot. Woven from the cut threads of men's lives, in the lamplight the cloak quivered and shifted with lost opportunities. Next to it, she spread out a length of fabric. She ran her hand over the hairy tangle of threads. She'd measured each one out but had yet to complete weaving. Moira reached into her pocket for the shears. It was time for some fates to be reassessed.

This wouldn't take long. She'd been doing it for millennia. Moira bent and snipped several threads close to the fabric. Careful not to let the cut threads fall to the floor, she placed them in a small white box, carved of the finest Greek marble. In time she would add them to her cloak.

Moira lifted a final thread between finger and thumb. It was already thinner and shorter than most of the remaining threads. Rather than cut it, she roughened the thread with the edge of her shears, tied several knots into it, then frayed the end. Moira laughed. She buried the shears in her pocket, folded the fabric away into her luggage, and wrapped the cloak around her shoulders. It was time to talk with the Furies.

Brownie wove his way back towards camp. It'd been an odd night and he'd needed an extra couple of beers to calm himself. The sun had set, but there was still enough light through the haze for him to see the track.

Up ahead, four women hovered on the edge of the track. What the hell? He hiccoughed. When he looked again, they were gone, replaced by a swirl of smoke.

Yer going crazy man.

'Not yet,' that unforgettable voice replied.

Brownie almost shit himself – again.

The haze swirled to reveal the woman from the bar, but she wasn't alone; on her left shoulder sat a little ruru owl. The fearsome talons of a kārearea falcon clutched her right forearm, which she held out like a falconer of old. On a stump beside her perched a fierce-eyed kāhu. He'd never seen one up close. The harriers normally soared high overhead.

All four of them stared at him like he was small prey.

Brownie shuddered and stumbled back a few steps. He hated birds. The only thing they were good for was eating.

'What yer doing out here? It's not safe fer a lady.'

'Oh, I'm quite safe, Mr Brown. Just stretching my legs after a long ride.'

How did she know his name and who the hell stretched their legs this far out of town? Brownie didn't like this one little bit, but his mother had thrashed into him the need to be polite. He swayed remembering her cane cutting welts into his thighs.

'Shall I walk yer back to town, ma'am?'

'No, thank you. I think it's best you get back to your camp. Accidents can happen if a working man does not get his sleep, can they not?' In the shifting light, the woman's youthful face sagged and wrinkled, and her eyes sunk into her skull. She looked like Death.

A chill ran down his spine and his legs wobbled. Brownie had the weirdest feeling he'd never sleep again. Damn the bitch. She could stay out here and get murdered. He didn't bloody care. He stumbled away. Behind him, wings flapped.

At the crossroads a mile north of town, he turned left and followed a path through a patch of unburnt forest down to the river. Brownie stumbled into the cluster of tents. The snores of his team had never sounded so good. Hopping from foot-to-foot, he whistled and did a happy jig.

Close-by, in the dark of the trees, a ruru called. Not the normal 'roo-roo' that gave the bird its name. Nope. This bird called his name 'brow-nee, brow-nee' over and over and over.

Brownie's guts churned. *Shouldn't'a had that last beer.* Shivering, he crawled into his small canvas tent, curled up under his thin blanket and squeezed his eyes shut.

No matter how he lay, Brownie couldn't sleep. When he did doze off, his mind filled with screams. Images of flames burning into his eyeballs jerked him awake. All night, the ruru called his name. Brownie tossed and turned so much his mattress of ferns moved, exposing the river rocks underneath. Three times he tried to rearrange the ferns, still the rocks jabbed his hips, his thighs, and his ribs.

Sometime before dawn, Brownie gave up and crawled out of his tent, grabbing the billy can on his way to the river's edge. One of his daily pleasures was his early morning piss in the river. He loved the sound of his stream hitting the water hard and steady. This morning though, he was sure someone was watching him. His piss was shy –

just spurting and splattering. Brownie sighed. He tucked his dick away, crouched, and splashed water on his face. Rinsed the crust from his gritty eyes.

In the murk, something moved on the far side of the river. A woman wrapped in a cloak stepped from the treeline. Impossible. He rubbed his eyes with his fists. When he looked again, the woman was just a damn kānuka bush swaying in the pre-dawn breeze. He was too bloody tired. Seeing things that weren't even there. Relieved, he turned and picked up the billy, stooping to fill it.

Somewhere upstream wings flapped and the infernal bloody ruru called 'brow-nee, brow-nee'.

Brownie stood and chucked the billy as hard as he could towards the sound. It clanged on the rocks. 'Shuddup, shuddup, shuddup,' he yelled.

'You shut the fuck up,' someone shouted from their tent. Jonah or Old Tom.

Crap. He'd pissed off the boys and hadn't even started their morning brew yet. He hobbled over the uneven rocks to retrieve the dented billy and filled it from the river.

Back at the campsite, he kicked a smouldering log from the edge of the fire pit back into the middle. He arranged a handful of dry twigs on the log and blew until they caught. Brownie was good at lighting fires. He fed the tiny flames with more twigs, then sticks, and when he was sure the fire had taken, he laid a couple of chunks of hinau on top.

Dark orange flames, tinged with blue, licked the wood. Exposed splinters blackened and curled away from the heat. Red sparks marched at the leading edge of the flames as they spread across the axe-split surfaces. Brownie smiled. In just a few minutes, the fire would boil up some billy tea and make a pot of porridge.

The chorus of farts and coughs coming from the tents meant the four others were awake. Isaac, the youngest, was the first to emerge. Like Brownie, he made a beeline for the river to relieve himself. The other three – Leftie, Jonah and Old Tom – preferred the privacy of the bush.

They were an odd mix but Brownie like them well enough. He'd joined them a year ago, after an unfortunate incident on a South Island sheep station.

That hut burning down had been a dumb accident. It could've happened to anyone. How could he have known the flicked match would land in a splash of lamp oil? And, even more to the point, it wasn't his fault some old drifter was asleep inside at the time. Still, Brownie would remember the burning man's screams as long as he lived. He'd left in a hurry, keen to put a body of water between him and those who thought he should be punished. He shook off the memory and set to stirring the lumps out of the porridge.

As they arrived at the fire, each man helped himself to some porridge and a cup of tea. They never spoke in the morning, not until the billy tea was drunk and the porridge pot emptied. No talking, no whistling, no humming a tune.

Wings flapped. Brownie looked up from his porridge. The bastard ruru was back. It swooped down river to land on a nearby branch. Its glare was worse than Jonah's. Even when Brownie looked away, he could feel its hungry yellow eyes drill into the side of his head. He glanced around at the boys, but they were paying the bird no notice at all. Then, it called his name, 'brow-nee, brow-nee.' Not one of them looked up. Brownie's left eye twitched.

Isaac gathered the dishes and trudged off to the water's edge to wash up. Jonah scowled at Brownie.

'What the fuck's the matter with you this morning?' His voice was a low growl.

'Didn't sleep,' said Brownie. 'Bloody ruru hooted all night.'

'Too many bloody beers mores the like,' said Old Tom, 'I heard ya stumbling in after dark, whistlin' and dancin'.'

'Nah, there were this woman and birds and…' Brownie stopped. They'd think him a damn fool.

'No bloody women on work nights. I told you that,' Jonah barked.

'Weren't like that, Jonah.' Brownie's eye twitched again. He scrubbed at it with his thumb. 'Saw Tāne smile.'

'Bullshit,' said Leftie. 'That old Māori doesn't know how to smile.'

'I swear he did…when that woman came into the bar, he smiled. I seen all his teeth.' Brownie stretched his lips to demonstrate.

Old Tom guffawed. 'Way too many beers.'

The others laughed. An old anger burned in his belly, but Brownie kept his mouth shut. He knew what he'd seen last night, and if the boys'd seen what he'd seen, they would've shit themselves too.

He changed the conversation. 'We burnin' the Sacks farm today?' Brownie loved burn days as much as he hated scrub cutting days. They'd cut back the undergrowth on Henry Sacks land over the winter and left it to dry for several months. It usually took a good year before the wood dried out enough to burn, but this year an early spring had been followed by a hot, dry summer.

Jonah stroked his greying beard and squinted at the sky. 'Looks good to me. No clouds and the breeze is from the east. Pretty much right for burning.' He pointed one of the two remaining fingers on his right hand skywards. 'Even that harrier thinks it's a good day. Sun's only just up and the bugger's already on the hunt.'

The kāhu circled overhead on strong, broad wings. Brownie's eye twitched and sweat erupted on his brow. For a minute he thought he'd chuck up his porridge. Couldn't be the same damn bird from last night, could it? Nah, that's just crazy thinking. He sprang to his feet and made a dash for the river to splash water on his face.

When he turned to walk back, they were all staring at him.

'What yer all looking at?' Brownie snapped. 'Let's get bloody going, eh?'

Moira rode out to meet with Angela Sacks after she'd enjoyed her second cup of tea for the morning. It was her own blend; she hadn't trusted the boarding house to have anything but fannings for their guests. Some months ago, she'd made the acquaintance of Jessica, Angela's sister, in Wellington. Jessica had described in disturbing detail the hardship of her sister's existence.

Moira had checked her fabric and had been pleased to find she'd given Angela a long, strong thread, but she didn't want to take any chances. Before arriving in Āpiti, she'd written to arrange a visit. In her reply, Angela suggested they could ride into the hills for a picnic lunch at Lake Morua. Her suggestion suited Moira well, since the lake was some distance from the farm.

Brownie flicked the match. It flew in a graceful arc to land in the oil-soaked pile of twigs. For a moment it looked like it wouldn't catch. Then a tiny flame crept along the trail of oil. Growing, it caught the dry tinder, devouring it like a hungry beast. Brownie did a little dance. He bloody loved fire.

They'd set up to burn from the west. The breeze would keep the speed of the fire in check. Stop it raging towards the house and sheds. Behind them they'd cleared a wide swath to ensure the burn moved in the direction they wanted. All he and the boys had to do now was put out any rogue flames.

Growling through the undergrowth, the fire licked up the trunks of the forest giants. Black smoke billowed in a tall column arching above the fire. Around it wheeled a kāhu, its cries piercing through the roar of the fire. Brownie's eye twitched and his joy melted away. He shook his fist skyward, 'Bloody bird.'

The fire wavered.

Brownie forgot the harrier. Something was wrong. The dense smoke swirled. It swayed almost vertical before curling first to the north then bent to the east. 'No, no, no!' The bloody wind never blew from the west – but it was. A gale was raging down the slopes of the Ruahine Ranges. Shit.

Brownie's mouth went dry, and a knot formed in his stomach. He turned to yell a warning at Jonah and the boys. Too late. His words were ripped from his mouth. The kāhu screeched as it rode the wind downwards in an ever-tightening spiral.

Urged on by the violent gusts, the fire became a roaring monster. Flames leapt up the gnarled trunks of ancient totara, matai and rimu. The wood screamed and cracked.

Somewhere ahead of the inferno, the boys would be doing their best to create a fire break. Brownie had to try and get to them to help. His best chance would be to get around the fire through the cleared land on the south side. He took off at a sprint, dodging through the still burning undergrowth, leaping branches, and stumbling over smouldering ferns and bushes. The smoke was confusing. He couldn't find a way through the burning debris to the edge of the block. Brownie followed the wall of fire, hunting for a way through.

His throat burning, he stopped to rip the bottom off his shirt and tie it around his mouth and nose. He heard a voice. Off to his right. One of the boys must have got left behind. Why the hell was he chanting? Brownie smashed his way through burning branches. He squinted though the smoke. Blinking tears out of his eyes, he stared again.

It was bloody Tāne.

He looked different – for a start he stood eight foot tall. His jet-black hair was pulled into a topknot, and he was naked apart from a short flax skirt and a large bone pendant. Tāne stamped his foot and rolled his eyes in time with his chant. In one hand he held a taiaha sprouting leaves, in the other a greenstone mere.

Brownie had seen a haka once before, and it'd made the hairs the back of his neck stand on end. This one made him wet himself. His left eye twitched without stop. He'd never believed in gods, but seeing Tāne like that in the middle of a bushfire…shit. Had his mother been right and he'd been wrong, all along? Gods did exist, and the one in front of him was very fucking angry.

Brownie did the only sensible thing – he ran.

Swallowing smoke and not caring where he put his feet, Brownie ran. Ignoring the heat, he chased the flames. Crashing through a bush, he stumbled out of the fire. Free of the tangle of bushes, ferns and branches he sprawled on the soft soil of the empty paddock. It was a bloody miracle. If gods existed, then so did miracles.

Brownie clambered to his feet. He had to help the boys. Pushed along by the force of the wind, he staggered towards the wooden shack that passed as the Sacks' homestead. The soft dirt sucked at his boots. He pumped his burning legs harder.

Tāne's chant kept time with his thumping heart.

The boys. He could see them. They were running to keep ahead of the flames, helping each other to scramble through the tangle of the cut underbrush. They were almost at the giant totara, the tallest tree left in the valley. They weren't in the clear yet, but looked like they'd make it.

A screech cut through the air, dragging his attention away from the boys. A kārearea plummeted. The falcon crashed at full speed into the fiery crown of a kahikatea. It emerged, clutching a burning branch in each talon. Flapping hard, it rose high above the forest then, tucking its wings in tight, dived. It dropped the burning branches one after another in the path of his fleeing mates.

Brownie screamed.

The boys stopped running. They were cut off, their way out blocked by a second wall of flames.

'Here,' he yelled so loud it ripped his throat. Maybe they could still make it? Maybe he could save them?

Jonah turned towards Brownie. Somehow, he'd heard the yell over the roar of the fire. Their eyes met through the dense haze of smoke for just a moment. Then Jonah was gone. Where he'd been was an enormous flaming ball. An epiphyte from the giant totara. The widow-maker had dropped from the tree without a sound. Jonah hadn't stood a chance.

'Nooooo.' Brownie dropped to his knees. He couldn't breathe. Not bloody Jonah. That bastard was too tough to die. He smashed his fists into the soil. 'Jonah,' he sobbed.

The wind stopped.

A bird screeched. Brownie looked up. From the top of the last unburnt rimu a ruru, a kāhu and a kārearea dropped to the ground. In a swirl of black smoke, they turned into hooked-nosed women with unnatural yellow eyes.

Brownie gaped. More fucking gods. For the first time ever he wished he knew how to pray.

He couldn't drag his eyes away as the gods whipped the flames into a tornado. Brownie covered his ears to block out the boys' screams. It didn't work.

Old Tom didn't even try to escape. He was spun off his feet and tossed high in the air. His scream high-pitched for a man his age. Old Tom's burning corpse thumped to the ground not far from Brownie. It smelled like roast lamb. Brownie gagged.

Leftie and Isaac ran towards Brownie, their sooty faces contorted. Isaac was faster. He might've made it, but Leftie grabbed at him. They fell, screaming. The fire swallowed them. Then one of them was on his feet. Brownie couldn't tell who. Staggering forward, whoever it was writhed and twisted as he burned. A blackened arm reached towards Brownie. Smoke swirled. Everyone was gone.

Brownie curled up in the dirt, hugging his knees tight to his chest. The men's screams burned themselves into his nightmares. There they joined those of the drifter from down south to become a quartet.

In the low notes, well below the high-pitched screams, Tāne's chant droned on.

Jim led the search party into the fire zone the next day. Even without the wind to fan it on, the fire had continued its journey eastwards consuming everything in its path. Henry Sacks' house and sheds had burned around him. They'd found his partially charred body still smouldering. His skull was crushed. They all agreed the man's horse had been spooked by the flames and kicked him in the head.

It was Jim who'd found that greasy little snake of a man, Brownie. He was curled up in a ball, crying like a baby and jabbering about gods and owls and women and all sorts of nonsense. A week later he was still talking gibberish, so the doc had him sent off to the asylum down Wellington way. No one would miss him.

After the fire, Moira travelled back south, heading to Wellington in search of a city-style version of democracy. She took the widowed Angela with her. At the Oroua River they'd bid good day to Tāne, who sat on a rock in the shade of the bush. After crossing the ford, Moira turned her three faces to her younger brother and smiled. Deep in its dark pool, the angry little taniwha stayed well hidden from the Gods of Fate and Forests.

Dr Parsons' latest patient, Mr Brown arrived mid-afternoon. He jotted in his notes that the patient's initial presentation was calm, despite a severe facial tic. The patient refused to engage in a meaningful manner during the admission process. Instead, the poor soul spent his time picking at the scabs of recent burns and muttering under his breath. The extent of the man's illness only became evident when Dr Parsons summoned the new nurses.

The three sisters, by birth not training, had been at Mount View Asylum for two weeks. Although they had come with the highest recommendation from one of his European colleagues, Dr Parsons didn't much like the trio of Nurse Erinyes. Each had a pronounced hooked nose and odd yellow eyes. They were competent nurses but were too severe in nature for his liking. Dr Parsons tried not to let their unusual looks and disagreeable demeanours impact his work and had avoided spending too much time with them.

The moment the nurses entered the room, the patient had screamed and thrashed. He'd also soiled himself. It had taken all three nurses, and a couple of extra-strong orderlies to hold him down. Dr Parsons had been forced to interrupt his note taking and administer an intravenous shot of whisky and morphine before the screaming stopped.

The patient subdued – Dr Parsons left him to the care of the nurses.

THE SEA CHANGE
BY NEIL GAIMAN

Now is a good time to write this down,
now, with the rattle of the pebbles raked by the waves,
and the slanting rain cold, cold, pattering and spattering
the tin roof until I can barely hear myself think,
and over it all the wind's low howl. Believe me,
I could crawl down to the black waves now,
but that would be foolish, under the dark cloud.

'Now hear us as we cry to Thee
for those in peril on the sea.'

The old hymn hovers on my lips unbidden,
perhaps I am singing aloud. I cannot tell.
I am not old, but when I wake I am wracked with pain,
an old sea wreck. Look at my hands.
Broken by the waves and the sea: and twisted,
they look like something I'd find on the beach, after a storm.
I hold my pen like an old man.

My father called a sea like this a 'widow-maker'.
My mother said the sea was always a widow-maker,
even when it was grey and smooth as sky. And she was right.
my father drowned in fine weather.
Sometimes I wonder if his bones have ever washed ashore,
or if I'd known them if they had,
twisted and sea-smoothed as they would be.

I was a lad of seventeen, cocky as any a young man
who thinks he can make the sea his mistress,
and I had promised my mother I'd not go to sea.
She'd prenticed me to a stationer, and my days were spent
with reams and quires; but when she died I took her savings
bought myself a small boat. I took my father's dusty nets and lobster pots,
raised a three-man crew, all older than I was,
and left the ink pots and the nibs for ever.

There were good months and bad.
Cold, cold, the sea was bitter and brine, the nets cut my hands,
the lines were tricksy, dangerous things; still,
I'd not have given it up for the world. Not then.
The salt centre of my world made me sure I'd live forever.
Scudding over the waves in a fine breeze,
the sun behind me, faster than a dozen horses across the white wave tops,
that was living indeed.

The sea had moods. You learned that fast.
The day I write of now, she was shifty, evil-humoured,
the wind coming now and now from all four corners of the compass,
the waves all choppy. I could not get the measure of her.
We were all out of sight of land when I saw a hand,
saw something reaching from the grey sea.
Remembering my father, I ran to the prow and called aloud.
No answer but the lonely wail of gulls.

And the air was filled with whirr of white wings, and then
the swing of the wooden boom, which struck me at the base of the skull:
I remember the slow way the cold sea came toward me,
enveloped me, swallowed me, took me for its own.

I tasted salt. we are made of sea water and bone:
That's what the old stationer told me when I was a boy.
It had occurred to me since that waters break to herald every birth,
and I am certain that those waters must taste salt–
Remembering perhaps my own birth.
The world beneath the sea was blur. Cold, cold, cold…

I do not believe I truly saw her. I can not believe.
a dream, a madness, the lack of air, the blow up on the head: That's all she was.
But when in dreams I see her, as I do, I never doubt her.
Old as the sea she was, and young as a new-formed breaker or a swell.
Her goblin eyes had spied me. And I knew she wanted me.
They say the sea folk have no souls: Perhaps the sea is one huge soul they
breathe and drink and live.
She wanted me. Ann she would have had me; there could be no doubt.
And yet…

They pulled me from the sea and pumped my chest
until I vomited rich sea water onto the wave-wet shingle.
Cold, cold, cold I was, trembling and shivering and sick.
My hands were broken and my legs were twisted,
as if I had just come up from deep water,
scrimshaw and driftwood are my bones,
carved messages hidden beneath my flesh.

The boat never came back. The crew was never more seen.
I live on the charity of the village:
There, but for the mercy of the sea, they say, go we.
Some years have passed: almost a score.
And whole women view me with pity, or with scorn.

Outside my cottage the wind's howl has become a screaming,
rattling the rain against the tin walls,
crunching the flinty shingle, stone against stone.

'Now hear us as we cry to Thee
for those in peril on the sea.'

Believe me, I could go down to the sea tonight,
drag myself down there on my hands and knees.
Give myself to the water and the dark.
And to the girl.
Let her suck the meat from off these tangled bones,
transmute me into something incorruptible and ivory:
to something rich and strange. But that would be foolish.

The voice of the storm is whispering to me.
The voice of the beaches whispering to me.
The voice of the waves is whispering to me.

HER GHOSTS
BY TRACIE MCBRIDE

The track Callie took barely qualified for the title; gouged through the bush by pigs and goats, it followed its own feral logic, weaving around tree trunks and under fallen branches and forging through sparser patches of undergrowth. Yet Callie moved as if she were alone on a deserted beach, her steps measured and her mind attending to nothing in particular. From time to time, she stretched out a palm to caress a leaf, a fern, a textured patch of bark. Were it not for the sound of the other volunteers, yelling 'Dita! Dita!' like the call of some dreadfully mutated bird, she could have merely been out for a leisurely bush walk.

She's down there. The thought entered Callie's mind as if it were common knowledge that had been sitting patiently in her subconscious until it was needed. She stopped, her head swivelling, her gaze scanning the thick vegetation blanketing the hillside that dropped steeply down to her right, seeing nothing but green.

There. There. She's there. It was more compulsion than thought now, and she almost stepped off the track in response, before catching herself and drawing a shaky breath.

'I think I see something,' she called out. There was a frenzy of rustling and snapping twigs, a large and clumsy creature making its way for her at speed, then Dan Harris was at her side, his wife Lisa close behind, wearing identical expressions of hope and concern.

'Where?' asked Dan, breathing hard from his exertions. Callie pointed vaguely down the hill. He leaned out and squinted, his blue eyes nearly slits in his tanned face. 'I can't see anything,' he said after a few moments. 'Are you sure it wasn't just a bird or…'

Lisa nudged him and stood on tiptoe to whisper in his ear. Dan regarded Callie for a long moment, looked back to Lisa who nudged him a second time, then looked back down the slope where Callie had pointed. 'Yeah, righto. We'll get on down there, then.' He unhooked the walkie-talkie from his belt and spoke into it. Within minutes, dozens of fluoro-clad searchers swarmed over the hillside like brightly coloured bugs. Callie stayed put. If she joined them, she would for certain be the one to find the missing girl, which would draw attention to herself that she did not want.

A hand shot up and with it a shout, 'I found her! She's unconscious, pretty banged up, but she's alive!' A ragged cheer rang across the hillside. The job wasn't over yet – there was still the challenge of more accurately assessing the girl's injuries, safely extracting her from difficult terrain, and getting her to the nearest medical facility in a timely manner – but the verdict of 'found alive' was the best news the team could get in the moment.

Still, Callie did not move. She surveyed the scene, frowning. How had the girl ended up halfway down a hillside? If it had been an accident, if she'd just tripped and fallen from the track, there would have been evidence of the tumble; damaged plants and foliage crushed as she rolled over them, a path of destruction as clear as an arrow pointing the way to where she stopped.

It was as if someone very strong had lifted the child over their head and hurled her down.

The atmosphere in the pub was thick with jubilation and relief. Footage from the news report – a slight figure on a stretcher being loaded into the back of an ambulance, two teary parents reacting to the good news, a panoramic shot of the dense bushland in which Dita had been lost and found – played silently on a widescreen TV mounted high on one wall. A happy ruckus broke out near the bar when Dan's broad, beaming face came on screen.

Callie had been swept towards the bar on a tidal wave of celebrating searchers. 'Cider, yeah?' her aunt, Marama, called from behind the bar when she spotted Callie in the crush and waved away her offer of payment. Callie took a deep swallow from her glass to reduce the spilling risk and weaved her way out of the press of bodies. Her own body coiled tight with anxiety; the pub on a Saturday night was her least favourite place to be, but her community's unwritten rules dictated that she put in an appearance.

A tiny vibration – *earthquake?* – shimmered through the floorboards. They experienced several minor tremors a year, and everyone accepted that a major quake was a matter of when, not if. Callie paused, looking around to see if anyone else had noticed. The party continued unabated. Callie rolled her shoulders to release the extra layer of tension and moved on.

'Callie! Over here!' From a corner booth, one of her work colleagues waved and pointed to an empty spot. Callie made for it and took the seat with a grateful nod. The others – primary teachers all – smiled and nodded back before resuming their conversation, making no effort to include her. They were all familiar with her peculiarities. In front of a classroom of eight-year-olds, she was bubbly and exuberant; off the clock, she was introverted to the point of reclusiveness. As always in her little hometown, Callie was both accepted as a member and left on the edge of the group as an odd outsider, a position she was content to occupy. Life here ought to, and usually did, feel safe. So why was she sometimes filled with this overwhelming urge to flee?

She sat, nursing her cider until it grew tepid, the hum of voices around her forming white noise behind her thoughts. At one point she rose to let her bench mate out of the booth. As she was already standing, she took the opportunity to go to the toilet, a journey that took her out of the main bar and to the other side of the much quieter dining room. On her return, she stopped just short of the doorway so abruptly that the woman following Callie walked into her with a small, startled yelp.

In the main bar, the atmosphere had turned glacial – Callie could feel it, although the cause of the mood change was yet to be identified – and she peered tentatively around the corner.

A group of six or seven young men had claimed a position at the bar. Their demeanours ranged from nervously guarded to puff-chested with bravado. The other bar patrons stared at them, mostly in silence, and a few of the young men stared back. At the group's head was an older man, somewhere in his forties at Callie's guess. His receding hairline was camouflaged with a buzz cut a couple of millimetres shy of completely bald. Despite the autumn chill, he wore a tight-fitting, sleeveless t-shirt, all the better to display gym-hardened muscles. He was a stranger to Callie, yet the sight of him made her instantly, intensely nauseated.

The man leered at Marama, and leaned on the bar as if he owned it. Marama – who actually did own it – returned a gaze of stone. 'I'll have seven pints of whatever shit you have on tap,' he commanded. 'And a shot of whiskey. Neat. Top shelf – if you have a top shelf.'

Marama folded her arms across her chest. 'Gonna need to see some ID,' she said. 'Not for you, obviously. For your boys.' Casting a scornful eye over the group, her expression shifted to one of recognition. 'Bobby?' she called to a youth in the middle. 'Bobby Bain?'

'I go by Robert now,' he answered sulkily.

'Sorry to hear about your granddad,' Marama said. 'Is that why you're back in town? To settle the estate? 'Last words I heard out of your mouth, you were 'never coming back to this shit hole'.'

Robert shrugged. 'He left me his farm. Not gonna turn that down. We've got plans–'

'Robert,' the older man said with a warning glare. Robert clamped his mouth shut and looked at the floor. The man returned his attention to Marama. 'Is it usually this busy in here? You lot celebrating something special? Oh, wait.' He pantomimed having a sudden recollection. 'Didn't you find a little lost girl in the bush?'

'Yep. Her parents paid for the first round of drinks for the search and rescue team, and I shouted the second. Didn't see you or your crew out helping to look for her though, so you'll be paying full price for yours.'

'I saw her parents on the news. White father, Indian mother.'

Marama raised an eyebrow. 'And that means…?'

The two stared each other down for one heartbeat, two, three. The man flashed a broad smile. 'You know what?' he said. 'I don't think all my men have their IDs on them. We'll come back another time. When we're better prepared.' He took care to flex his biceps as he pushed off the bar. They made their way out in a pack, nudging other patrons with just a touch more force than needed.

The leader swung his head in Callie's direction as he passed, and she flinched. He did not pause, only bared his teeth in a feral grin. Then they were gone, the joy in the pub sucked out the door with them.

Callie bent over, forearms braced on her knees, and drew in deep, shuddering breaths. She had not wanted to face him, *no, no, no*, but why she couldn't say. Something bad was brewing, and, judging by the muttering and scowls in the next room, it didn't take someone with special intuition to feel it.

The pub emptied out quickly after that. Without being asked, Callie helped to clean up, clearing glasses and wiping tables. Usually, tasks such as this served as a mindfulness exercise for her, settling her thoughts and emotions into a more manageable state, but tonight it was of little help. A headache throbbed at her temples, her stomach churned, and she had no idea how long she had stood wiping the same table when the last of Marama's staff called out their goodbyes. Next thing she knew, her aunt was taking the cleaning cloth from Callie's hand and gently pressing her shoulder, urging her into a seat.

'You look like shit,' Marama said. 'Thought you could use these.' She placed a glass of water and two Paracetamol on the table. Callie took them up gratefully. With a delicate groan, Marama sat opposite her and took a sip from her own glass, her customary end-of-shift rum and coke.

'Lisa tells me you found the girl,' Marama said. She leaned towards Callie, her two meaty forearms braced on the tabletop.

'No, not really, I just…'

'They're all talking, you know. About how there was no way you could have seen her from where you stood.'

Callie shrugged and said nothing. Marama huffed and stretched, took another sip, and pretended to look out the window before taking another tack.

'I've watched you go on search and rescue operations in the bush around here literally since you were born,' she said. 'Only six weeks old, and your mum had you strapped in a front pack while she joined in. You two were first on the spot so many times, people thought your mum was psychic. Probably started because of her red hair and pale skin, but for a while there was a story doing the rounds that she was descended from Scottish witches.'

Marama chuckled. 'And maybe she was, for all I know. Anyway, as you got older, your mum would go on searches without you sometimes, or else your dad would take you. And then the pattern became a little less clear, at least to most people who had their eye on the wrong part of it. Of course, we both know that your mum had all the psychic ability of a sack of spuds. But you – now, that's different. Remember when your dead granny used to visit you?'

A chill ran up Callie's spine. She covered it with a scoff. 'Come on, Aunty,' she said, 'so I used to have vivid dreams. You know I wasn't really seeing ghosts.'

'Do I, though?' Marama's scrutiny was making Callie squirm. 'I know that your father used to see them, and your grandfather told him not to talk about it in case people thought he was mad. And I know your dad gave you the same advice when you were little. I don't think it's doing you much good, though, trying to pretend you're not psychic.'

Callie sighed. 'What is this about? If you think you've had it all figured out all this time, why bring it up now?'

Emotion flitted across Marama's features, and Callie shrank from it; the pity on the older woman's face was almost too much to take from someone she'd always seen as a human-shaped rock. 'Because I worry about you, that's why. Both your parents dead, nobody to guide you or give you answers even if they had answers to give in the first place. You know, there once was a time when you would have held a high-status position in the tribe. You would have been respected and valued for your ability. Now…now nobody wants to admit it even exists. Least of all, you.'

Marama shifted uncomfortably in her chair. It wasn't just concern for Callie's well-being that had prompted the discussion. Callie steeled herself for it.

'The Marsdens could really do with special insight right now, too,' Marama continued. 'The cops aren't letting anyone near that little girl except for her parents and the hospital staff, and everyone's meant to be keeping their mouths shut while they're investigating, but you know how it is in a small town. People talk anyway. And they're saying that physically Dita's gonna be okay, nothing that a bit of rest and TLC won't fix, but mentally, she's not quite right.' Marama tapped one temple with a forefinger. 'Dita reckons she was kidnapped by a ghost.'

'You don't believe that, do you?'

'No, no, of course not. But *somebody* took that girl. And whoever it was, what if they do it again? And what if they go further next time? Would you really want that on your conscience, knowing that you could have stopped it, but didn't because you were too scared to try?'

Callie's special ability didn't work the way Marama thought it did. Messages came to her unbidden and weren't always useful, or their meaning might not immediately be clear. Still, her aunt's request weighed heavily on her mind that week. Her dreams were plagued with disturbing, chaotic images that dissolved from memory the instant she awoke, leaving her only with a vague sensation of wrongness. She continued to feel tremors that nobody else seemed to notice; it was as if she was walking on rubble which could, at any moment, give way under her feet and send her plummeting into a deadly chasm. She held it together at work for the most part, but a couple of times when the classroom was empty of students, she caught herself staring out the window with no idea how long she'd been standing there.

Even the mood in the staffroom was troubled. Rumours abounded about the goings-on at the Bain farm.

'My boyfriend Tony reckons they're building a big fence around the house. Three metres tall, topped with razor wire, the whole bit.'

'I heard that they're guarding the place with specially trained attack dogs. My cousin Donna is a vet nurse, and she says it's some super aggressive breed that they imported from Germany.'

'A boy in my class – you know Wiremu, really clever, you taught his older sister last year – he told me he was out flying the drone he got for his birthday, and it crossed over the border between their farm and the Bain's, and they shot it down. Then when his dad went to talk to them about it, they threatened to shoot him next.'

'Do you think they could have had something to do with Dita Marsden's abduction?' Callie was as shocked as everyone else to hear these words come out of her mouth. The room went silent, and all eyes turned to her. 'Maybe it's just a coincidence, that this lot turn up in town at the same time as a child gets snatched off the street and thrown down a hill. Or maybe…'

'Or maybe we'd better be careful what we say.' This was from Gary Jorgenson, a teacher in his first year out of university who, it was widely tipped, was unlikely to last a second year before moving back to Auckland. 'It's a bit of a cliché, isn't it? Strangers come to town, some kid wanders off, falls down and hits her head, suddenly everyone's putting two and two together and coming up with five?'

His words were for the wider audience, but his glare was reserved for Callie. 'The last thing this town needs right now is a witch hunt.'

Saturday morning came. Callie went through the motions of her weekly grocery shop in a fog. Hearing her name called behind her in the short checkout queue, she shook herself to full awareness and turned to see the worried face of Mia Ngata. Callie had taught Mia's twin daughters a couple of years back. The girls weren't with her today, but Mia's youngest, a boy who had just started kindergarten, had a tight grip on Mia's pants leg and sidled shyly behind his mother as Callie offered him a smile.

Mia spoke again. 'Did you hear another kid's gone missing? Vincent Chang. His family live up on…'

'I know Vincent,' Callie said. 'He's in my class this year.' Her fists tightened around the shopping trolley handle so tightly, her hands hurt. The tension and pain spread through her entire body. Another ground tremor vibrated through the floor, and this time Callie wasn't alone in feeling it. Glass jars rattled on shelves, and alarm creased the faces of everyone in the supermarket. An ill-balanced cereal box hit the floor with a loud smack, making Mia and her son flinch. The boy began to cry.

The tremor subsided, and those who had swiftly taken shelter under counters and doorways emerged with nervous chuckles. Callie did not wait to partake in the post-quake discourse; another child was lost, one of *her* students, and the drive to protect him was as powerful as if she had given birth to him herself. She released her laden trolley, left it where it sat, and ran.

The urupā where most of Callie's whānau were buried could be accessed by road, but Callie had always preferred the more direct route, which was a steep and narrow stairway cut through bush into the side of a hill. The treads, hard-packed dirt edged in timber, were treacherous when wet as they were today. Callie recklessly bounded up them two at a time. She emerged into the clearing at the top, panting and sweaty, and took several breaths to regain a measure of composure before making for the gate in the fence surrounding the small cemetery. The fence, a simple post-and-wire construction, sagged with neglect, but a large flask tethered to the gate was clean and full of water, and the graves were well-tended.

Both your parents dead, nobody to guide you, Marama had said. That only showed how little people understood.

Callie's first impulse had been to visit her father's grave, but as she entered the urupā, the atua pulled upon her from all sides. Her father called from his resting place near the entrance. His mother reached out from two rows back. To her right, a dark and angry presence raged, urging her to seek utu. And from somewhere near the back left corner, a faint whisper of a karakia beckoned like a siren. She moved to the epicentre of the graveyard, planted her feet, and closed her eyes, her overwhelmed psyche allowing little else.

A rumble started, so low it was on the edge of human hearing; another quake, a big one this time. The ground heaved like a great beast trying to shake off vermin. It threw Callie to her hands and knees. She dug her fingers into the soil and clung to the earth as if she might at any moment spin off into space. Time lost meaning as she endured the dual onslaught from the land and the ghosts.

When at last the ground stilled, she opened her eyes. A deep, jagged furrow carved the urupā in half, running scant centimetres from her fingertips. Headstones had been dislodged and scattered, and at least one grave had been disturbed badly enough to leave rotting coffin wood exposed. The atua still spoke, but now their voices had coalesced into a single, coherent message. Callie rose from the dirt as if in a trance. She knew now where to go.

The atua told her – *You have always known.*

Callie could tell before she could see it that she was close to the Bain homestead by the cacophony of panicked yips, barks and howls. She jogged up and over a small rise towards the noise. The rumours about the fence had been true, but the quake had virtually destroyed it. Some sections of fencing stood at crazy angles, while others had been felled completely. A pack of dogs – one for each man, at a quick estimate – were not purebreds, but an assortment of pig dogs and mongrels.

Despite the barrier of the fence being only notional now, the dogs kept to their side of it. They circled, snarled and cowered, their eyes rolling wildly in terror.

Callie walked into their midst without fear. The nearest dog, all scars and muscle, approached her at a near-crawl, his tail held low and wagging. She extended a hand for him to sniff. The sniff turned into a lick, and the wagging intensified. Callie spoke to him in a soothing tone, nonsense phrases mostly, and scratched him behind one ear. The dog leaned into it, eyes half-closed with bliss. Encouraged by his reaction, the other dogs followed suit, pressing close around Callie for her benediction.

Callie looked toward the house. One end of it had collapsed under the force of the earthquake, looking like it stood in a war zone. Two figures approached from around the corner of the undamaged end. One was small and slightly built – a child. Vincent. Shoved from behind, the boy stumbled, whimpered, and righted himself before quickening his pace.

But not too quick; Callie gasped at the thick rope noose hanging loosely around the boy's neck. Her gaze travelled along the rope to the person holding it. She blinked, taking a moment to decipher what she was seeing.

Vincent's captor was featureless, shrouded in white. A pair of heavy work boots strode beneath the hem of a flapping white robe. Except for two cut-outs for the eyes, the hood, which rose to an exaggerated triangular point, entirely obscured the wearer's face.

Kidnapped by a ghost. That's what Dita had said. The girl's observation now made horrible sense.

Vincent's eyes widened. 'Callie!' he cried. The shrouded figure gave the rope a vicious jerk, and the boy staggered backwards to a halt, his hands grasping at the noose which had drawn perilously tight. He stood quivering, his gaze conveying a terrified plea for help.

A hand reached up to pull off the hood, and Vincent's kidnapper revealed himself. It was the man who'd turned Callie's stomach in the pub the previous weekend. Only now, the sensation of nausea had turned into a roiling pit of heat. Callie had suppressed the emotion for so long, she didn't recognise it first. *Fury.* It diffused through her limbs, flushed her face, and beaded her skin with sweat.

'Well, look who it is!' he said. 'The town witch!' Against her thigh, one of her new canine friends vibrated with a low growl. Before Callie could respond, another person – Bobby Bain – came jogging around the corner of the house.

'Dylan, I need your help, the other guys are…' He stopped short and gaped at the trio. 'Dylan,' he started again, slowly, carefully, as if speaking to a toddler holding a loaded gun, 'what are you doing?'

'I was going to take this little yellow bastard into town and string him up from the nearest lamp post, but the earthquake might have disrupted my plans somewhat.' Dylan shrugged. 'Never mind. I'll do it here. At least I have a witness.' He nodded dismissively at Callie. 'Even if she is just a half-caste whore.'

Callie shook her head, amused and appalled in equal measure. 'Dude, nobody says 'half-caste' anymore. You might want to get in your time machine and go back to the nineteenth century.' Both men ignored her.

'No,' Bobby said softly. He repeated it louder, more firmly, yet with a little start as if he were afraid of his own sudden courage. 'I didn't sign up for killing kids.'

'Really, Robert? Because I thought I made it quite clear that this group had to be prepared for violence to take back our rightful place in this country.'

Bobby licked his lips and looked nervously from face to face. 'Yeah, nah, I didn't think that…'

'Don't you worry, boy.' Dylan emphasised the last word with an extra coat of contempt. 'I won't make you dirty your delicate little hands with this. Anyway, it's not like you can stop me.'

Bobby was already backing away. 'I'm sorry, Callie,' he said. 'I have half a dozen blokes trapped under rubble. I have to at least try to get them out.'

With Bobby out of sight, Dylan gave another yank on the rope, this time pulling Vincent completely off his feet. The boy made terrible gasping, choking sounds as he scrabbled futilely at the noose. Slowly, never dropping his gaze from Callie's, Dylan walked backwards, dragging the child before him, Vincent's sneakered heels digging grooves in the dirt.

'STOP!!!' Callie's bellow echoed off the hills. She stamped her foot on the ground, and the ground spoke back with a rumble and a shiver. The tremor was long and strong enough to throw Dylan off balance. He let go of the rope. With the sudden slackening tension, Vincent pulled the noose over his head and scuttled out of Dylan's reach.

But Dylan only had eyes for Callie. Or more specifically, what she could feel amassing at her back.

The atua had followed her from the urupā; they were in her, perhaps they had always been in her, and now they were emerging to confront the foe. Her long, untethered black hair floated up from her head. Power crackled through her body. An ancient curse, the meaning of which she felt in her bones rather than consciously understood, flowed from her mouth. At her feet, the dogs crouched and snarled. Dylan hauled up one side of his robe to reach a sheath on his belt. He drew a hunting knife from it. With a snarl as savage and fear-driven as the dogs, he raised the blade and lunged for Vincent.

Callie unleashed.

Three forces struck Dylan in quick succession. Another earthquake, the strongest one yet, flung the man flat, yet Callie remained unaffected. It was as if she existed as an extension of the earth rather than a discrete being, and she rode the land's convulsions with ease. One atua, the most powerful, struck the man's mind, shredding what remained of his sanity. Callie almost felt pity for him as he shrieked and flailed at his bodiless assailant. The rest possessed the dogs, riding them in a wall of fur and fangs. They set upon their former master, tearing flesh from bone, ripping open belly and throat and cutting his cries mercifully short. Dylan still held the knife in his hand yet made no attempt to defend himself, almost as if he welcomed that savage final assault.

Callie dropped to her knees and beckoned Vincent to her. He rushed into her arms, and she drew him in tightly, covering his ears to mute the sounds of the dogs, not that he could likely hear much over the sound of his own raspy sobs. She didn't know how long they held each other, but at length she recognised a kind of calm in the air. The earth had quietened, and so too had Vincent, his cries reduced to the occasional soft sniff. One dog remained, his white fur slick with blood. He whimpered in confusion as he circled Dylan's gory remains, then turned and slunk off after the others who had fled for the cover of bushland. From the house came the sound of human coughing and shifting timber; at least one of Dylan's gang had made it out alive, and despite their leader's atrocity, Callie hoped for more.

Callie held Vincent gently away from her to examine him. She winced at the rope burn around his neck; otherwise, he moved freely and responded to her voice, his eyes grave but clear.

'Come on,' she said. 'Let's get you home.'

They walked in silence for a while, two scarred and bruised people travelling across a scarred and bruised landscape. Then Vincent clasped Callie's hand and drew her to a stop.

'Callie,' he croaked, 'were those your ghosts?'

She sighed and considered her answer. *Tell him the truth, Callie,* her father whispered. *I'm sorry I ever advised you otherwise.*

'Yes,' she said with a smile. 'Yes, those are my ghosts.'

WHAT BONES THESE TIDES BRING

BY NIKKY LEE

The ocean is angry today. Its waves pound the sandbar; pummel the beach in a roar of white static. I tiptoe over the sand, basket in hand, studying what the water has brought me. Driftwood here, cuttlefish there. Into the basket they go. Driftwood for the fire, cuttlefish to trade to the carvers.

Overhead the sky rumbles, and the wind sends sheets of stinging sand against my legs. I push on. Water claws its way up the beach before the tide drags it back in silting, swirling currents that would drown even the Olwerld's strongest swimmers.

Still, I search the black sand, one eye on the angry water. One freak wave and it's over. I'll sink like the Olwerld did. Yet despite the danger crashing not fifty metres away, my gnarled fingers trail through weed and kelp, over rocks, searching for a catch.

Because when the ocean is angry, it coughs up the best trinkets.

The best bones.

At last, something smooth and rubbery brushes my hand. I double down, digging into the sand, feeling out its shape with my fingers until I recognise it. A boot.

I unearth it in a spray of sand and salt, and the roar of the ocean fades away as I run my hands over it, barely able to contain my excitement. Cracked leather, rubber sole, laces long gone. Definitely Olwerld. I burrow my hand inside the same way a bird might eat a snail, fingers scrabbling through the sand as I hunt for the morsel inside. But with every scoop I lift out, the lower my spirits sink. If there were Olwerld bones in here, I should have found them by now. I reach the heel, nothing. Arch, nothing. The toe is empty too, and I up-end the boot and beat it out on the beach. Noth–

A faint 'plick' of something hard bounces off a beach rock. I dive to my hands and knees, scouring the sand again. Where? *Where, where, wh–*

My fingers close around a tiny bone no bigger than my thumbnail. And the moment they do, I feel the weight of it hit my chest. *Yes. Someone's home.*

A gust of wind brings me back to the beach. The rain that has been threatening all morning has arrived in big, fat drops, pelting the sand like hail. I tuck the bone into the pouch around my neck and slip it under my oilskin.

'I'll wake you up soon, sweetie.'

I blink open my eyes. A dim room blinks open with them. Blurred and dingy. Another blink and the room sharpens: damp plywood walls, threadbare carpet. A cast iron fireplace squats in the middle of the room flanked by an array of pots and pans. Overhead, a single lightbulb hums. It flickers. Once.

Where am I?

'Welcome back, sweetie.'

I whirl on the voice, coming eye-to-eye with a weather-beaten face full of hard lines and yellowed teeth. A tangle of grey hair tumbles from the woman's head, wrapping over her shoulder in a snarled braid. In one hand, she holds a small iron-looking box, lid open, and I glimpse an array of baubles inside before she closes it.

'Do you remember your name?' she asks.

'Riley,' I say, without thinking. The moment it is past my lips, the woman sucks in a breath, as if she's breathing in the scent of my name. Weakness grips my knees, and my vision goes hazy again. *How did I get here? Where is here?*

Overhead, the lightbulb's hum rises to a buzz.

'It's okay,' she tells me. 'Relax.'

And against every instinct, I do. The building tension in my neck and shoulders slackens; the churning knot in my stomach stills.

'Good,' she says. 'The first awakening is always hardest.'

Awakening? But before I can ask, she points over my shoulder. 'Tell me what that is.'

Confused, I follow her gesture to a floor-to-ceiling set of shelves on the wall behind me. Every inch is crammed with junk: old nails, curled up bits of wire, a dog's collar, several tattered and mould-covered books, a birdcage – all of it and more piled on top of each other like a hoarder's shrine. There must be close to a hundred knickknacks on those shelves, but somehow, I know exactly which item she wants me to name. Second shelf from the bottom, third item along. A small box and screen with laminate curling off its sides.

'It's an old TV,' I say. 'Analogue.' I crouch before it and lean in for a closer look. The screen is too dusty to show my reflection. 'I haven't seen one of these since I was a kid.' I make to wipe the dust away, but something in me jerks my arm still.

The woman speaks again. 'And that?'

My attention is pulled along the shelf. To a flat device lying beside a teddy bear with both button eyes missing and stuffing bursting through the seam of one arm. I examine the dark screen and the black mould trapped around the edge of the casing.

'Smartphone,' I say, and my hands automatically pat the back pocket of my jeans for the familiar shape and weight I already know is missing. Another lost phone. I bite back a groan. Mum is going to *kill* me. Panic stabs through me. *Where is Mum?* The last thing I remember was my hand in hers, our fingers wrapped so tight, and so cold. I try to picture the scene, pull the memory out of the haze of shapes and sounds in my head. It's so close, like a forgotten word on the tip of my tongue.

Our hands clasped. Mum's fingers around mine as I pulled her along. That's right, we were running. Running from something. Something big. Terrifying. Until Mum doubled over in the street, gasping.

'Riley, slow down, I can't–'

'Post digital then.' The rasp of the old woman snaps me back with a start, and the thread of memory breaks. I claw after it. Something was hiding in that moment. Something important. But the memory is gone. I blink around the room, look at the hunched woman again. Really look. Her knitted jumper has holes at the elbows. Two odd shoes grace her feet. But what catches my attention is the iron box in her hands. It's the size of a large jewellery box, vintage looking with swirling patterns on its lid, which she clicks shuts as she places something inside.

'Who are you?'

Her grin is all teeth. 'You can call me Mable.'

'What is this place?'

Her grey eyes fix on me, irises dark and swirling. Like storm clouds. Like the sea. Panic I can't explain stirs inside me. *Like the sea.* The hairs on my arms go on end. Something big looms at the edge of my memory, but like my childhood monster under the bed, I'm too afraid to look.

Outside, the shrill cry of a fantail cuts through the air.

'Go back to sleep, my sweet,' Mable coos.

My eyelids droop before I even realise what she's said. *Wait, no.* I fight against the overpowering urge to sleep. But it's too late. My mind is drifting. *Wait!* I manage to crack an eye open and find my perspective's changed. It's as if I've shrunk to the size of a button, a full-on *Alice in Wonderland* moment. Mable's enormous face hovers over me, so close I can see the dimpled pores on her wind-blasted cheeks.

Wait! I try to scream, but nothing comes out. I try to rise, but my body is gone.

'You'll feel better next time I wake you, sweetie,' Mable says.

And something heavy and iron slams shut above me.

Her bone is cold when I retrieve it from my bone box and spark her awake again. Unlike the first time, her body coalesces hard and fast, flaring into consciousness with a form so solid I can barely see the floor and walls through her. Seas be, she's a strong one. *And all mine.* It's all I can do to contain my glee as she glares and finally asks the right question.

'What are you?'

I sink into the old rocking chair, placing the box on my lap and curling my hands around it. 'I'm a bone collector.'

Her blank look confirms what I suspected. She's from *before*. The chair creaks as I rock, and I wonder how much I should reveal. How far I can push. A broken spirit is no use to anyone.

The ghost's ethereal eyes – a faint translucent silver – fix on me, clearly waiting for an explanation. So, I uncurl my hand to reveal the yellow bone in my palm.

She goes still. Perhaps she senses her connection to it. Perhaps, deep down, she already knows she's dead.

'Is that...?'

'A bone.' I watch her. *Gently does it.* 'Yours.'

Her form shivers, edges bristling. She points to her foot. 'It's not my–' And stops. Stares at her boot and the floor we can both see through it. She doesn't scream. Just slumps. Curls into herself on my carpet and burrows her face into her knees. She doesn't cry. *Brave girl.* Braver than others I've broken the news to.

At last, her gaze seeks me out through her knees. 'How?'

I crook an eyebrow. 'You don't remember?'

'I remember running. I–' Her focus drifts, expression stilling. '...there was water. It was everywhere.'

My chair releases a squeak as I stop mid-rock. 'Wait, you were *there*?' I say it too quick. Too harsh. Not the right tone for a ghost I'm trying to coax awake. But she lifts her head, even as her translucent limbs tense.

'Was I where?'

I mutter a curse. No putting that cat back. 'The end of the world. The Olwerld. Your time.'

The ghost stares at me. 'It ended?'

'It did. Many died. Billions.' I tap a gnarled finger on her bone in my palm and she twitches. 'We woke up the ocean and he swallowed us up. Including you, it seems.' *A scholar would pay a pretty penny for you indeed.* But this ghost is mine. For me.

A throaty *aarrk-aarrk-aarrk* cuts through the air, making us both jump. Gannet. Even through the door, his warning is clear. *Strangers are coming.* Without thinking, I grab the bone and plunge my power into it, grasping the spirit's essence and pulling it up and out.

Riley gasps, clutches herself. 'What are you–'

I thrust her essence into the first shell I see: the Olwerld teddy bear.

There's a hiss of static as I release her and the speaker inside the bear's chest crackles, releasing a slow '*I wuuuuuv yooou moooommmmaa*' before my power closes around her like a fist.

'Shhh,' I tell the ghost inside the toy. 'Don't fight. Just watch.'

A haggard, bearded face greets me when I open the door. But it's not the beard nor the faded camouflage jacket that I recognise first. It's the eyes. I've not seen many living people with dead eyes, but Warden Wyman has them. There's a hard emptiness in them that chills me, and not for the first time I wonder what happened to make him that way.

'You've come I long way,' I observe.

He holds up a duffle bag. 'Outta juice,' he says, pushing his way across the threshold. Behind him, Gannet releases an *aarrk* and darts out of his shell – a taxidermied gannet I leave on the doorstep – and slaps his way in after Wyman. His transparent feet leave no prints on the carpet.

I ignore the ghost bird – he's part of the furniture now – but Wyman's gaze follows it like feral cat sizing up a kill. Things must be bad in the settlement if he's eyeballing a measly bird spirit. I point to the driftwood table before the fireplace. 'Show me.'

Wyman unzips the duffle, revealing a battered radio transceiver. 'Cole says the kit's fine. But the power's gone.' His last words angle at me like an accusing finger.

I meet his glare, and something flickers in those dead eyes as they shift from me, to my bone box on the rocking chair, then back to me. Fear. *Not all dead then*. I smile sweetly. 'Are you trying to say I sold you a dud?' My swollen knuckles creak as I uncurl my palm and wait.

Wyman hesitates, then grudgingly hands over a carved owl. The wood is polished smooth with age, the paint long faded. Still, I feel it's significance. The weight of its mana. This was important to someone once. Treasured. Like all shells are. It's no bigger than his palm, perfect for a man on the move as much as he is. It's why I sold it to him to house his ghost.

'Did you rest it as I instructed?'

He nods. 'It doesn't work.'

I turn the owl over in my hands, then nudge a bit of my power into it. Not a lot. Wyman won't get a free recharge unless he pays. Just enough to make the spirit inside spark.

A ten-year-old boy coalesces on the table, his cut-off jeans and singlet exactly the same as the last time I'd woken him. Unlike last time, his shape is horribly faint. A suggestion of a boy, really. More silhouette than spirit.

I purse my lips. 'Rested it, did you? You all but burnt it out.'

'I did rest it! Every night, just like you said.' He's gaining steam, voice rising, shoulders squaring. 'It worked the radio fine the first month, but now–' He hucks up a wad of spit on my floor, right at the silhouette's feet. 'Useless. I paid you six months of supplies. You promised me the best. This ghost can't even turn on a bulb.'

'Sit *down*.' I snap my power at the man, brushing the inner essence that makes Wyman *Wyman*. Spirit, soul, whatever. The same part that remains *after*. It's not much of a touch, more a reminder why bone collectors are respected. Revered. Not lectured like a browbeaten sap.

Wyman immediately stops. Everything. His breath. His heart. His whole body stiffening.

'Do not lecture me, *boy*.' I hold him more a moment more, then release him. The air whistles out of his lungs and his knees buckle. He catches himself on the arm of my rocking chair, nearly pitching over again. I jab his chest, forcing his attention to my accusing finger and away from the tremble in my legs. Working with ghosts is one thing, working on the living is quite another. The living take a lot of power.

'How *long* did you let it rest?' I demand. 'How many *hours*?'

Wyman gawps at me. 'Three hours,' he manages at last. 'The radio is unmanned from midnight to 3am.'

Three hours? Seas be. It's a miracle it lasted a month. 'A ghost isn't an Olwerld machine, Wyman. It needs rest. *Decent* rest,' I add as Wyman opens his mouth. 'No spirit can power a machine twenty-one hours day for a month without burning out. Look at it.' I wave at what's left of the ghost. 'It can barely keep itself corporeal.' I fold my arms and harrumph. 'You think you didn't get quality? Most wouldn't last a week.'

The Warden seems mollified by that. At least, he's gone quiet, though his gaze fixes on Gannet again, those hard eyes watching my ghost bird in a way that puts my hackles on edge.

'We need the radio,' he says. 'Everything goes through it. Trade negotiations, supply runs, hunts, defences. It's our hub, our life-line to the other settlements.'

He looks at me with that hard desperation again. His settlement is on the edge, and it is Wyman's job to see it survives. That was the problem. When men like Wyman got desperate, they got dangerous.

And stupid, I think as he glances at Gannet again. Hiding the girl had been a good idea.

'It's going to cost you,' I warn. 'If you want round-the-clock radio, you're going to need more ghosts.' I scoop up my bone box from the rocking chair and give it a rattle. There's the unmistakable 'plink plink' of bones inside. 'I have two dog shades each capable of generating three hours' power. That should be enough to let your ghost rest.'

Wyman shakes his head. 'Shades are unreliable. Can't have it cutting out on us. We need a steady power supply. I want another like the boy. One of your best.'

Of course you do. Greedy bastard. I don't look at the teddy and the ghost girl sheltered inside it. She's the strongest I'd found in years. Fully sentient. Near solid. Like hell I'd hand her over.

'I'll need time,' I say. 'Bones like that are hard to find.' At his growing scowl, I add, 'You could offer up some of your own. Fresh dead tend to stick around.'

His scowl vanishes, and the disgusted look that follows says everything. There's a reason why settlements all cremate their dead.

'Old dead,' he says. 'No one from the last decade.'

I shrug. 'It'll cost you more. Can you afford it?'

Wyman's silence goes on so long I wonder if he's reconsidering the dog shades. Eventually he shifts, pulling a slip of paper from his pocket. He hands it over. I claw it open and read, then open my bone box and tuck it inside.

'You'll see it's already signed,' he says, and if I hadn't just read his offer, I might have mistaken the edge in his voice as anger. But it's not. It's fear.

I hold out my hand, and he hesitates. 'A contract is a piece of paper, easily lost,' I say. 'This requires as handshake.'

He shifts, clear uneasy. Shifts his weight, glances at the door once, as if contemplating escape – he wouldn't be the first – then sighs and holds out his hand. 'It's all yours.'

I grin. 'I accept.' And as our palms touch, my power bites down.

I feel oddly rested when Mable pulls me from the teddy. Muscles all soft and limber, like I've climbed from a hot bath. Only I don't have muscles anymore, not really. I hold my hands up and stare through them, making out a crooked kitchenette and an ancient rust-streaked fridge in the room's corner. My stomach squirrels into my spine.

Okay, Riley, be cool. I suck in a shaking breath. Or whatever it is I breathe. *Don't freak out.* The lightbulb overhead flickers, sways again in the ceiling's draft.

With Wyman and his radio gone, Mable has started…well, pottering is the best I can call it. She collects her iron box and with a flick of her wrist, sends the ghost bird into an old record player (middle shelf, fourth item along). The player starts up, and when Mable places the tonearm down on a scratched and warped vinyl record, a tinny song crackles from the speaker. Humming, she lowers herself back into her rocking chair.

'You must have questions,' she says.

She's right. A dozen questions crowd my mind. It's a war between my brain and my mouth to pick one.

'What, who, the boy I mean,' I gesture at the door. *Focus, Riley.* 'That. What was that?'

'What you think it was?'

I want to say it looked like she and Wyman were using a ghost like a fucking battery, but that was insane. *Right?* Mable folds her hands over the iron box and waits. Right? I clear my throat, and as I do, the lightbulb starts up its hum again. *Oh sweet Jesus.*

'You use us for power.'

Mable nods. 'The sea destroyed the Olwerld's power. Luckily, we found a replacement.' Her knobbed fingers flex towards me. 'A resource we had plenty of.'

Because, of course, humanity would think to exploit the dead. Anger ripples through me. Was that going to be my fate, too?

As if sensing my thought, Mable offers a thin smile that kills my anger cold. 'That is the way of it now. The dead's duty is to the living, you've had your time. The living have to work with what we have.'

'But–' I begin, still trying to wrap my mind around what she was saying. There were no ghosts before. At least, none that were real. I want to cry 'you can't' or 'I won't', but what comes out is a strangled, '*How*?'

Mable shrugs. 'Mana, chi, chakra, spirit, however you call it, I control it. *And by extension you.*' She waggles her fingers and a pressure trickles down my spine. 'That's what a bone collector is. When the Olwerlder's disrupted the balance, the cities sank, ghosts rose, and this power rose with it.'

Her words tumble over me. *When the cities sank…* Goosebumps prickle my neck.

Mum's hand grips mine, so cold. So wet. 'Just float, Mum,' I say. 'I got you.' My limbs are heavy, my boots dragging me down. We float in the dark, waiting for the sun to rise as the current pushes and pulls us. Wait for the sun, *I think. Wait to know which way to swim.*

My tongue turns thick in my throat. I don't remember seeing that sunrise.

I push the memory down and replay Wyman's visit in my head. There's so much I don't understand, but one detail sticks out above the rest. The handshake. The way Wyman slunk out of the hut after had felt *wrong*, like looking at an arm and knowing from the bend in it that it was broken.

'What did Wyman agree to?'

Mable grins yellow teeth at me. 'The only thing he had left to bargain with.'

Horror blossoms in my chest. *His ghost. His soul.* I stumble back, was she going to…

The bone collector snorts. 'Don't look at me like that. He'll live his life just fine. All my contracts do. But when his death comes, it will belong to me.'

I take in her lined face and grey braid. Wyman is easily forty years her junior. She'd be long dead herself before she could claim the goods. Unless…

A sensation like crawling spiders tickles down my legs. Unless she *would* be around in another forty years. Sweet Jesus, exactly how old was she? Then a more insidious thought. *Was a bone collector even human?*

Mable raps a knuckle on the iron box in her lap. The sound of it rings through me, like she'd clapped a cymbal in my face. 'Enough questions for today. Let's get you trained up.'

The more skilled the ghost, the more valuable you are. This is the lesson Mable drills into me.

'Put some spirit into it,' she likes to say, cackling at her own joke as I mush my essence through the machines on her shelves.

I master the record player first. Unlike the teddy bear, this machine is cold and *stiff*, like trying to turn a half-rusted screw.

Mable is utterly uncompromising. 'That's because it's not a shell. It's a machine,' she says. 'If bird spirit can work it, you most certainly can.'

Only when I realise that I've pushed too much of my essence at the machine does it finally click. I syphon off a sliver and feed it in. Bit by slivery bit. The player spins up and Mable places the arm onto the vinyl. A jazz ballad crackles out, its saxophone and baritone singer barely rising over the pop and hiss of the ancient vinyl.

'A good start,' she says when she yanks me out and places me back inside the bear sometime close to midnight. 'Gannet can barely manage an hour. We'll try something new tomorrow.'

And despite knowing I'm only hastening my impending servitude, I can't help but feel a glimmer of triumph. It's a long night. Ghosts don't need to sleep. And Mable has somehow bound me to the plushie. So I turn and examine the tiny device nestled inside the bear's stuffing. I've scarcely brushed the machine before it releases a burst of static, then 'I'mm huuuuungry.'

'Girl,' Mable warns from the sofa that also doubles as her bed. From inside the bear, I feel her power reach for me: a giant hand ready to clench me silent. 'Don't make me put you back in your anchor.' She taps the iron box resting on her chest. Plushies can't shudder, but my essence recoils. I don't know what she means by 'anchor', but I can guess. When I'm not busy funnelling power into a machine, the box calls to me. A part of me is in there. One of my bones. From the way it clinks when Mable carries it, there must be dozens, maybe hundreds, of others like mine in there.

By the end of the week, I've mastered the TV, the TV remote, and FM radio – even if all I get is static. The week after, it's a rusted convection oven with more holes in it than a sieve. Mable lectures me on anchors and shells.

'When I hand you on, I'll give your owner a shell to keep you in,' she says. 'Your anchor stays with me.' She rattles the box, which I'm coming to realise she very much enjoys doing, the same way a pianist might strike a single key to listen to the note's resonance. A childhood memory washes through me at that thought. *Me sitting on Mum's lap before a scuffed old piano, hands resting on top of her fingers as they flow across the keys.*

Mable's fingers click before my face and I blink. 'Leave the past alone, sweetie.'

The following week, it's the smartphone. And that's when the trouble starts.

The smartphone lights up in my hand. *First try. Seas be.* I was right not to give up the girl. She's too strong for amateurs. Not even Wyman's ghost had been able to make the screen do more than flicker. I tap the cracked screen and am confronted with the lock screen. It's been years since I've seen it.

'Good, sweetie. Very good.' I reach my power out to feel her essence inside the casing. It's positively vibrating with power. Part of me urges to act now, use the ghost and be done with it. But another part stays my hand. *Why not see how far she can go?* it whispers. *Think what a developed power like hers could do for you. Another fifty years, easy. Maybe more.*

I admit it's tempting. The level the girl is at now would give twenty, maybe thirty, years. Far better than the year here, month there I'd been living with for the last decade. I rub my aching knuckles. The pain was back again. Dull in its way, but growing. Reminding me of what waited if I didn't act soon.

The phone buzzes in my hand.

I yelp and drop it. It lands on the carpet with a thud but doesn't switch off.

'Sorry,' my ghost says. 'Thought I found a way around.'

With a scowl, I pick up the phone and turn it over in my hands. It has never buzzed before, but the lock screen still glimmers up at me. As much as I want to know what's behind it, I've long resigned myself to the fact that there is no breaking the Olwerlders' security. I reach out my power to pull the girl from the device before she fries it – something I never thought I'd have to with *any* ghost – when I feel her dig in, like a fish fighting a hook on a line. Then she *pulls* back.

'I think I can bypass it.'

My jaw drops. Too distracted by the lure of the device, she doesn't notice. Inside the phone, I sense her pushing and probing her essence through it. Until, a second later:

'Oh I *see!*'

The lock screen vanishes.

'Girl–' I begin.

She ignores me and rifles through the device. *Flash, flash*, goes the display. Things open and close faster than I can follow. When I extend my spirit to hers, I feel the hunger burning insider her. The need to know.

She's searching for something.

Images appear. Her ghost touch flicks through strange vistas. Sunsets over still water. Buildings tall as mountains. Stone and concrete and bright lights. Faces, so many faces. She stops on one. Two smiling adults and their children outside a house. Not a hut, a proper Olwerld house.

'It's not here,' my ghost says, her voice quiet.

I use her pause to close my power around her essence, working her hold of the device loose as a parent might detach a child's grip from a toy. 'What's not here?' I ask as I pull her free.

Her face is wet when she coalesces. 'Answers. What happened.' She sinks to the floor, hugging her knees. 'It's all gone.'

Overhead the lightbulb's hum returns. It flickers and I glower at it. The last thing I need right now is the ghost in my lightbulb burning out. I collect my bone box and crouch beside her.

'Smart devices take a lot of energy, sweetie,' I say. 'You need to rest.'

Never mind that her form is still solid, and aura bright. But she nods, wipes at her eyes. Her mind's too wrapped up in mourning for the world that was to notice me open the bone box.

I send her straight to her anchor. Straight to sleep. And when I shut the lid, I slump into my rocking chair, the knowledge thumping in time with my pounding heart.

This ghost has gone far enough. I cannot afford to wait.

For the first time, I dream. Not in pictures, but feelings. Warm and muzzy, like sleeping in the sun on a summer's day. The kind of dream you know is a dream. And there is a sense of someone, *someones*, nestled close. *The bone box.* She's put me back with her other bones.

Dimly, I sense Mable move us. A rattle, and I roll into someone, catching a whiff of wine and laugher as we cross paths. A bump, and I plunge into someone else with a brisk, jolting cold and the taste of seawater in my mouth. Panic surges through me. *Not the sea.* But it's too late; the nightmare rises and swallows me hole.

'Stay with me,' I tell Mum. We float on our backs. It's not survival stroke anymore. Just survival. 'Just a little longer.'

I hope I'm right. I'm past the point of cold. Sometimes I think I hear other voices across the water, but whenever I lift my head to look I see no one. No lights. No boats. No figures floating in the water but us. There *must be others, I think. The storm had battered our suburb.*

'A storm possessed,' the news anchor had said. But we'd left too late. The water caught us in the street. Swept us away.

Now, the sky sprawls clear above us, stars so bright it makes the darkness between them feel bottomless. I work my numb lips. 'Don't let go, Mum.'

She doesn't speak.

Doesn't breathe.

She hasn't for hours.

I squeeze my fingers around hers. Her fingers are going stiff. 'Don't leave me.' I whisper, and I swear something squeezes back.

'I'm right here, Riley.'

I start awake in the dream.

This is not how it happened. I know it's not. Because, instead of sinking, Mum shakes off her body and turns to me, transparent hands taking mine, and says: 'I'm here.'

The nightmare tumbles away, and I feel her there. Next to me.

'Mum?'

'I'm *here.*'

I don't have room to wonder. The hows and whys of it fall away as the full realisation crashes into me. She's here. Dread clenches around my heart. She's *here.* In Mable's bone box. *No. No, no, no.* I don't say it, but with our anchors touching, she already knows.

'Oh Riley, I'm so sorry.'

It takes time to prepare. I move the shells from the shelves, stacking them outside on my rickety veranda around Gannet. I caulk the window seals with pitch. Shove a rag up the chimney of the fireplace. Salt the thresholds. All of it sealed, so my sweetie has nowhere to go.

I go over my work again, just to be sure. Knives secured in the kitchenette drawers, poker outside. Nothing for her to grab onto in case she's got a touch of poltergeist.

At last, I'm ready.

I place my bone box on the driftwood table. Open it. The bones are crowded together, phalanges, carpals, metacarpals, tarsals and metatarsals, even a malleus from an ear. I trail my fingers through them all, searching for the right one. I find her hiding at the bottom, a larger patella suck to her side.

'There you are, sweetie.'

Her ghost flares awake the moment I touch her. Her form is so solid it almost blocks the light from the bulb above.

'Did you know?' she demands. The tears are still on her cheeks. *Damn, damn.* I'd hoped the rest would mellow her out, but something's got her in a right fuss.

'Know what?' I ask, genuinely baffled.

Not the right answer, apparently. With her bone in my hand I feel her anger simmer under my fingers. Then grief wells up behind it, so raw it scalds my skin. It takes all my control not to drop the bone with a hiss and a curse.

'You have her!' she explodes, pointing to the patella I'd pried her from. 'My mum is in your stupid box.' Her fists curl at her sides. '*Let her go.*'

It takes a moment to follow. Her mother? I glance at the patella, rifling through my memories. The light ghost? I'd had her for, oh, what, sixty years? Not particularly powerful. Scarcely more than a shade. Flickers of sentience. Enough to run a bulb for an evening. But, now I think about it, I'd found them both on the same beach. *Oh hells.*

The bulb hums above us.

'Quiet down,' I growl at it.

The girl advances on me. *Advances.* The cheek! Her form looms large and my temper snaps. I poor power into my hands and squeeze her anchor.

'Enough! You are dead. Your mother is dead. Your duty is to the living. Now *quiet*!'

She stumbles, legs folding under her with a cry. Mostly surprise. Maybe a bit of pain. I harrumph and reach for my bone box, picking out the patella from the pile. Best to work with her mother's shade asleep. Even if it does mean I'll have to work in the dar–

A pressure pushes against my senses, fighting off my hold. I whirl on the ghost. 'Seas damn it, girl!'

She lunges at me. 'I'm *not* your puppet.'

I reach for my power, digging deeper, harder than I have done in many, *many* years. And there I feel it, the scrape and twinge as I hit the bottom of its well. But it's enough. I smack her away, blasting her through the driftwood table and sofa bed.

'You think you're the first to defy me?!' I step towards her, gathering the dregs from my well again. *Time to end this.*

The lightbulb explodes above us. Not a mere shattering and tinkle of glass. It blasts out, hammering a dozen shards into my back with a waft of righteous glee. A blade of it lodges in my neck. Lodges deep. My hand flies to the wound, clamping over the blood already slicking down my throat.

Fuck! Fuck, fuck, fuck!

I drop the girl's anchor and plunge my free hand into the bone box. No sense wasting such a powerful ghost on something like this. My fingers find the one I want in seconds; I know all my bones by feel. I grab it, put it in my mouth and bite down.

My vision swims. Bone crunches between my teeth. It's a flimsy carpal, easy to eat. Dust and bone fill my mouth, along with the flush of heat through my veins. Ghost essence.

In the corner, the buzz of the ancient fridge cuts out.

The ghost's essence drops into my well. A tingle washes over my limbs. *Heal me*, I command it. The wound in my throat burns, then tickles as the skin knits shut and puckers into a scar. I cough and straighten, wiping my bloodied fingers on my skirt.

My sweetie stares at me. I didn't think ghosts could go pale, but she manages it.

'You *eat* us?'

'When I must.' I shrug. 'When I need it.'

Our gazes land on her anchor on the carpet and horror takes over. I smirk. *End of the road, sweetie.*

'No!' She flings herself forward – not for her anchor, she must know she can't hold it. She goes for *me*. Her grip closes around my wrist, and there's a surprising strength behind it. *Seas, if this girl had lived, she might have been one of us.*

I grab her anchor. Cop a glancing blow to my cheek. It's strong, but there's no weight, *no flesh*, behind it. It's like fighting a cloud. Still, she climbs *up* me, tearing at my hair, clawing at my eyes. I yell and trip over the driftwood table and thud to the floor. Pain smarts down one hip and leg. Her transparent fingers work at my clenched fist as I lift it to my mouth.

'I'm going to enjoy eating you,' I snarl, and shove her anchor into my mouth.

Crunch.

Her form quivers. I feel her fight to hold herself together.

Crunch.

She vanishes. The first wave of power drips on my tongue, searing as it goes down.

'*Please, stop.*' Her voice is small. Close by.

Not a chance. I bite down again, grit and bone dust coating my mouth.

Her essence roars into me. Where the shade before had been a flush, this is a wave. It crashes through my muscles and bones, filling my well to brimming. The contrast between is startling. I'd almost forgotten what it was like to eat a proper ghost. *Finally.* I roll onto my back. *This is what I'd needed.* More essence, more soul to fill me, *power* me.

Worth the wait, the ridiculous indulgence.

The girl's essence sloshes inside me. I laugh, my squeaking giggle the only sound in the dark room.

Another fifty years, easy.

I stand. Dust off my jumper and relish the springy suppleness in my limbs. 'Ha,' I say to the empty hut and reach for my bone box.

The essence *twitches* in my well. My breath snags. Just digestion. Perfectly norm–

Nausea hits like a hammer. I double over, gasping as the essence shifts inside me. She's *moving.* Working inside me, wrapping herself around my well – *around my soul* – like a constrictor.

'What is–'

She squeezes. The strength flees my legs, and I clatter to the carpet. Another squeeze. My body twitches, my control falling away. She's balled my essence up, and I feel her working, pushing, pulling, straining.

She's pushing me out. Forcing *my soul* out of my core.

Stop! I scream, but nothing comes out. I dive into my power, try to push back. But it's not enough. It's too tight. I'm too empty. And she's too strong.

My essence is forced up my chest, down my left arm. Into my hand. My right arm spasms. Left leg kicks. She's testing them. Syphoning power through my muscles.

Don't you dare!

My/her mouth spreads in a grin. We lurch up. Sway, stumble, sway. We stagger into the kitchen. She pulls open the drawers.

Stop!

My/her hand closes around something cold. Steel. Sharp.

She forces me down further, into my pinkie. Her essence pins me there, vice-like as she splays my/her fingers.

My butcher's knife swings into view. Lifts above my/her head. Then it drops like a guillotine.

N–

The beach is quiet today. Even the gulls are silent. Like they know something is here that shouldn't be.

I've built the bonfire high. Its heat sears Mable's skin, curling the end of her braid as I lean close and overturn the bone box into the flames. Our bones clink as they drop, then pop like burning logs. There's an odd a stomach-dropping moment of weightlessness when their connection to Mable and I melt away.

I hold Mum's patella in Mable's good hand. The other is wrapped in bloody rags, clutching the collector's ragged pinky.

Put me back! her soul rages, spitting a flow of steady curses. She doesn't stop, not even when I throw her finger onto the fire. *You will rue this day, girl. I swear it! I will end you!* She keeps going until the fire finally cracks her anchor, cutting her off with a hiss.

The next is harder. I hold the patella to my shell's lips, feeling the warm mussiness seep through my thoughts. 'You stayed with me to the end.' *Both times.* 'Thank you,' I tell Mum, and give her bone to the flames.

I make sure every anchor is ash before I wade into the sea.

The waves whisper as they pull at my feet. One step brings the water to my waist. The next, it crowds my head, soaking Mable's braid.

Inside me, the last remnant Mable's power begins to unravel. The knot of extortion contracts loosens, then dissolves.

Enjoy your death, Wyman. Lucky bastard is probably too caught up trying to find a working radio to notice.

I lean back and float in the sea, letting the current pull me from the shore. Gannets wheel in the blue above. One of them rides the wind on translucent wings.

I smile, feeling myself come unstuck from the bone collector's body and swirl with the water. No shell. No anchor. With a sigh, I close my eyes.

It is time to rest.

Glossary of Māori & Local Terms

arvo	Aussie	afternoon
atua	Māori	spiritual beings, gods, ghosts, or powers
bevvy	abbr.	beverage
blowed, (to be)	colloq.	to be bothered, to be inclined to
cab sav	colloq.	cabernet sauvignon, red wine blend
duffel (bag)	military	canvas bag
EFTPOS	anag.	Electronic funds transfer at point of sale
e noho ra	Māori	farewell
e taku ipo	Māori	my darling
Gladwrap®	brand	cling film / plastic wrap
iwi	Māori	tribal group
karakia	Māori	prayer, chant, song
kia ora	Māori	greeting, hello
kōauau	Māori	flute
kumi	Māori	giant lizard monster
long-drop	colloq.	outdoor toilet, a deep hole in the ground
mānuka	Māori	New Zealand teatree, *Leptospermum scoparium*
mana	Māori	prestige, honour, power, status, talent
matuku	Māori	heron, bittern
Milo®	brand	Nestle chocolate drink, iconic in New Zealand
ngahere	Māori	bush, forest
oriori	Māori	lullaby
patupaiarehe	Māori	fairies, mischievous wood spirits
pāua	Māori	shellfish, abalone
ponga	Māori	tree fern, silver fern
pounamu	Māori	greenstone
Poutini	Māori	a famous taniwha

Pākehā	Māori	white New Zealander, European
Papatūānuku	Māori	Earth mother goddess, the land
puke, pukish	colloq.	to vomit, feel like vomiting
rub along, (to)	colloq.	to get along together
smoko	colloq.	tea break, smoking break
Tama / tama	Māori	proper name, boy, son
tamariki	Māori	children
taniwha	Māori	supernatural serpent monster
te moe pai	Māori	sleep well, sweet dreams
trampers	colloq.	hikers, walkers
ua nui	Māori	big rain, rainstorm
urupā	Māori	cemetery, burial ground
uni	abbr.	university
ute	abbr.	utility vehicle, farm vehicle
utu	Māori	revenge, response
whānau	Māori	family
Whaitiri	Māori	female spirit, goddess of thunder

Biographies

Editor

Lee Murray is a writer, editor, poet, and screenwriter from Aotearoa. A *USA Today* bestselling author, her titles include the Taine McKenna adventure series, supernatural crime-noir series The Path of Ra (with Dan Rabarts), the fiction collection *Grotesque: Monster Stories*, and several books for children.

Her many anthologies include *Hellhole: An Anthology of Subterranean Terror, Black Cranes: Tales of Unquiet Women* (with Geneve Flynn), and *Unquiet Spirits: Essays by Asian Women in Horror* (with Angela Yuriko Smith). Her short fiction appears in prestigious venues such as *Weird Tales, Space & Time*, and *Grimdark Magazine.*

A multiple Bram Stoker®, Australian Shadows, and Sir Julius Vogel Award-winner, Lee is a Shirley Jackson Award winner, a NZSA Honorary Literary Fellow, a Grimshaw Sargeson Fellow, and 2023 NZSA Laura Solomon Cuba Press Prize winner. Read more at leemurray.info

Foreword

Lisa Morton is a screenwriter, author of non-fiction books, and a prose writer whose work was described by the American Library Association's Readers' Advisory Guide to Horror as 'consistently dark, unsettling, and frightening.' She is a six-time winner of the Bram Stoker Award®, author of four novels and over 150 short stories, and a world-class Halloween and paranormal expert. Her recent releases include the *Calling the Spirits: A History of Seances*; and, from Applause Books (Oct 2023), *The Art of the Zombie Movie.*

Lisa lives in Los Angeles and online at lisamorton.com

Contributors

Kathryn Burnett is an award-winning screenwriter, playwright and writing coach. Her TV credits include *My Life is Murder*, and *The Brokenwood Mysteries*. She has written several dark/horror projects for the screen, but this is her first foray into the dark corners of short story.

Read more at kathryn-burnett.com

Helena Claudia is a young writer hailing from Tauranga. Since 2019, she has been living in Pōneke. Helena's passions lie mostly in non-fiction and research-driven work, but she dabbles in speculative fiction and poetry when inspiration strikes.

She is currently serving as the Youth Representative for the New Zealand Society of Authors, Te Puni Kaituhi o Aotearoa.

Gina Cole is a Fijian/Pākehā, queer writer living in Tāmaki Makaurau. Her short story collection *Black Ice Matter* won Best First Book Fiction at the 2017 Ockham New Zealand Book Awards. Her fiction, poetry and essays have been widely anthologised and published. Gina graduated with an LLB (Hons) from Auckland University in 1991, an MJur in 1995, an MCW (First Class Hons) in 2014 and a PhD in Philosophy from Massey University in 2021.

Her science fiction fantasy novel *Na Viro* (2022) is a work of Pasifikafuturism. In 2023 she was appointed a Member of the New Zealand Order of Merit for services to literature.

William Cook lives and writes in New Zealand. His genre-spanning work includes novels, short fiction, poetry, and nonfiction. His dark psychological horror and thriller fiction include the novel *Blood Related*, and the collections *Babylon Fading* and *Dark Deaths*. Other popular titles include the *Psychological Horror Stories* series and *Gaze into the Abyss: The Poetry of Jim Morrison*.

Read more at www.williamcookwriter.com and download his free collections, *Dreams of Thanatos* and *Serial Killer Thrillers*.

Debbie Cowens is a teacher who lives on the Kāpiti coast. She wrote the comic mystery *Murder and Matchmaking*, co-authored the award-winning anthology *Mansfield with Monsters*, and her story 'Caterpillars' won an AHWA Shadows Award. She lives with her husband, son, and cat, and she enjoys writing in the brief hours when neither teenager or feline are occupying her computer.

Neil Gaiman is an author of short fiction, novels, comic books, graphic novels, poetry, audio theatre, screenplays. Among his works are the comic book series *The Sandman* and the novels *Stardust, Anansi Boys, American Gods, Coraline*, and *The Graveyard Book.*

He has won numerous awards, including the Hugo, Nebula, World Fantasy, British Fantasy, Locus, and Bram Stoker Awards, as well as the Newbery and Carnegie Medals.

Learn more at neilgaiman.com and on twitter @neilhimself

Del Gibson lives in Wellington and has had 26 short stories published, as well as several articles and poems. Her horror shorts have been published in anthologies *Flash of the Dead* and *Flash of the Fangs* (edited by Parth Sarathi Chakraborty) from Weird Shadow Press. Del is actively engaged in the writing community and runs a popular Facebook group called Horror Central and collaborates with YouTube Podcasts where her short stories are read out by narrators. Del also reviews horror movies, books and music on YouTube Live streams, and on her social media platforms.

Jacqui Greaves has lived an adventure-filled life, spanning a range of careers and countries. She's wrangled kindergarten children, driven buses, researched humpback whales, spoken at the United Nations, visited Antarctica, and farmed deer. These days she writes strange and sometimes sexy fiction. Jacqui has so far published a novel, two novellas, numerous short stories, and a bunch of scientific papers. Her current work features a murderous menopausal space-farer – it's not meant to be autobiographical. Jacqui doesn't believe in happily ever after, so shares her house with a cat.

Find her at: @jacquiG@mastodon.nz, www.instagram.com/nzjacqui and www.jacquigreaves-author.com

Denver Grenell is a writer of horror and dark fiction who lives with his family in a small rural town in New Zealand. A life-long horror hound who got back into writing after a long break, he is now making up for lost time, furiously expelling every idea that has collected inside his skull over the years. His stories have been featured in various anthologies from Crystal Lake Publishing, Black Hare Press, Bloodrites Horror, Hawke Haus Books as well as on Hawk & Cleaver's *The Other Stories* podcast.

His debut collection of short stories *The Burning Boy & Other Stories* is out now through Beware the Moon Publishing. The survival horror novel *Red Ruin* was co-written with Ian J Middleton and was a finalist for Best Novel at the Australian Shadows Awards 2022.

Read more at: www.bewarethemoon.co.nz

Tim Jones is a poet, author and anthologist who lives in Te Whanganui-a-tara/Wellington. He was awarded the New Zealand Society of Authors Te Puni Kaituhi O Aotearoa Janet Frame Memorial Award for Literature in 2010 and the NZSA Peter & Dianne Beatson Fellowship in 2022.

Tim's recent books include poetry collection *New Sea Land* (Mākaro Press, 2016) and climate fiction novella *Where We Land* (The Cuba Press, 2019). His poem 'Restraints' was included in *Ōrongohau | Best New Zealand Poems 2022*.

His novel *Emergency Weather* will be published by The Cuba Press in 2023.

Nikky Lee grew up as a barefoot 90s kid in Perth, Western Australia on Whadjuk Noongar Country. In 2016, she moved to Aotearoa and now lives in Auckland with a husband, a dog and a couch potato cat.

Her short fiction has been shortlisted six times in the Aurealis Awards, with her post-apocalyptic fantasy novelette 'Dingo & Sister' winning Best Young Adult Short Story and Best Fantasy Novella in 2020.

Her 2022 debut novel, *The Rarkyn's Familiar*, won a Sir Julius Vogel Award for Best Youth Novel, three Indie Ink Awards and was finalist in the 2022 Aurealis Awards and the Foreward INDIES Book of the Year Awards.

Paul Mannering is an award-winning New Zealand writer living in Canberra, Australia. He is the author of The Tankbread series (Permuted Press) The Drakeforth Series: *Engines of Empathy, Pisces of Fate, Time of Breath*, and *Heroes of Heresy* (IFWG Publishing), horror fiction *Hell's Teeth, EAT*, and *The Trench* (Severed Press), and numerous short stories.

He is the producer and narrator of podcast audio dramas at BrokenSea Audio.

Owen Marshall has published or edited more than 30 books, including novels, short stories, and poetry. A former teacher, Marshall held the Katherine Mansfield Memorial Fellowship in Menton, France in 1996 and won the Deutz Medal for Fiction at the Montana New Zealand Book Awards in 2000 for his novel *Harlequin Rex*. In 2000 he received the ONZM for Services to Literature in the New Year Honours and the CNZM in the Queen's Birthday Honours of 2012. He received the Prime Minister's Award for Fiction in 2013.

Born and raised in Te Kuiti, Marshall currently lives in Timaru.

Tracie McBride is a New Zealander of Ngāpuhi descent who lives in Melbourne, Australia. A member of the HWA and the AHWA, her work has appeared in over 100 print and electronic publications, including the Bram Stoker Awards®-nominated anthologies *Horror for Good* and *Horror Library Volume 5*. She has two short story collections in print, *Ghosts Can Bleed* and *Drive, She Said*, and her work has won or been shortlisted for various awards including the Sir Julius Vogel Award, the Aurealis Award, and the Australian Shadows Award.

Learn more at: traciemcbridewriter.wordpress.com

Kirsten McKenzie fought international crime for fourteen years as a Customs Officer in both England and New Zealand, before leaving to work in the family antique store. Now a full-time author, she lives in New Zealand with her family and alternates between writing time travel trilogies and polishing her next thriller. Her novels include *Ithaca Bound* and the Old Curiosity Shop series. Her spare time is spent organising author events and appearing on literary panels at various festivals around the world.

Find out more at: www.kirstenmckenzie.com

Celine Murray is a queer, disabled New Zealander with a multi-faceted cultural background, including Chinese, Māori, and Scottish ancestry. A writer and poet from a young age, she published her first collection, *Seven to Seventeen*, at 17 years old. She is the winner of a Sir Julius Vogel Award for science fiction and fantasy for her novella *Peach and Araxi*. At university, Celine pursued her interests in linguistics and communication and now holds a Masters of Speech and Language Pathology.

Though just beginning to dip her toes into the world of horror, Celine has a longstanding enthusiasm for death, with work experience in the death industry.

Dan Rabarts is an award-winning author and editor, four-time recipient of New Zealand's Sir Julius Vogel Award and three-time winner of the Australian Shadows Award. Together with Lee Murray, he co-writes the Path of Ra crime-noir thriller series from Raw Dog Screaming Press and co-edited dark fiction anthologies *Baby Teeth: Bite-sized Tales of Terror*, and *At the Edge*. His five-book steampunk-grimdark-comic fantasy series, *Children of Bane*, is published by Omnium Gatherum Media. Dan's science fiction, dark fantasy and horror short stories have been published in numerous venues worldwide.

Dan also regularly narrates and produces for podcasts and audiobooks. Find him at dan.rabarts.com

Bryce Stevens has collaborated with some of the biggest names in international horror. A former editor of *Terror Australis Magazine* and *Bloodsongs Magazine*, with Christopher Sequeira and Steve Proposch he has co-edited *Cthulhu Deep Down Under*, *Cthulhu Land of the Long White Cloud*, *War of the Worlds: Battleground Australia*, and *Caped Fear: Superhuman Horror Stories*. His work has appeared Ellen Datlow's Years Best Horror Honourable Mention and Recommended Reading lists on multiple occasions.

Of Māori descent, Stevens has been writing horror tales under the pen name David Kuraria since 2015.ghost hunter.

Marty Young is a Bram Stoker Award®-nominated and multiple Australian Shadows award-winning writer and editor, and sometimes ghost hunter. His fiction and anthologies have been nominated for and won numerous awards, while his essays on horror literature have been published in journals and university textbooks across the world.

Marty was also the founding president of the Australian Horror Writers Association from 2005-2010, and one of the creative minds behind the internationally acclaimed *Midnight Echo* magazine, for which he also served as executive editor until mid-2013. As of 2023, he is the co-chair of Asylumfest, an all-new annual Australian horror con.

Marty's website is www.martyyoung

The Clan Destine Press Anthology Suite

A driver picks up a hitchhiker on a dark road; a restorer develops a strange bond with a cursed doll; a visit to a cabin in the woods goes terribly wrong...

We all know how those stories end – or do we?

In *This Fresh Hell*, every story begins with a well-known horror trope but ends with a twist, bringing new life and unexpected resolutions to old ideas. Fears are interrogated, ghosts re-examined, and monsters reconfigured. From chilling to quirky, these stories will appeal to dedicated horror fans and those dipping into the genre for the first time.

Editors Katya de Becerra and Narrelle M. Harris invited writers from Australia and around the world to reignite and subvert horror tropes. The result is 19 genre-bending stories by:

Eugen Bacon, Elle Beaumont, Jason Franks, Claire Low, Raymond Gates, Sarah Glenn Marsh, Greg Herren, Annie McCann, Chuck McKenzie, L.J.M. Owen, Gillian Polack, Tansy Rayner Roberts, Clare E. Rhoden, Candace Robinson, Sarah Robinson-Hatch, Claire L. Smith, C. Vonzale Lewis, and A.J. Vrana.

ISBN: 978-1-9229043-3-1 (hb)
978-1-9229043-4-8 (pb)
978-1-9229043-5-5 (eB)

ISBNs: 978-1-9229041-6-4 (hb)
978-1-9229041-7-4 (pb)
978-1-9229041-8-8 (eB)

A clamour of rooks. A mischief of magpies. A storytelling of crows.

All the corvids – rooks and ravens, jays and jackdaws, crows and magpies – have the best collective nouns: from tidings and titerings, bands and trains, to a parliament, a party, and an unkindness.

Clamour and Mischief is a veritable storytelling of adventures featuring corvidae, the bird family known for its intelligence, cunning and connection with folklore and urban legends.

Our storytellers come from around the world and include award-winners and fledgling authors in their professional debut.

Herein are 16 striking stories imbued with the humour, darkness, wisdom and magic of the birds which inspired them.

Stories by: Raymond Gates, GV Pearce, Eugen Bacon, Geneve Flynn, Alex Marchant, Jack Fennell, RJK Lee, Lee Murray, Dannye Chase, Narrelle M. Harris, R.D. White, Jason Franks, Katya de Becerra, George Ivanoff, Tamara M Bailey, Gabiann Marin.

ISBNs: 978-0-645316-84-1 (hb)
978-0-645316-85-8 (pb)
978-0-645316-86-5 (eb)

The rising dread of damn good mysteries.
A horde of criminally good horror writers was invited to take a walk down the mean streets of crime. Their task: to make your blood run cold, to scare you witless and to make your skin crawl. And most of all to make you think.

The rising dread of a good mystery doesn't really need anything supernatural to keep you on the edge of your seat. But put the two together – crime fiction and horror – and all sorts of nasty business comes out of the woodwork. Sometimes literally. The stories herein include urban monsters, Victorian-era mathematicians, contemporary lawyers, near future police, and outback ghosts.

Edited by Alan Baxter – award-winning author of horror, supernatural thrillers and dark fantasy, liberally mixed with noir and mystery – our Damnation Games are played by 19 Aussie, Kiwi and international authors:
Gemma Amor, Joanne Anderton, J. Ashley-Smith, Alan Baxter, Aaron Dries, Gemma Files, Geneve Flynn Philip Fracassi, Robert Hood, Gabino Iglesias Rick Kennett, Maria Lewis, Chris Mason, Lee Murray, Cina Pelayo, Dan Rabarts, John F.D. Taff, Kyla Lee Ward, Kaaron Warren.

ISBNs: 978-0-6450021-2-6 (hb)
978-0-6488487-6-9 (pb)
978-0-6488487-7-6 (eB)

Who Sleuthed It?

*Fingers and feelers and paws and wings
Solving thrillers and chillers and secretive things.*

An anthology in which animals help their animal friends, or human sidekicks, solve diabolical crimes and whimsical mysteries in 19 stories by Australian, American and Irish authors.

Kerry Greenwood, Elizabeth Ann Scarborough
Meg Keneally, Narrelle M. Harris
Livia Day, David Greagg, Atlin Merrick
Fin J. Ross, Vikki Petraitis, Tor Roxburgh
Lindy Cameron, CJ McGumbleberry
Chuck McKenzie, Jack Fennell, Craig Hilton
L.J.M. Owen, GV Pearce, Kat Clay
and Louisa Bennet

The Only One in the World

Since his first appearance in 1887, Sherlock Holmes has been the quintessential English sleuth, alongside his loyal companion and biographer, Doctor Watson.

But what if they had come from some other place in the world, or another time? How would they differ from Conan Doyle's creations? How similar might they remain?

Holmes and Watson are herein re-imagined in new cultural contexts, different genders and sexualities, and in stories rich in foreign detail that still reflect their origins.

Thirteen writers from around the world, with cultural or historic expertise, explore the possibilities with stories set in Germany, C17th England, Ireland, Australia, Russia, South Africa, India, Poland, USA, Ancient Egypt, Viking Iceland, and even the entire world.

You'll discover Holmes and Watson are not only unique in original canon, but the Great Detective remains singular in every world!

Stories by: Kerry Greenwood & David Greagg, Greg Herren, Atlin Merrick, Jack Fennell, Lucy Sussex, Jason Franks, Natalie Conyer, Lisa Fessler, Katya de Becerra, Jayantika Ganguly, LJM Owen, Raymond Gates and JM Redmann.

ISBNs: 978-0-6489586-2-8 (hc)
978-0-6488487-8-3 (pb)
978-0-6489586-3-5 (eB)

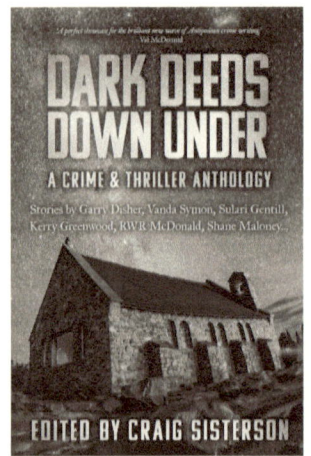

Dark Deeds Down Under features the very best of modern Australian and New Zealand crime writing.
Spend time with some of your favourite Aussie and Kiwi cops and sleuths – Hirsch, Corinna Chapman, Sam Shephard, Rowly Sinclair, Murray Whelan – and the edgy stars of some cracking standalone tales.

Travel the criminal trails of two countries from the dusty Outback to South Island glaciers, from ocean-carved coastlines and craggy mountains to sultry rainforests or Middle Earth valleys, and via sleepy towns to the seething underbellies of our cosmopolitan cities.

The 19 dark deeds herein are perpetrated by:
Alan Carter, Nikki Crutchley, Aoife Clifford, Garry Disher, Helen Vivienne Fletcher, Lisa Fuller, Sulari Gentill, Kerry Greenwood, Narrelle M. Harris, Katherine Kovacic, Shane Maloney, Renée, R.W.R. McDonald, Dinuka McKenzie, Vanda Symon, Dan Rabarts & Lee Murray, Stephen Ross, Fiona Sussman and David Whish-Wilson.

ISBNs: 978-0-6453167-9-7 (hc)
978-0-6453167-8-0 (pb)
978-0-6453168-0-3 (eB)